The Whole Disgraceful Truth

Genealogy

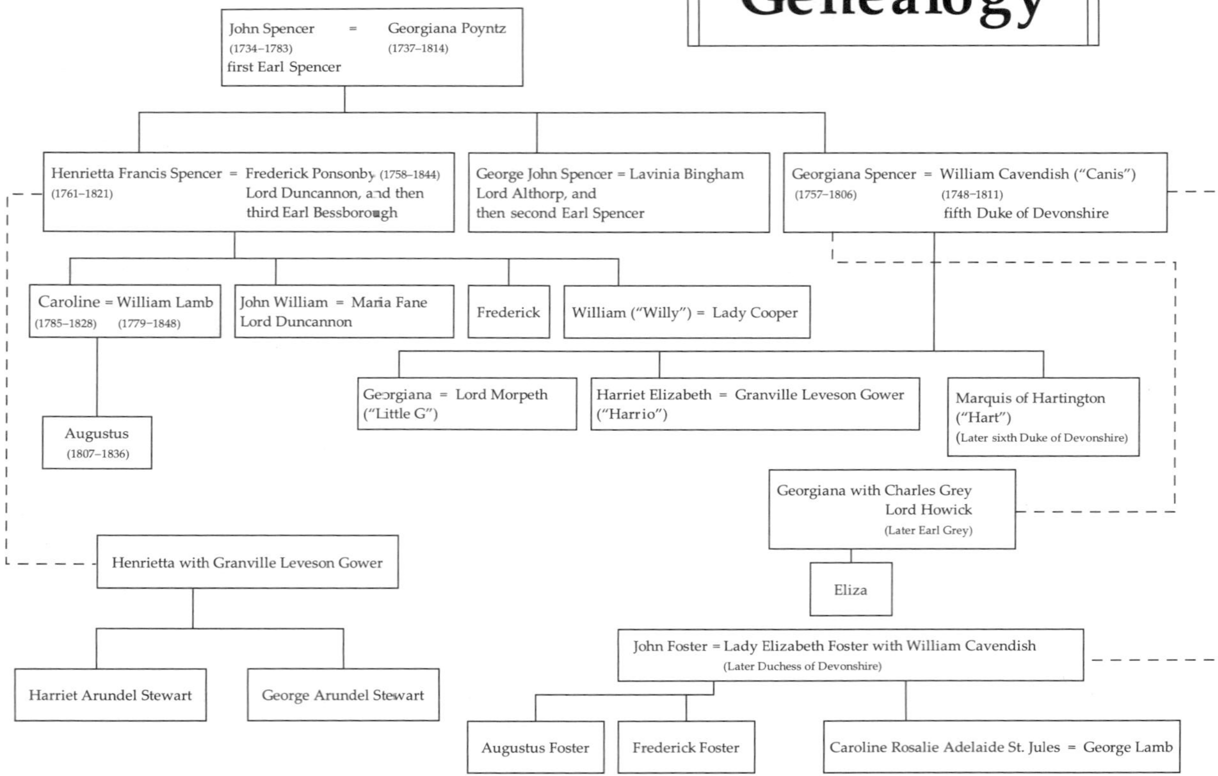
John Spencer = Georgiana Poyntz
(1734–1783) (1737–1814)
first Earl Spencer
Henrietta Francis Spencer = Frederick Ponsonby (1758–1844)
(1761–1821) Lord Duncannon, and then third Earl Bessborough
George John Spencer = Lavinia Bingham
Lord Althorp, and then second Earl Spencer
Georgiana Spencer = William Cavendish ("Canis")
(1757–1806) (1748–1811)
fifth Duke of Devonshire
Caroline = William Lamb
(1785–1828) (1779–1848)
John William = Maria Fane
Lord Duncannon
Frederick
William ("Willy") = Lady Cooper
Augustus
(1807–1836)
Georgiana = Lord Morpeth
("Little G")
Harriet Elizabeth = Granville Leveson Gower
("Harrio")
Marquis of Hartington
("Hart")
(Later sixth Duke of Devonshire)
Georgiana with Charles Grey
Lord Howick
(Later Earl Grey)
Eliza
Henrietta with Granville Leveson Gower
Harriet Arundel Stewart
George Arundel Stewart
John Foster = Lady Elizabeth Foster with William Cavendish
(Later Duchess of Devonshire)
Augustus Foster
Frederick Foster
Caroline Rosalie Adelaide St. Jules = George Lamb

The Whole Disgraceful Truth

Selected Letters of Lady Caroline Lamb

Paul Douglass

palgrave
macmillan

THE WHOLE DISGRACEFUL TRUTH

First published in 2006 by
PALGRAVE MACMILLAN™
175 Fifth Avenue, New York, N.Y. 10010 and
Houndmills, Basingstoke, Hampshire, England RG21 6XS
Companies and representatives throughout the world.

PALGRAVE MACMILLAN is the global academic imprint of the Palgrave Macmillan division of St. Martin's Press, LLC and of Palgrave Macmillan Ltd. Macmillan® is a registered trademark in the United States, United Kingdom and other countries. Palgrave is a registered trademark in the European Union and other countries.

ISBN 1–4039–6958–2

Library of Congress Cataloging-in-Publication Data

Lamb, Caroline, Lady, 1785–1828
The whole disgraceful truth : selected letters of Lady Caroline Lamb / [compiled by] Paul Douglass.
p. cm.
Includes bibliographical references and index.
ISBN 1–4039–6958–2 (alk. paper)
1. Lamb, Caroline, Lady, 1785–1828—Correspondence. 2. Novelists, English—19th century—Correspondence. 3. Politicians' spouses—Great Britain—Correspondence. 4. Byron, George Gordon Byron, baron, 1788–1824—Relations with women. 5. Great Britain—Social life and customs—19th century. I. Douglass, Paul, 1951– II. Title.

PR4859.L9Z48 2006
823′.7—dc22
[B] 2005044603

A catalogue record for this book is available from the British Library.

Design by Newgen Imaging Systems (P) Ltd., Chennai, India.

First edition: April 2006

10 9 8 7 6 5 4 3 2 1

Printed in the United States of America.

For Jeremy and Regan—no finer people in the world

I have written to William to tell him not any falsehoods not as you say any stories to conceal my guilt but the whole disgraceful truth. I have told him I have deceived him I have trusted solely to his mercy & generosity—yet as I have not said you any of you know anything about it do not mention it to him unless he does to you . . .

—Lady Caroline Lamb to Lady Melbourne, 1810

CONTENTS

LIST OF ILLUSTRATIONS

ACKNOWLEDGMENTS

This volume is possible only because of the generosity of the staff members of many archives and libraries. The institutions are listed in the Manuscript Sources portion of this volume, and acknowledgment of the source of each letter has also been provided. However, I wish gratefully to acknowledge here the help of the many kind and expert individuals who have given me advice, research assistance, and arranged permission to transcribe and print the letters of Lady Caroline in the archives they represent or own. I am also grateful for the support of San Jose State University, and of the students who have interacted with and challenged me about Lady Caroline over the past nine years.

Virginia and John Murray, thank you. Without your support, this book could not have appeared at all. Letters from this collection are reproduced by kind permission of the John Murray Archive.

Many thanks go also to:

The Lord Bessborough.

James Cooper, Director, and Captain John Cunningham, Royal Navy (Retired), of the Stansted Park Foundation, West Sussex.

Peter Wilkinson and Alison McCann of the West Sussex Records Office, Chichester.

Christopher Ridgway and Alison Brisby of Castle Howard Archives. Grateful acknowledgment is here made that letters are printed in this volume from the Castle Howard Archives by kind permission of the Hon. Simon Howard.

John Meriton, Deputy Keeper in the Word and Image Department of the Victoria and Albert Museum. Grateful acknowledgment is made to the Trustees of the Victoria and Albert Museum.

Zoë Stansell of the British Library, London.

Jill Barber and Christine Shearman of the Hertfordshire Records Office, Welwyn. Letters printed here are by kind permission of Hertfordshire Archives and Local Studies.

Diane Naylor and Andrew Peppitt of the Devonshire Collection, Chatsworth. Letters printed here are by kind permission of the Duke of Devonshire.

Bruce Barker-Benfield of the Department of Special Collections & Western Manuscripts, Bodleian Library, Oxford University.

Wayne Furman of the Office of Special Collections, The New York Public Library.

Pollinger Limited, representatives for Lord Lytton and the Lovelace Papers on deposit in the Bodleian Library.

Leslie A. Morris, Curator of Manuscripts, Houghton Library, Harvard University.

Stephen Jones of the Beinecke Rare Book and Manuscript Library, Yale University.

Michael Plunkett, Director of Special Collections, the Albert and Shirley Small Library, University of Virginia.

Jane Cunningham, Head of Photo Survey, the Courtauld Institute of Art, London. Andrew Peppitt, Archivist, the Devonshire Collection at Chatsworth, Bakewell. Helen Trompeteler, Picture Librarian, the National Portrait Gallery, London. And of course, the editors and production managers I have worked with at Palgrave-Macmillan: Farideh Koohi-Kamali, Amanda Fernandez, Lynn Vande Stouwe, Julia Cohen, William Fain, and Maran Elancheran.

Marilyn Gaull was the editor of *Lady Caroline Lamb: A Biography* (Palgrave 2004), and she has played a crucial role in the completion of all my work on Caro. This expresses my deep gratitude to her. Peter Graham and Peter Cochran gave me invaluable feedback, and I thank them here (again) for their generosity. I must also thank Michael O'Neill, Fred Burwick, Bernard Beatty, and Frances Wilson for commenting cogently as I progressed in my selection of Lady Caroline's letters. At the very beginning of my research, Margot Strickland, author of *The Byron Women* (Peter Owen 1974), shared with me many materials relating to Lady Caroline's life and letters. I am still deeply grateful for her help. I have also benefited from correspondence and conversation with Rosemary March, Cindy Lawford, and Catriona Mills. Mike Snell of New York City has for years been sending me information and commentary that has enlarged greatly my understanding of the relationship between Lady Caroline and Isaac Nathan, and I thank him. Along the way, I benefited from the help of a number of assistants who did research and transcribed letters: Eve Culver, Allison Macphee, and Ryan Campbell. My brother-in-law, Kevin Keller, leant a hand with the preparation of the Index. Thanks, Kevin.

I am very grateful for the assistance of colleagues with expertise in special fields, especially those who translated for me from the French, Italian, and ancient Greek texts, including Professors Danielle Trudeau, Sebastian Cassarino, and Marianina Olcott of San Jose State University, and Professor Blanche McIntyre of Oxford University.

My deepest thanks go to my wife, Charlene, who contributed to the completion of this project by doing research and editing. Te amo.

EDITORIAL METHOD

Lady Caroline Lamb's stream of consciousness style presents challenges. I have followed the method of introducing as little alteration as possible so as to preserve both the feel and the ambiguity of her flying sentences, while also trying to help the reader avoid needless confusion. The object has been to let her speak in her own voice, creative spellings and all.

The originals of several letters not being available to me, I have included some from printed sources. A number of the letters (printed or in manuscript) have had to be dated by contextual clues. All speculative dates are bracketed. The list of "Letters with Sources" at the end of the volume offers any rationale used in dating or challenging the accepted date of a particular piece of correspondence.

I would like to have included letters from Caroline's correspondents to fill out the picture, but that would have meant sacrificing her words. In selecting letters, I have sometimes preferred those requiring less explanation, but in general the primary guide to selection has been the insights the letter offers into Lady Caroline's life or her period. Brackets always indicate editorial emendation or explanation. Where the text is unclear, I have put into brackets a possible reading with a question mark to indicate its speculative nature. Where the text is indecipherable, I have put into brackets and italics the word "*illegible.*" A genealogy, a listing of principal figures, and a chronology are also offered to support the interested reader.

Introduction: Lady Caroline's Life

Lady Caroline Lamb was born Caroline Ponsonby on November 13, 1785 in London. She was the daughter of Frederick Ponsonby, Viscount Duncannon, and Henrietta Elizabeth, whose sister was Georgiana, Duchess of Devonshire. Henrietta (known as Harriet) and Georgiana were famous beauties who wielded political as well as social power. Caroline had reddish-blond hair and delicate features, excellent teeth, and freckles on her cheeks and nose. When Lord Duncannon inherited his father's title and became Earl Bessborough, Caroline received the honorific title of "Lady," which she kept until she died. She was a member of the very highest of an immensely privileged aristocratic class. She knew the Prince of Wales. She was presented to the queens of France and Italy; and as a child she told Edward Gibbon (the author of *The Decline and Fall of the Roman Empire*) that his face was so ugly it had frightened her puppy. Thus began the reputation for outrageous behaviour that followed Caroline the rest of her life.

Caroline received a very good early education. Her mother was a natural teacher, and her grandmother, Lady Spencer, a woman of formidable energy and standards. The two women lavished attention on precocious Caroline, who at age four or five could draw a map of England freehand and had begun to read. She quickly picked up basic French and Italian, and at six she began to study music. At six and a half, Caroline spoke French "very tolerably" (according to her father) and could play a tune on the harpsichord. By the time she was seven she had begun to read French and Italian.[1] At eight she was writing letters in French. Agile and athletic, Caroline nonetheless seemed elfin. She lisped, and mimicked the dialect of the Devonshire household—a nasal drawl seasoned with baby talk. Today, she would probably receive speech therapy.

---

[1] Bessborough and Aspinall, *Lady Bessborough and Her Family Circle*, 15, 56, 70, 99.

Caroline's natural childhood desire for attention put her in a panic when her mother suddenly began spitting blood and suffering spasms that sent her to Italy for a rest cure. The seven-year-old girl went along and reacted badly to this and to the accidental deaths of a young boy and her grandmother's beloved dog. Worse still, her mother fell in love with Granville Leveson Gower, a handsome young officer, and began a long affair with him. Jealous Caroline had suddenly to compete all the harder for Harriet's attention. Her misbehavior irritated her tutors, who prescribed harsh punishment. Her grandmother and mother counteracted the tutorial regime with permissiveness, and Caroline suffered further emotional confusion.

No one who lived through this period—especially not a precocious young girl whose mother was a personal friend of Marie Antoinette—could fail to be profoundly affected by the collapse of the French aristocracy. Caroline became dimly aware of her ambivalent social position and the limitations of her role as a female. Rebelliously, the seven-year-old girl demanded to climb Mt. Vesuvius, despite the volcano's unpredictable tendency to drop large hot rocks randomly around the landscape. Her mother said "No."

Just before her eighth birthday, Caroline passed a worm in her stool but seemed fine. Two weeks later, more worms appeared. She developed a persistent fever and could not keep her food down. She became delirious with fever and almost died. "I feel a thousand fears," Caroline's grandmother Lady Spencer wrote of her granddaughter's emaciated condition.[2] Though Caroline recovered, she had developed nervous behaviours, like compulsively asking questions that fretted her mother and grandmother. The family returned to England, and over the next few years watched Caroline with concern. As she approached adolescence she was regularly sequestered with a trusted governess, and her cousins Georgiana and Harrio began to think of her as a pariah. She managed to conquer her questioning and to be reintegrated in the family. Thus, her mother felt ready to give her a traditional coming out in Paris in 1802, shortly after the signing of the ill-fated Treaty of Amiens. Caroline had avoided being shunted into a familial backwater, but it was a near thing.

Two years later, Caroline rediscovered William Lamb, second son of Lord and Lady Melbourne, whom she had met as a girl. The two became infatuated. When William's elder brother Peniston died, making

[2] Lady Spencer's journal for 1793. Devonshire MSS. Chatsworth [UK], fifth Duke's Group, ff. 2014.185–252.

William heir to the Melbourne estate, Caroline accepted his proposal, then sought vainly to persuade her grandmother to endorse the match. Lady Spencer saw no advantage to the family in Caroline's marrying a relative newcomer, but she decided not to actively oppose her granddaughter's desires, and William and Caroline married in 1805. Although this marriage was one of mutual passion, Caroline had lived for years in a female cohort including her mother, aunt, and female cousins. She felt the loss of this companionship keenly, and complained to her cousin G that she felt "still a little sore on the subject of being separated from you all." Caroline quickly became pregnant, but her first child, a son, died within hours of birth, and then she had daughter who died after premature birth. In 1807, Caroline and William produced an apparently healthy boy, Augustus, who unfortunately soon showed symptoms of epilepsy and retardation. To her credit and William's, they kept Augustus in the household, giving him every chance to develop normally, despite his frequent *grand mal* seizures.

Caroline and William loved their child and each other, but they often fought. Their relationship was one of tutor and pupil, for William projected the image of an experienced man of the world. He was an agnostic and political conservative (despite his membership in the Whig party) who pronounced himself not a pillar of the church, but a buttress who supported it from the outside for the sake of domestic stability. Lady Caroline's naive piety took a beating, and she began to ape the fashionable ennui of her class. Her morals eroded, and in 1810–1811 she had a love affair with the notorious Sir Godfrey Vassal Webster—got caught, and embarrassed her mother-in-law by confessing to William, who forgave her.

In March 1812, Caroline read an advance copy of Lord Byron's newly published *Childe Harold's Pilgrimage*, wrote to him, and began a very public affair that nearly resulted in an elopement in August. Lady Bessborough collapsed, but she and Lord Bessborough dragged their daughter off to the family estates in Ireland to forestall further bad behavior. Caroline still believed Byron would run off with her. She had at this time a sharper understanding of the hypocrisy of Britain's liberal "Whig" culture than he, and she was prepared to leave England permanently. Byron would do so eventually, but not yet—and not with her. He wrote her a letter intended finally to "snap the knot," and Caroline suffered a nervous breakdown. She celebrated Christmas 1812 by lighting a bonfire and tossing replicas of Byron's gifts and letters onto it while local children recited her poem comparing Byron to Guy Fawkes.

After this bitter break-up, Caroline began a novel manuscript and formed friendships with people close to Byron, like his publisher, John Murray, and Isaac Nathan, the young Jew with whom Byron was writing "Hebrew Melodies." Byron married one of William Lamb's cousins, and when their marriage foundered, Caroline felt divided. She defended Byron against public humiliation (he was accused of sodomy), and yet tried to protect Lady Byron from losing custody of her child. William's family made a concerted effort to bring about a separation and wrest custody of Augustus from Caroline.

In summer 1816, just after Byron departed England forever, Caroline published a novel, *Glenarvon*, loosely based on her affair with Byron. It was set in Ireland and took as its background the bloody repression of the Irish uprising of 1798. It also satirized a number of familiar London households. She portrayed Byron as a traitor to the Cause of Irish Freedom. The book hit like a bombshell. She was "cut" and shunned by virtually everyone. Her in-laws found a doctor who diagnosed Caroline as "insane." Under extreme pressure from his mother and sister, William came close to a separation, then demurred. It seems clear now that he supported his wife's writing.

Caroline struggled on for the next eight years, in and out of hot water with her relatives. In 1818, the daughter of one of her mother's cousins became pregnant—not an unusual event at Devonshire House, but because she had already acquired "a bad reputation by hanging around with young unmarried men," and had "committed the unpardonable sin of being talked about," as Dorothy Howell-Thomas puts it, she was considered outrageous in the mode of Lady Caroline.[3] Lady Bessborough adopted the baby girl, who was named Susan Churchill.

Caroline went on to publish two satires of Byron's *Don Juan*: *A New Canto* (1819) and *Gordon: A Tale* (1821). She wrote two more novels. *Graham Hamilton* (1822) tells the story of a young man who sacrifices his moral code and ends up an outcast who emigrates to America. Her last novel *Ada Reis* (1823) is a phantasmagoria of witchcraft and wizardry in which the title character makes a deal with satanic forces and pays the ultimate price. Lady Caroline also wrote a good deal of poetry that was published in small magazines and annuals, and numerous song lyrics that were set to music and sold by Isaac Nathan.

When Lady Caroline's beloved mother, Lady Bessborough, died while traveling in Italy, in November 1821, Caroline was devastated. She travelled to Chatsworth for the funeral and interment, but could not bring herself to attend the services on New Year's Eve. Lady

---

[3] Howell-Thomas, *Lord Melbourne's Susan*, 26.

Bessborough's little ward, Susan Churchill, now three-and-a-half years old, became Caroline's responsibility. William accepted this duty willingly. He also agreed that they would become godparents to Isaac Nathan's newest child, Louisa Caroline Nathan.[4]

The news of Byron's death in 1824 crushed Caroline. She witnessed his funeral procession as it passed through the neighborhood of Welwyn, near Brocket Hall and the Melbourne family estates. She also read for the first time a poem Byron had written years before in frustration at her antics that cursed her with "remorse and shame" for betraying her husband and tormenting Byron after he broke off their affair. Though she exaggerated the impact of these events upon her psyche, the record shows that she produced little writing after this date. She worked at a wide variety of novel projects and even published a women's pocket-diary—a sort of calendar and receipt-book rolled together with inspirational quotations from famous writers. She also formed literary friendships with William Godwin (father of Mary Shelley), the Italian novelist Ugo Foscolo, and several liberal (or "Bluestocking") writers like Lady Morgan and Amelia Opie.

Caroline's husband finally agreed to a separation from her, then reneged again, allowing her to return to live quietly at Brocket Hall, her favourite place. Her health had declined under the abuse of alcohol and laudanum (liquid opium). She began to retain water as her internal organs gradually deteriorated. By 1827, she was an invalid under the care of a full-time physician. William had been given the post of Secretary for Ireland, and was away when she entered her final days. He made a dangerous crossing of the channel and was at her side when she expired on January 25, 1828. William, who had stuck with her in spite of everything, wrote that he felt "a sort of impossibility of believing that I shall never see her countenance or hear her voice again."[5] She died before her father-in-law, and therefore never became "Lady Melbourne," nor saw William rise to become prime minister under Queen Victoria.

Lady Caroline's reputation as a writer is not high. Her novels have often been described as hysterical and melodramatic, charges that her fiction only partly warrants. She had an uncanny ability to blend fact and fiction, and her satirical edge was sharp. Years after her send-up of the Holland House Whig *salon* had appeared in *Glenarvon*, people were still calling Lady Holland "the Princess Madagascar" behind her back. Her powers of description and social activity were superb.

---

[4] Nathan, *Fugitive Pieces and Reminiscences of Lord Byron*, 153.

[5] Ziegler, *Melbourne*, 105.

Caroline lived in a great era of letter-writing, and became obsessed with all its paraphernalia: nibs, ink, paper, pencils. Over her lifetime she owned scores of stamps for the purpose of affixing wax seals to her letters. One said, simply, "Caroline." Others exhibited the image of a bull, a lion, or a lamb (being pierced by many spears). She stamped her letters with these and others showing a castle tower among the clouds or just a cross-hatched design with the motto "Toujours." One is a head profile that might be William Lamb—or Lord Byron; it is impossible to tell.

After Lady Caroline's death, her ward Susan Churchill was sent to boarding school in Geneva to finish her education, even though William might easily have boarded her with a family and made her a governess. He gave his consent to Susan's marriage in 1837, and lived to see her prosper. I agree with Susan's biographer, Dorothy Howell-Thomas, that "[t]he very fact that William and Caroline, to whom tradition attributes so tormented a family life, so little consistency, responsibility, and generosity, brought her up and set her on her way to adulthood, and watched over her with affection to the end of their lives, speaks as only facts can."[6]

Caroline's only surviving child, Augustus, lived a full life, despite his handicaps. In November 1836, William (now Lord Melbourne) was engaged in paperwork at his desk while twenty-nine-year-old Augustus lay upon the sofa nearby. He had appeared to be asleep, but suddenly spoke in a quiet voice to his father: "I wish you would give me some franks [postage stamps] that I may write and thank people who have been kind in their inquiries."[7] In a few hours he was dead. The fact that Augustus lived in the love of his parents, relatives, and caretakers for three decades, despite his overwhelming medical problems, also speaks to us between the lines of the letters in this volume.

---

[6] Howell-Thomas, *Lord Melbourne's Susan*, 2.

[7] Dunckley, *Lord Melbourne*, 236–37.

CHAPTER ONE

Childhood and Youth

LETTERS OF 1797–1804

The importance of Lady Caroline Lamb's relationship to her grandmother and mother, and even to her brothers and her cousin "Hart," Marquis of Hartington (later the sixth Duke of Devonshire), has been widely recognized. The significance of her attachment to her cousin Georgiana, called "Little G," is much less understood. From an early date, Caroline shared intimacy with G, or "Jarry," as she calls her in letters written after her eleventh birthday. The intimacy continued after G's marriage to Lord Morpeth (the future sixth Earl of Carlisle) in 1801.

Caroline grew up a rambunctious, tomboyish girl who loved badminton, board games, horses, and dogs—many dogs, to whom she gave names like "Tango," "Bambina," and "Jock." She also lived from infancy in a world colored by politics—as allusions to "reform" "Old Pit[t]" and "taxes" show. Strangely, one of these early letters, written on twelfth night, says "I'm mad that's bad . . . I'm bad that's mad," a foreshadowing of her famous description of Byron as "mad, bad, and dangerous to know."

Typically in Caroline's letters, rhyme always threatens to take over, and the emotional pendulum is always swinging.

1. Lady Caroline Ponsonby to Lady Georgiana Cavendish (Little G). 7 JANUARY 1797.

[. . .] Oh sweetest devel tis now my turn to write to you what you should burn is hario ill I'm sorry for it [. . .] Oh lord what troubles in this be and naught but gambling wine and [glee?] will cure it what am

I writing come sing row de low row de low we leave for our heroes pleasure of fighting.

I'm mad
that's bad
I'm sad
That's bad
I'm bad
That's mad

A ridle
The damson tree
Damn the trees on

You know damson tree
Well put

Damn tree son
That makes treason
Though 'tis good to say
Damn tree son

Ah little little little me
Writes to devel devel G [. . .]
mon Dieu tis twelve night a damp moon chilled me
oh good gods I here declare never more in letters for to swear
oh G this sorrow now I feel I cannot from you quite conceal
here I beg entreat and claim never from you to hear the name
or any word near half so bad as what we use or what we had
tis shame dishonour base and wrong to thus continue all along
what we should not at first have begun but now we'll end it as its
wrong but swear with me on this moment that by the Earth and
by the reform never more to swear and then do it if you dare

Caroline fought regularly with Mary Johnson, a sturdy and determined woman, though afflicted by stuttering, who had been hired in late spring 1796 to govern Caroline's misbehavior.

2. Lady Caroline Ponsonby to Lady Georgiana Cavendish (Little G). 21 January 1797.

Dear Jarry:

The devel take her what shall I do with such a she devel confound her hang her ye gods what a life I lead with that plaguy girl Jarry you wont see my brother when you come home I'm sure I wish Mrs. Johnnnnnnnson with all her stutterage was at the devel d—'d disagreeable d—'d tiresome and d—'d illnatured oh good God Jarry I never knew such a confounded formal affected old maiden stutering little tyrant as that Mary she is so precise if one is five minutes after the time my God of heaven what a scold I really could be spiteful to her she is realy so confoundedly positive I thought I could have bit her with rage [—] if any thing happens of impertinence as she calls it why then she's as red as fire she stutters pite piter piter pCarpipidy pte pte Caropipiline pte piter has pi pi piter piter long been pter pte pter in twa twa tway this way p and pe pi piter piter ptwa ptwa [. . .] I I I am positive [—] I think to myself the Devel would have a good wife [. . .]

The Bessborough and Devonshire households had games and toys in abundance.

3. Lady Caroline Ponsonby to Lady Georgiana Cavendish (Little G). 25 September 1797.

Dear Jarry

The order of the ladder is over I gained the shipwreck [—] Johnsons life of the poets pleasure's of memory Young's night thoughts[1] a collar for Patza and a bird. Thank you for your letter I lost it and in looking for it I found your secret which I will try to send you. We played at Pope jone[2] every night almost for money till nine or a little past, my brothers went yesterday to Harrow before they went they hunted some rats and John threw me a dead one which blooded me [—] last night I looked at Jupiter the star through the telescope it looked like a full moon Mama is going to write to you in this letter she goes to town today give my love to my cousins and Hart pray tell Miss T[rimmer] I will write to her soon I read your secret but cannot make all out I am your affectionate cousin,

Caroline Ponsonby

September 1797 Fryday. Roehampton.

Tango Patza Bambina Prince Venture Vixon Ceazer Suvent Jock[3] have most of them got the mange and are obliged to be dipt very often

---

[1] Samuel Johnson's *Lives of the Poets* (1779–81), Samuel Rogers' *The Pleasures of Memory* (1792), and Edward Young's *Night Thoughts* (1742–45).

[2] Pope-Joan, a card game named after the legendary female Pope of the 9th century, played on a round board divided in eight compartments.

[3] A roll-call of Caroline's dogs.

in the fat tar pit to cure them poor old Leppen is dead—I am setting traps all over the house to get a mouse.

At age twelve, Caroline was apparently more aware of the political reform movement than of her mother's encounters with Granville Leveson Gower.

4. Lady Caroline Ponsonby to Lady Georgiana Cavendish (Little G). November-December 1797.

Dear G

a reform a reform[4] did you write a reform. then good bye cousin no more Gary or G from me Sweet G we will reform but not till we meet what must good children write no news no bore no sights no devils no nothings no nonsense there is a G a brave one too that fears a painted devil[5] we can reform we are not corrupted at any time but I disdain to reform at this time I will reform in heart but not in hand I will reform myself but not my letters.
oh you lilly liverd girl

hang all Harrio's lectures to the wise such as old Pit[6] let him get on with taxes lectures and the like while we in one hand glass in t'other wine cry health to all who lectures none [. . .] oh Gary why do you ask me to date where I am as I very seldom know I believe to day is the fifteenth 16 or 17 of either November or December I think we are at Roehampton but what is that to do tomorrow we shall be in town and next day we see the procession but then next day for aught I know to the contrary we may be here [with] Lord Grenvill Lesen[7] or what ever his name is [. . .] goodbye dear Garry heighho for jenuary dear what a pitty Christmas eve is on a Sunday [—] I thank you for your kind wish that I was with you but I wish you was with us there is papa mama my brothers I and I am always going out in Town and then when I come here we play at battlecock and shuttledore[8] and mama reads Shakespear in the

---

[4] Lady Caroline's mother was deeply interested in parliamentary reforms, like Charles Grey's 1797 bill to clean up elections.

[5] That is, Lady Elizabeth ["Bess"] Foster. Lady Caroline and her cousins Little G, Harrio, and Hartington hated Bess, mistress of the Duke and friend of the Duchess of Devonshire.

[6] William Pitt the Younger (1759-1806), politician and statesman, who had suspended *Habeas Corpus* in the early 1790s, declaring all English "reformers" had taken the side of France in a time of war.

[7] Granville Leveson Gower, Caroline's mother's lover, who later married "Harrio."

[8] Battlecock and shuttledore—old children's game from India—basically badminton without a net.

evening When she goes with [Ann?] up stairs to sleep John Fred Will[9] and I generally raill out a song with a machine that would frighten you in the great hall while the Men drink in the dining room them men generally are poor Papa and some dogs lying by the fire. we go out a great deal here.

C[aroline] P[onsonby]

Sometimes her letters became almost incoherent—though still in rhyme.

5. Lady Caroline Ponsonby to Lady Georgiana Cavendish (Little G). [1797–1798].

Dear G

Im distracted as you see by my letters Im mad Iv no patience to write good god Jarry [. . .] all the devels demons say make Hartington say in his days he never knew what love could be till he did know his sister G then let him swear by suns by skies that if he can believe his eyes or else deucedly mistaken be if he e'er saw a girl like G and none in swearing doth exel and that he swears by ladies well except one else that is named C she can almost as well as he [—] Dearest devel do not be bored to read this letter take it and burn it in some furnace or fire [. . .] powder into dust and if there must be that why then there must [—] die die forever oh this stupid foolish little bit of paper.

Caroline's tutors apparently expected her to read novels of notorious length and difficulty.

6. Lady Caroline Ponsonby to Lady Georgiana Cavendish (Little G). [1797–1798].

Dear G:

do you know what o'clock it is for here it is so dark though today is remarkably clear [—] have you been to your Chesterfield Ball have you seen or danced with a pipe Lady I'm in a great fuss having lost hope, not however the knife. how do you go on about minerology. my box is never come—ask Miss Trimmer when it is have you done Clarissa[10] you

[9] Lady Caroline's three brothers, John William (Lord Duncannon as heir to the Bessborough estate), Frederick (later a hero of Waterloo), and Willy (her favorite), two years her junior.

[10] Samuel Richardson's epistolary novel, *Clarissa* (1747–48).

will be surprised to see so many little dabs of Letters, but it's silly wit—when do you come?

yours ever
CP

7. Lady Caroline Ponsonby to Lady Georgiana Cavendish (Little G). [1797–1798].

Dear Jarry

I intreat you to tell no earthly being I ever wrote or you to me any kind of letter [. . .] I went to Mrs. Lambs at White hall accompanied with my tag Mary[11] today we all go that's to say the Lambs Caro and me to Lady E Monk[12] to dance. they come to take me esp. William Lamb[13] has a very bad cold Lord Melbourne had a badish headache yesterday [. . .] the croupe [is] a very choking illness it is a suffocation in the throat I hope you will recover of it it is a very dangerous disorder my uncle Spencer had two children that died of it [. . .]

CP

can I get any thing for any of you in town?

Like their French counterparts, British aristocrats rightfully feared the revolt of the working classes. Patriotism dominated many family discussions and activities of Caroline's youth and early adulthood, as did literary events, like the emergence of the Edinburgh Review.

8. Lady Caroline Ponsonby to Georgiana, Lady Morpeth (Little G). [1802].

Dearest G

though I have been rather late in acknowledging it I was nevertheless extremely obliged to you for your letter—how I wish you could have

---

[11] Her "tag," was Mary Johnson, hired to discipline Caroline.

[12] Lady Elizabeth Monck, a friend of Lady Caroline's mother.

[13] Lady Caroline's future husband. Caroline's later statement to her friend Lady Morgan that she fell in love with William when she was only twelve or thirteen may have been true. See *Lady Morgan's Memoirs*, 2: 210-13.

seen the Presentation and convention of the Colours—both of which were affecting and interesting in the greatest degree—My Aunt[14] spoke low but well—and Duncannon distinctly, he looked extremely well but really the newspapers give so minute and moving an account that I shall not plague you with any other though I imagine theirs must damp all enthusiastic Ardour. yesterday we went to see all the Corps pass in review before Lord Harrington who with a very military air and scrutinizing look made observations on them—however he turned round to us with a gracious smile and sayd we might be proud of the Marylebonnes and so we are! Lord Petersham left his aide decamp Burwick to take care of us and has nearly won my heart by his Manners and face which are both superior to most people's. In the evening we remained en famille with Lord Abercorn[15] who is grown so extremely gracious (particularly to Mama) he seldom leaves us when he is in Town for two days [. . .] Lady Melbourne who came to Town for a day or two is confined to bed by Dr. Blaine who very awkwardly dropped a stone on her foot—this is a secret, don't Blab it about [. . .] Caro & I have been walking in Green Park & we called at White Hall—Lady Melbourne was better though still in pain—I admire the Heroism with which she bore it for no body knew she was suffering in the least the whole time she stopped at D[evonshire] House—her beauty I thought much gone off lately—but I am convinced in her best days she never looked so beautiful as this morning—quite small, young and Blooming!

Have you seen the Edinborough Review—I hear it is very good—written by some young men of that place and full of very just Criticisms on many new plays and Books. Grand Mama[16] has taken lodgings in St. James, that much to the discredit of her family as it seems as if we had shut our doors upon her—the truth is there is not too much room, D[evonshire] House can hold no more. I am in bed and my room no bigger than a coal hut within Harrio's—we are full of horrors at this invasion but amidst a thousand heroical speeches Harrio swears she will fly even to America sooner than die here in the easiest manner imaginable.

I hope Bertha's or some of Lady Elizabeth's admirers will arrive at D[evonshire] House who knows but their productions incline them to favor us—Lord Melbourne has spoilt my pen but say'd it will do to send

[14] Probably Lavinia, wife of Lady Caroline's Uncle John, second Earl Spencer.

[15] John James Hamilton, ninth Earl Abercorn (1756–1818).

[16] The Dowager Lady Spencer.

you every message from him that might be sent—you will think this a very stupid letter but consider how a Cold, Barley water, & a hot room stupify [. . .]

Believe me Dearest G your always and affectionate
Caroline Ponsonby

CHAPTER TWO

Marriage

LETTERS, 1805–1809

Lady Caroline was married to William Lamb on 3 June 1805. Her cousin "Hart" was devastated by the event, because he had believed he was going to marry Caroline. He never married, and evidence in her letters shows that Caroline never stopped trying to conciliate him for the failure to fulfill a childhood fantasy. The marriage was not really desired by Caroline's mother or grandmother, but it had potential. William expected to inherit the fortune of his aging father, Lord Melbourne, and he seemed to know how to handle his volatile bride. The couple were given a relatively small allowance and apartments in Melbourne House—a wonderful residence near Downing Street, but one that afforded them little privacy or independence. Caroline would wait her entire adult life in expectation of becoming "Lady Melbourne," for William's father outlived her by a few months.

Though Caroline loved William, she felt the loss of the women's circle that had enwrapped her to this point. Her character also eroded under the influence of London's amoral society and her husband's agnosticism, as we see in a letter written as early as January 1806, six months into her marriage, addressed to Lady Holland, a dominant figure of the gynocracy (as Byron called it). Lady Holland hosted regular gatherings of politicians, artists, and writers at her home, but her status was marginalized because she had divorced Sir Godfrey Webster before marrying Lord Holland. Despite warnings from her mother-in-law, Caroline formed a warm friendship with Lady Holland.

In 1807, after a miscarriage and the premature birth of a daughter who did not survive, Caroline and William had a seemingly healthy boy, whom they christened Augustus. The Prince of Wales himself attended the celebrations and stood as the child's godfather. Soon, however, Augustus showed signs of epilepsy and mental retardation. We can only speculate on the origins of Augustus's problems, but one possibility is that he suffered from a parasite he received from his mother or ingested in his food.[1] *Caroline never stopped hoping Augustus would recover.*

Caroline's brother Frederick was wounded in the British campaign in Spain. Like a number of British citizens, she felt frustrated and angry over the poor handling of the military operation in 1809. She was also frustrated by the seeming invulnerability of Lady Elizabeth Foster, the Duke of Devonshire's long-time mistress, who had held onto her position in the household even after Georgiana, the Duchess (also Lady Elizabeth's closest friend), had died in March 1806. Three years later, in October 1809, Caroline could only fulminate to Hartington as the hated "Bess" managed to marry the Duke and take the place of their beloved Georgiana.

In the interstices, Caroline made closer acquaintance with the literati of the age, including figures like Sidney Smith (a founder of the Edinburgh Review*) and William Blake. She also discovered that William had been infatuated with Little G before he fixed upon Caroline. She made the subject an open one between herself and G, but anxiety about William's previous affection for her cousin never quite left Caroline thereafter.*

It is hard to say how much Caroline was bothered by the marriage of William's brother George Lamb to her illegitimate cousin Caroline St. Jules in 1809. From this moment Caroline became "Caro William" to distinguish her from her doppelgänger, "Caro George."

Another strange event in the family was the marriage in 1809 of Caroline's cousin Harriet ("Harrio," Little G's sister) to Lady Bessborough's long-time lover, Granville Leveson Gower. Whether out of general sensitivity to the situation, or because they feared her misbehavior, the couple made sure not to invite Lady Caroline.

1. Lady Caroline to Georgiana, Lady Morpeth, Future Sixth Countess of Carlisle. [18–20 June 1805.]

[. . .] you told me the happiest time in your life was three weeks after being married. I am not quite arrived at that period—but am very much contented with my present state & yet I cannot say I have never felt happier—I think content & a sort of pleasant calm express this better than any other word I have felt moments of much greater happiness but then they were not so real [—] they were snatched up with a great deal of fear both before & behind that they would soon be over as was indeed

[1] Dickinson, "Augustus Lamb (1807–1836) and His Tutor, Robert Lee," 48.

the case—such was the breakfast at Chiswick when I walked round the garden holding Williams arm and when I wished to put a stop to time—being at that moment as happy as I ever wished to be—& yet though I loved William then with a more romantic & enthusiastic attachment I did not know or even flatter myself with believing he was so worthy of being loved as I find him—indeed I am surprised as you say why we had such an opinion of his moral Character—if he had not always acted with the greatest & strictest propriety yet I believe he never for a moment either justified such actions to himself or meant them—he is kinder more delightful & more attentive than even I expected. he reads to me sometimes from nine in the evening till two—walks & stays with me all day & I have not found one single moment hang heavily with me since I have been here—& yet I will not say I am the happiest person alive. I feel I shall be & feel too that in the whole world I could not have found a person who would have suited me in every respect so well as he does, but I am still a little sore on the subject of being separated from you all—I feel I daresay like a soul just arrived in Paradise—very happy no doubt as they must be happy to be there but still a little cut off from all it had once been accustomed to love & live with—Do not mistake me though or think this will actually be the case for I mean to plague & follow & live with you just as much as ever & perhaps more as my sulky fits have been thoroughly routed

I often talk of you to William & am more delighted than I can tell you with the Frankness and affection with which he speaks of you. We agreed that if he had denied having felt a very strong attachment to you he might have been less guilty of the charge of inconstancy but would have had many more faults to answer for—he is frankness itself, However & does not scruple to say he loved you very sincerely[2] How after that confession you ever happened to chuse another I cannot pretend to guess but for your & my own account I am delighted for though I am sure William would never have given you any serious cause to repent it yet his situation & both your ages then would have made it very disagreeable in short impossible and his Character was much less formed than it is now & even now I think he will improve every year & that is saying a great deal as it is not every body who does so by growing older—[. . .] I am afraid you will think me rather garrulous with age—by the length of my letter but they say that infirmity comes on with years

[2] In another letter of this period to Georgiana, Lady Caroline writes, "Seriously you do not know my Dear Dear G how very much I love you & my Husband I fancy would confess as much if he dared but that is a sore subject with him" (Castle Howard MSS J18/35/68).

and though I am seriously no longer very young yet there is no age I do not feel some hundred years and if I was asked by surprise how long I had been married I should certainly say four or five years [. . .]

Yrs most truly and affectionately,
Caroline Lamb [. . .]

Here perhaps is a clue to the collapse Hart suffered on 7 May when he learned of Caroline's betrothal, and his mother's physician Walter Farquhar had to be called in to sedate him.

2. Lady Caroline to the Marquis of Hartington. 23 June 1805.

Brocket Hall

The wand was broke her elves dismiss'd
The Deamons yell'd—the serpents hist
The skies were black the thunder roar'd
When sad Titania left her lord
And thus in plaints both loud and long
To stones address'd her mournful song.

———

To Oberon a long adieu
And with him all his fairy crew
To jests & pranks & spikes & sticks
To Betsey Green & Willy Hicks
To lance & shield & Capes for knights
To Scibson [Bapehs?][3] magic rites
To Houses built twixt earth & skies
To mausolees for Dragon flies
Adieu to these to thee adieu
And with thee all thy fairy crew—

[. . .]

Oh how could I these joys forgoe
And all for such a Creature too

---

[3] Variants of this name appear at several points in Lady Caroline's correspondence with her cousin, the Marquis of Hartington (later the sixth Duke of Devonshire). It probably refers to a fictitious character of their childhood.

A man whose very gentlest breath
might blow a thousand elves to death
So black so fierce & such a voice
I own I marvel at my choice—

[. . .]

Thus spoke Titania then she sigh'd
Doomed to become a mortal bride
What since befel her no one knows
but certain 'tis overwhelmed with woes
she deeply mourns her broken vows.[4]

Caroline turned to her cousin for basic advice about sex and pregnancy.

3. Lady Caroline to Georgiana, Lady Morpeth, Future Sixth Countess of Carlisle. [AUGUST–NOVEMBER 1805.]

Thank you for your letter my Dearest G & be assured as long as mine are acceptable in prose they shall not fail but really I can send you nothing else as I have forgot all about the verses which were then in my head, full I remember of sympathy & peculiar German too & extinguished sentiment & glow my love. [. . .] It is delightful at Brocket but my wishes do not particularly center here. I am like a horse in clover looking out for a new pasture though I shall never find a better—am I with child G tell me fairly what you think & how you felt when you were so first [—] had you ever little unaccountable pains many fears that you were going to miscarry[5] were you nervous apt to be frightened very hungry every day very sleepy and very languid did a great deal of exercise give you a pain in your back were you restless———pray tell me also for I have nobody else to ask though it seems rather an extraordinary question to ask but is it bad for you to sleep with your husband at the time in the most significant sense of the word—I am anxious to know for I must let nothing be done that can hurt my darling boy who I love already better than any thing—

[4] Hart felt Caroline had promised to marry him, and while this may have been his misperception, Caroline seems to acknowledge she encouraged his fantasy.

[5] Lady Caroline's fears were fulfilled. On 1 February 1806, she gave birth prematurely to a little girl who died.

William Lamb, by Sir Thomas Lawrence. 1805. National Portrait Gallery, London.

we are reading tolerably little & I see too little of William—today I lead quite a pleasant life but today for the first time I went out to shoot with him it was pretty to see the Dogs & my beautiful husband with all his black hair over his brows & a great colour from the eagerness & animation he felt pacing over all the stubble fields with his gun on his shoulder & me on his arm sometimes we rode & then he brave and stoutly led my Horse. I was delighted till I saw one partridge killed & another wounded which though at too great a distance really to see I imagined & greatly disgusted I went away

Tell Car I am still as I was at Holy Well that is I am convinced the Mother of a beautiful boy [. . .] I am sure I feel the boy move—

Burn this immediately & if you tell Lord M[orpeth] a word of what I have said to you tremble at what I shall repeat to William.

The young married couple made an extended visit to Lord and Lady Abercorn's residence in Stanmore, where amateur play productions became the focus.

4. Lady Caroline to Georgiana, Lady Morpeth, Future Sixth Countess of Carlisle. [OCTOBER–NOVEMBER 1805.]

You are determined I find to write such wicked letters that I must either give you up for ever or scold you very——jealous——merciful heaven what words! if I was jealous you should drink slow poison every morning and if I was jealous I should hate you instead of which somehow or other you know I l . . . . o . . . . v . . . . e you lady and therefore no more—

William as you guessed is to make love to Lady Cahir which all things together I think make a better comedy than the ones they are going to [perform?] his parts are Captain Absolute, Rivals,[6] ruffian Captain in George's play,[7] Mr. Oakly in the Jealous Wife[8] the Thom[as] Benevolent of Oroonoko[9] in that tragedy and the other plays are not yet fixed on how they will act I do not know—George is perfect he acts according to custom with all his head and does Acres[10]—Lawrence will do well he has many stage tricks and they say a very good idea of acting—as for William he has not even read his part yet so we cannot judge but if he acts as he does any thing else he will impress every body [. . .]

[6] Richard Brinsley Sheridan's *The Rivals* (first performed in 1775) features Captain Absolute.

[7] *Whistle for It*, a musical comedy that opened to poor reviews shortly after this amateur theatrical trial at the Priory, Stanmore, home of Lord and Lady Abercorn.

[8] George Colman's comedy, *The Jealous Wife* (1761), is based on Henry Fielding's *Tom Jones*.

[9] Thomas Southerne's *Oroonoko*, first produced in 1695, was based upon Aphra Behn's *Oroonoko, or the Royal Slave* (1688).

[10] Bob Acres, a character in Sheridan's *The Rivals*.

I have married not a man but an Angel [—] take from him his beauty (which by the bye increases every day) his being the cleverest and most sensible of all men and yet I say if you look over the whole world you will never find his fellow—he is kinder more gentle more soothing more indulgent talks nonsense better and coaxes me more than a woman could and with all that he is in short perfection I have not found hitherto a fault in him and yet I have been five years looking for one—you will excuse this little rhapsody—it does as well as your treatise on hearts—for I think neither of our essays had much to do with the head—you will wonder what has loosened the joints of my fingers & made me run on so flippantly but the reason is plain—my own William Lamb is gone to Brocket for another review—since I wrote William left me for two days & a night for his detestable yeomanry dinner—I did not know before how cold & melancholy it was to sleep by yourself [. . .]

At the Priory, Stanmore, the drama of Caroline's first pregnancy receives almost equal billing with the plays in production.

5. Lady Caroline to Georgiana, Lady Morpeth, Future Sixth Countess of Carlisle. [October–November 1805.]

Dear G

I think the next bad thing to neglecting writing a person is to make excuses for it therefore as I have committed the first offence to my own G I will have nothing to do with the other [—] did you ever read a fairy tale concerning a palace which was so contrived that whoever entered it could never by any means get out again—this was a magician's but to show how much it was taken from real life turn your eyes to the Priory [—] here we came to pay a visit of about three days at most & here no power on earth but death can get us away from perhaps till the first week in January—Lord and Lady Ab[ercorn] are kindness itself the very essence of all that is delightful or obliging but the very mention of removing for a day clouds the whole sunshine of the skies and such a storm ensues as was seldom witnessed but by the inhabitants of Sicily they have taken us by a weak side and play upon a thing that never fails to succeed my being at a very critical moment and not in a very strong state—I believe the danger is over but I was allarmed for I grew languid & had pains in my back weakness all over and ceased to be sick they confine me all day in an horizontal posture to a couch and in general make me dine upstairs[11]—William is quite well and a great favourite here Lord Abercorn says he seldom saw a man he could compare with him and Lady A[bercorn] less cautious and perhaps less true says she never did [—] this is the more flattering as I hear it from all quarters and not only from their mouths which might otherwise be suspected—Lord and Lady Aberdeen flirt together au notre mode—Lady A[bercorn] says if you will not repeat the joke "I come out from dinner and am almost always obliged to pull my veil over my face on one side Kat and Lord Aberdeen set on an arm chair so close that it is no matter whether they are embracing or no for I defy a person to find out when they are not & if I turn the other way I see Caro & William very comfortably gone to bed in another part of the room on the couch" [. . .] if every body was placed in their different situations as suitably as vegetables Lady A might be singing old songs of sentiment by a book [—] Caroline Lamb might be lying among the stars in the universe and William might be at the feet of Georgiana but I hope not of Georgiana

—MORPETH—[12]

Caroline took care to reassure her grandmother of her good behavior—though Lady Spencer had plenty of opportunity to observe otherwise.

6. Lady Caroline to Georgiana, Lady Spencer. [9 DECEMBER 1805.]

How good it was of you to write again to me, my dearest grand-mama, & how much good your letters seem always to do me. I often think of the time I spent with you at Althorp & Bath with pleasure. We used to be so very comfortable, & I believe besides good society, the being always occupied makes time go very pleasantly.

I have been keeping rather different hours—though the Priory is far from a late place: for while many go to bed even before eleven, few sit up after twelve. [. . .] Wm. & I get up about ten or ½after or later (if late

[11] Lady Caroline's pregnancy was difficult. She portrays herself as under others' control here, but her mother and cousins described her as terrified of doing anything to harm her baby.

[12] Anxiety about William's affection for Georgiana is obvious in Caroline's letters of this period: "William sends you his love also and all good wishes a friend can imagine & he is my Pretty G's friend & I am your friend & we are these three good friends together" (Castle Howard MSS J18/35/87).

at night)—have our breakfasts, talk a little, read Newton[13] on the Prophecies with the Bible—having finished Sherlock—then I hear him his part—he goes to eat & walk—I finish dressing & take a drive or a little walk with some of the inhabitants, generally Lady M[ary] Hamilton[14] who is a remarkably sensible & amiable girl, then come up stairs where William meets me, & we read Hume[15] with Shakespear till ye dressing bell, then hurry & hardly get dressed by dinner time [. . .] I am quite happy & Wm. bids me tell you he thinks I am growing quite good. I do not know what to say, I think there is much room still for amendment, but anyhow I will not do amiss for want of pains, I promise you. [. . .]

Adieu my dearest grandmama, pray remember me very kindly to my dearest aunt & cousins & mad^elle[16] Believe me your most dutiful & affectionate granddaughter. I am quite recovered now from my indisposition, but keep extremely quiet. I have got milk. The child has not moved yet.

On 31 January 1806, Caroline went into premature labor. Her baby boy was born early in the morning on 1 February, but lived only a few hours. William had won an election the previous day in Leominster, arriving home to find his child dead and his wife exhausted. Sadly, her Aunt Georgiana died on 30 March, complicating her recovery, which featured manic outbursts followed by contrition.

7. Lady Caroline to Georgiana, Lady Morpeth, Future Sixth Countess of Carlisle. [April 1806.]

My Dearest G

I feel so afraid of your not liking William and think it is all my foolish jokes which I promise you are quite over now & he has not heard your name without proper decorum & gravity since I lay in I was not going to say any thing you disliked the other day only I was really anxious to beg you not to tell Ld M[orpeth] you know by experience how disagreeable any third person is in such stupid jokes & I do not think they

---

[13] Thomas Newton (1704–1782), Bishop of Bristol, wrote a dissertation on the Prophecies.

[14] Daughter of the first Marquess of Abercorn by his first wife, Catherine, daughter of Sir Joseph Copley. She died unmarried in 1814. In British peerage, a marquess ranks below a duke and above an earl.

[15] David Hume (1711–1776), philosopher and historian.

[16] Probably Caroline St. Jules, Lady Caroline's illegitimate cousin, who married George Lamb in 1809.

would amuse him—the moment I found it plagued you I left it off [. . .] I may often say little impudent speeches or speak too loud and too much[17] but all this is for want of thought & will be corrected in a year or two I daresay—if you could see my heart I feel sure you would all love me much better & though I have a thousand faults I may say I think with truth that I never said or thought any thing from ill nature or will to any body [—] I hope you are now none of you angry with my manner to Lady Elizabeth [Foster][18] believe me I feel every thing about her but too strongly & yet I will add that I feel still more the greatest compassion for her I think she has lost her best friend[19] & I feel secure she has no other aim or plans than to live quietly with us all I know she feels any kindness very strongly & am sure she would dislike giving pain to those who are kind to her more than to those who are otherwise I do not know if I was mistaken I was very much pleased to see your manner the other day—it would be impossible for you my own G to be otherwise than kind to any body [. . .]

By June, Caroline had become pregnant again, and the news had helped to settle her.

8. Lady Caroline to Georgiana, Lady Morpeth, Future Sixth Countess of Carlisle. [SEPTEMBER 1806.]

[. . .] Thank you Dearest for your pineapple & if you like our wheat ears, William will occasionally send you some—indeed what you say is very true but I believe not just to me, for I am so far from repining at any little disappointments I may have experienced that I only try how I can be grateful & good enough for the great happiness I possess indeed my own G[—]William would make up for a great deal & I think we both know what it is to have good husbands—as to me, I have tried most seriously to follow all your good advice & do not think one word of it was wasted upon me. I try & keep as free from all irritation & disputing as I possibly can & though I feel enough how far I am from what I ought to be I think I may venture to say I am very much improved. Wm & I have had no quarrels of any consequence since I fancied myself with child & I believe a Month before which you know is very near four months all

[17] One of the indicators of bi-polar disorder.

[18] Caroline strongly disliked Bess Foster.

[19] Georgiana, Duchess of Devonshire had died 30 March 1806, as noted.

together & I do not believe now I know how to quarrel with him he is so very indulgent & kind. perhaps however I boast too much. we may have had some casual little words in that time though but few I assure you & certainly nothing serious—William made me quite low today though for in talking of former times of Woburn many years ago & of Fox & the Duke of Bedfords kindness to him, he grew so out of spirits that he quite cried—as women do & has but just recovered his spirits—however they are returned as usual for he is reading a Greek play out loud & making such a noise I scarcely know what I am writing [. . .]

Caroline Lamb

William Lamb's mentor, politician Charles James Fox, died on 13 September 1806, at Chiswick House, a residence of the Duke of Devonshire, who had invited him knowing he needed comfort as he faced the end.

9. Lady Caroline to Georgiana, Lady Morpeth, Future Sixth Countess of Carlisle. [14 September 1806.]

Little Hampton

We were all very much affected with the melancholy account we have heard today—there is no philosophizing with one's feelings or we had so little help before we had little new to hear but there is so dreadful a sound in the words It is all over that no body can judge till the moment how they will bear hearing it—William is most extremely affected by it—Mr. Fox was so strong was so very kind to him that he has lost almost his best friend indeed with the Duke of Bedford the two who had most influence over him and to whom he looked most up to—what with seeing Frederick and what with hearing this melancholy news—I could not read your dear letter for some moments and William carried it out with him before I was aware of your injunctions but I did not repent for he said it was the prettiest letter & the prettiest he had ever seen & though he said he cried very much at the details in it he would never have forgiven me for not showing it [to] him even if I had known before you wished me not indeed my own G I agree with you in all you say & your poor M[other][20] if she had been here would have wished more than any

[20] The Duchess of Devonshire had died on 30 March 1806.

thing that Chiswick should have been the spot for so great a Mind to reign itself in and to afford the quiet and delightful moments to the little remaining time he had to live—Dear Mr. Fox how good & kind he was to us he comforted us for our loss[21] & little thought how soon we should have to lament his—we can form but a trifling idea of the loss he will be to the nation & to every thing political but we have learnt to know how all his friends and relations & all who loved him will suffer I think if people are not kind to Mrs. Fox hereafter I shall esteem them brutes & fancy their prudish virtue & starched unkindness will be looked upon as worse in the sight of God than even her most degrading faults We who all loved him and know his wishes will be kind to her but I sadly fear that false Lady Holland[22] after a show of civility for a time will make her feel her helpless situation one thing however I am determined to do and that is if she takes St. Anne's from Mrs. Fox I will never speak to her again How pretty I think your verses they express so exactly what I felt but could not find words to speak pray burn my letter & never tell any thing I say to you, if you will not—I shall write to you as openly as if you read my heart & shall tell every thing till I hear it tries or displeases you—Mama as you may imagine is very low but she likes to talk with me and tell me every thing & no body is so particularly pleasant to talk with as she is I did not know till lately half of the comfort such a friend was I hope we shall long continue to have her God Bless you Dearest write some time to me & believe me most affectionately and truly yours Caroline Lamb

Caroline miscarried, losing a little girl, who was buried in Hatfield with her brother. The day after her twenty-first birthday, Caroline felt mainly anxiety about the negative opinions of her cousin G and sister-in-law, Emily.

10. Lady Caroline to Georgiana, Lady Morpeth, Future Sixth Countess of Carlisle. 14 November 1806.

Brocket Hall

[. . .] I cannot wait any longer without writing a line to you Dearest G as you are so odd a person I believe you will take some new fancies

[21] That is, the death of the Duchess.

[22] Charles James Fox was the Uncle of the third Baron Holland, to whose wife, Elizabeth, Lady Caroline alludes. Apparently Fox's wife had some claim on the Hollands' property (in St. Anne's) which it was in the power of Lady Holland to frustrate.

against me if you do not hear from me occasionally. I must not profess any more but if you knew William's accusations I believe you would be satisfied of my love [—] he says he believes I love you better than him at least he knows I can keep no secret from you—this however I very strenuously deny I only will hope that you have affection enough for me to believe I am no flatterer & would not take all the pains I do to exculpate myself in your eyes if I was not very anxious to merit your good opinion the only motto I give to you is therefore be blind—that is do not search out the faults I try to conceal from you and object to me—because I am more amiable to those I love than to those to whom I am less attached—Emily[23] has just come here I never knew a person so much improved as she is in Mind person and manners & I think very few people as amiable or as pretty her only fault is ill nature & that I think is very much gone off it is not either ill nature of the heart but of the tip of the Tongue only I am just one and twenty and you do not know how bold it appears to me I must indeed try and grow all that I ought to be & I hope you will find I am improved in many points when next we meet I ride every day & am got in excellent health again but I am sorry to think how soon you will be graded and Emily & I have been putting the odds forward against it in a balance and we find it morally impossible you should escape—what does Ld M[orpeth] think of Buonaparte's praise and what do you think of that bloody man [. . .] my poor Mama writes me very melancholy letters & I wish you were back again to salve and comfort her [—] she calls you and Harrio her dear children and says if any thing could have made her feel more affection towards you than she us'd to it is that misfortune which overwhelms both at the same time seems to place yours more immediately indeed under her care Oh my G what a sad world this is bonneur plaisir d'amour meme tout passe tout plaisir[24] Harrio wrote me a very kind letter [. . .] Mama has sent me a drawing of her[25] which I am to keep till you come then it is to be yrs [. . .]

William was offered the honor of delivering the first address at the opening of Parliament, and Caroline worked at getting along with her in-laws.

---

23 Emily, Lady Cowper, William Lamb's sister, and a bitter opponent of Caroline's through most of her life.

24 The melancholy here is attributable to Fox's death, for he was William Lamb's mentor and sponsor.

25 Georgiana, Duchess of Devonshire (died 30 March 1806).

11. Lady Caroline to Georgiana, Lady Morpeth, Future Sixth Countess of Carlisle. 26 NOVEMBER 1806.

Brocket Hall, Welwyn.

Thank you a thousand times my Dearest for your kind letter I began to think you a long while answering mine but concluded you had so many correspondents like me you had no time to answer them all I am always glad when you are at Castle Howard as I know it does you good and with Dear Lord M. whom I hope you will remember me to—as William does not like my hand I have got a writing Master and really when I see my own letters I think "this cannot be I" as the Old Woman did [. . .] Emily and I went to the Hartford Ball last Night both dressed and looking very pretty she the prettiest both dancing in great spirits all the evening—I the longest. We came home at near four quite tired neither of us having danced I believe above once since we were married—Emily is grown beautiful and more amiable than any body—her ill nature is never from herself and depends much upon her Company the truth is any body who indulges themselves in the habit of telling stories of others must always grow more or less ill natured [. . .] Wm has promised to move the Address[26]—I only hope he will do it well though my Ambitious hopes of his success are entirely destroyed by Buonapartes Conquest[27] who will destroy parliament, people, England and all if he goes on at this rate [. . .]

12. Lady Caroline to Georgiana, Lady Morpeth, Future Sixth Countess of Carlisle. [26–27 NOVEMBER 1806.]

[. . .] if Brocket Hall being in greater beauty than I ever saw it Wm & I being its only inhabitants & this the only opportunity I shall have of inviting you are inducements pray do come for one Night at least & bring with you Caro and Harrio if you like or whoever you please only write one word before that I may order you a good dinner—& if Ld M[orpeth] has not time to come pray try & do so for once without him but I rather hope this will not be the case for I do like your husband so

[26] William was to make the opening address of the parliamentary session, a privilege offered to him by the Whig leadership. Caroline is worried because he was a poor speaker.

[27] Napoleon's army had won a series of victories in the Jena Campaign for control of Prussia, which had ended with General Blücher's capitulation on 6 November 1806 at Ratkau.

much that if I had not one of my own—I have often thought I was in danger of nourishing a hopeful passion—seriously after Wm I do not know a Man I admire & like so much & this is no flattery to you for I say so to every body. pray tell him that his present to me is more admired than any thing I wore it last Night at the Hartford Ball [. . .] William is quite delightful & I as happy as the word can express Lord & Lady Melbourne are really kinder & more attentive to me than any thing you can imagine & my dressing room is a little Paradise [. . .]

Caroline now suspected she might be pregnant again, a prospect both happy and troubling, for her first two pregnancies had ended disastrously, and she feared losing William's devotion either way.

13. Lady Caroline to Lady Bessborough. 14–15 January 1807.

My Dear Dear Dear M[other]

excuse the little hastiness of my temper yesterday for the Coachie not being my own was a thought strong enough to have interrupted an oration of Cicero [—] I continue very well though a little disappointed at not having fainted away today. I cannot think why. Caro[28] and I dined early and went to the Play last night which was pretty good sport and some pretty singing, though the words of Brahams[29] best song were enough to make a mulato sick—

Says a smile to a tear
On the Cheek of my Dear
how come we how come we together
like a Bright sunny ray
through a showery day
in a Morn in a Morn of spring weather

The latter part's mine for want of the memory of the other lines which were however no better, if so good—Mr. Sheridan[30] called on me

[28] Caroline Rosalie Adelaide St. Jules, who would marry George Lamb on 17 May 1809.

[29] John Braham (1774?–1856), tenor, and composer of Jewish descent and colleague of Isaac Nathan.

[30] Almost certainly playwright and politician Richard Brinsley Sheridan, Lady Caroline's mother's lover, whose intense interest in Lady Caroline led some to speculate he might have been Lady Caroline's father.

yesterday, was very pleasant & seemed to have no mysterious intents. Ld Stair[31] & Mr. James agreably enlivened us at the play where Caro[32] sat flirting with George [Lamb], & I like Susannah and the elders discoursing with them. I could not help remarking the difference between a lover and a husband [—] George had been near an hour and a half at the play before William appeared who when he came was very agreable & infinitely more entertaining than Ld Stair—we met Lord & Lady [Borino?][33] hand and glove, for they never are asunder—how comes this wonderful phenomenae why when the honeymoon is over does Lord B. remain a Lover—I am so poetical that it is a mercy I do not write my letter like Dolly the Cook's maid and perhaps I should if I had a little less time for I always think one does & says more when one is pinched for dear life to a minute [—] the accounts of Francis would have ceased to be allarming & ended in death if I did not suppose Bently's memory and nurse's had failed [—] he brings me word his pulse is at 19 this is so much more probably a hundred and nineteen or ninety that I have made myself easy about him, but have written to Pemberton[34] for further details—if Lady Dun[cannon] is with child[35] the jokes about Pemberton will be endless, as we both consulted him at the same time to make us so and he has the reputation of infallibility I must just go and fetch a watch—I will be back in a minute. Berry & G are the next subjects Miss Berry[36] came here yesterday tolerably agreable & entertaining G arrived soon after and we had a very pleasant conversation together Lady Melbourne sent you many kind messages yesterday & invited you to dine here, which, considering her fore knowledge of your expedition to Holywell was more kind than well judged—G. & Ld Morpeth took little George[37] to the play last night. I am glad of it but afraid she will have been very low God bless my own pretty Best & Dearest M. I will write again

---

31 Possibly John Dalrymple, sixth Earl of Stair (1749–1821).

32 Caroline's illegitimate cousin, as noted.

33 Possibly the second Baron Boringdon and first Earl of Morley (1772–1840). His marriage to the daughter of the Earl of Westmorland in June 1804 was, ironically, dissolved by Act of Parliament in 1809.

34 Christopher Robert Pemberton (1765–1822), physician.

35 Maria Duncannon and Lady Caroline were indeed both pregnant.

36 Mary Berry (1763–1852), author of *Social Life in England and France from the French Revolution* (1831).

37 The Morpeths' eldest son, afterwards seventh Earl of Carlisle (1802–1864.)

tomorrow in the meantime believe me most truly & affectionately & dutifully yrs,

Caroline Lamb—
I am quite well today—

Early in 1807, Caroline confirmed she was once again pregnant. She started making a book of verse and stories for her cousin G, to whom she continued writing in the most intimate terms.

14. Lady Caroline to Georgiana, Lady Morpeth, Future Sixth Countess of Carlisle.

[January–March 1807.]

Thank you Dearest G for your verses which as you say may have faults but are very pretty however notwithstanding and somehow or other I never can help crying when I read them—there is something I have always told you that interested me so particularly about you, Chatsworth and William at that time that it always seems to me like a melancholy attachment of my own in very happy times and if I was to tell you half how agitated and almost miserable it makes me to think of you some years ago as of my own thoughts or of Wm who I did not know or of Chatsworth and Hardwicke you would believe that it was some little species of insanity which they say people have in one particular subject [—] when I was last at Roehampton with reading some of Wm's verses to Amanda[38] I worked myself up to what Rousseau calls *l' point fatal de le imagination* till I could only recover myself by crying & blubbering out loud—therefore I maintain that memory is a most painful gift and that any day I might choose to indulge myself (for there is a sort of pleasure) in looking back I feel quite miserable though I do not think I feel this to so great a degree as I did when I was much younger [—] from about twelve to seventeen I had this to so painful a degree this irritabilitie that I remember making myself just as miserable at the recollection of Lucca baths of Lady Abercorn & her attachments and sorrows of [*illegible*] even and Margate later as it has since to a greater degree of Chatsworth, you and afterwards of myself and Brocket Hall [—] I am even pretty near sure I should never have known how to fall in love myself if I had not

[38] William Lamb may have written poems dedicated to or about "Amanda," as a euphemism for Caroline's cousin Georgiana (Little G)——or Caroline may have invented the character of Amanda, who appears in the book she made for G, perhaps as a tribute of some kind.

either learned or fancied I'd learned how from you [—] confess in point of happiness nothing is so pleasant as that point in time when you are too young to know or confess what you feel but really and truly begin to love Rousseau describes all this better than any body and makes you feel a little the same emotion as what he describes as you do at what you yourself have coloured and remember now [—] that you may burn this very affected letter immediately I will write several secrets at the bottom such as

Lady Elizabeth Foster is not Good—God bless my soul is that a secret?

George [Lamb] has been ill treated—is that a secret?

G is the dearest woman in the world

Wm the Dearest Man, Papa my brothers Ld M[orpeth] and Mama with Uncle Devonshire, excepted

Wm adored you—you were ungrateful

G adored William who was constant

Well let us rejoice there are four happy instead of two & please pegs (young G's oath) there will be five when I am brought to bed[39]

I am making you a book for your [*illegible*] but shall never give it you unless you will promise never to show it—William sends you a kiss he shall not give it you unless I may likewise kiss Ld M

Dona Q[ue] tanto al mio bel sol pia cesti pia ce pia cera[40]

In the book she created for her cousin G, Lady Caroline put the following letter as a preface.

15. Lady Caroline to her cousin Georgiana, Lady Morpeth. 16 MARCH 1807.

My Dearest G:

as we have often talked together—on the subjects I mention in this book—I cannot help thinking you will accept of it though some things may not quite meet with your approbation—I have put in it some of my verses also—not that I think them worth offering to you but because I wish you to keep them, & other things in remembrance of two people

---

39 Caroline means that she and Lord Morpeth are also among the happy ones, because William failed to secure Little G's hand in marriage. Thus, there are two happy couples, and once Caroline delivers her baby, a fifth happy soul will join them.

40 A garbled transcription of an aria lyric by Faustina Maratti Zappi (1679–1745). The lyric also occurs more accurately and completely in another letter Lady Caroline wrote to her cousin dated 16 March 1807. It expresses the jealousy of one woman toward another.

who love you very truly and hope they are not indifferent to you—Sometimes when you look on this if you should be inclined to think less well of me let it plead for me in your affection—as I acknowledge here many imperfections & would not even claim your friendship on any merit I possess but merely on feeling a very strong desire to correct my faults & such a particular value for your esteem & love that I think it will be hard if I cannot gain them—

I am afraid writing this will appear ridiculous to you; and therefore I rely on your kindness that you will keep it sacredly for your own eyes and not think yourself authorized to shew my secrets even to your husband—for if you even think it ridiculous how much more will any other person less indulgent—I have sometimes vexed you my Dearest G with foolish jokes—but these were between ourselves and shall never be again if you desire it—all I wish is that if I die, or any other way am seperated from you, the remembrance of my faults may be forgotten by you if possible—and the remembrance of my love for you, my adoration almost of W^{m} & Mama and the sincere regret I felt for any wrong thing I had ever done be alone preserved—do not let any thing alter the sentiments you once said you should always feel for William—as my husband I should hope he would be considered by you as a friend, but from other circumstances and former acquaintance I hope you will value him for himself. You must not be angry when I confess that you having once possessed his heart adds a good deal to the natural love I bear you and adds a sort of romantic and melancholy idea to the remembrances of those times, which I see is felt in a still greater degree by William when ever he alludes to them—to so great a degree that he acknowledges all after-life seems gloomy in comparison—the truth is life as it advances is accompanied with reflection experience and generally with misfortune—we look back to days that were light up by hope & undisturbed by apprehension, to those days of innocence security & continual delight.

when perhaps our young hearts first glowed with love & every generous sentiment youth naturally feels, and the contrast *may* be sad if we compare them with those of even the happiest maturity—our extra ordinary situation here, the uncertainty of our life, & those still dearer to us—the darkness in which our Future existence is involved—the dreadful fear of judgment on every action of our life, the still more dreadful one of not meeting those we loved on earth, hereafter—these reflections must be continually checking our happiness—even suppose it undisturbed by other severer causes—one thing alone in this world of gloom and disappointment can counterbalance every evil—a perfect reliance on that Being by whom we were created—an implicit belief that he neither will deceive us, or permit us to be miserable but for our good—a total rejection of all scepticism all reasoning!—we know nothing!—we can know nothing—let us do our best & trust in him—to him too do I commend not only us and all those we love—but those more particularly who know not the comfort of relying on his protection—who though following his commandments & receiving his blessings every day—are alienated from his throne & seek in the Mazes of reason for Theories and explanations involved in eternal darkness and only to be enlightened of his appointed time—oh may he see fit to turn their hearts before it be too late to forgive their errors in consideration of their noble virtues & to guide us & them through the trials and temptations of this world in such a manner that we may hope to meet in peace & joy in a better—and now God bless you my own Dearest G I am very melancholy or I would not have begun your little book with so dull and dirge-like an [opening?] but indeed this Month makes one melancholy and long evenings by ones self & the wind whistling through the windows—at one oclock too does not tend to enliven—

Donna che tanto al mio bel sol piacesti
Che ancor d'preggi tuoi parla sovente
Lodando ora il bel crine, ora il ridente
Tuo labbro ed ora i saggi detti onesti [. . .][41]

Though still fearful about her pregnancy, Caroline found she had company, for her brother's wife Maria was indeed also expecting.

16. Lady Caroline to Georgiana, Lady Morpeth, Future Sixth Countess of Carlisle. [Spring 1807.]

Thank you my Dearest G for your kind note and for walking with your dear boy to see me [. . .] let me tell you my ails and aches which thank

---

[41] A lyric by Faustina Maratti Zappi (1679–1745), Italian poetess. Lady Caroline alludes several times to this lyric, which expresses one woman's jealousy for another. It begins: "Woman, liked so much by my handsome Sol [could be a short form of *Solo* (my only one), or *Sole* (my sun)], who still talks often of your qualities, praising your beautiful hair and your smiling lips and your virtuous way of talking . . ." It concludes; "Keep silent; keep silent if you want to tell me that he still loves you." I am indebted to my colleague, Professor Emeritus Sebastian Cassarino, for translating these verses.

heaven are rather better for the country Lady Duncannon[42] however is a female Hercules compared to me & the prodigious circumference of her person quite annihilates my small increase. I do not know whether Wm intends to speak Monday he said last week perhaps he should if he had any thing to say and a good opportunity—the subject is so old no body can say anything new but it is so interesting a one at the same time I rather hope he will however I should be frightened to death for fear he should not succeed and lose by a bad speech all the praise gave so liberally at first for yr life do not mention to any one that he is even likely to speak for I know him so well I feel sure if it was mentioned to him he would quite give it up[43] God Bless you Dearest

Caroline's pregnancy had run almost to full term. She marveled at the fact that meek, unmarried little Caroline St. Jules now seemed sexually experienced, an "education" apparently administered by William's brother George.

17. Lady Caroline to Georgiana, Lady Morpeth, Future Sixth Countess of Carlisle. 3 August 1807.

London

My Dearest G

I do not know of any surer spoiler of the Pathetic than anybody in the act of being sick & perhaps Harris forgot to tell you how you released us from soulévement de coeur[44] when by opening yr door abruptly the M[ornin]g you set out we found you in the very act. notwithstanding this I can assure you I was some time recovering my usual spirits & felt a great desire to amuse myself more than ordinary, for which reason instead of going home I jogg'd over the roughest stones in London to Painter Lawrence[45] where I found Wm setting for his picture [—] if I had been writing a novel, I should add accidentally or to my infinite surprise, however I arrived there to his, which does as well & may teach him the danger of assignations even though streets or seas divide—as I may come in unexpectedly and end the whole tragically—his picture is less beautiful

---

[42] Maria Fane, wife of Lady Caroline's eldest brother, John, Lord Duncannon.

[43] William Lamb's inability to speak extemporaneously seriously hampered his career in Parliament. He faced public speaking with the greatest anxiety.

[44] "Soulévement de coeur"—the rising of the stomach.

[45] Thomas Lawrence (1769–1830), British painter.

than the original and that is all [. . .] Caro G[46] has been very kind to me since you went & walks with me almost every day. I think she is much more experienced than she used to be—or than I was before I married—oh those Lambs how they do enlighten one's mind [. . .]

Augustus Lamb had been born on 29 August 1807, and all had gone well. William and Caroline agonized before deciding to have the baby inoculated with Cow Pox as a precaution against acquiring the Chicken Pox or Small Pox.

18. Lady Caroline to Georgiana, Lady Morpeth, Future Sixth Countess of Carlisle. 13 OCTOBER 1807.

London

[. . .] My little boy has had the Cow pocks very effectively I hope for it has pitted him sadly & made him look thin & pale.[47] he really is a beautiful Baby but feverish as he has been these four days past. William is growing very fond of him—but of course is less so than I am in outward demonstrations. I daresay Harrio's coming will please my Uncle but never meant he was angry, only he said he shd like her to come to Bath if they went—but I rather think that plan is given up at least others are talked of now—which I am glad of [—] it not being absolutely necessary for his health as Harrio must have disliked Bath very much—you cannot think how every body here praises Caroline—she has not only one of the most amiable & sweetest dispositions I ever met with but her mind seems so improved her ideas enlarged & her conversation more from her own head than it used to be. trust me the Lambs are the best of Masters. they can teach every thing but not to love them & Frederick [Lamb] even take him for better & for worse has more perfections & merits than any common man besides—by the bye how I wish [. . .] Harrio would marry and mend him—then we should all 3 live in the same House sign our names alike & it would be an odd fact[48]—for what signifies wealth & state

---

[46] That is, "Caro George," Lady Caroline's illegitimate cousin, Caroline St. Jules, who would marry George Lamb in 1809. The family had already fallen into the habit of distinguishing the two Carolines in this way, it appears.

[47] The cow pox was given to children intentionally in hopes of inducing immunity to it and other forms of the disease. It is from these early experiments that we derive the term "vaccination" (from "vaca," for "cow"). It is not impossible that this vaccination complicated or induced some of Augustus's subsequent health problems.

[48] Caroline imagines herself and her two cousins, G and Harrio, all being called Mrs. Lamb.

now—the [*illegible*] & the Gold Smiths[49] will be English nobility if permitted to keep their treasures by cleaving to Buonaparte every thing else will be either ruined or swept away am I not as prophetic as Miss Trimmer?

God Bless you Dearest G
post going

Car Lamb

Tuesday [—] the Christening is to be to day
little boy pretty well

19. Lady Caroline to Lady Bessborough.
30 October 1807.

[. . .] I have a little pain in my chest, they think from taking too much exercise & carrying the dear heavy boy, who improves á vue d'oeil.[50]

yr own
CL

Caroline continued a voracious reader.

20. Lady Caroline to Lady Bessborough. 24 April 1808.

I have really been so occupied with the sorrows of Mary Queen of Scots you must excuse my not having written before. I had always read the other side except in Hume, & was surprised at the conviction Robertson seems to carry in every line of her guilt. His must be a very immoral book for in spight of that one always feels so very much interested for her.[51]

I have also read the Modern Philosophers,[52] which in spight of a little vulgarity & too much sameness, I like extremely. Julia's character is beautiful & tho' Harriet Orwell gives one rather too much the idea of a blushing maid with a workbag, & I cannot fancy anything very romantic in the way of love—with an apothecary, yet her character is, I think, extremely well drawn & I like Bridgetina very much.

[49] Albert and Benjamin Goldsmid (spelt "Goldsmith" by Lady Caroline) were Jewish lenders who helped finance England's war with France and Napoleon.

[50] Literally, "at view of the eye."

[51] William Robertson published his *History of Scotland* in 1759.

[52] *Memoirs of Modern Philosophers* (1800), a novel by Elizabeth Hamilton.

We have all been reading le Siege de la Rochelle.[53] As I leave others to make their own remarks, I shall only tell you my own opinion, which is, that though I think it almost more interesting than any book I ever read, I think the methodistical stile it is written in & the whole of her reflections very dull. [. . .] William has been praising your son of that name very much, & says if he would talk a little more he sees no bar between him & perfection. Seriously I never saw a person, independent of his relationship to me, so agreable, & his figure his [*sic*] quite beautiful. Do not tell him this even to please him, as he will believe it & spoil it in a variety of ways. I am convinced nothing is worse than praise, except finding fault, unless it is for things one can help. [. . .] I fancy we shall come to town Wednesday I thought it expedient to write you a longer letter than usual—"a stitch in time"—you remember the proverb, & I hope this will prove a most effectual darn, for I hear you have not thought me a very entertaining correspondent of late, my letters to you being like chease parings, just enough smelt to shew from whence they came & yet far from what anyone would wish to keep. God bless you dearest. Pray come to London in good sorts & spirits & we will be very gay.

A year after Augustus's birth, everything seemed fine.

21. Lady Caroline to Lady Bessborough.
21 AUGUST 1808.

[. . .] I hope if you return through Wales, you will not fail to call on the Lady Elenor Butler & Miss Ponsonby, who, I hear, are quite delightful.[54] Lady Elenor all sprightliness, brilliancy & carelessness; Miss Ponsonby clever, accomplish'd, gentle & agreable. Their cottage is beautiful & their only maid a wonder of fidelity & ability—she having given them all her little savings when they were distress'd & done everything for them ever since.

I am afraid my new page will be obliged to go away soon, he having behaved very ill. Augustus continues well & I grow very rondelette. [. . .]

---

[53] *Le Siège de la Rochelle, ou le malheur et la conscience* (1808), by Madame de Genlis, had been translated into English that same year by R.C. Dallas, a friend of Lord Byron's.

[54] Lady Eleanor Butler (1739–1829) and Sarah Ponsonby (1755–1831), best known as the Ladies of Llangollen, the Welsh village where they lived after having "eloped" together in 1778.

Caroline's interest in the costumes of her pages may have been indistinguishable from her interest in dressing as one.

22. Lady Caroline to Mr. Baker, Her Tailor. 25–26 October 1808.

J.W. Baker:

I do not know whether you alter clothes if not you may return them, I will have them done by a person here, but if you do I send you the directions which I beg you will attend to particularly—the new suit of clothes you made for Tom Hughes and which he only wore twice may be altered for Thos Bently the next suit he has if you do not think this will be too small & if so there is no more to be said at present, but if you think they will be too small I want them to be cut out for the same boy you made the Hussar suit for [. . .] which is to be the shape and size of the last—the red cloth waistcoat & the drab one must each have 3 rows of buttons down the front and the drab waistcoat red down the seams and button holes. They must both be made to button close up to the neck cloth & the drab belt with red seams and buttons made to go to either—the jacket you made is not quite a proper shape—not slop'd off enough on the sides before the belt & waistcoat near an inch & a half too long waisted—the trousers also too tight at the bottom and too short so that they are not concealed as they should be under the belt—this does not signify for what has been done hitherto but I wish you to attend to it in future [. . .]

As Augustus grew, Caroline also gained weight—a good sign.

23. Lady Caroline to Georgiana, Lady Morpeth, Future Sixth Countess of Carlisle. 30 September 1808.

Welwyn

[. . .] my little boy is really grown as blooming stout & lively as your little Georgiana which is saying everything he has more Colour in his lips and cheeks than he did when quite a baby & is mottled all over he is no thinner but quite lively & well so that every body who sees him now for the first time says what a fine stout healthy boy he is—when I have said this much I have said all for though a year & a month old tomorrow he can neither walk alone nor speak a word—but laughs like a Lamb and grows very like me *en beau* & fat—I continue perfectly well we have been very comfortable indeed & my own William is returned the only thing that makes me uneasy is that I have nothing at all the matter with me—never am sick eat ravenously & should not know I was in any way differing from Wm but that my Cloathes grow rather tight for me and yet I look as ugly meagre & ill as if I was so [. . .]

On 17 May 1809 George Lamb and Caroline St. Jules were married and seemingly happy, while Caroline and William had been out of sorts with each other as their fourth wedding anniversary approached.

24. Lady Caroline to William Lamb. 27 May 1809.

My Dearest William

After Dear boy[55] was gone to bed I set out for Pansangher having begun Adele de [Tenangze?] which amused me so much I was there in no time—I found the Bride & Bridegroom[56] in high health & spirits though they really behave themselves in such a decorous manner I should imagine they must have been married before. L^{y} & Ld Kinnaird[57] are here the latter much better than I ever hoped to see him. Pansangher is very pleasant in all respects & I only want my Angel boy & Man to be perfectly happy [. . .] I must leave off or I shall have nothing to say to you Dearest Mannie when you come—pray arrive *rayonnant* with good humour & health Stomach was a little out of order I think when on went hope it is better—Ranger ran away from me yesterday & Francis found him Parading about the top of the parks with some stray poultry. I would not bring my pretty Phillis[58] with me as you wished me not—Sir Philip Francis wrote to Ld Kinnaird to decline dining with him he can only wish Ld Kinnaird may act well through his dinner or his dinner through him they read last night some of the new Montague letters you cannot think how clever they are—unlike the stile of a girl of fourteen but really as so many married women are so like children in body & mind it is well now & then the reverse should take place—Tunc. I have just been stung. [Greek phrases, roughly translated as "the writer has had a lapse," "and the little bee/beast makes both honey and grievous wounds."] God Bless you my own Dearest sweetest man. I will study to

---

55 That is, her son, Augustus, not yet two years old.

56 George Lamb and his bride, Caroline, St. Jules, illegitimate daughter of Lady Elizabeth Foster and the fifth Duke of Devonshire, who was born the same year as Lady Caroline Lamb.

57 Lord Kinnaird was brother to Douglas Kinnaird, Lord Byron's acquaintance.

58 Ranger and Phillis were two of Caroline's dogs.

be as pleasant a friend to you as Caroline George[59] is to her husband—& so I pray do not regard her with any other eyes than those of fraternal affection which let me add is no great thing in point of love my own Brothers excepted—we seemed all of us acting a play last night—in a new House—old people & all met together from odd quârters—I think lately my dearest William we have been very troublesome to each other which I take by wholesale to my own account & mean to correct leaving you in retail with a few little sins which I know you will correct also do not say java—condemn me not to silence, assist my imperfect memory & occasionally call me friend-girl Darling (though Mrs. Clark shares that appelation) & all such pretty names as shew great love. I will on the other hand be silent of a morning—entertaining after dinner—docile—fearless as a heroine in the last vol. of her troubles strong as a mountain Tiger & active as those young savages Basil's boys to whom by the by you will give one shilling apiece—you should say to me *raisonnéz mieux et repliquéz moins.*[60]—own Queen—Car Lamb

25. Lady Caroline to Lady Bessborough. 28 July 1809.

If you are quite well I should take it as a great favour if you would just write me the principal dates & events, wars, risings, &c. from Romulus till the time of Constantine the Great. If you are unwell, do not do it, but if you have the time, I cannot tell you of what use it will be to me, as I understand your hasty sketches, and it makes me remember the history which Wm. is now reading to me.

I am anxious about you, & beg you will make Mrs. Peterson[61] write one line to say how you are, or my papa, as it would be cruel to leave me without saying you are quite well again.

26. Lady Caroline to Lady Bessborough. August 1809.

We had a very odd dinner at Mrs. Day's on Tuesday. Ld. Henry Seymour[62] was there & I liked it very much, though I could not help

---

[59] The family had already been referring occasionally to the two Carolines as "Caro George" or "Caro William," but the wedding formalized the practice.

[60] Literally: "reason better and reply less or less quickly."

[61] Sarah H. Peterson, Lady Bessborough's personal maid throughout her life, from age fourteen in 1783.

[62] Second son of the first Marquess of Hertford (1746–1830).

regretting the expence those poor people put themselves to in order to give us a magnificent entertainment. I must do them the justice to say I never eat so good a dinner, though the grief I had all the time in reflecting that nothing but a quartern ague or putrid fever on my part could possibly cancel the obligation, made it nearly disagree with me. After dinner a Miss Green, sister of Mrs. Ed^{d} Jerningham sung. She has a fine voice, bad manner & wonderful knowledge of music. I was then set down to loo with the Comptroller of the Customs, the parson of the parish, Ld. Henry Seymour, & the doctor, who all quarrelled about how I should play, & to my inexpressible horror & amazement I heard Ld. Henry vehemently assert that Ly. Caroline should play her trumps when she pleased & without in the least regarding or acquainting the public, & should say " Pam, be civil" according to the old Walpole way of playing it. The Comptroller of the Customs as warmly maintained that Lady Lamb must play a trump if she had one in her hand, though it might prove her own perdition. Words grew high & I grew frightened, when they all turned to me & asked me if I ever had play'd at Loo before. "Yes," I replied, "at the Princesses last night"—"And what sort of Loo was that?" they said eagerly, "what sort of Loo was that ?" "A very different one," I answered, & they all eagerly asked in what respect. "A much quieter one," I said, & it allay'd the rage for the moment & made them all laugh, but after a time it broke out again worse than ever, like Mrs. Jordan in Three Weeks after Marriage[63]—for as soon as Lady Lamb had been allowed to play & the laughing at her remark was over, they began coolly to examine who was in the right, which put them all again in a worse rage than before, so that after a few rounds I was glad enough to get home [. . .]

Though of uncertain date, the following letter exhibits Caroline's tendency to outrageous behavior at the many social events she was now attending.

27. Lady Caroline to Lady Holland. [FALL 1806 OR LATER.]

Dearest Lady Holland let me dine with you some day soon. Bespeak me—I am engaged till next Monday—I have been much amused having put on boys shoe buckles a red Emery wig a boarding school frock so that I looked like a boy dressed up for a girl & in that character told

[63] Arthur Murphy (1727–1805), debuted Three Weeks after Marriage in 1764, and it had been revived as recently as 1806 at Drury Lane Theater in London.

everyone that I personated Lady Caroline Lamb had died my hair red &—I jumped like a Harliquin laughed heartily & had no mercy on any one—likewise heard pretty home truths saw who were my friends & shrugged my shoulders at those whose malice more abundant than their wit treated me Cavalierly—having tired myself with these juvenile freaks I slipped behind a curtain & pulling a gown & cassock hid for that purpose over my frock returned in the character of Sidney Smith & as well as I could personated a Scotch Reviewer a Yorkshire Clergyman—a London wit—but here I faild for to make people laugh I must have had some sparkles of his—I preached Repentance however & sinnd as he does with one eye while I turnd the other up —

Caroline's brother Frederick was a member of the 12th Dragoons, known as the Prince of Wales's regiment, and thus deeply involved in the Peninsular Campaign against Napoleon and the French.

28. Lady Caroline to Lady Bessborough.
14 August 1809.

[Cowes, Isle of Wight] Monday evening, [14 August 1809].

I cannot bear the anxiety, my dearest mama, of remaining here after this last account from Spain. The Duke was kind enough to send me the most particular accounts he had, but they only add to the suspense I suffer. Only conceive my dear brother's regiment was the only cavalry engaged.[64] Good God, how dreadful it is to have him there, & what must you suffer if I feel so miserable & anxious.

I was for instantly setting off for town, but Wm. dissuaded me. I shall, however, try & come tomorrow or next day, but if your letters do not satisfy me, you may certainly expect me. How sorry I am for Genl. Mackenzie[65] who was so excellent an officer, & how very very dreadful the fate of the German Legion has been. Pray send me word whether Corisande's[66] brother is in Spain, or any one else I am anxious about. I trust Colonel Seymour is safe. Indeed, mama, I cannot bear to be away from you at such a moment. I shall certainly come to you immediately.

---

[64] At the battle of Talavera, 27–28 July 1809.

[65] Major-General John Randoll McKenzie was killed at Talavera.

[66] Corisande de Grammont, a childhood emigrée who had been raised with Caroline and her cousins, had married Lord Ossulston, afterwards fifth Earl of Tankerville (1776–1850), in 1806.

Wm. does not much care about Petworth,[67] & I cannot stay unless you send me a very satisfactory account. If the French army is really dispersed & my own brother is safe & not likely to be again engaged, I will stay, & depend on you for letting me know immediately, but I do long to see you & comfort you & be anxious with you more than I can say.

I am just returned from a fagging day of 6 & thirty miles sight-gazing. I was going out to tea when Mr. Day told me there was news arrived. I really felt a sort of terror when I heard it was from Sir Arthur Wellesley,[68] that I cannot describe—it is in some measure relieved, but the anxiety with which I wait for letters is not to be told [. . .]

thank God for the safety of my own dear brother, thank God for it a thousand times. Would I could feel as happy as I ought, but the dread of more news, & the sorrow I feel for the misery this has caused to so many thousands of people, quite prevents the joy I ought to feel at our success. My own brother, I never had a fear about how he would behave; had I a doubt I should not have endured the cruel anxiety I have done. You will, of course, send me every possible detail, every name you may hear mentioned, for I see every face I meet anxious & enquiring. A poor man called here this moment & found his nephew's name among the killed. He said he dared not go home with the intelligence.

God bless you my own dear M. You shall decide about my coming or staying.

The cost of the war in lives and property surprised most Britons, and they reacted, like Caroline, with anger to reports of Spanish malingering.

29. Lady Caroline to William Lamb. 4 SEPTEMBER [1809].

My Dearest love

[. . .] I began Sir John Mo[o]res letters again[69] and am very much struck if the account is true with the bad management there seems to have been at first setting out. I cannot also conceive how with such letters & opinions

---

[67] Family home of George O'Brien Wyndham, third Earl of Egremont, William Lamb's father through his affair with Lady Melbourne.

[68] Sir Arthur Wellesley (1769–1852), later first Duke of Wellington.

[69] James Carrick Moore (1763–1834) ed. of *Sir John Moore* (1761–1809) *A Narrative of the Campaign of the British Army in Spain* (1809).

daily coming forth such a general infatuation about the Spaniards could prevail—what occasioned your Mother Mrs. Fell my Mother & so many other of all orders and parties to tell such a pack of stories which seem to have been perfectly groundless—I can allow a great deal for the enthusiasm but such conduct as the Spaniards seem in general to have shewn towards us is certainly a great damper to such feelings [. . .] what a shame it seems to devote our brave armies in a hopeless cause for a weak ungrateful people—& my dear brother too! in Sir J Mores letter to Mr. Frere[70] where one can see he is in a tiff at his appointment he agrees with you about titles wrongly bestowed for he says—he trusts he will excuse any thing omitted in his letter thinking it better to give no Titles at all rather than the wrong one—by the by my blood curdled with the quantity of black bile Freres' pompous insignificant impudent letter brought forth. I could not stand it at all, such a nonchalant Coxcomb—I almost wish he had been with the German legion [—] we should have then seen what sort of figure he would have cut at Talavera[71] [. . .] I have been playing all day with that pretty little Augustus of yours, he is the dearest child I ever saw & shows where you are gone by pointing to the sea. Mister Colman informed me in person last Night that you were safe at Southampton in health & spirits by 20 minutes past ten, which information he repeated 3 times with a yes of triumph at the end [. . .]—God Bless you love, your own faithful Wiffins.

Caroline now took a more aggressive teasing tone toward her cousin Hart.

30. Lady Caroline to the Marquis of Hartington. 29 September 1809.

With a cross heart a bad pen red Ink & no time I write these few lines to you my little kind cousin. will you have any thing to say to me about the opera. will you pay me the subscription you promised to make for Widow Santon & will you tell me whether you are angry or what is the cause why if I may use the expression, you have quarrelled with yr. own bread & butter. I have read the rights of Woman, am become a convert think dissipation great folly & shall remain the whole year discreetly & quietly in the Country. Caroline George is the delight of Brocket Hall. give her 3 kisses for me & mind I never will give you another while you

---

[70] John Hookham Frere (1769–1846), English diplomat and poet.
[71] The battle of Talavera took place 27–28 July 1809.

live—you are a bad good for nothing boy & I will not tell you how dear G[ran]d Mama looks though I am now at Holywell, what Miss Trimmer and Phiz Martin are talking about nor any of the news I have just heard—your very much offended Caroline Lamb—

I have seen a Lady who fancies herself in love with you, but I will not tell you who it is as I mean to give my consent to your marriage with her. Maria & the Cabinet are still Labouring[72] but neither of them fairly delivered—

Caroline assailed Hart repeatedly for not holding a firmer line against the usurper, Lady Elizabeth Foster (who was about to marry the widowed Duke of Devonshire).

31. Lady Caroline to the Marquis of Hartington. 11 October 1809.

My Dearest Hartington

that you are affronted with me I really believe or you could not after 4 attacks so obdurately continue silent I have seen many a long letter of yours addressed to other people & I lament that you think it such an annoyance to write to your first & best friend that you will not even condescend to say a word to me the last letter I wrote to you my good G[ran]d mama chose to send and observd there were rather strong expressions in it it was all about what now I find is declared & however little right I may have to Censure that old Witches conduct I shall never hear her called by the dear name she has assumed[73] without regret & disgust [—] & disgust very strong though I will do all I can to conceal it Pray tell me how Caro broke it to you & what that emblem of innocence thinks now of Lady E Foster is it still possible she can still be like the Pharisees who had eyes and saw not & ears & heard not or has she all along cunningly & slyly been aware of the whole intrigue—I detest such petty artifices as Bess employs—if she will be wicked let her be so in the

---

[72] Lady Maria Duncannon was about to deliver a baby. Spencer Perceval, who had just been appointed prime minister on 9 October 1809, had found it difficult to form a cabinet, and had to perform his previous office of Chancellor of the Exchequer, lacking a replacement.

[73] Lady Elizabeth Foster was about to marry the widowed fifth Duke of Devonshire, thus assuming the title of Duchess of Devonshire, which had belonged to Hartington's deceased mother (and Lady Caroline's aunt) Georgiana. The marriage occurred by subterfuge on 19 October 1809. Lady Caroline called an "odious tricking business at Chiswick." The Reverend Preedy married her to the Duke believing he was repeating a previous ceremony (British Library Add. MS 51560 f. 127).

face of day but when I think of the scene of deceit plot iniquity & wiles this serpant has made use of I shudder at the thoughts—& you have begg'd her pardon & advised her to take this step Oh hypocritical Hart fret & storm behind & fawn on that Wily woman when before her [—] I cannot bear it—not that I approved the violence of your conduct before or all that foolish way of talking of your father & her which I think was encouraged in you but I admire a firm sincere mode of conduct one that may be depended upon for life and that if one leaves you three months one may not expect to see entirely changed—the wind is not more unstable than you [—] a breath alters your very principles & Vanity has more influence over you than the best feelings—I know I am offending you by this mode of speech but were you here I would give it you well, express myself fully & have you at my feet—at a distance I only expect slights & silence—some new bubble has attracted yr fancy & till it bursts with all its varied colours I must wait in patience for an answer—I have a world of news but shall tell you nothing & moreover am as cross as Patch at the Triumph of Hypocrisy & the petty intrigues I see every where carried on—I am sure the Melbournes knew of this long ago & I am sure also my good Cous[in] that you told old Bess you would not disapprove of it—oh she is a deep one—she has flummeried up a certain young Marquis from his Cradle. she knew well that the storm where it blew hardest would be over soonest & the former influence remain stronger than ever. this mistress of yr Papa's knows how to throw her chains about you she has a word here & a word there & few can set aloof above her—I must say for myself—that when you were all so violent I was calm. What I knew before did not strike me a second time as a new thing but the cool contempt & indifference I felt from the time I knew that Hypocrite's character never left me & never shall though civility for my Uncles & humanitys sake will I hope always keep me from being disrespectful

God Bless you dear Vain angry cousin

You once loved me as I always shall you write or not write & when I see you I know you will take all steps to kiss me & appease me. but we shall see if I cannot in my Turn be cold too

yr affectionate
Car Lamb

in the name of our old saint Scibson Bapeh[74] let me conjure you to write me

---

[74] As noted, variants of this name appear Caroline's correspondence with her cousin Hart. It apparently refers to a fictitious character of their childhood.

32. Lady Caroline to the Marquis of Hartington. 9 NOVEMBER 1809.

Hertford

My Dear—Hartington

Your silence is absolutely provoking & if you do not write to me three lines now I will send you another bitter letter as the only means of giving you Tongue—I can find no box to subscribe to this year agreeable to my wishes—will you take one with me & we will fill it with pleasant people & you can have a Ladies seat, & I will set about getting subscribers answer me yes or no c'est tout ce que je demande[75]—I have got your ring for me have you got my picture—answer me directly or believe me I will be affronted I saw your sisters yesterday in high preservation they are coming to call here tomorrow—if you pass this way & do not see me either at Panshanger or Brocket I shell be furious—Let me know when you come & I will meet you at La dear Douarière's,[76] if not at B[rocket] Hall if not here—write write write write write write write write—I will add nothing but write till I have an answer & will send you a double letter unfranked twice a day by the post with write in it if I get none—Bad boy I'm going to Corise[77] at Hatfield in a Chaise & pair—yr very otherwise than affectionately

Car Lamb

I will give you some more pills if you do not write—

Even Caroline became reconciled to the marriage that was now planned (at Lady Bessborough's own desire) for her mother's long-time lover, by whom she had two children, Granville Leveson Gower (Viscount and then Earl Granville), and her cousin Harrio.

33. Lady Caroline to Georgiana, Lady Morpeth, Future Sixth Countess of Carlisle. 17 NOVEMBER 1809.

St. Albans

My Dearest G

give the inclosed to your sister who was so kind as to write to me herself. now as she had time you must & therefore pray tell me when he

[75] "It is all that I ask."

[76] Douairière: "The Dowager," Lady Spencer, Lady Caroline's grandmother.

[77] Corisande de Grammont, now Lady Ossulston.

proposed to her [—] what he said & if you are not all as happy as possible [. . .] seriously few events could give me as much pleasure first because I love Ld G[ranville] & then chiefly & really because I feel sure he is the only person for Harrio to marry & I have been quite impatient for that event [. . .] I think G[ran]d Mama is delighted at it & I do hope & trust & feel sure it will be the happiest of all possible Marriages ever

C Lamb

34. Lady Caroline to the Marquis of Hartington. 27 December 1809.

My Dearest Hartington

Nothing but a long expressive letter from you can remove the affront I labour under at being excluded from my own Cousins Wedding[78] Mrs. Scafe is shocked at it pray send me a favour & Cake if not I shall positively turn Green with jealousy & yellow with melancholy [. . .] send me an account of the Ceremony. no soul writes me word what happened. who was affected. how Ld G behaved if Harrio was unhappy. how she was drest. what she wore. let me know all these things & mind you come and see us at Christmas—was Mama at the ceremony & [. . .] did they dance afterwards—how's your eye—God Bless you little cousin Hartington. yr cursed bracelet has fell off near six times since you put it on—it has a most villainous clasp—I blush to see it, but remember it is only mine for one year

yr most sincerely affectionate cousin
Sophia Heathcote

[78] Caroline had (intentionally?) not been informed of the wedding, which took place 24 December 1809.

CHAPTER THREE

Infidelity

LETTERS, 1810–1811

Augustus's seizures and fevers provided a constant source of anxiety, which Caroline tried to palliate with the levity of verse.

1. Lady Caroline to the Marquis of Hartington. 21 JANUARY 1810.

Friend of my heart accept this letter
The child thank God is rather better
But spight of Doctors drugs & pill—
has been most wonderfully ill
'Tis true he did not wheeze or Hoop
But yet we thought he had the Croupe
His breathing was so short & thick
We were oblig'd to make him sick
But Lucas says the Cough & heat
Today have sounded a retreat,
So that I may in safety say,
The inflamations giving way.
Ime writing to you lovely Spark,
With Nurse & Sally in the Dark.
so that I neither care nor ken
which way I turn my crazy pen.
But when some light assists my hand
Ile draw the picture you command

paint Flora in a flowing robe
with either breast just like a globe
her skin like snow on frozen river
her Hair the colour of your liver
her wide jaw bone and figure tall!
leave it to me, I'll paint it all
But as I am much press'd for time
accept the sense & leave the Rhime—

& tell la chere Douarière[1] that I trust she will not think of coming here this great great while but wait till I come to her which I hope to do in a few days—it grieves me not to see you but as I know you doat or dote upon me I am contented, and so God Bless you I will set about your drawing tonight. I have scarcely been out of the Boys room since you left me & am so full of Nursery jokes I hardly know how to write sense certainly that was a very pithy joke of yours when you said understanding was not yr cousin [. . .]

In 1810, Lady Caroline broke her wedding vows after meeting the son of Lady Holland (by her previous marriage) Sir Godfrey Vassal Webster. Webster was a war hero who had fought in Spain, like Caroline's brother, Frederick Ponsonby. He had returned with the skull of a French soldier which he had reputedly converted into a macabre-looking gold-encrusted drinking cup. He had a bad reputation. Even the Whips Club, with its lax rules and standards, would not accept him. He was twenty and an object of clandestine interest by many young women. Caroline was twenty-four. When the affair was discovered, she tried to get her mother-in-law, Lady Melbourne, to forgive her.

2. Lady Caroline to Lady Melbourne. April 1810.

My Dearest Lady Melbourne

I must indeed have a heart of iron if it was not most deeply wounded and affected by your letter and conversation by my Mothers sorrow and by the unparalleld kindness and patience of my friends and will you then make me this offer, shall I again be receivd be loved be confided in by you all. God knows and sees my heart the sacrifice is greater than it

[1] "The Dowager," Lady Spencer, Lady Caroline's grandmother, who often visited Caroline.

should be but I will make it. by this very post I write to Sir Godfrey I tell him the same to you and my resolution is as irrevocable as it is painful yet you may trust me. I will see him & as he is faithful to his promises of not writing I cannot tell where [. . .] but hardened & selfish as I am I can most truly & too painfully feel for your reproof & the grief & infamy I am bringing on myself & family—I solemnly on my knees call God to witness that (unless ill) I return here on Tuesday & consent neither to write to or see Sir Godfrey any more but <u>in Public by accident</u> & as a <u>common acquaintance</u> I even go further I will <u>avoid</u> him & I will write no more—no indeed indeed I will not [—] it shall end here [. . .] God knows I am humiliated enough & did not expect I should ever act in this manner, some heads may bear perfect happiness & perfect liberty mine cannot & those principles which I came to William with—that horror of vice of deceit of any thing that was the least improper that Religion which I believed in then without a doubt & with what William pleasd to call superstitious enthusiasm—merited praise & ought to have been cherished—they were safeguards to a character like mine & nobody can tell the almost childish innocence & innexperience I had preserved till then—all at once this was thrown off & William himself though still unconscious of what he has done William himself taught me to regard without horror all the forms & restraints I had laid so much stress on—with his excellent heart right head & superiour Mind he might & will go on with safety without them he is superiour to those passions & vanities which mislead weaker characters & which however I may be ashamed to own it are continually misleading me—he called me Prudish said I was straight laced amused himself with instructing me in things I need never have heard or known & the disgust I at first felt to the worlds wickedness I till then had never even heard of in a very short time gave way to a general laxity of principles which little by little unperceived by you all has been undermining the few virtues I ever possessed—Williams love for me is such that he is almost blind to my faults yet that first ardour that romantic passion which we both experienced was far too violent to last—contrary to the general opinion on this subject it has lasted far longer on his side than on mine & with its enthusiasm has ceased also its inconveniences my temper is calm we never quarrel never shake the House with storms of passion as we did for the first three years—I can command myself now & he rejoices in the change yet he looks not for the cause—gratitude affection even love remain in my heart but those feelings which carry with them such a charm and existed so many years unabated had lately been on the decline—forgive me Lady Melbourne for telling you all this I would wish to account for a conduct which appears to me as inconceivable as it is without excuse [—] to your strong mind all I have said will appear very foolish. yet remember I write with full confidence in your compassion every thought of my heart without reserve or reflection—had I been placed in a different situation had you shewn me less kindness & confidence what might not have become of me thank God I am saved in time though I do not take any merit to myself yet hope by my future conduct to gain some—[. . .] I solemnly engage myself by every thing most sacred I write it that it may bear witness against me that for one year at least from next Tuesday I will neither write to hear from nor see Sir Godfrey unless [asked] or by the consent of my family—his gifts however I shall keep & shall take it a kindness if they are not abused or lookd on with disgust perhaps some future day I may of myself restore them—

yours most gratefully <u>un</u>dutifully & affectionately
Caroline Lamb

To Lady Melbourne's horror, Lady Caroline decided to clear her conscience by confessing everything—or almost everything—to William.

3. Lady Caroline to Lady Melbourne. [April–June] 1810.

My Dearest Lady Melbourne

Sir G[odfrey] gave me a bracelet at Argyle street with his hair & just before I went I desired him to put it on which he did behind one of the doors The next Morning I made a jeweller come & rivitt it so that it could not come off without breaking the chain—this Morning I took fright all my sins came upon me a sudden terror came into my head as I lookd on my little blooming Augustus that I might be punished for my conduct by the loss of what I neglected—your kindness my Mothers my husbands—my own husbands all occured to me. I tore the bracelet off my arm & put it up with my chains in a Box by itself I have written to desire some one will fetch the dog & on my knees I have written to William to tell him not any falsehoods not as you say any stories to conceal my guilt but the whole disgraceful truth I have told him I have deceived him I have trusted solely to his mercy & generosity—yet as I have not said you any of you know anything about it do not mention it to him unless he does to you but write to me my Dearest Lady Melbourne write & tell me you forgive me for I am indeed very miserable very repentant I inclose you a letter I beg you will read & get [sent?] to you I made the promise of not writing again therefore you may inclose it to say you send it I am very superstitious and believe all those who are wicked are. this Morning the dog the beautiful little Peppeo playing & running about me snapped at the child but did not bite him—it was this occassiond my fear great God I thought if this dog should go mad & bite Williams child what would become of me I went into the garden & took a long walk the dog suddenly droppd before me in a fit foaming at the mouth—it turnd my heart sick I trembled all over I took it home & prayd that I might be forgiven then it was I tore my bracelet off & wrote to William I wish he could shew you my letter as you would see in it that I have told no stories used no deceits but that I have made one request which I hope he will not refuse that of not naming the person—whom I have not only assured him was no ways to blame but like wise told him that he has warnd me of my danger & was as anxious as possible that the whole should cease here—

They think the dog is Mad. I am sure this cannot be but it is very dreadful to me very very alarming—till Sir Godfrey returns you shall take care of his presents for me & then return them God Bless you my Dearest Ly Melbourne, pray do not name the Person to William or say any thing about it & write to me immediately

yrs most truly from what dangers I have been saved Good God I tremble when I think of it I was indeed on the brink of perdition & about to encounter misery infamy & ruin with perfect levity.

Though preoccupied with fallout from her adulterous relations with Webster, Caroline derived pleasure from studies she shared with literate women like Lady Oxford.

4. Lady Caroline to Lady Holland. After 11 July 1810.

My Dearest Lady Holland

[. . .] [Lady] Oxford writes thus to me—"Let us my sweet friend improve the passing hour & turn our minds from the vulgar & trivial to the contemplation of true wisdom. I would wish to cultivate a friendship which promises me such delight if you are of the same way of thinking write freely & secure in the integrity of our own hearts [we] will defy a censorious World & laugh at sour looks"—she likewise seriously recommends the dead languages to my attention being convinced that her favourite Greek would alone repress or depress the ardour & activity of my congenial soul—I am much captivated with this Ladies[2] good sense—it flows with all the Honey of flattery which I am yet childish enough to like the taste of [. . .]

It appeared that Caroline had repaired relations with her lover's mother, with whom she shared feminist sentiments.

5. Lady Caroline to Lady Holland. After 14 July 1810.

My Dearest Lady Holland

[. . .] I give you as much account of the Health of the family as if you were our Physician but really little else travels down to me my Cousins & Virtuous friends not being over addicted to scribbling—do not think I put you in the other class because I had the pleasure of receiving a long letter from you today it is only an appellation I give them out of Contrast to myself & other more liberal minded women who like Mary Wollstonecraft[3] stand up for the rights of the Sex & wear our shackles with dignity—these Lords of Creation who pretend in England to trample us under foot are just as much our slaves & just as little can do without us as any others with less big pretentions—only like other noble animals we let them bridle & Curb us for want of knowing our strength we are just entering the eighth Book & I agree with you in what you say of it only think every particular skirmish too much dwelt on which is natural but tedious—I read the new Testament in Greek with great success & am edified with the slow but sure progress I make in that language you cannot think how learned I should grow did it but agree with my head to apply [. . .]

Caroline showed off her learning to Hart and William.

6. Lady Caroline to the Marquis of Hartington. 21 July 1810.

Most Delectable—

What may seem singular is that I had just written a Greek letter to my Brother in law it was the labour of a week & a Chef d'oeuvre—not

[2] That is, Lady Oxford.

[3] Author of *A Vindication of the Rights of Woman* (1792) and mother of Mary Shelley, the author of *Frankenstein*.

being a Porson[4]—I took yours mighty quickly as his answer, nor was undeceived till an abler Assistant my Black William assured me it was from the son of Devonshire—he was much [letter torn] & assures me it was pure most pure—& thinks pitiful you should not read and write a great deal so few being at your Age so fair a way to distinguish themselves at the truly Attic [. . .] God preserve you most sneezable yr very giddy Cousin

William Rufus-Rex

She also sought to excel at inventiveness and charm.

7. Lady Caroline to the Marquis of Hartington. 31 July 1810.

My most sanative Elixir of Julep—my most precious Cordial Confection—my most dilutable Sal Polychrist & mash mallows paste. Truly comfortable spirit of Hartshorn Tincture of Rhubarb & Purgative Senna Tea—it is impossible my most exquisite Medicine chest for me to describe the delightful effect the potion you sent me this Morning had upon me. prescribe such powders to all the [Greek] who die for love of your Lordship's tricolourd eyes, & remember Cousin of my heart & heart of my cousins that your all faithful gallipot was only waiting for a line to dose you with letters every day, & how dost do my dear Roderick due precious windy & rainy weather we have had in these quarters *sans jest* thou hast a parlous wit & I believe I shall never be warm again after my own heart—my tusks ache madly—would I could Louch at you—poor meagre Bone. I wreakd not how like we had all been to lose you in the Land of Erin go Brah. Write if you cherish the virtue Mercy—for I must hear from you one way or tother. Lewis & Mac of Clanronald slept here in their way to the Highland monstrous pleasant the latter & greatly boring the former. there is a picture of me doing full length, you would steal if you could louch at it—never was any thing so beautiful or so cheap, shall give me yourself for a mere nothing on your return 6 guineas a kitcat. Gd Mother very well went to sleep there on Tuesday & Wednesday—monstrous pretty party & supper gave on Sunday as a farewell, & now mean to adjure the delights of the flesh & all the pomps & vanities of this Wicked World

Love & cultivate Spencer Ponsonby
God preserve you my Dearest

---

[4] Richard Porson (1759–1808), scholar of ancient Greek.

Tartar Emetic your own
Syrop of Elderob
write very soon
tell my Brother I shall write very soon to him—

Caroline's affair with Webster wouldn't die—or she wouldn't let it.

8. Lady Caroline to Georgiana, Lady Morpeth, Future Sixth Countess of Carlisle. 10 August 1810.

Melbourne House
Friday

My Dearest G

[. . .] I have a bad head ache and am just setting out for Brocket Hall where I left William & did you ask me whether I felt sure of my future conduct—alas I have acted so ill that I have lost much of that vain confidence I used to boast of, but if feeling once more little short of adoration for Wm & perfect perfect happiness can prevent my making myself odious & wretched then I think I may say I am sure I will act very differently in future—you cannot think how painful it is to me to recur to that subject how once I liked to talk of it is the only thing surprises me, but indeed William's behaviour to me since has been such that I must have been bad indeed not to have been touched by it. God Bless you dearest never allude to this but if ever I behave in the same way again or anything like it cease to care about me I shall not be worthy of any one's regard

yours ever & most affectionately,
CL

Caroline knew she had lowered herself in Hart's opinion.

9. Lady Caroline to the Marquis of Hartington. 2 October 1810.

My Dearest Hartington

I am really quite uneasy about you hearing from all sides odd tales about you—some saying you Cough others that you are feverish and in short all agreeing that you are not quite well—now my heart of hearts

I conjure you on my knees I entreat you if you are not quite the thing to come immediately to Town & any how write to me as I cannot live if I do not hear from you & if you hear I am dead I know well enough you will regret me—here I am safe but not over well—however I neither had my neck broke or got into the Newspapers tho' I behaved a little wild—riding over the Downs and about the sands with all the officers at my heels in a way not very decent for one of my Cloth—I am like the song of Rosa in love with every body & am always abused for it while I thought her a Goddess she thought me a fool & in fact she is most in the right—What a world it is dear sweet boy, what a flimsey patched work face it has—all profession little affection no truth. that you love me I feel sure dearly & deeply though you now & then see my faults but indeed it is but bad speculation to gaze on the black of every object. mine are unfortunately all on the surface I am pitted all over but it is but skin deep—many a fair outside covers a blacker heart—dear little man—take care of yourself & when we meet in a better & happier World we will be unco virtuous—how you prate have you nothing better to say for yourself ? [. . .] I diced a few shillings for you & won by the name of Eleanor—but gave my prize to a small Maid—God Bless your highness long life & happiness attend you—pleasure strew her flowers for you—Health upon your steps attend. Cozen Dear, Adieu Adieu—I inscribe myself your friend. La Douariere[5] has just been here quite well, Selina rather yellow—

The cowslip & the lemon pale
with Selly's cheek might vie
But never maid that was not frail
had such a jet black eye—
[. . .]
there is Caroline Jules,
with her laces & thules
is good yet makes many men sigh
while her sister runs wildish
And seems rather childish
but oh she's a roving eye—

My metre is rather lacking in sense so farewell dearest sweetest & most precious Cuzino fratello, write to me pray & believe me

---

[5] That is, Lady Caroline's grandmother, Lady Spencer.

She maintained the façade of having dropped Webster and wrote Lady Holland and Hart in the usual bantering tone.

10. Lady Caroline to Lady Holland. 18 October 1810.

My Dearest Lady Holland

write to me I conjure you—& now having shewn you how desirous I am of hearing from you is it not a hundred to one that you will not send me a letter who ever granted a favour to a trying melancholy reproachful lover—not you I am sure so do just as you will I leave it to your own option & then perhaps you will write of your own accord [. . .] Miss Clarissa Harlowe is just dead[6] & I really am so much discomposed at it & at Lovelaces grief to whom I do not think she behaved quite handsomely that I can prate no more nonsense & conclude as Lord Abercorn did one of his speeches that if I have tired you it is no more than what I have done myself—pray let me know how Lady Landsdowne is & where & how you are my very amiable Patroness when you are tired of your Dame d'honneur tell her so that she may seek in time another Queen to whom to pay her devotions—yrs with simplicity

Emily Cowper
oh how improbable

I have been 3 years & 7 months reading Clarissa and have now half another vol to finish this is having a quick mind a superabundance of activity of which I am at times accused [. . .]

11. Lady Caroline to the Marquis of Hartington. 10 November 1810.

I've been nearly in a teff
But you care not a crumb.
I love my Cousin deaf
But I hate my Cousin dumb.[7]

---

[6] Caroline had reported starting Richardson's Clarissa almost twelve years before—she was not the first nor the last to struggle through the novel.

[7] Hart suffered from a progressive hearing loss that had begun when he was a boy.

Shockd at your conduct
for which I see no rhime
I wishd you in a ponduct[8]
& hope it was no crime.
Is the Dutchess breeding
'Tis rumourd every where
But no such late seeds needing
we've got a precious heir[9]
& long may he flourish
his kinswomans delight
many babes may he nourish
some black haird & some white.
Ld Cowpers wife has brought forth
a little healthy brat[10]—
this year I shall not stir North
So think no more of that—
Nothing could be sadder
than the news about the King[11]
he was a little madder
on putting on the ring—
our Party shewd their bile
by making it a jest
it would not take they changed style
and attend for the best—

I've got a gnac at rhiming
but cannot write in prose
'tis like the church bells chiming
& lulls one to repose.

Your letter sweet Coz made me strech my lips to my ears we vulgarly call this laughing & so, if you wish to cause me merriment straight ways send me more nonsense—there is a comfort in writing it to one who

[8] Can the conflation of "pond" and "viaduct" possibly excuse this rhyme?

[9] Caroline alludes to the possibility that Hart's stepmother, Bess, who had supplanted Hart's mother Georgiana, could, if she conceived at her advanced age, still bear a child who would supplant Hart as heir to the Devonshire estate.

[10] In November 1810, William Lamb's sister Emily, Lady Cowper, gave birth to a son.

[11] George III had entered a bout of madness from which he seemed unlikely to recover. The result in February 1811 would be a bill creating the Prince of Wales as Regent, to rule in his father's stead.

will take it down as a Cockatoo swallows a spoonful of Castor oil—which I know is your case, for in many respects you resemble that sagacious Bird. how could you be false & deceitful to me.

oh hartington thou base deceiver
still importunate in vain
giving to the rich receiver
what you steal from want & pain.
you like the world the opprest opressing
tread fever on the slenderest toe
& when you choose to inflict a dressing
'tis where none can resent the blow—

Why did you abandon me & Mrs. Conyers & go & offer yourself like an Apostate to that Corisande-O—[. . .][12]

yrs
Molly Teacok—

is Brother at Chatsworth & how long does Pappa stay there!

Caroline's affair with Sir Godfrey Vassal Webster lasted longer and generated about as much heat as the one she would commence with Byron in March 1812. A full year after claiming to end her affair with Webster, Caroline confronted Lady Holland with the fact that they had been carrying on as before, and presumed to instruct her in motherhood.

12. Lady Caroline to Lady Holland.
Before 16 [or 11?] April 1811.

My Dear Lady Holland. I am going to act in a manner that may appear very improper to you—I have no one to advise me therefore if it is so forgive me [. . .] I have seen too much of your son[,] I have drawn him into a correspondence with me which was dangerous for both—his whole conduct has been as generous and as superior to most Mens as you could wish [—] my conduct unfortunately was as blameably the contrary [—] my Mother has long suspected that I was not going on well [—] any one might see it for I took no pains to conceal it [—] I liked Sir Godfrey & was rather proud of what I ought to have been ashamed of [—] the day before yesterday my Mother saw me receive one of his letters [—] I told

[12] Corisande de Grammont, now Lady Ossulston.

her vainly it was from another person [—] she would not believe it. the consequence of all this is that we have mutually promised to give up all correspondence all appointed meetings & what induces me to confess to you what ought never to be mentioned is that I cannot help thinking you have seen less of him & been less kind to him than you other wise would on my account—I have come to you less also—knowing that however unjust the accusation would be God knows the World might say you encouraged us & let us meet at your House—which has never once been—I therefore hope you will see more of him in future have him with you gain his confidence & save him if you can from a set of wretches who live upon him ruin him & lead him into all sorts of wrong—he has a good understanding an excellent heart & warm good feelings [—] turn them to account & remember I will never come near you again sooner than prevent your seeing as much of him as you ought. I was the only friend in the World who gave him good advice & now I am gone. you who are a much fitter one must take my place. you will of course never mention my name to him [. . .] but do not from policy abuse me before him or try and make him think ill of me [—] do not by talking of my love for William & his kindness for me try to make him think I was hypocritical and acted from Caprice & vanity towards him—after what has passd between us these attempts would fail & time & silence only can bring all right again—yet no time will ever bring me back the perfect innocence & enjoyment I once possessd nor shall I ever hear Williams name or meet his eyes without feelings of bitter reproach [—] yes Lady Holland I will own it to you at the risk of degrading myself for ever in your eyes no affection no gratitude for that dear kind husband saved me—no principles of Religion & Virtue [—] it was your son only & to his generosity to his forbearance to his real friendship for me I owe my preservation from dispair & infamy—I shall leave Town for a few days tomorrow & I once more think I trust myself in safe hands by the unbounded confidence I have shewn you & Ld Holland—as to William he is & I pray God he will ever remain ignorant of what would break his heart[13]—and I wish to clear myself & Henry[14] in your eyes—he never but <u>once</u> was the means of any letter passing between me and Sir Godfrey tho' I have no doubt he knows something of the matter from the cross and chain he brought me—I will be prudent in future I promise you for

---

[13] Presumably William would have been heartbroken to discover that his wife's earlier confession and repentance had led her right back to the same offense with the same man.

[14] Henry Webster, Sir Godfrey's brother.

all our sakes I will [. . .] I shall hope you will one or both of you answer my letter to say you forgive me & will think well of me in future yrs most sincerely C Lamb [. . .]

Lady Caroline did not want to accept the justifiable anger of Lady Holland, though she is forced to acknowledge that she is no different from other cheating wives.

13. Lady Caroline to Lady Holland. May 1811.

Dearest Lady Holland—I will answer for it if you look the World over you will not find a Being in it loves you with as true & constant an affection as I do & if you chuse to consider me lowerd on account of my being the friend of ⋆ your son whom every body seems to scout[15] because he chuses to have an opinion of his own & not to be led as most others are by the oracles of Fashion I am sorry—because you will find á la longue that I am not one so easily to be put down[,] that I know what I am about have a fine spirit & am not to be intimidated by Words—I see many shake their heads when they look at me exclaiming ah she knows nothing of the World & the truth is that I know too much of it & will not condescend to obtain its praises by the little arts some practise those who abuse me do it behind me—for they know I could retort only that I am not of that disposition—nor would I care to defend myself by pulling down others—on the contrary sins & follies I take them to myself & only request that I may be loved by those who did love me & not judged of with others for I will not act like them so the comparison does not hold—I will not give up my acquaintance with Sir Godfrey but I promise you it shall not go on in any way to give offence I am not foolish enough to talk of innocent Friendships & German Trio's[16]—I am not wicked enough to live with one Man & like another [—] I am not lost enough to break every bodies heart & my own by abandoning my husband & child—therefore be easy & assure yourself all will end here if my friends will not talk & if they do bless them I forgive them as who would not in their place—I have one word more to say [—] I cannot help thinking Sir Godfrey could explain the whole [*illegible*] transaction about money but I daresay he will not—hate me or no I am yrs most sincerely & Ld Hollands most affectionately

Car Lamb

⋆a monstrous silly Passage—the common cant of every Woman in similar circumstances!

---

15 That is, to deride him.

16 "German Trio"—in other words, a ménage à trois.

From the tone here, one would think all had again been repaired between Caroline and her lover's mother, Lady Holland.

14. Lady Caroline to Lady Holland. 29 May 1811.

The She Sheridan[17] to her Madonna—can I live without you. Le soleil qui brille pour tout autre est a jamais obscur pour moi[18]—dear & beautiful Lady—are you not a little grieved at my absence—that is what comes of mes alliances—I am like a flame of Fire or a lamp of oil & those I attach myself too Ice—even I a poet I should address you like Crowley with all those pretty metaphores such subjects give rise to[,] but why freeze a little Dame d'Honneur for a fault if it be a fault of which the best natures only are capable—I am like a vestal who thought of other concerns than the pure Flame she hoped Heaven would keep burning—do not condemn me to being burned alive—wait a little & I shall return to dust without any unusual assistance—it is where we are all journeying nor titles nor honours nor Physic nor walzing can keep us aloof one hour beyond our time—if you think me moralizing impute it to my having been of late much in the Company of one Sidney Smith a serious pious man—more formd for the austerities of the Cell than for the brilliant Circles of Fashion where as he says devoted Victims flit before him like the shining visions of a dream—he has conversed with me much & has so expatiated on the Innocent amusements of a life in Yorkshire that I purpose Mrs. Sidney willing to retire there for some months—tell Ld Holland the Duke of Gloucester with whom we dined yesterday praised him warmly that good but dull Prince is overjoyed at being Chancellor[19] the word is ever on his lips—sparkles in his eyes & spreads animation over his white cheeks—I saw him speaking low & tenderly to Lady Donegal I listened and the word university quieted my suspicions—after dinner what occurd? ruin to the character of the young & innocent—Walzing was the subject of discussion—Princess Sophy agreed with me that we had better stick to the dance of our own Country—but the Duke insisted on one turn—the Band

---

[17] An odd phrase, linking herself to Sheridan, whom some have suspected of being Caroline's father.

[18] Literally: "The sun that shines for all others is forever obscure for me."

[19] That is, the Prince of Wales is delighted to have been declared Regent ("Chancellor").

playd O mein Liebe augustein[20] & off we went—an extra step of his Highness put me out. vainly I remonstrated round & round we turnd & I never thought walzing so criminal in my life tho' I have always been of opinion & still am that those who like it like it because it is doubtful—those unco good young Women who shudder at the thought of vice like to venture to the edge of the precipice down which so many of their frail companions have been thrown—they simper over an improper Book—ride & flert as Lady Ossulstone calls it in Rotten Row[21] turn round & round half afraid they are doing wrong & then go home to their Lords pleased like the Pharisee of old that they are not like this sinner whom passion & feeling alone impelld reluctantly to ruin & infamy [—] Lady Ossulstone gave me some advice the other day—pretty Innocents—I like to hear them prate to me it is like a person who has been studying Machiavel taking up Mrs Trimmers lessons[22] in one syllable for making naughty children good—

I too am much inclined to Flert
but then tis with a Gentleman—
I ride—but you ride in the dert
With all the black legs that you can—
now I do keep in Rotten Row—
Though that displeases little O[23]—

I likewise walze & think no wrong
Lor[d] O sees harm but I see none
for if you do not walze too long
& turn the same with every one—
How can there be the least of evil
if the Man turnd out the devil
then I will walze let who say no—
For who cares much for little O—

& let her Walze & Flert with all the Courtly finikee witless things that call themselves Gentlemanlike in the wide world—Ile be off for Arabia

---

[20] "Ach du lieber Augustine" was a popular waltz dating from this period.

[21] Corisande de Grammont, a French émigrée who grew up in the Devonshire household with Lady Caroline and then married Lord Ossulston, whose name Lady Caroline spells creatively with an "e." Rotten Row: London's oldest bridle path, through Hyde Park.

[22] Sarah Trimmer (mother of Selina Trimmer, the governess of the Devonshire-Bessborough households) was a well-known author of didactic books for children.

[23] That is, Corisande, Lady Ossulston.

where I think I shall find Men & manners more to my own liking—one can bear to be smashed by a Mountain & killed by a Basilisk but nobody can stand being bit at by a fly [—] what are these things in Neckcloathes who dare call their foolish brainless Clods by the term Gentleman—pretty Gentlemen they who have lookd in their glasses and fritterd away their hours from 5 till 4 & twenty in the Company of those who are as insignificant as themselves—an imaginary World whom they have created & whose bye laws they Revere has shackled their feelings till Fashion has fashionably the qu'en diráton seems solely to keep them from a state of stupefaction a shoal of minnows of coach which it is too much honour to look upon & poor moralizer what art thou a solitary Fly

God Bless you

ever & most truly yrs—

William and Caroline's wedding anniversary (3 June) was a disaster. Lady Caroline encapsulated the contradictory nature of her behavior when she spoke of her "last reconciliation" with Lady Holland in the following letter.

15. Lady Caroline to Lady Holland. 4 June 1811.

My Dear Lady Holland as you had affection enough for me to seem vexd when I was angry with you I think it my duty in point of gratitude not to let any resentment lurk at the bottom of my heart without mentioning it to you—I am frank—you are prudent—& we behave to each other accordingly [—] now in our last reconciliation you vexd me more than during our quarrel—you said hard things to me under the appearance of kindness & by that means prevented my noticing them—once for all therefore I would explain them & then have done with them forever [—] I can quite quarrel but I cannot be your friend by halves—it rests with you to chuse which—but if you like me & wish me to be as I was once—you must believe what I say—for if indeed I have forfeited all right to be believed in what I affirm I am not worthy to be spoken to—the two things you accused me of are false—I have a right therefore to deny them—you affirm that you quite clear me from all you once feard—that I took you in it is true as I did all my friends & half London [—] that I did it to excite interest & succeeded—that I had acted my part well—shewed my cleverness & now might like a good little Woman amuse myself with something else—these were your very words they have been all this time like weights in my stomach—& finding that I cannot forget them I beg leave at once to explain them to you & you may do as you will about the rest—I have had no wish to excite any emotion in any one—I have just followd the impulse of the moment as I generally do—made myself a great fool—& vexd those who cared about me—if you knew the value I set upon their good opinion & upon possessing a good reputation & upon pleasing a husband who whatever you may think I all but adore[,] you would not fancy on light grounds that I would willingly sacrifice every thing for mere vanity you would at least believe that I got myself into more difficulty than I thought for by impudence & that I do not find it so easy to get out of it all as you are pleasd to think but I am of opinion that these transactions degrade & never excite either interest or admiration—they may & do raise the Man in the opinion of some but they lower the Woman to the very dust of the earth & my Pride is somewhat hurt at being named with a set of creatures who have neither passion nor ability—I mean your common door danglers & supper flirts—I did not therefore act ill to excite emotion I acted ill as I act always because I cannot help it [—] because like the good Man in Midas "remember when the Judgment's weak the prejudice is strong"[24] & my passions have so long been used to master my Reason that although it exists it is not every body who knows it does—promises are but so many additions to sin I therefore make none but if you chuse to believe me you may—I will profit by the lesson I have had & my future life shall be dedicated to Wm & my family & my future efforts to conquering every feeling that ought not to exist in a well regulated mind [. . .] [I] know too well that when a Woman places herself in the power of any Man whether young or old—unless they really love her (which is a rare exception) they treat her as they think she deserves & the most Gentlemanlike are not ashamed when they think it will not hurt themselves to treat her with familiarity & disrespect—Godfrey has behaved very differently to me—I know he would rather see me happy than have his Vanity gratified at my expence—if I see him no more which must now be the case I hope those will fill my place who will advise him as well & be as sincerely his friend as I shall ever be Adieu & believe me yrs affectionately if you wish it

Caroline Lamb

William Lamb for the first time last night witnessed what he never before believed—it was our Wedding day & as he left me Walzing at 2 oclock he reminded me of it & of the vows & protestations I had then made—& are they all changed in a few years—no believe me—I remaind however till 1/2 past 5 & as I drove home my heart reproached

---

[24] A phrase from Kane O'Hara's burletta, <u>Midas</u> (1764), Act 1. Sc. 4.

me & tho tired to death I could not sleep—if my Friends feel pain let them ask themselves whether de gaite de coeur[25] I give them a momentary anxiety which must fall short of what I inflict on myself—I regret the infatuation that seems have overcome all my principles & right feelings but if a life of very constant attention & thorough amendment can make up for the past believe me it shall immediately take place my husband is angry with me I do not wonder—

Now as a first proof of confidence I ask you to burn this & unless to Ld Holland to say nothing about it to any one of your 100 friends if you do I shall know & I shall in future act accordingly

Lady Caroline Tired and Dispirited. From a painting by Eliza H. Trotter. Exhibited 1811. National Portrait Gallery, London.

[25] That is, wantonly. Lady Caroline's friend, the Reverend Sidney Smith composed a Waltz titled "Gâité de coeur" in this period.

Caroline tried to maintain a calm "normalized" relationship with Lord Holland, though she suspected he had heard from his wife about the affair with Webster.

16. Lady Caroline to Lord Holland 27 June 1811.[26]

Thursday night

I am at home with William Lamb
And he I think is rather better
He says he does not care a d–mn
Whether I prate or write a letter

So as you sent this morning early
And as you know I love you dearly
And as I am not prest for time
I answer you in Doggrell rhime
[. . .]
By Heavns I'm sick of Dissipation
And want some serious occupation
[. . .]
See Wellesley whose compelled to fall
To little Party from a Crowded Ball.
There I am going—where with flattering tongue
Men will make pretty nothings seem like wrong
Whisper its very hot or What a Crowd! &
prudent—bid you answer—not so loved
Then give you rings & chains—they know the art
To win a Woman's vain and fickle heart.
But Ime grown wiser & can laugh to see
What fools they make themselves & would make me.

My Pen is tired & so no doubt are you
With truth & love sincere I bid Adieu
& every pleasure which a lenghthened life
can offer you your children & your wife

---

[26] This letter appears to be a down payment upon Caroline's promise to Lady Holland in a letter of the same date: "I mean henceforward to be a Pattern Wife & Grizelda if necessary," even while she admitted her penchant for dissipation: "[I]t is just a week since I have closed my eyes before 6, 7 or 8 in the morning" (British Library Add. MS 51560 f. 155).

I from my heart do pray for—this believe
& my dull Rhymes with courtesy receive.

Despite being in the wrong, Lady Caroline would not accept any slights at Lady Holland's hands, like being disinvited from a party—for here, her pique boiled over.

17. Lady Caroline to Lady Holland. [JULY 1811.]

I do not know whether Sir Godfrey Webster may think proper to send the letter I desired him to give you but in case his Mothers prudence steals into his mind I shall write you another and send it you myself. in the 1st place I beg leave to remark that I told you positively last night that I could not come and therefore your extreme anxiety to prevent me might have been wholly set aside—but Further I desire you will once for all hear my determined resolution—I will never set foot in any ones House who instead of being happy to receive me thinks it proper to make conditions—you may easily make your choice & I call the God of Heaven to witness I will to my death abide by it—but remember Lady Holland I do not wish to be disrespectful in my manner of speaking to you—however I may think you have behaved to me as my Mothers Friend I shall never offer you any childish or public incivility—but neither by writing or by conversation or by any other means will I from this hour hold the smallest communication with you—I am just—& whatever my faults when I see a person actuated tho' against me by a spirit of rectitude of Religion of strict undeviating principles I bow to an authority which however rigid I must admire—but when I perceive mere Worldly prudence conquer every feeling of affection kindness & humanity—I have done & I would as soon Waste my affections on a stone as on such a character—to tell you that whatever has been said whatever might have been said of you I would have stood firm to you tho the whole World had deserted you is what you know & knowing it I would have you learn that no human power shall ever dissolve the Friendship or allow the sentiments I feel for him some call your son but you do well to renounce a Mothers name—& to leave him to the false friends & bad Company your neglect of him has early brought him to—for were you to call him son & speak of him still as I have sometimes heard you it might be deemd no greater impertinence in me to remind you of the Duties of a Mother than in you to taunt me with those of a Wife—I will sooner give up wealth comfort peace of mind & every other good & follow that Man than I will bear to hear him continually made an object of scorn & abuse & denied the common privilege of meeting & speaking to me when I please—as to the gnats & mites that dare to peck at me let them look to themselves—I will turn upon them before long with the vengeance which one bated & pursued at length is taught to feel & level them to the dust from which they sprung—what are these things that dare to speak of me—at best only my equals & by what I can find many of them inferior to me in the satiric powers they would stab me with—grant me but health & life & if I chuse it you shall see them flatter & follow me & lick the dust I tread on—Lady Holland if this is the case I shall be courted by you [—] that which is loved becomes lovely in your eyes—& as this is the case an ambitious mind may still hope to obtain or keep your affection but to speak the candid truth I am too great an admirer of the warm & sincere heart to lay much stress on such professions [—] keep them therefore for the new favourites of Fashion who shall sail smoothly & propitiously down her silver Tide—keep them for those who dare not think for themselves & acknowledge other jurisdiction besides that which God & their own conscience imposes—that I did love you once I showed you & to this I attribute the change in your manner to me whatever the cause from this hour we part—wishing you all happiness to yourself & your whole family—I remain more sincerely than you deserve—

yours
Caroline Lamb

to you who deal in short but cutting sentences this Heroic Epistle may appear ridiculous [—] laugh at it as you chuse I know the anger of a Human Being is most contemptable do not therefore think I wish to intimidate you I merely speak a language no wonder you cannot understand [—] the language of a warm & wounded heart wounded by you in a manner no after talking can repair—nor is it merely now this present note tho' that set all on fire but the sparks were kindled long before & unlike general conflagrations behind me it will be long before they burn themselves out—there is one thing I wish those who pretend to care for me would know [—] if I am playing a desperate game let them remember I am as firm as I am fearless & nothing but tenderness & gentleness shall move me—at such a moment I could have hoped to have been other wise employd—but it is no matter [—] my feelings are no doubt of very little consideration to you—

Caroline immediately offered a contrite apology for her attack and wished everything to be as before.

18. Lady Caroline to Lady Holland. [JULY 1811.]

6 oclock
Devonshire House

My Dearest Lady Holland

I entreat you to forgive the very very improper letter I wrote last night that I am miserable for it you may believe by my now writing this that I think you justified in not wishing me to meet Sir Godfrey there I acknowledge also—& that by my foolish resentment & anger I only added to the rest of my very blameable conduct I likewise own—do therefore as you will I will not let another hour pass without asking forgiveness for my offence & I think you most fully justified in refusing me—I go tomorrow to Brocket & if either of us should die I shall on my death bed be miserable for the letter I wrote last night—to say my spirits were horrid that I was unhappy angry is no excuse—were you to forgive me happen what would I would Gallop over to see you at eleven tomorrow morning before we set out

yours however you may treat me most sincerely most affectionately
Caroline Lamb

Pray don't forgive, jusques a midi[27]

Lady Holland was too tired (at least temporarily) of the emotional ups and downs of their relationship to permit this episode to pass, however.

19. Lady Caroline to Lady Holland. 6 AUGUST 1811.

My very Dearest Lady Holland I was in the Carriage & have got out to tell you that I am miserable quite miserable at what I have done [—] your kind note is worse than a thousand abuses [—] that I love that I esteem that I value your friendship believe [—] that I abhor myself for my weak passion & for every thing I have done these 2 years past—you may you must think & think if it is any satisfaction to you to know that I am now setting out with a heart half broken you may rejoice—for indeed indeed I am unhappy humbled mortified & only wish I could throw myself at your feet & claim that forgiveness from your own dear hands which you have had the generosity to send me

[27] *jusques a midi*, "until mid-day."

in writing God Bless & preserve you & may I live to see you & to thank you

ever & most affectionately

yrs
Caroline

With Webster finally out of the picture, Caroline tried to paint one of domestic bliss for her cousin G.

20. Lady Caroline to Georgiana, Lady Morpeth, Future Sixth Countess of Carlisle. 25 October 1811.

[. . .] this House is beautiful but there are no dogs & to me that is unpleasant—Wm Lamb chases the Fox & pheasants—I ride a great deal & see much of the Neighbours—Augustus is my bosom friend [. . .] he is also Wm Lambs delight—we are united like 3 flames or 3 oaks or what you will. Time permits no more at present from your loving Cousin [. . .]

The subject of Bess Foster never failed to provide a distraction from any concerns of Caroline's family.

21. Lady Caroline to the Sixth Duke of Devonshire. 14 November 1811.

I know why my Duke felt melancholy—he has the heart of an angel & he knew he had been too hasty too suspicious—[28]

let not suspicion's Eager serpant tooth
destroy the noble confidence of youth—
& spoil with cunning love & prudent art
the genuine feelings of thy open heart—

you felt that you had ferrited the maim'd Fox out of its last hold—the safe corner to which it still clung from the dangers & taunts of a rigidly

[28] After the Sixth Duke of Devonshire (Hart) initially turned Lady Elizabeth Foster out of Chiswick and Devonshire House, he replied good-naturedly that he had not been guilty of "cruelty to the oppressed," and indeed had done what he could to reassure Lady Elizabeth about her future, and teased Caroline by concluding: "Always tell me when a qualm comes across thy mind about my purity," signing himself "Devilshire" (Bessborough and Aspinall, *Lady Bessborough and Her Family Circle*, 218).

just World—you had been told it would encroach & you dropp'd a hasty exclamation, & it made you sick to think you had done so—I am sure of it & I feel the same—Cousin of mine we have one fault, we both act precipitately [. . .] now you see, young Devon—I write the very thoughts of my heart so be not offended I shall tell you all—& your own motto of Honi soit[29] must be my safeguard—not that I think friendship authorises unkindness as some very sagaciously imagine but merely confidence & sincerely so now to God the Father—
I met Miss Trimmer[30] the other day

> Like a fair peach that never has been tasted
> its sap its bloom & all its flavour wasted
> droops our Selina on her virgin Tree
> unlov'd unloving any living he—
> but this is neither here nor there to thee—
> [. . .]

Despite an initial failure to meet, Lady Caroline and Lady Morgan became friends for life, and Lady Morgan's The Wild Irish Girl *(1806) would later partly inspire Lady Caroline's* Glenarvon *(1816).*

22. Lady Caroline to Miss Owenson [Lady Morgan.] 1811.

London, 1811

My dear Miss Owenson,

If it had not been near making me cry, what I am going to tell you might make you laugh; but I believe you are too good-natured not to sympathize in some manner with my distress. It never occurred to me that I should forget the direction you gave me, so that having ordered the carriage, and having passed a restless night, I was but just getting up when it was ready. I ordered it to fetch you; where, was the question—at York, was the only answer I could possibly give; for York, alas, is all I

---

29 *Honi soit que mal y pense* [Shame on him who thinks this evil], the motto of the Order of the Garter, oldest and most important of the orders of knighthood in Great Britain. Its head is the sovereign, and the garter (inscribed with the motto) appears on the royal arms of Great Britain. As a result, the phrase is sometimes erroneously described as "the motto of Great Britain."

30 That is, Selina Trimmer, governess in the Devonshire-Bessborough household. Caroline often commented on her drab and hangdog appearance.

remember. Now they say there is a York lane, three York streets, a York place, a York buildings, and York court. I knew no number, but immediately thought of sending to Lady Augusta Leith;[31] the Court Guide was opened, it was for 1810; Lady A. Leith consequently not where she now is, and where either of you are I cannot think; but as I was obliged to go into the country, I wrote this, and take my chance of its ever getting to you. Should you receive it, pray accept of my regrets and excuses, and do not treat me as ill as I have you, but remember your kind intentions some evening. I shall be back Saturday, I believe; but General Leith goes Tuesday.

See me before you leave town, and send me your number and street, I beg of you; the impression you have made is, I assure you, a little stronger, but I never can recollect one direction—do you think the new man could teach me?

Yours very sincerely, C. Lamb.

My direction is always Melbourne House.

---

[31] The wife of Major General Sir James Leith (1763–1816), who fought with Wellington in the Peninsular War. The Leiths seem to have been thick with the Lambs.

CHAPTER FOUR

Byron

Letters, 1812–1813

In early 1812, Lady Caroline read an advance copy of Byron's first hugely successful poem, Childe Harold's Pilgrimage *and wrote to him.*

1. Lady Caroline to Lord Byron. 9 March 1812.

Childe Harold

I have read your Book & cannot refrain from telling you that I think it & that all those whom I live with & whose opinions are far more worth having—think it beautiful. You deserve to be and you shall be happy. Do not throw away such Talents as you possess in gloom & regrets for the past & above all live here in your own Country which will be proud of you—& which requires your exertions. Pray take no trouble to find out who now writes to you—it is one very little worth your notice & with whom you are unacquainted but who from the first has admired your great & promising Genius & who is now so delighted with what you have written that it would be difficult for me to refrain from telling you what I think.

As this is the first letter I ever wrote without my name & could not well put it, will you promise to burn it immediately & never to mention it? If you take the trouble you may very easily find out who it is, but I shall think less well of Child[e] Harold if he tries—though the greatest wish I have is one day to see him & be acquainted with him.

Having received no immediate reply, Caroline wrote again in verse.

2. Lady Caroline to Lord Byron. [11 March?] 1812.

Oh that like thee Childe Harold I had power
With Master hand to strike the thrilling Lyre
To sing of Courts & Camps & Ladies Bower
And chear the sameness of each passing hour
With verse that breathes from heaven and should to heaven aspire
Then all confiding in my powerful art
With Friends attentions & expressions kind
Ev'n I might Hope some solace to impart
To soothe a Noble but a wounded heart
And pay homage due to a superior mind
Nor think with prying eyes & Idle Jest
I'de wish to search the secrets of thy breast
or that a Womans Vanity should move
Me to affect—thy confidence & love—
ah no—I love nor will that word profane
Which those who know it not make light and vain
Strong love I feel for one I shall not name—
What I should feel for the could never be the same—
But Admiration interest is free—
And that Childe Harold may receive from me.

Despite the avowal of merely platonic intentions, Caroline's letter got Byron's attention. By late March their affair was on.[1]

3. Lady Caroline to Lord Byron. 27 March 1812.

Good Friday

The Rose Lord Byron gave Lady Caroline Lamb died in despight of every effort made to save it; probably from regret at its fallen Fortunes. Hume at least, who is no great believer in most things, says that many more die of

[1] Much later in life, Lady Caroline told Lady Morgan that, when she first observed Byron, she wrote in her journal that he looked "mad, bad, and dangerous to know" (Morgan 2: 200).

Lord Byron in Albanian Dress, painted by Thomas Phillips. National Portrait Gallery, London.

broken hearts than is supposed—when Lady Caroline returns from Brocket Hall, she will dispatch the Cabinet maker to lord Biron with the Flower she wishes most of all others to resemble, as, however deficient its beauty & even use, it has a noble & aspiring mind, &, having once beheld in its full lustre the bright & unclouded Sun that for one moment condescended to shine upon it, never while it exists could it think any lower object worthy of its worship & Admiration—yet the sunflower was punished for its temerity but its fate is more to be envied than that of many less proud flowers it is still permitted to gaze though at the humblest distance, on him who is superiour to every other & though in this cold foggy atmosphere it meets no doubt with many disappointments & though it never could never will have reason to boast of any peculiar mark of condescension or attention from the bright star to whom it pays constant hommage yet to behold it sometimes to see it gazed at to hear it admired will repay all—she hopes therefore when brought by the Little Page it will be graciously received without any more Taunts & cuts about "love of what is New"—Lady Caroline does not plead guilty to this most unkind charge at least no further than is laudable for that which is rare & is distinguished & singular ought to be more prized & sought after than what is common place & disagreeable—how can the other accusation of being easily pleased agree with this? The very circumstance of seeking out that which is of high value shows at least a mind not readily satisfied—But to attempt excuses for faults would be impossible with Lady Caroline—they have so long been rooted in a soil suited to their growth that a far less penetrating gaze than Lord Byrons might perceive them—even on their shortest acquaintance—there is not one, however, though sorry indulged, that shall not be instantly got rid of if Ld Byron thinks it worth while to name them—the reproofs and abuse of some however severe & just may be valued more than the easily gained encomiums of the rest of the world. [M]iss Mercer, were she here, would join with Lady Caroline in a last request during their absence, that besides not forgetting his new acquaintances he would eat & drink like an English man till their return. The lines upon the only dog ever lov'd by Ld Byron are beautiful. What wrong then that having such proof of the faith and friendship of this animal, Ld Byron should censure the whole race by the following unjust remarks!

"perchance my dog will whine in vain
"Till fed by stranger hands—
"But long e'er I come back again
"He'd tear me where he stands[2]—

4. Lady Caroline to Lord Byron. [MARCH–JUNE 1812.]

My mother is returned & she looks quite beautiful & well how little you know her—did you know her you would idolize her. She is just what

[2] From *Childe Harold* 1:13 (a song between stanzas 13 and 14).

you would like most upon earth—Lady Melbourne is coming to Brocket I hear—she shall not have her life embittered by such a one as I am if I feel jealous of her I will remember her age and respect her & if she speaks harshly I will recollect my faults and not answer—She has every fine quality and much good—but if I have too much of it I think she is too wholly without sentiment & romance—she also wants that softness which my mother and yourself have that Vielle Court manner which is to me prettier & more conciliating than any other [. . .]—My Mother who always has the fortune of being left children has now got the care—guess of what—of an Hermaphrodite to which till this hour she had not believed could exist—what an unplanned appendage to her family—she was consulted as to its name—it is not yet Christened—it is of both sexes & a remarkably fine interesting child about six months old perfect in every respect Shall it pass for male or female—which will be the safest: if you can throw any light upon this subject do but for your life do not name it to any one—because in the first place it will seem as if I wrote to you which you know I never do—& in the next it will appear a mighty strange sort of Topic of discussion from me to you—& be discust. Yesterday I received a letter from Lady M saying these words—Caroline is there no end to your strange adventures, will nothing cure you—I hear but I do not believe that you have a female Page—if so do not hope to make me laugh—you always think you can make people laugh at yr follies but these are crimes.

So now for anguished days again—but I love Lady M & think she has the law[3] on her side & therefore I will be very submissive & kind—for your sake also—for she is only too dear to you [. . .] your very dutiful Friend and affectionate servant

"Caroline"

The poem in the following letter was addressed to Annabella Milbanke, William Lamb's cousin and—though no one yet suspected it—the future Lady Byron, but it was intended only for Byron's eyes.

5. Lady Caroline to Lord Byron. [MAY 1812.]

Cousin of mine thy verses stray & Quaint
Shall soon unrivald all his favour share

[3] That is, Lady Melbourne, Lady Caroline's mother-*in-law*, of whose intimacy with Byron Caroline was jealous.

For love requires but little art to paint
Such one as thee in colours bright & fair

Thou hast the charms of innocence & youth
Thy thoughts & passions under firm controul
Thy lips untainted pure as spotless truth
& faith & Principles to guard thy soul

[. . .]

Live for the Present happiness of life
What I from folly have thrown far from me
Be fond Mother & a faithful Wife
And all the joys once mine I wish to thee

Considering I was not a pupil of Blackets[4] give me credit for writing off such an address my Horse waiting my G^{d}mother calling my boy crying my husband swearing my Maids scolding—though metre sense music poetry are rather withheld but it is not to all that these are granted & from an Infant I wrote Rhimes as you see—much as shoe blacks & bell men & love sick Maidens when abandoned oftentimes break out in—take Annabella's far worthier productions be not over in love with her this one Evening and afterwards you must do as you will—I send your ring would it were more to my liking but before long I will have one quite so—ever yours I am ill this Morning—but I shall come living or dead to the Play—& take you up in my way write to me—

6. Lady Caroline to Lord Byron. [April–June 1812.]

as you like curiosities I send you a relic of Lady Caroline Ponsonby aged 14[5]—& I request you keep it for her sake—I saw Walter Scott last night—he did not remember me I think at first [—] I much wish to ask him to name some Evening within these 14 days & I will engage some persons who wish to meet him to come here. I trust you will be of that

---

[4] Cobbler-poet Joseph Blacket (1786–1810) lived in Seaham, home of Annabella Milbanke. Lady Caroline had reluctantly given some of Annabella's poetry to Byron, who wrote a note praising Annabella's work and comparing it favorably to Blacket's.

[5] Lady Caroline had enclosed a cutting of her hair from that early period of her life.

number—if you go to Lydia[6] tomorrow I will meet you there & will you bring him—I go early to Devonshire House—

yrs
CL

Several times during that spring and summer of 1812, Byron and Caroline fought and made up. Samuel Rogers, a poet and friend of Byron's, who had earlier commented dryly on "the manoeuvres of certain noble ladies" who tried to use him to get access to Byron, now found himself occasionally stuck in the middle of lovers' quarrels.[7]

7. Lady Caroline to Lord Byron. [APRIL–JUNE 1812.]

My dearest Byron

There is no cause for alarm—but I have had a wretched night and am still painfully irritable. I am therefore going out and to occupy myself in the air.

I am exceedingly grieved I gave you so much uneasiness. I will endeavour by all possible means to avoid a return of any thing so painful between us—In justice to myself however I may say that I should not feel this irritation if it were not for my present circumstances. These seem both cause & effect—

but I sincerely do wish for ever to give you no pain, and as I know how well the human mind can accommodate itself to any thing, I have no doubt that the present source of my perpetual vexation will soon be at an end. With every feeling of the sincerest affection—your attached

CL

8. Lady Caroline to Fletcher, Byron's valet. [APRIL–JUNE 1812.]

Fletcher—Will you come and see me here some evening at 9, and no one will know of it. You may say you bring a letter and wait the answer. I will send for you in. But I will let you know first, for I wish to speak with you. I also want you to take the little foreign page I shall send in to see Lord Byron. Do not tell him before-hand, but, when he comes with flowers, shew him in. I shall not come myself, unless just before he goes away; so do not think it is me. Besides, you will see this is quite a child,

---

[6] Lydia White, a bluestocking hostess to whom Lady Caroline later dedicated her third and last novel, *Ada Reis* (1823).

[7] Rogers, *Recollections of the Table-Talk of Samuel Rogers*, 190.

only I wish him to see my Lord if you can contrive it, which, if you tell me what hour is convenient, will be very easy. I go out of Town to-morrow for a day or two, and I am now quite well—at least much better. When does Holmes come again—if you see him tell him I wish to speak with him & send this not knowing where else to send for him.

In one of her most infamous letters to Byron, Caroline enclosed a clipping of her pubic hair.

9. Lady Caroline to Lord Byron. 9 August 1812.

Next to Thyrza Dearest
& most faithful—God bless you
own love—ricordati di Biondetta
From your wild Antelope

I asked you not to send blood but yet do—because if it means love I like to have it—I cut the hair too close & bled much more than you need—do not you the same o pray put not scizzors points near where quei capelli grow—sooner take it from the arm or wrist—pray be careful—& Byron—tell me why a few conversations with the Queen Mothers always change you I think by the bye that you would make a bad Minister a worse Ambassador—you would in the first case be always acting from pique—& resentment & in the latter soft words & pretty lips would make you another Duke of Buckingham—when you left me I must one night be in your arms—and now not even see you but in presence of a witness—oh I could scold—but as you think proper only this I assure you—se ti vedo ed il Principe e la ti Baccierò[8]—dicendo Honi soit qui mal y pense[9] e addio mio Bel & Buono amico[10]—Newstead—that is a pity[11]—why not have kept it & taken Biondetta[12] there & have livd & died happy—yet you give us both up no tie can bind but Newstead bears your unkindness in sullen silence—I will kneel and be torn from your feet before I will give you up—or sooner be parted with.

---

[8] Roughly, "If I see you at the Prince's, I will kiss you."

[9] "Honi soit qui mal y pense," the motto of the order of the Garter: "Shame be to him who thinks this evil." See Chapter Three, footnote 29.

[10] Literally: "and Goodbye my handsome and good friend."

[11] Caroline had heard that Byron would be forced to sell Newstead Abbey, his ancestral estate.

[12] That is, Lady Caroline herself, who signed herself "Biondetta" above. The name is an allusion to *Le diable amoreux* (1772), a novel by Jacques Cazotte in which the devil appears as a fair-haired, cross-dressing female "page boy." ("Ricordati di Biondetta," meaning "remember your Biondetta.")

The affair almost came to an elopement in August when Caroline fought with her father-in-law, ran away, and had to be brought home by Byron himself.

10. Lady Caroline to Lady Melbourne.[13] [12 AUGUST 1812.]

Dear Lady Melbourne—

Lord Melbourne came into the room said he should tell Wm every thing—& in the most insulting manner assured me Lord Byron would not take me if I wishd [—] in short he despised me—as to that I am as sure of Byron as I am of any thing on earth—but I will not for worlds involve him in my ruin forget my existence all of you—I shall instantly set off for Spain & join Fred L[amb]—& Lady Augusta Leith [—] I will behave in no way to disgrace my family & it is but a temporary absence [—] comfort my Mother take care of my boy & believe me yours—ever

Caroline's mother, who collapsed and began coughing blood, insisted Caroline leave London and travel to the family estate in Ireland, and she was ultimately successful, though Caroline too became physically ill and even mentally deranged under the stress.

11. Lady Caroline to Lady Melbourne. [13 AUGUST 1812.]

My Dearest Lady Melbourne

She had a good night—& I really feel satisfied the more as Sir Walter[14] has orderd her to be cupp'd[15]—now Duncannon says his only hope is in you that he will stand <u>bail</u> for me this once—& take me under his care if you will but persuade Sir Walter not to let her leave England[16]—& he will be persuaded if you are of this opinion—living altogether comfortably & quietly

---

[13] This note was almost certainly written and sent back to Melbourne House after Lady Caroline ran away on 12 August 1812, provoking a wild sequence of events that culminated in Byron himself returning her to her family.

[14] Sir Walter Farquhar (1738–1819) Scottish physician who attended the Bessboroughs and Devonshires as well as the Prince of Wales.

[15] Lady Bessborough had suffered a serious collapse after Lady Caroline's running away from home the previous day. "Cupping" drew blood to the surface of the skin with heated cups that created suction as they cooled, and then leeches or knives might be used to bleed the patient.

[16] Lady Bessborough was determined to get Caroline out of London and over to Ireland, at the risk of her own health.

either at Roehampton or any where she pleases is surely far better for her than taking a long journey—sea sickness & every other inconvenience—I know she has set her mind upon it—but you can you must persuade her not—we are all most anxious and I far the most as I feel I am the cause [. . .]

As she prepared to leave for Ireland, Caroline pretended it was her own idea and still sought a meeting with Byron. Byron had not pushed her away at this time, indeed, he had written a very emotional letter: "My dearest Caroline—If tears, which you saw & know I am not apt to shed, if the agitation in which I parted from you, agitation which you must have perceived through the whole of this most nervous nervous affair, did not commence till the moment of leaving you approached, if all that I have said & done, & am still but too ready to say & do have not sufficiently proved what my real feelings are & must be ever towards you, my love, I have no other proof to offer; God knows I wish you happy, & when I quit you, or rather when you from a sense of duty to your husband & mother quit me, you shall acknowledge the truth of what I again promise & vow, that no other in word or deed shall ever hold the place in my affection which is & shall be most sacred to you, till I am nothing I never knew till that moment, the madness of—my dearest & most beloved friend—I cannot express myself—this is no time for words—[. . .]"[17] *She responded in similarly overheated terms.*

12. Lady Caroline to Lord Byron at the Albany. [15–23 August 1812.]

Dearest Lord Byron—be pacified and hear me. I am without excuse [—] I trust my self to your compassion [—] if you tell any one that I attempted to see you I am lost irretrievably lost—if not be quite assured I will neither write nor send nor see you—I really leave London immediately alas at my own request—I merely called in Hopes of seeing you one instant just to ask you to forgive my having broken all my promises—be quite secure that I will intrude no more, be happy—but as I depend solely upon your generosity do not embitter the feelings of all my friends by telling them what a lost and worthless being they have lavished all their kindness upon—I myself have wished to leave Town—had it not been so I would not have called but I think you are offended with me. I fear it & this thought makes me most wretched [—] let my absence my

[17] *Byron's Letters and Journals*, 2:185. The letter was reproduced as a lithographic facsimile by Lady Caroline for Thomas Medwin after publication of his *Conversations with Lord Byron* (1824).

silence my obedience in future atone for the past—oh Lord Byron think how inexcusable it must appear to others when it does so to you—& pray forget what I have done—grown more alarmed more wretched than you can think—I am really utterly lost if this is known if you keep the secret of my dishonour still I fear you must dispise me.

To see Byron again, Caroline was willing to endure the intrusion of her mother-in-law, whose intimacy with Byron made her highly jealous.

13. Lady Caroline to Lady Melbourne.
[ALMOST CERTAINLY AUGUST 1812.]

My Dearest Lady Melbourne

I hardly know in what manner to address you after your repeated goodness to me—but I will at least save you the suspense you cannot but feel & if you will permit me to take leave of Ld Byron one day before I leave him—perhaps for ever & certainly for a much longer time than you think if this may be allowed & indeed whether it is or not unless you turn me out of the House—I will neither draw ruin on his head nor cause you & my Mother & him I ought never to name to be made uneasy & miserable hitherto you say I have lived for my self—henceforward I will live for others—I will not consider what is pleasure but what is right—I shall see L^d^ B this Morning—he will acquiesce in all I wish—he has behavd to me most kindly most honourably—most as he ought—if either of us have said things of the other or of ourselves in moments of anger do not think it was to deceive. it was I know not why—madness on both sides—perhaps too great kindness or weakness or his strong attachment or both [—] at least madness on mine—try & forgive some part in short do as you will I neither ask nor expect it at present till my conduct shews that I can forget every thing but the affection & generous kindness Wm my Mother & yourself have shewn me nor to speak of many others—God Bless you & if I dared pray—I would say me also for who needs blessing more—

your ever affectionate & most grateful <u>child</u> in conduct & in love—

Caroline Lamb

once more—the day before I go this is my last request—& no more deceits & lies on my part I am sick of them—

While Caroline was in Ireland, she still exchanged numerous letters with Byron, who could not bring himself to shut the door completely on her. Her emotions ran the usual gamut of defiance, contrition, agony, and distraction, and she thus appeared to Lady Melbourne, and through her to Byron himself, as duplicitous. Her letters were remarkably consistent, however, as she defended her sometimes inconsistent behavior, requiring only (she said) that Byron acknowledge he had really loved her. She was outraged when Lady Melbourne suggested Caroline had once sneaked a look at one of Byron's letters not intended for Caroline.

14. Lady Caroline to Lady Melbourne. 28–29 September. 1812.

My Dearest Lady Melbourne it is 4 days since we have heard I conclude owing to the winds from any of you—pray tell me what Wm ought to do—have you heard or thought of St Albans—is Parliament dissolved[18] if so tell Miss Webster[19] to give her Bulletins to you & do not expect many letters from me as it would be unmerciful to make you pay for my stupid letters—we came here today the approach to this Castle is dreary romantic solitary & very fine—all about Bessborough bears the appearance of plenty health chearfulness & cleanliness all here of former Grandeur & times gone by [. . .] will you give a kiss & my love to my dear little Boy it is near ten days since I had the happiness of hearing he was well [. . .]—I could say something but the Atlantic rolls between us & we may chance never again to meet & therefore it is unkind oh so unkind to quarrel across seas—I am not very well neither very ill—but this place is damp & dismal I gave you a long account of it but I did not like my letter believe me ever gratefully & affectionately

Caroline Lamb [. . .]

15. Lady Caroline to Lady Melbourne. 15 October 1812.

My Dearest Lady Melbourne—tax yourself with no <u>kind</u> letter it did not come [—] two of a very contrary sort I have receivd—once more I assure you upon my honour I never opened or intentionally read any letter of yours—I found a part of one on the floor [—] it was in a hand I was used to receive to my self—I made no secret of it [—] I have

---

[18] Parliament was indeed being dissolved, and William wished to run for a seat, but lack of money prevented him.

[19] Thomasina Webster, governess and surrogate mother for Augustus Lamb.

committed no wrong[20]—hitherto I have behaved with perfect honour deceived by every human being I never have returned in kind their ill treatment—but as you say it is not for me to complain & you shall none of you ever more tax me with too much openness—I have borne a great deal & will bear no more—that which is not spoken is more to be dreaded than that which is seen—I shall write no more—only entreating you not to write unkindly to my Mother who says instead of delightful letters from you she receives at present nothing but a few short guarded lines—& why? upon my soul she is innocent & ignorant of every thing of this—she never names one I do not ever speak of—& as to my having accused him I hope I did not—if I said he was unkind to me because I wishd to behave well—I did him great wrong I beg his [and] I beg your pardon—I scarcely know what I wrote do not tell him I said this I conclude I have deserved the treatment I have met with & I will bear it without complaint but it was so unnexpected & it wounds me so deeply that you must not think I can write to you or any one again Lady Melbourne I here do solemnly swear to you by all that you may hold most sacred if it were not for my Mother & the kindness I have received from you all from this day forth you should never see me again—oh that I had not been weak enough to return when Lord Byron brought me back[21] that I had never returned but come it late—it will come at last—& such an exit I will make from this scene of Deceit & unkindness that it shall expiate even my atrocious conduct as you call the canting sorrow of which you accuse me—Lord Byron has now seald my destruction & it shall follow—mark these words & when it comes remember It was not the mere impotence of frantic grief—but the secret firm resolution of a heart bitterly & deeply injured—I never more will write to you & thanks for the letters I have received I shall not reproach you for them I deserve unkindness from you [—] I never have I hope I never have accused Lord Byron—he or you best know why he behaves ill to the Woman he so lately professed to love—he is changed perhaps[,] is that a reason—no we are not master of our affections this love for another is no crime but I neither expected nor can bear insult hatred suspicion & contempt—I will not bear it [—]

---

[20] Lady Caroline had been accused of reading a private note of Byron's to Lady Melbourne, and the accusation rankled throughout her stay in Ireland. In another letter of this period she protested: "I assure you upon my most sacred word of honour I never in the course of my existence opened any Ladies letter or note or read any letter not addressed to myself" (British Library Add. MS 45546 ff. 40–41).

[21] Caroline alludes to Byron's having fetched her back home after she ran away on 12 August 1812.

he may love who he pleases I shall never reproach him but he should not treat me with cruelty & contempt

16. Lady Caroline to Lady Melbourne. 14 October 1812.

My Dear Lady Melbourne—

[. . .] you may all think I am merry because I dance jigs—I have thrown it all away no body loves me now or ought—I wish to be dead [—] they who wish it are not long in having their prayers heard—I would send you a song upon a Funeral but I do not like to make you pay[22] for any stupid nonsense of mine—remember me to those that remember me & say nothing of me to others [. . .] Wm is out of spirits about Parliament but he is right without involving himself or L[d] Melbourne in debt he could not have come in[23]—otherwise it is a great disappointment—I wrote you a letter but it was a stream of tears & I remember you—saying this looked affected—you see yr observations are not lost upon me[24]—I inclose you a little note for Emily—ever yours

17. Lady Caroline to Lady Melbourne. 13–17 October. 1812.[25]

Kilkenny

Here we are where all are gay one hour & sick with fever the other—as to me I can neither be ill or well I neither sleep nor eat nor am able to do any thing I am more out of spirits than it is possible to say—you bid me write to my mother I can write to no human Being—I receive no letters I wish to receive none—do not fancy I ever can return or remain in England do not deceive yourself or talk harshly & unkindly to me my mind my nerves my whole constitution is so irritated that Wm says he does not know what to do with me—& Jane the same—ask him if I am

---

22 Lady Caroline assumes Lady Melbourne must pay the postage for letters she receives.

23 They now knew Parliament had been dissolved on 29 September, leaving William Lamb frustrated: "It is actually cutting my throat," he wrote his mother. He wanted to ask his father for financial assistance, but felt he could not (British Library Add. MS. 45546).

24 Lady Caroline was keenly anxious not be "thought a love sick deserted Lady," and declared, "I am free & independent of Lord Byron—I do not wish to move his compassion," in another letter of this time (British Library Add. MS 45546 ff. 40–41).

25 Letter is smeared as if she had wept over it.

selfish or stubborn as you always say these are savage words & go to my very soul—I cannot forget their harsh sound—from you from him they come & dread driving me to utter dispair [. . .] I can bear this but a little longer Lady Melbourne I struggle to conceal my feelings to my Mother I am not ungenerous I am not selfish—but I cannot will not bear this state much longer remember I warn you I do not menace—I am respectful I wish to be so—but you are not here to witness what I suffer [—] Wm has been on the point of writing to you several times [—] so has Jane [—] I do not sleep—I cannot eat I can dance can ride but strangers even think me miserable they suppose it is leaving my Child [—] my Mind is irritated—I will go away—or die—depend upon it—I do not act as that Mr Eden[26] did I never will I warn my friends in time—but there are calamities God inflicts we can bear them—others we ourselves have brought we cannot bear—I have no complaint to make against any one—but I think myself cruelly treated I feel it to my soul—indeed I hide every thing from Mamma—indeed I do not think only of myself Wm knows Wm says I do not—I only say this Ld Byron need not shall not write it was his own desire—I remember once my not doing so one day caused him misery he will leave England without seeing me if he does it I only say this you have all of you lost me forever I shall never recover [from] that letter never never—do not write or speak to Lord Byron do not I implore you—I shall know if you do & I do entreat you not but do not you also write harshly to one who is near mad & soon very soon will be gone Wm promises me I shall see him once more it is only once I wish only for one moment—had not my Brother prevented me before I came all had been well—do not name me to Lord Byron for God sake do not—do not write so cruelly to me

As in her correspondence with Lady Holland, Caroline often wrote in haste and regretted it.

18. Lady Caroline to Lady Melbourne. [OCTOBER 1812.]

Bessborough

My letter to you is not gone—thank God for it would have grieved you to see it—you never read one so horrible—devoting myself to wickedness & infamy out of revenge! God Bless you & calm the Passions it has

---

[26] Mr. Eden's identity is unknown.

pleased him to try me with—we must call to order order & reform![27] send me back Lord B[yron]s letter[28] & do not shew it shew this to Emily or Caro [—] pray My Dearest Lady Melbourne now that I am calm I regret the letter I wrote yesterday which perhaps might be excused if you knew all—now this is a trust upon honour & I feel no doubt of you therefore I will speak to you as I would before God from my very heart—you are right in all you say about my Love I know it is too violent—but there is this to be said the only two Men who ever lov'd me insisted on it—would not be content with less & did all all in their power to make me love so by more than returning it—those two are most different in character but after them no others can please—It is dangerous to be attached to one of this sort they both acknowledge it because all after must appear a blank—Wm you say feels for me even more than affection & I do the same for him it is impossible not—but that sort of passion though it lasted with us for above three years must as you remarked cease to exist or change its object—with him a new pursuit engrossing all his Time & powers prevented me this mortification with me—I am sorry to observe a different conduct made me deserve the strongest blame—but grant the fact that my attachment to Lord Byron grew in time to be as strong as you say—that is to madness & excess—you must easily believe that his conduct so unnexpected so sudden has nearly killed me—Wm forgetting all jealousies really feels for me because you may ask him whether I have not tried to think of others & to forget myself but I wish to speak reasonably to you if I can—my Dearest Lady Melbourne your behaviour throughout has been generous & you will I am sure now I am grievd not alter—your letters have been received by me with scenes of passion & tears—last night the storm in my room was as William remarked not exceeded in violence by the storm of thunder & lightning without—the consequence in a calm on both sides this morning & if it will not tire you I will now explain myself—you say I shall be sorry to hear Lord Byron is in spirits—believe me I wish him all happiness health & spirits—& I do forgive him from my very soul for making me the play thing & victim of his varying

---

[27] "Reform," the battle-cry of the Whig Party, had been part of Lady Caroline's vocabulary since a child. See letter dated November–December 1797, beginning "*a reform a reform . . .* " The word became synonymous for her with personal reform, an effort to avoid "those tearing spirits which always lead me into Folly," as she wrote in another letter in fall 1812 (British Library Add. MS 45546 ff. 50–51).

[28] Caroline had written Byron shortly before from Kilkenny, where she was from 13–17 October 1812 before returning to Bessborough House and then Dublin.

passions—never fancy I wish to cause grief to anyone. as I said when leaving Augustus half the pain of parting is gone when we feel that it is not shared—but though I do think few Women & no Man ever took blame to themselves as I always do without throwing it on the other side—I will not let be believed that I intrude myself upon those who are tired or exceed in the violence & unreasonableness of my attachment it is not two months back when at Brocket I missed writing a single day I received such letters of dispair & accusation from himself & now because after writing constantly at his own request he ceases without one word of explanation & I have not heard from him since the 12 of last month—he affects astonishment at my sending an express—Dearest Lady Melbourne—it is better this should end here—Lord Byron is amiable generous & full of talents but he is of a character to desire those who love him most—even his friends say there is no standing it how then should one of my character—the violence & rashness of which he encouraged & liked while novelty lasted—I have a letter I could send but it would be wrong & I will act honourably by him whatever he or any one else may do by me—the one I inclose is rather of an older date it can do him no harm as it merely professes what he has often said—I entreat you to read it & to return it me—if you chuse to betray my confi[dence] & to shew it him—or to tell him of it—just remind him that he did the same by me—& to you—besides there is not a word in this he could dislike your seeing therefore read it & return it—& observe that in my life I never threw any of my faults upon those that however blameable lov'd me—within these two years many confidences of this kind have been reposed in me—& not one human Being has ever heard them—my answer has been—this may or may not be true on your part but I think it fair to tell you so far from making me vain or giving me pleasure it makes me angry I will never mention what you say if you never more will say the same & believe that I speak the truth when I assure you it never can be returnd I do not wish to make a fool of you or of my self—now all this behaving fairly & not as a Coquette—I have beside the proof—as it silenced very impertinent people & they have been respectful & yet friendly ever since—now if I were as vain & as selfish as some think would I not just have hinted this or by some manner of means have allowed it to be thought & yet I take no pride for not doing so for I think a contrary behaviour mean—with respect to Lord Byron I can only say wrong or right I did love & admire & believe in him from my heart & soul—whatever he wishd I wishd how could I without one hint on his part know that he thought my letters a trouble to read & disliked writing—I told him in Town that I was afraid it would tire him I proposed not writing [—] all I asked was not to be kept expecting what would not come—for this is the only thing I cannot bear—& now Dearest Lady Melbourne—when I say he is changed—I am not fool enough to believe that he is so—or but what if I see him again the whole of this will begin—I know what his reasonableness is he can talk & act so for a day—& then he will tell me oh never mind what I say you have changd & if you are [not?] to me as before by heavens I will go & never see you again—or else he will ridicule Platonics as he calls it—& in short I know pretty well how he will behave—& if I were to say I could resist this—I should say what was false—therefore I have made up my mind to avoid him till I am more reasonable—I only wish one thing I should like him to think well of me—I should not like him to know in what furious passions I have thrown myself—I trust all to your kindness & do hope you will not shew him or name to him any thing I have said—particularly by way of reproach—I wrote him what I thought a calm short letter before the little note or just after the little note I inclosed you from Kilkenny—in which I said that I was sure writing was troublesome & therefore begged him to do so no more—he is angry with me I fancy & will take me at my word & I promise you I shall not write any more to him—now when I first received his cruel letter I resolved to behave as ill as I could & the opportunity in Ireland is not wanting—here it is considered as such an honour to be noticed by an English Lady that all the men are sighing & looking in the manner of Brownlow north from morning till night—there was one who was from England & who was therefore much considered he came up to me with pretty verses & various other begin[nings] I did not attend to—till revenge gave me the wish—it was only to walze with me he asked only once & he would consider himself as the happiest oh the most perfectly happy of men—& I mov'd a foot out to do it—then Lady Melbourne a terror came upon me of the meanness of this sort of little vengeance & I thought to what a degraded character I was sinking & I started up with a look of Heroism must have astonished every body in the room who were waiting thinking I was using all the pretty arts of affectation—& I said I will not walze in a voice & manner more like a Lady in Bellingate than a Lady in a Ball room—& I feel glad that I have not through pique done what would <u>have</u> lowerd me in my own feelings—I do not mean walzing—but engaging myself in this manner—for though Lord Byron said in his last letter "you may do what you please—I release you from all your promises["]—yet after all if love for him has led me wrong no worse passion shall—I will check all this & try & get back my heart & affections if not as pure as good as before at least something more wise to offer them again to the only Man has shewn me real affection for surely no other would have borne what Wm has—& even now though my ill conduct has rousd his temper & made him at times furious & harsh yet upon the whole how very kind he is—last night I cried for two hours & he held my head himself—& never asked me one question—nor did he the whole time at Kilkenny though I disturbd him every night for it is 3 weeks since I have slept or attempted to close my eyes before [4?] in the morning or eat or been well—I really do think I have been almost in the same state I was after lying in—but it is over I hope now & I will try & bear every thing & not only bear it but make it useful—I have only 3 things to ask you—one is not to tell Lord Byron I either was angry or reproachd him or sent you this letter—the other that you will shew this to Emily & Caro—this one I now write—not Lord Byron's not a word in it but mine as it will express to them what I express to you—that I am unhappy but not now unreasonable & that I hope they and all my friends instead of being resentful against me will only see in my fate how little happiness any attachment gives out of ones own family—I know neither Emily nor Caro would ever act as I have done & I honour & love them for the manner in which they do behave—but let them while they blame me continue to feel for me and if I do return & live with you all assist me in avoiding what all those who have acted as I have are liable to—I mean plunging further & further into guilt—restless unhappy—perhaps mortified—those who like me suffer themselves to follow every impulse & have no command—will to drive away thought & probably from being unhappy—go on till these crimes exceed thought & then they either kill themselves or cause the death of others & there an end of such characters!

being talked of with one Man is also a nice excuse for all others to seek you—why else do we see in the World the most beautiful & attractive of human Beings passed by with respectful & distant admiration—while some who have no recommendation but facility of access—are followd & sought—I have placed myself in a difficult situation but I have what few on Earth have—a generous noble kind husband & such friends that there is not one of them I would not willingly give all I have on earth to & die though I think that the least offerring to make them happy—as to my Mamma she is angelic—no one ever can ever will know what that Woman is—or how entirely I love her [—] Lady Melbourne my own Lady M—While a wrong passion fills the heart it absorbs every other—it is this makes me appear selfish [—] Men not only will be lov'd—but will be lov'd exclusively require every sacrifice & swear that they require none—I have been wrong and I am grieved for it but do not on that account throw me from your heart no nor Emily & Caro who are my sisters my friends from children whom I do love most dearly I have been a disgrace a dishonour to you hitherto but I will try hard now to make up for it—Lady M—while I am writing this a letter is brought me it is from Lord Byron I shall not read it till tomorrow—but whatever its contents it makes not the smallest difference in what I have said not the smallest—God knows I feel still towards him all I ought not & therefore no doubt he will ever have power to make me miserable—but I am sure he will not—before I read his letter or know whether it is kind or cruel—let me say this I acquit him of all intentional wrong towards me—for like me I believe he follows every momentary impulse—I wish him to be most happy & will serve him if ever it is in my power—& moreover every request of his as they were such as they will only be further safeguards to my future good conduct—shall be scrupulously adherd to by me—I will avoid the very [beginnings?] of wrong no fear of being call'd prudish my faults are not that way—but I will do all this for Wm for my own for your sakes for Virtues & purities sake as well—as for Lord Byrons—what I am to others so by Heavens I will be to him

The Bessboroughs determined to return to London, and yet Byron had still not definitively told Caroline their affair was over. Perhaps at the insistence of Lady Melbourne or his new paramour, Lady Oxford, he wrote now, sharply, to "snap the knot" as he said.[29]

19. Lady Caroline to Lady Melbourne.
4 November 1812.

My very Dearest Lady Melbourne—as our setting out is delayd[30] I write which I otherwise should not for having begun several letters to you & finding them all upon looking over exceptional to say the least—I burnt them [. . .] you seem to think that I am surprised Lord Byron should change to me & prefer another [—] can you suppose me so vain so presumptuous as to have thought or expected or exacted fidelity & truth in an attachment of this sort [—] the very circumstance preventing my

---

[29] *Byron's Letters and Journals*, 2:193–94.

[30] The Bessboroughs had come to Dublin on 1 November, but on the 6th they went to Bishopscourt and stayed three nights before returning to Dublin, from whence, for some reason—perhaps weather—they did not depart until the 12 November.

belonging to him would have renderd such a compact very unjust—& I do hope to not be so unjust as to make this be thought—over & over again I have said to him—this cannot last & particularly on your side—cannot & must not & all I do entreat is that when over you will not as some Men do cut me wound me desert me—but treat me with kindness & gentleness—I need not tell you how he promised it[,] how he abused those who could do otherwise when you are away [—] he said all will be done to make you change but it is only you I am afraid of for myself there is no fear—but I an[swered] suppose you should—& suppose business or other attachment or an idea of right or any other motive makes you see fit to leave me—all I ask you is to say so fairly & not to be harsh & unkind to one you know & see does not wish to involve you—Lady Melbourne while there was danger of this he did not seem so very fearful and my own opinion is that whatever he may say to all of you he would have been glad if I had left all for him—certainly he shew'd no backwardness to this & when I told him of his saying he would take me if I threw myself upon him but it would make his misery[,] he used to laugh & say—do you not see I say all this to keep them free from suspicion—but even grant he did fear it & he <u>ought</u> [—] for miserable we should both have been beyond idea—grant I say that he did fear it—was there any danger of it just now when having heard from him saying something of an affaire [and being] annoyed at my return [—] I wrote with my usual vehemence—& said such an idea made me sick & that having once got over the pain of parting with him I never would return but so long as I know him attached to me I would keep to every wish of his though separated from him & live only to make up to William for the past [—] I gave him leave to marry to do what he pleased & only said I hoped he would still remember me with affection not the less for having resisted involving him & my whole family in misery [—] I then accused him of having betrayed several secrets of mine & ended saying what satisfaction & amusement his letters gave me—this was the letter I wrote on the 6th of September after my arrival at Bessborough[31]—& about 3 days after I received a letter more kind than ever—but it was the last, for after that came the empty Frank & afterwards the letter to Mamma saying Cheltenham waters had cured him & he hoped we should stay in Ireland a long while & that she would write to him neither about Ly A Ly B or Ly G ever but about herself for whom he felt the greatest possible interest—he said his spirits were beyond all idea & he was going—& there he left off—I have never heard since but when he sent the express & one letter

---

[31] They had arrived at their Irish estates on 4 September 1812.

besides quite evidently to vex me all about some other person—4 pages ending with these words—["]so far for the dearest & best friend I ever had & as to yourself Lady Caroline correct yr vanity which is become ridiculous—exert your Caprices on others enjoy the excellent flow of spirits makes you so delightful in the eyes of others & leave me in tranquility["]—how right you are in all you say Dearest Lady Melbourne but how difficult I find it to bear this—you must not think however that I have given way always to grief or that I shewd Wm any letter of Lord Byron's—I meant to do so—perhaps I thought I had when I wrote for I was almost mad but he will tell you himself that I never did this & as I do not think I have behavd with dishonour to Lord Byron do not ever suppose that I spoke of Wm without affection & kindness & respect & love [—] if I might say so I believe in my heart Lord Byron was jealous of that love [—] he said he would give nothing for a heart could feel for any other living object but himself & knelt to me that I might say if any thing happend to Wm that I would belong to him & I would not—it is the only thing I ever refused to say & when he wrote those promises of attachment I put in mine except Wm upon which when he read the word except he tore the Book [to] pieces & said I will have no exceptions [—] if you even dream of another I will make your heart ache & burn [—] he always ended by saying "now you will tell Lady Melbourne I abuse your husband will not you["]—& I used to be ready to cry—do not ever repeat all this & do pray burn my letter & do not fancy when I ask you not to tell it that I fear Lord Byron will deny it—for he could not deny it but I wish it all forgotten [—] what signifies reproaches & unkindness—he & I have much to answer for but as I never will flinch from the censures I deserve I do not like to be accused of what I am free from—never when menaced to the utmost would I deny to Lord Byron one word that was true—& that Evening when you found me up stairs in such a state of agitation you do not know how cruelly he had treated me—because I would not say that I hated Sir Godfrey Webster[32]—& because he said if I had given him a single present of any kind he would dispise hate fly [from] me forever more—I did not answer & then he went into such a furious passion & swore at me & said tell me is it so & I said it is no use telling you what is false—it is true—but Sir Godfrey never made love to me—from the first he loved another he never even shook hands with me but as an acquaintance[33]—but did you like him he said & I answered yes! & then

[32] Caroline had confessed to Byron her affair with Webster.

[33] It is not impossible Lady Caroline's affair was platonic, but we must doubt it.

he did abuse me & scorn me & mock me so & call me such horrid names that I threw myself down in the way you found—& there was just such another scene because I would not say I lov'd him better than Wm Lamb & his constant answer was—by God you shall pay for this for I will wring that little obstinate heart—& pray now I have told you all this do not be angry with me & say I force my confidences upon you & do not tell any of these things to one can turn them all against me—for tho' the consciousness of being in his power should never make me act one way or other—yet I have still enough attachment for Lord Byron to wish he may not absolutely hate me—for this reason believe me I abstain from reproaches or indeed from writing—& also assure yourself that if he is attached to another Woman—I shall neither be surprised nor offended—the unkindness of which I complain springs from a vindictive jealous suspicious temper—his loving another is but natural at his [age?] & a fault I of all others can best excuse—tho' even one that would entirely prevent my ever renewing any acquaintance with him—as like himself I would be first or not at all—as Augustus is tenacious of letters[34] I will write you one addrest to him all about what may be more entertaining than this but till now I have really been incapable of writing on any subject [. . .] God Bless you my very Dearest & Kindest Lady Melbourne I shall indeed remember how good & how forbearing [you ha]ve been—[do] excuse me or if you cannot—try at least & forgive [—] I am ever your most grateful & most affectionate

Caroline Wm Lamb

Though Caroline had put on a brave face to Lady Melbourne, she took the blow of Byron's rejection hard.

20. Lady Caroline to Lady Melbourne. [FALL 1812?]

[. . .] do not mistake what I said—I feel the difference of my situation the most undeserv'd difference & I beg you to hate me & forget me for I am a disgrace to you all—I ought not to come to London [—] do not wonder if I waver about it—I dare not go there be assurd I dare not every street every place reminds me of my conduct & if others forget it—it is their kindness [—] I never shall nor will I bring among the

[34] To placate Augustus, Lady Caroline told him that though she did not write often, he need not be jealous, for she wrote "to no *other Child*" (British Library Add. MS 45546, ff. 50–51).

unsuspicious & innocent all that is base & detested—Lady Dalrymple Hamilton says I must see her but how can I when we parted she gave me a heart which she said I was to wear for her sake & whenever I was going to do any thing flighty & imprudent I was to look at it & be wise—I told him of it & how I lov'd that heart for which reason he wishd for it & when I asked it him again merely for the sake of sparing explanations to her & because it was peculiar he said he had lost it or given it away[35] [. . .] here is the ring Lady Melbourne—which was to have followd my fortunes through life & been buried with me when all this ends [—] may it not give you the suffering it has caused me but do not ridicule this whim or refuse to wear it let me see when you come that it is on your hand it is the only thing he gave me I have ever worn lately—& I did swear so oh never never to take it off & he said in his letter that he had still his on—but ever after that I wrote my name Caroline Byron & he calld me his Wife & it was yet fresh from the stamp hardly polishd that it might be quite new gold as he said—all his other rings are markd with his name but this has no mark. now remember—& <u>never</u> tell to any but never take that ring off while you exist this you must promise[36]

yours Caroline

Returned from Ireland, Caroline organized a pre-Christmas bonfire in the village of Welwyn, not far from Brocket Hall. Village maidens danced around a fire on which Byron burned in effigy, and as they danced, they tossed onto the flames facsimiles of Byron's letters and gifts to Caroline. For the occasion, Caroline composed a poem to be recited by one of her pages, beginning, "Is this Guy Fawkes you burn in effigy? Why bring the traitor here?[. . .]"[37] *Subsequently, she made a first visit to John Murray's offices in an attempt to gain possession of one of the portraits of Byron she felt she was owed. While she had been in Ireland, she had begun writing a novel. This apparently became a form of therapy for her as the winter wore on.*

21. Lady Caroline to Lady Holland. [February 1813.]

My Dearest Lady Holland ask Mr Allen to write me a few lines just to say how you are—I am not very well—but we keep such divine hours

[35] Byron had indeed scattered most of Caroline's gifts among other friends and paramours. In his memorable phrase, "the trinkets are travelling" (*Byron's Letters and Journals,* 2:255).

[36] Byron claimed that Lady Caroline concocted the ring ceremony: "she *bestowed* [the ring] upon *herself* & insisted on my placing it on her finger" (*Byron's Letters and Journals*, 3:355).

[37] Quoted in Blyth, *Caro: The Fatal Passion*, 146.

we must grow healthy in time I should think—I looked at the novel as you were so good as to say you would read it—it consisted of nine vols—scribbled by various Pages—I waded through it with difficulty & found by erasing all that was bad & all that was dull—and all that was unnecessary that I just reduced it to 3 Pages—one of which was borrowed from an old Author the other was beautiful but too Poetical for the present taste & the 3d is still at your service & may serve equally for the beginning middle or conclusion of any work whatever whether tragic or comic [—] is not this at least being candid—so leaving off all hopes of turning Author I write now to you—trusting to your honour or anything else as worth trusting to—that you will contrive to make somebody write me an answer that is a statement of how you are[,] what you see do hear & think—Goodbye to you Dearest Lady Holland I am now writing a Comedy & you are one of the Dramatis Personae we get up at 8 litterally & go to Bed at 11 & sleep as it happens I seldom [. . .] snow drops & Crocuses have peeped through the wet mould which incessant rains have made into a moving Pool—all this I know from heresay—For I have not moved six paces square from the door—having driven myself into a state of truly pitiable weakness—

yours ever & most affectionately

Caroline Lamb

Wm is very well & we are very comfortable—Augustus[38] looks radiant & is growing tender hearted—he is Wms delight—& never from him [—] walks with him reads to him and cuts as many jokes as George Lamb [—] he looks really beautiful in his new dress—which is plain & not as I daresay you think all over gold & silver—

Writing therapy could only hold the hurt and anger at bay for so long, however, and Lady Melbourne's continued intimacy with Byron prompted more letters reviewing the past.

22. Lady Caroline to Lady Melbourne. [BEFORE 24 MARCH 1813.]

Lady Melbourne

to abide by his will—to try & gain command over myself & without once yielding to pique or anger—henceforward to shun beginnings to

[38] Augustus Lamb was now 6 1/2 yrs. old, and subject to regular grand mal seizures.

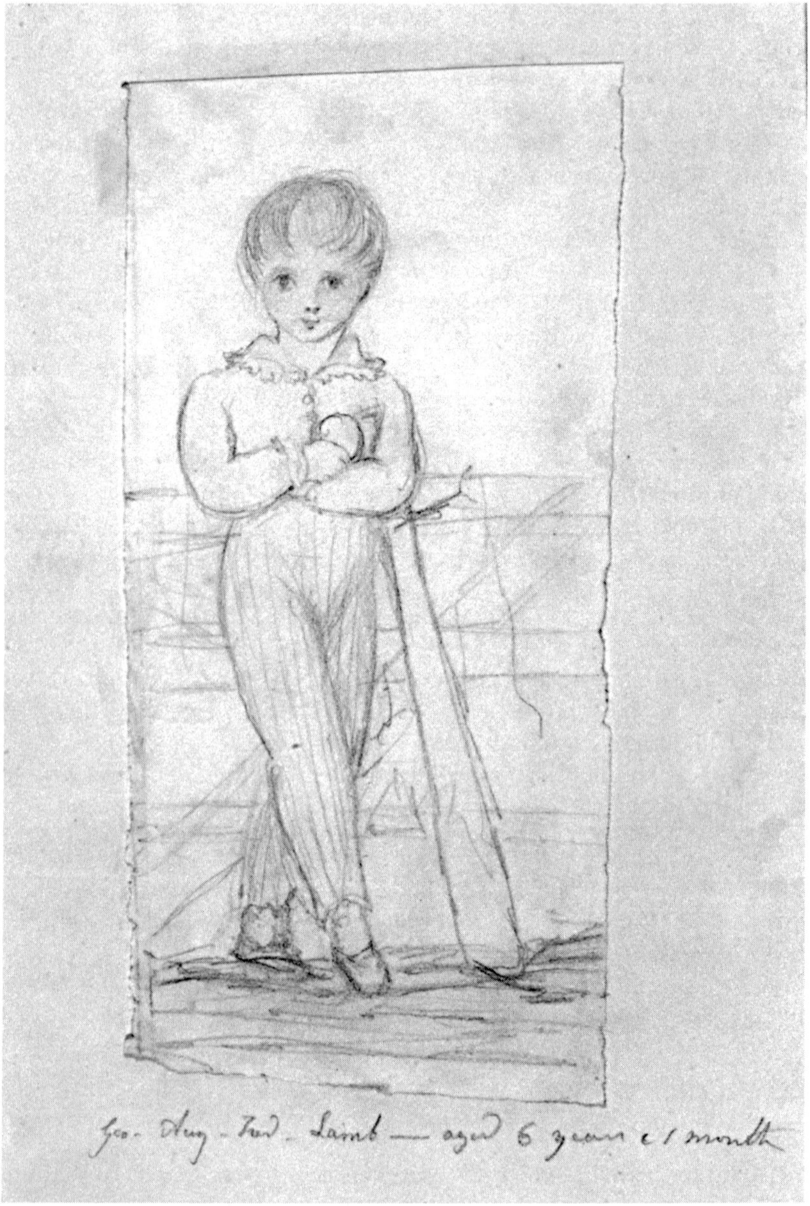

Sketch by Lady Caroline showing her son Augustus, with the caption "Geo. Augustus Lamb—aged 6 years & 1 month." By permission of Hertfordshire Archives and Local Studies.

wrong & live only for a family I love & honour & owe every thing to—but Lady Melbourne if this were all I could bear it—[. . .] without one Idea without one supposition about Lady Oxford [—] I wrote to her saying my Dearest Aspasia[39]—only think Byron is angry with me will you write to him will you tell him I have not done one thing to displease him & that I am miserable—tell him I wrote him a cross letter I know—but I have a thousand times asked his pardon—he is tired of me I see it by his letter I will write no more never teaze him—never intrude upon him only do you obtain his forgiveness—I received no answer & went to Dublin—there a letter came to me from Lady Oxford as I thought it had her seal I opened it tho' I knew it could not be an answer to mine as there had not been time—but it was a letter from him saying—Lady Caroline—our affections are not in our own power mine are engaged I love another—were I inclined to reproach you I might for a thousand things but I will not—they really are not cause of my present conduct my opinion of you is entirely altered & if I had wanted any thing to confirm me—your Levities your caprices & the mean subterfuges you have lately made use of while madly gay—of writing to me as if otherwise would entirely have opened my eyes—I am no longer yr lover I shall but never be less than your friend—it would be too dishonourable for me to name her to whom I am now entirely devoted & attached— & he put Lady Oxfords seal one I had myself shewn him & laughed with him about & he dated his letter Presteign[40]—I have no complaint to make against him or against her such are the facts & now you shall hear what my wishes are—& if you think them unreasonable I will try & give them up—I did wish to see him because I think it would in every way be better—but I now feel this ought not to be & my only desire is that you should engage him to write me a few lines just to recall those very harsh accusations—or if he will believe these things against me—just to say he forgives me & we part in peace—because if I were to die I should be miserable at doing so without this. he says also that I have abused & ridiculed him [—] ridicule him I could not & I do hope & trust I never did abuse him—but if in moments of bitter agony I have suffered my self to do so—he ought[,] he must now that we part—surely if you ask him he will forgive it—not that I plead guilty to this because to my knowledge I never did—Lady Oxford will of course have done all she could to

[39] "Aspasia" was Lady Oxford's nickname, alluding to the brilliant consort of Pericles, the "maid of Miletus."

[40] Eywood, Presteign, was the home of Lady Oxford.

set him against me dwelling on my behavior about Sir Godfrey I only wish him to think well of me—& to recall those very severe very unkind expressions which quite embitter my existence—as to offering him any slight or mortification which he mentions—were it in my power even which it is not surely he must know I never would—no nor to Lady Oxford or any other even were she to insult me—I believe I said in a letter to you once do not tell Lord Byron of my violence—I fancy you did not even know of it & I feel convinc'd that however rejoiced you may be at this being ended you will never say anything may give me further pain—tell him I have been violent no doubt & absurd—but surely my situation was such that he may in some degree excuse my doubts of him with far less cause [—] was he not for ever taunting & doubting me—& it is much better this should end much better & whatever I feel now—I cannot[,] will not regret it—nor ever seek to renew it or even to see him till I am quite sure such meeting may not lead to any thing the least wrong [—] as to my letters & presents—he says it is an insult to ask for them—then let him keep them—but let him remember how sacred a trust he by that means imposes on himself [—] not on my account for that is now of no consequence but for all of yours & Wms—his own presents dear as they are I will not keep because they are of too great value but in returning them God knows I mean no insult—I cannot however run the risk of his having to say—I cost him dear—the reason this occurred to me which sounds a coarse expression is because in talking of being attached to some Ladies—Lord Melbourne one day said people say a mistress is expensive by G—a mere flirtation with a Lady of Fashion costs double it was one day at dinner he said this & I wondered till now what he meant—& Byron shall not have to say this of me—as to every thing else I do not defend myself—whether I have been as guilty as it was possible or so wrong that it is impossible I should ever again call myself innocent—he knows—& whatever he thinks fit to accuse me of when it was untrue I would bear without denying but had I sought to involve him or to go away—will he deny that I had daily hourly opportunities & offers—they tell me he never wished it—it may be so—but if so he went very near to doing what he wished not & I leave it to him to say whether if I had at all wavered—I should still have been here once indeed upon principal I thought it would be best to go—I said I would see what effect such proposal had—my Mothers illness at Holland House was the consequence from that time we argud & I wrote him word & he knows I was sincere when I said it was impossible—do you remember when

Bellingham[41] was hangd—that Evening I was with Lord Byron many hours 3 things I swore—never to let our attachment end in wrong—never to go away with him never even to say I preferd him to William—I was serious in the vow I made & how far I broke that vow is immaterial & the more as every circumstance convinces me Lord Byron wishes the worst to be thought & what worse is there [—] what guilt greater than mine in the sight of God or Man—let me at least not add to such heavy sins those of levity of Hypocrisy—I will never more deviate from truth—but I could willingly have left you all—dear as you are—It is the wish of my heart to go from you into any Country far off when I may never see any more of you again [—] Lady Melbourne it was almost too hard a trial sending me here alone with Wm [—] nothing but his generosity could have induced him to bear the scenes he has daily & nightly witnessed—but I am now better & will try & be calm [—] Lord Byron has it in his power to make me so in future—I beg you not to write now—do not let him be tormented but when you see him state the plain truth & only ask Mamma & Wm whither a day passed without tears while I was away [in Ireland] & tho I got into tearing spirits for the moment when the duke or others were by—was Hypocritical to say he made me unhappy—as to my Vanity [—] he fostered it himself—& thus ought he to wonder at its existence—recrimination is useless for God sake do not say to him one word that is like a reproach—only defend me from the charge of meanness—duplicity—& Levity [&] with respect to him only say if I have unheedingly spoken of him without respect & affection I never more shall—& as to trying to see him or insulting him or anything of the kind—need he[,] can he believe it—no never any more will I intrude never—but there is one favour I would ask—you will say it is weakness & childish—[now hear?] me—Lord Byron gave me 3 pictures of himself two by Saunders[42] into my own hands one by a Friend of his & he asked me to send him one for the engravers the other to be altered the other for his Aunt he also wrote me word from Cheltenham he had a little one for me—now out of 4 given I request for one—any one he may think like do not say this because it looks like a reproach merely state it as my request that he will either restore one of Saunders pictures or give me

---

[41] John Bellingham murdered Prime Minister Spencer Perceval in the House of Commons, having mistaken him for Granville Leveson Gower—a strange circumstance. Byron stayed up all night to observe the public hanging of the assassin at dawn on 19 May 1812, Newgate Prison.

[42] George Sanders (1774–1846), who painted a portrait of Lord Byron in 1809.

another—I could if I wishd it have taken it from thence as it was sent there in my name—but I never will have it but from himself nor at all unless he quite likes it—will you now excuse this letter & may I depend upon your honour that you will not shew it to him Lady Melbourne remember if no promises are sacred what are we to trust to in existence—can you wonder at my suspicions & mistrusts oh if you knew all I had heard you would not wonder—but I do enjoin you in this instance as you hope truth & faith will be kept by you—by your love for your children which I believe the strongest feeling I do entreat you this once neither to show this letter—nor to take extracts out of it nor indeed to say one word to Lord B [that] may in the least appear like complaint or a reproach on my part or as if I betrayed the confidence he reposed once unlimitedly in me—God Bless you are you not tired [—] yet I have much more to say [. . .]

Caroline also asked for a tribute clipping of Byron's hair. He acquiesced, then tricked her by sending a clipping of Lady Oxford's hair instead.

23. Lady Caroline to Lady Melbourne. 24 March 1813.

Bath

My Dearest Lady Melbourne—

[. . .] you say he promised you the hair this is all I wish for & as you think I deserve it—the letters I will look over but it is painful to do so—I sent him the Copy of a paper signed the 14th of August I never saw him since or for a fortnight before—it was if you recollect after my Mothers illness a good while—& just before we went to Ireland—it says Caroline I engage by all that is sacred whatever may occur whether I may be forcd by others to give you up or to form any new engagement—I will abide by this so help me allah & your God—your Gifts I will consider as sacred & either restore them to you—or return them myself no other shall ever possess—your picture I will never part with—mine I freely gave you & you shall ever keep it with my will & consent—if induced to marry or to like any other which I do not believe credible—I do engage to write & consult you first & fairly to tell you the change in my thoughts & affections—in every instance your feelings shall be solely considered by me & through life you may depend on me as being not only your lover but your most devoted & attached friend—I do not write this during the violence of passion or from any possible motive but the true feeling of a heart solely yours & it is my belief unalterably yours I ask but a few things in return but even should you be prevailed upon to act differantly you may depend on me—I shall have a melancholy pride in fulfilling your desires though you may forget mine—yours Byron—I sent this to him merely to shew him that I had some little reason to be surprised at his conduct [—] he answers with a thousand Jokes about lovers perjuries & says he concludes by my still dwelling on past occurrences that I have not found any new connection ?! [. . .]

Byron yielded to Caroline's desire for a "final" meeting, despite Lady Melbourne's objections. The effort to cool Caroline's passions backfired, however.

24. Lady Caroline to Lord Byron.
[Draft of a Letter, May 1813?]

one only word. You have rais'd me from dispair to the joy we look for in Heaven—your seeing me has undone me forever—you are the same—you love me still—I am sure of it your eyes your looks your manners your words, say so. —Oh God can you give me up if I am dear—take me with you take me my Master my friend I will serve you take me with you—who will fight for you serve you in sickness & Health live but for your wishes & die when that can please you who so faithfully as the one you have made yours & bound to your heart of hearts. yet when you read this you will be gone. you will think of me perhaps too as one who gave you sufferings & trouble—Byron my days are past in remembering what I once was to you—I wish you had never known me or that you had killed me before you went. God Bless & preserve my friend & master

your
Caro

It seems odd that Byron continued to communicate with and even to see Caroline when he had expressed to his friends and Lady Melbourne such a strong desire to be done with her—but that is what happened.

25. Lady Caroline to Lord Byron. [Before 5 July 1813.]

as I will not disobey you and Lady Melbourne I give her this open—if when she has read it she sees no wrong in it I hope she will give it you—for I believe she is the only person alive who does not try to make mischief between us—of course she has tried to break off our acquaintance but I do not accuse her now of having used unfair means—I did do so—before you both I acknowledge it—but you must not judge of me for I have sufferd enough—you are both right in not allowing me to see much of you at present—I trust however that you would find me alterd in many respects I think I could behave better than you either of you imagine but as I [?] no doubt you know best what is right I will submit only requiring the performance of a promise that I drew from you when we met which I do trust you will both think it right to keep—& also if the requests I have made to you are not improper ones tell them to Lady Melbourne & she will act by me as she thinks well & just if I give her no occasion to do otherwise—perhaps you will both of you laugh at this letter—well you may but it is difficult to write such a one at all & yet I wish it because it must prove I have no underhand views—I know I have written to you & I think you did wisely in only answering that you must not write—but I will try & abstain from it while I am in Town & when I go back to the Country you say you will then let me hear from you sometimes & when you are abroad—not so as to tire you—or be a torment but when you write to Lady Melbourne if you are so good as to send one line to me to say you are well it is all I ask & I will be satisfied Lady Melbourne says if I live till you return I may then see you as much as you please—I hope it will be much—but it is a long time to wait however I see it must be & I hope you will both believe me when I say I will try & make myself contented as it is settled—for I am very grateful to you for saying you forgive me & to her for permitting me to see you—it has made the greatest possible difference to my peace of mind & you shall neither of you have cause to repent but I grieve to find how every one except Lady Melbourne has tried to lower me & harm me in yr opinion there are very mean arts of bringing about an end which I hope they will never be able to achieve quite though they did enough—it has given me such a rancour & ill humour that as I do not know who to accuse so I set & hate all society collectively & all your friends individually and as to that sly yellow fiend[43] [—] I never will speak to him again—they have all tried to blacken me & will again & they are too & too skilful not to succeed besides I put myself in their power—in the power of every one for when they tell me you said such and such things of me I fire up & say ten thousand times worse of you & of

[43] Samuel Rogers (1763–1855), poet and friend of Byron, known for his emaciated appearance. Caroline made him a cadaverous sycophant named "Tremore" in *Glenarvon*.

Lady Melbourne & of every body to which alone of all accusations I plead guilty & for which I shall evermore grieve—but I can only say as you have had the generosity to forgive me without one reproach—& as Lady Melbourne was the means by which I gained this good—I will rather be cut into pieces than ever speak unkindly or with disrespect of either of you again—at one time I was even jealous of her—I confess it I thought she was gaining your confidence & esteem & I was losing both I acknowledge this & I was not wrong—for I too have had wrongs to forgive though I believe my self to have been completely mistaken in those who did harm me—now all feelings of Jealousy are past because indeed they cannot exist situated as we are—I even think we might be friends & as you would have other attachments there could be no fear—but still as Lady Melbourne has not confidence enough in me to allow of this & as I make no doubt you will both act as kindly by me as you may & ought I will never more seek it till it is thought proper—but you need not believe my enemies—when they tell you things of me ask Lady Melbourne and see what she says—as to Sir Godfrey Webster you may hear ten thousand things about if the ill natured & malicious chuse to tell it you—for I plead guilty to very absurd very wrong conduct—but you know all—I told you every thing & appeal to himself for the truth & he is sure to say the worst he can of me—but it is hard to have things referrd to before our acquaintance—I never have deceivd you & therefore was in hopes I should not be accusd of artifices such as [drawings?]—I shall not go to Lady Heathcotes[44] & Lady Duncannons therefore pray go to both & never stay away upon my account for if I wish it I will let you know—but were we to meet you may be assurd I would not speak to you nor look at you once—I wish we were—only to show Lady Melbourne how I would behave—there is another thing I wish to say while writing to both of you—& it is this if I stay away or refuse to Walze[45] or to shake hands with people I am accusd by Lady Melbourne of doing it but of a romantic abused wish of pleasing you—now be assurd I do not flatter myself that you care in the least about it—perhaps even you would be glad to hear I was dancing & amusing my self because you are I am sure goodnatured enough to be sorry if any one is

---

[44] But she did go to a ball thrown by Katherine, Lady Heathcote a short time after writing this letter. It took place 5 July 1813, and there Caroline is supposed to have stabbed herself in pique at Lord Byron. Her account of the incident is contained in an 1824 letter to Thomas Medwin in Chapter 9 of this book.

[45] Byron professed to hate the Waltz, and his lame foot made dancing in general an unpleasant social activity. Caroline, who loved the Waltz, had agreed to forego it for his sake.

unhappy whom you in the least care for—but I do promise yourself & Lady Melbourne my motive for all this is quite different from what you may either of you think—it is because I feel how very ill I have behav'd & what levity of manner & what foolish vanity & spirits I once had—before I knew you—& remembering this—I do not wish to fall into the same errors again—besides I cannot think a Woman who has once acted as I have can be too reserved in future people of course will laugh—and deride me & call it an affectation of prudery to attone for an excess of the contrary conduct but if this affectation continues no one will in the end blame it & no one will have the power to reproach me for what is past—the least thing now will be misconstrued every unguarded word or look of mine will be lookd upon with severity—I see the sharp censures all ready to start into words in every cold formal face I meet—then do not you imagine I have the vanity to presume that you still care what I do—though I hope you will never be displeased at hearing that I do the best I can to make up for the past & do not let Lady Melbourne think it is from a wrong motive or to cherish vain imagination & regret that I follow the line of conduct I have resolv'd upon—she says love is all imagination nothing else—& what is this saying it may explain the seat of the evil but it cannot remove it besides every thing in life is more or less imagination but Love need not always lead to wrong—it does too often it has with me—but may it not also guide to right & to duty & may I not be impel-l'd to act better than I should naturally & to conquer a very turbulent & faulty character by those same feelings—believe me I may & shall—you must not be angry that I have written you so long & so dull a letter you know when I saw you I could not & I dared not speak then do not be offended if I write [this?] & as I shall not be here to urge it to your to Lady Melbournes kindness & affection I trust for the fulfilment of my requests—grant them if it seems good to you both—& God Bless & preserve you & her I shall never cease to feel grateful & you will not from the day you saw me evermore hear of my doing things contrary to your wishes—I also make you this new promise I will never write to any Woman—indeed I have no cause for I think I have been very ill used by them if I have any thing to say in future it shall be to yourself but do make those you can influence burn the letters that are in [their?] power—for I will never more write be assurd

As Lady Caroline's relationship with Murray grew, she began a set of illustrations for Lord Byron's Childe Harold *that she hoped the publisher would eventually print.*

26. Lady Caroline to John Murray. [MAY–JULY 1813.]

Dear Sir

You will acknowledge that however troublesome I have been it is not often that I write a reasonable letter to you and as I am going to do so now I beg you will answer it—I have since I left you had a severe struggle with myself & you have been cause of it—I think from your manner you imagine that it would be a great indelicacy in my suffering the vignettes to be published—of course it would have been without my name but I have not dealt quite openly with you in this respect—the hundred pound I named to you will be paid if they are not published—this however was not much consideration for I own to you the pleasure of making drawings for Child[e] Harold is what most delighted me—the man to whom I am engaged has settled everything with [*illegible*] all is ready & I believe begun—it now rests with you to determine & I promise upon my honour I will act as you determine—shall I make this sacrifice to what perhaps is right & give it up or may I let them take this chance without putting my name or having any thing further to with them—if I give up publishing them or sooner purchase them back will you to make up to me for the disappointment promise to assist me in making a Book of them for him & one other for me—[. . .] you must write to me by return of post direct your letter to me inclosed to Lord Cowper Panshanger Hertfordshire where I shall be tonight & speak frankly I will return your letter—I swear that I never yet show'd one that you sent me—to mortal eye—believe me yours sincerely

Caroline

Byron feared that Caroline, who had forged a letter in his name, might publish their correspondence and include almost anything, and it appears from this letter that his fears were not completely baseless.

27. Lady Caroline to John Murray. 7 OCTOBER 1813.

It is too wet for me to come—are you going to hear the Dirge for poor Moreau[46]—shall you be at home tomorrow at eleven I wish to see

---

[46] Jean-Victor Moreau (1763–1813), general who clashed many times with Napoleon, sustained severe injuries at the Battle of Dresden, 27 August 1813, and died a few days later.

you—Why did you not answer my letter—I am about to publish a work—250 letters from a young Venetian nobleman—addrest to a very absurd English Lady—they are beautiful & might serve all other noblemen. they exhibit every feeling the Strong attachment & great ability can give there is a mixture of humour & with in some—will delight you they are no common love letters believe me for they addrest no common absurd Lady—& therefore required something more than ordinary—there is also one letter written by the same youth which may be inserted separately—it is a complete answer to the above—a renunciation of every Iota of the 39 articles of faith[47] [. . .]

Caroline had a portrait of herself done by Thomas Phillips. At her request, Phillips portrayed her in a page's outfit holding a plate of fruit and in the presence of a spaniel. The portrait represents the scene from Jacques Cazotte's Le diable amoureux *(1772) in which a man of twenty-five (Byron was twenty-four when he met Caroline) is seduced by an "enamored spirit" (a devil) who appears to him in the guise of "Biondetta," a fair-haired woman dressed as a page carrying a platter of fruit and accompanied by a spaniel. Phillips had also painted Byron, and when their pictures were displayed together, they achieved an odd effect that created gossip.*

28. Lady Caroline to John Murray. 9 November 1813.

as you have [been?] so much my friend may I ask you one thing. Do you think my Picture as a Page standing by Lord B . . . will have a bad effect. a stranger saw them and told of it saying I was there holding him first & he in a monk dress. She whom he told it to thought it was all in one Picture. This shows how things are mistaken & imagined—I was asked whether I was painted at Phillips as a Page holding a plate of fruit to Lord Byron as a friar! will you tell Phillips to put my picture out of sight—really he who professes to be so prudish might have obeyed my orders in this respect which were given very decidedly long ago—after which he liked his performances so well that he produced it—and every one going in sees us two together—

William Lamb assisted John Murray in a translation of Madame de Staël's d'Allemaigne *into English, much to Caroline's pleasure, for she wished to cultivate*

[47] The Thirty-nine Articles of Faith were included in the Book of Common Prayer, and, though not imposed on clerics, were nonetheless expected to be affirmed by them upon ordination. Many considered them too Calvinistic.

a relationship with both publisher and author. In the mean time, communication with Byron went on fitfully, and he was, unbelievably, still prepared for an elopement, if Caroline made no other course possible.

29. Lady Caroline to John Murray. [Fall 1813.]

William will ask about Carlton House—and the proof sheets[48] if it will not offend the translators never mention it—The men you speak of are clever but are they good French scholars—I want to see you if I can I will call if not call on me—I could not dine at Mad. DeStaals yesterday we go there today—How I like her—

30. Lady Caroline to John Murray. [28 December 1813.]

I have to thank you for an attention which I feel most extremely I should say for many—do not load me with more—reserve your kindness for his works alone they never can fail of being dear & welcome to me—you have sent me the Vestale[49] which I will return carefully when we have gone through it—it is very beautiful. the music is quite in the best style of composition. At this moment it was most acceptable as we have a great deal of time and are a great many people & have nothing to say or do—Mad. de Staal tried to like us but I am convinced found us all much too "mortal" for her—drinking swearing laughing walking hunting riding—& bathing being the chief delights of this place—to air & water I think she seems to have an antipathy not to mention soap [and] exercise [. . .]

31. Lady Caroline to Lord Byron. [1813.]

Here is a hearts ease for you gathered by the Holy Well Spoken of in Mam. de Grammont—do you remember the first I gave you—the first Rose you brought me is still in my possession you will find it in the Trunk with all yr other Gifts all that I could preserve—once more God Bless you—may you be very happy—do not be offended I shall torment you no more—I love & honour you from my heart as a friend may

---

[48] Of the translation of de Staël's work on Germany, *d'Allemaigne.*

[49] Gaspare Spontini's opera *La Vestale.*

love—no wrong I hope—as a sister feels as your Augusta feels for you[50]—ever yours Dearest Lord Byron.

32. Lady Caroline to Lord Byron. [1813–1814?]

You have been very generous and kind if you have not betray'd me, and I do not think you have. My remaining in Town and seeing you thus is sacrificing the last chance I have left. I expose myself to every eye, to every unkind observation. You think me weak, and selfish; you think I do not struggle to withstand my own feelings, but indeed it is exacting more than human nature can bear, and when I came out last night, which was of itself an effort, and when I heard your name announced, the moment after I saw nothing more, but seemed in a dream. Miss Berry's very loud laugh and penetrating eyes did not restore me. She, however, [was] good natur'd and remained near me, and Mr Moor[e], though he really does not approve one feeling I have, had kindness of heart to stay near me. Otherwise I felt so ill I could not have struggled longer. Lady Cahir said, "You are ill; shall we go away?" which I [was] very glad to accept; but we could not get through, and so I fear it caus'd you pain to see me intrude again. I sent a groom to Holmes twice yesterday morning, to prevent his going to you, or giving you a letter full of flippant jokes, written in one moment of gaiety, which is quite gone since. I am so afraid he has been to you; if so I entreat you to forgive it, and to do just what you think right about the Picture.

I have been drawing you Mad. de Staal, as the last I sent was not like. If you do not approve this, give it Murray, and pray do not be angry with me.

Do not marry yet, or if you do, let me know it first. I shall not suffer, if she you chuse be worth you, but she will never love you as I did. I am going to the Chapple Royal at St. James. Do you ever go there? It begins at 1/2 past 5, and lasts til six; it is the most beautiful singing I ever heard; the choristors sing "By the Waters of Babylon."

The Peers sit below; the Women quite apart. But for the evening service very few go; I wonder that more do not,—it is really most beautiful, for those who like that style of music. If you never heard it, go there some day, but not when it is so cold as this. How very pale you are! What a contrast with Moore! "Mai io l'ho veduto piu bello che jeri, ma e la belta della morte," or a statue of marble so colourless, and the

---

[50] An intentional allusion to his rumored incestuous relationship with his half-sister Augusta?

dark brow and hair such a contrast. I never see you without wishing to cry; if any painter could paint me that face as it is, I would give them any thing I possess on earth,—not one has yet given the countenance and complexion as it is. I only could, if I knew how to draw and paint, because one must feel it to give it the real expression.

At some point during this period, Caroline wrote in French to Byron offering the "services" of two girls from his "forsaken mistress." Fiona MacCarthy discovered this note and comments in her biography of Byron that it formed part of "an intricate masquerade of male and female, page and master."[51]

33. Lady Caroline to Lord Byron. [1812–1814?]

Antoinette and Georgine are both at your service. The Father and Mother really hope you will hire one, but they say the younger one is the healthiest, and sweet and affectionate like nobody else. She cried when you refused to take her and said: I think Milord was upset when he saw my earrings. Please take one, because it is your forsaken mistress who gives her to you. The girl will follow you, will take care of you, and will always be loyal to you. Love her for me, and send back to me the one you don't want to keep. Farewell, my dear Master, my heart is sad because I am going away for so many years. Take care of yourself and may God bless you. Always yours, your Mistress and servant [. . .][52]

---

[51] MacCarthy, *Byron: Life and Legend*, 171.

[52] Translation from the French by Professor Danielle Trudeau of San Jose State University.

CHAPTER FIVE

Byron: The Aftermath

Letters, 1814–1815

Lady Caroline's friendship with John Murray continued to deepen. She encouraged him to go fishing at Brocket and took him into her confidence in ways that must have been often uncomfortable, given Murray's close business relationship with Lord Byron. She continued to read, correspond with other writers, and work on her novel.

1. Lady Caroline to John Murray. [1813–1814.]

Catalpa[1] is the name of the Exotic. It is rare & beautiful & its perfume sweet as the vows of Lovers & the prayers of good Men—do you ever pray—if so ask of Heaven for absolution of those souls that are lost—laws are only human—no one should judge of others—what is the meaning of right & wrong—all is but appearance—who that looks innocent can be thought guilty—what is guilt—there is no such thing as conscience—people may go in the World and what is the use of thinking if I cannot sleep in my Bed why then should I try to lie down there are balls & Assemblies & operas & plays—& who dances more gaily than I can—who shall dare say I am not good or happy—yourself you dare not think it—come & see the Ballroom Friday Thursday I sup out tomorrow there is a great Ball Saturday a supper—till the week is full of amusement be happy let us all be merry What is life given us for but to

---

[1] Catalpa, a deciduous, hardy shade tree of North America and Asia with large leaves and big white flowers.

enjoy it—God Bless you Sir—& if there be a God pray that he may bless even me also—

2. Lady Caroline to John Murray. 25 January 1814.

Dear Sir: You have been very near losing your Correspondent—& it ought to show you that even in this World if we escape dying of a Broken heart we may at all events finish with a Broken head—such a fall as I had yesterday it has furnished to cast disorder into a Brain already sufficiently whirling—I am really ill—but write this to tell you that if the Drawings come today by Poppa my father as I expect I will send them you back immediately—the Regent writes to say he shall be here tomorrow—it is passing strange his coming in this weather but there is no accounting for tastes. Melbourne has invented a Machine not the infernal Machine but one as wonderful it chases the snow four Horses draw it & we are by this means the only people not blocked up—excuse my writing more as my head is really in pain I slipped & fell—against a corni[che] just above the temporal artery—do not tell any one otherwise it comes round.

Yours,
Queen Mab[2]

The Prince Regent pledged to visit Brocket Hall despite bad winter weather, which Caroline found bracing. She was becoming more and more confident in her literary judgments.

3. Lady Caroline to John Murray. [February 1814.]

[. . .] Miss Edg[e]worth[3] must not be run down because she has like most people misunderstood her own powers—she never can pretend to any thing that is the least [particle?] of Genius she has not one single spark of it which time or opportunity could kindle—but in its place I think she has a very reasoning head much humour, & great discrimination—she paints like the Dutch school true to the life—I only quarrel with her choice—she introduces us to the society of those who are disagreeable & she

---

[2] In *Romeo and Juliet*, Mercutio jokes that Mab, bringer of dreams, has made Romeo lovesick. Caroline might have seen Percy Shelley's *Mab: A Philosophical Poem*, which was privately printed in 1813.

[3] Maria Edgeworth (1768–1849), prolific Irish novelist, author of *Castle Rackrent* (1800), a precursor of Walter Scott's historical novels.

delineates characters we regret ever to meet with—like Crabbe[4] she delights in drawing mediocrity vulgarity & meanness—this can never please—in her present production[5]—there is more than an ordinary share of it—& no great humour to make up—no interest to carry us through—I for one cannot finish it but those more persevering will—

I really am glad that you have prevailed upon him to leave out the "Mister"—I wish any one had power to persuade him to leave out a panegyric which even in a private letter would appear like flattery & as you say injure him it addresses—that warm affection which breathes from the heart shews itself very differently—he will not <u>now</u> feel the harm he does himself by these "notes" & prefaces—but the time will come when he will regret it—in this cold and cavilling age, enthusiasm is a far less natural feeling than love of ridicule & censure—great Poetic Genius like every thing else that raises itself above the level makes enemies—they who flatter most & lick the dust in the hour of success are the first to turn—Lord Byron injures himself in a manner which grieves me—but not knowing how to command his tongue—I sometimes think his own words but too true he has many flatterers but few real friends—you may judge by my writing thus openly whether I have confidence in you—indeed I have & I feel secure that you will never repeat one word which I have said—& which only would as all else <u>is</u> be misconstrued—perhaps you will extend this discretion upon your part further & make as great a secret of my writing to you as I do of your writing to me—for believe me any thing in this World is made mischief of & the only Virtues or talents necessary for a safe passage through it—are these—to speak the truth—& nothing but the truth when one is obliged to speak at all—to be silent in general—& <u>never</u> to repeat in one society what one hears in another—no not even praise—it is neither fair nor necessary nor will great talents make up for the want of these rules—Madame de Staal for example with all her intellect is deficient in this respect—her truth I do not deny—she is I think very true very sincere & neither exag[g]erates nor equivocates—but there is an insatiate curiosity torments her—she will <u>burrow</u> her self into all the Tracasseries of her most distant acquaintance & in the hopeless desire of setting every thing right—she fails as Don Quixotte did before her & leaves all to use a vulgar expression "by the ears"—I cannot stand it [—] We came to an open rupture about Lord Byron and yet I abused him respecting his conduct to me even as

---

[4] George Crabbe (1754–1832), called by Walter Scott, "the English Juvenal."

[5] Probably *Patronage* (1814).

I felt—but I said he was & ever would be most dear to me—& I do not besides see why strangers are to ask one those sort of questions to Gossip about on all sides & then prate of it to the person again—this is unwise believe me it is very unwise—she is safe with me as I shall return no more—dead men tell no Tales & I am like them gone—& for ever—but mark my prophesy—she will ere long get herself into some serious scrape—people are not made of marble they not only feel but they remember & in general they resent—she has no tact, no discretion—she believes every thing hears every thing—& enquires into the most private concerns—to say that I have quarelled with her would be ridiculous as if a butterfly were to abuse the sun—because it could not stand the lustre of its beam—but I fly from what I can only admire but never love—& I shall keep silent in future when I find I am misunderstood. You must not fancy by this that Mad[ame] & I are not friends—we are but she hates him—& why does he needlessly make himself ennemies? "The soft triumver"—"sol" pauses on the hill"[6] I wish altered—sol is at all times a common place term, tell your friend to speak English it is a goodly language & while he writes in his Mother tongue he had better use the terms we are us'd to—"Gull" & the Bulbul and a young Galeongée[7] are just so many baits to draw sneers—which however disposed are always better avoided—I think the Bride of Abydos full of these lesser faults but the Corsair is quite beautiful—indeed he has a very splendid Genius—& I cannot but feel a deep & lasting anxiety that he should be himself in all things it is all I ask—you owe his quotations from Dante and the beginning of the Bride to me—& not to Mad. De Staal—for I sent him Dante last year so that you see I was not useless even to his genius [. . .] The snow is from 2 to 3 foot here in the north I have heard of its being 20—but conclude the 0 was added on—I am ever with most grateful thanks yr

Caroline

It is rather tiresome the Regents having a sore throat as all those who were coming here are kept at bay—he seems very desirous of coming—& I shall think if he does—that it is paying a very great Compliment to Lord Melbourne—for were I a Regent & not being one still more unless in a case of life & death I would not travel this Weather. I hate to go slow do not you—it is the only thing I much care about—I run—gallop—or drive as if for a wager—otherwise I can not if I stay at Home a year—I

---

6 See Byron's "The Curse of Minerva," lines 23–24: "Not yet—not yet—Sol pauses on the hill. / The precious hour of parting lingers still."

7 The Bulbul and the Gal[i]ongée (a Turkish sailor) are from Byron's poem "Bride of Abydos."

never have the windows shut even in Winter—keep the feet warm the head cool & the heart free & you may defy the World the flesh and the Devil—Mad de Staal—that is my creed—but alas not at all times my practice

Byron's "Lines to a Lady Weeping" had just been published with The Corsair. *This poem attacking the Prince of Wales for making his only daughter weep at the dinner table had originally been published anonymously on 7 March 1812 in The Chronicle. Byron was now assailed by the Tory Press because his authorship had been proved, and Caroline wrote to Murray on the subject.*

4. Lady Caroline to John Murray. [February 1814.]

How you surprise me—write me but one word more [—] it is not true that he sent word to you that he was very angry "Weep daughter" was cut out of the other editions—is it not true that he stood firm to what he had done & took the blame wholly upon himself—this I trust is true [. . .] you have known him as a friend as a Patron—I knew him as more—were he now to turn your foe—to laugh at you openly—to make you his jest his scorn—it would wound you—but oh for one moment think what it is for a Woman to bear who from the language of idolatry and confidence—is at once betrayed—taunted expos'd to all—& made hateful even to her nearest friends—happily for me—their love was too firm to be shaken but had it been otherwise where should I be now a Being utterly disgrac'd—abandoned by him for whom all was left—& lost to every other—I cannot think of this without horror—let others beware—by my fate—whoever they are they could not have been more flattered more courted more lov'd—apparently—whoever they are they cannot have been more cruelly undeceived—. my letters shown, my words misrepresented, my gifts offered & worn by such a Woman as Lady Oxford! I can feel & I can resent—oh believe it—time while it quells enthusiasm & love awakens worse feelings—& however guilty to others—there is no excuse—no not one for him—I shall say to him as Elvira did to Pizarro[8]—if you cannot act well at least act nobly—if you must not be among the good—be at least among the great—I pray him this—I pray do not betray one already but too much injured & betrayed—

Yours very sincerely
Caroline

[8] Richard Brinsley Sheridan's last play was *Pizarro* (1799).

Let me hear from you—& do you who are his friend & he has but few real friends do you soothe him & try & not offend him—he will get over all this—I cannot think it is this which vexes him so much

Caroline's relations with her uncle, Lord Spencer, had never recovered from news of her affair with Byron.

5. Lady Caroline to Lord Spencer. 13 May 1814.

My Dearest Uncle, I have just received the cup & papers, for which I thank you extremely & I assure you it has been for these 10 months past & shall be my endeavour to regain the good opinion of the Friends I have left—I never wish to allude even to what has passed. Only when I hear so many things rumoured which I know to be quite untrue may I not have reason to think that you also have heard them & believe them [. . .] every one it is said who puts themselves into the wrong always thinks they are wrong'd—& so no wonder I think this my case—but it is this feeling which prevents my being humble or penitent. I have been made mad, & then the acts to which I was driven are coldly brought against me—they—accuse me, who know that I have been too much injured to defend myself, & when I hear these things instead of being gentle I am indignant & furious [. . .]

Caroline obviously still felt she might salvage some sort of relationship with Byron, for she continued writing to him as if they understood one another despite their enforced separation.

6. Lady Caroline to Lord Byron. [1814.]

These flowers have no Hope of pleasing you, they come trembling with fear in case you should be offended at their being sent [—] is it possible that you looked kindly on me at Miss [*illegible*] I durst not believe it—but my heart felt your goodness though it was my duty to you & to all not to show it thank you also for not having spoken ill of me to HobHouse—his noticing me the other night made me ready to cry—when any friend of yours speaks kindly to me—I dread what they must think of me—for I am about ready to fall at their feet—Judge then what my feelings were—when I saw or thought I saw you smile on me—perhaps some day if I live—you will give me back some part of your friendship—indeed I will deserve it—& if any one has the generosity during our long absence to speak one word for me—to you—may every possible happiness & blessing come upon them for it—so few do—one person only said that you had spoken of me with such affection to them that they believed you had lov'd me seriously—& that person has been most dear to me ever since—even if it was not true it was good and kind to say it—"Friend" as the quakers [Langearten?] says "Judge not of me too severely"—& be assured that while this heart beats, gratitude for your former kindness & affection that cannot alter will be in me—whatever I may have been—I will be such as you may not dispise—because yourself said that if never in word or look or thought a Woman acted ill a second time no one ought to feel contempt—at least I think you said this—[. . .]

I never saw two Women more in love with you than my favourite Lady Hamilton & her sister.

They talk of you in a manner I cannot bear to hear—they say you have the prettiest manners the sweetest voice & the most beautiful face—I read to them in your voice[9] & they nearly cried & kissed me till I was suffocated all for love of you.

7. Lady Caroline to Lord Byron. 3 June [1814.]

That it is not in nature to resist that there is nothing in Heaven or earth or under the earth like <u>you</u> and that if I am condemned to sail in sulphur hereafter I shall think it hard & cruel for why did God make a Being like you if he did not give us strength not to admire & love it are you sure that you are a Man—I doubt it—[*illegible*] for this letter—how many angry looks from Lady M. how many frowns will be my fate—& perhaps from you—the mouth will be turned with its corners to the ground—however I cannot be worse off as someone said when they were in the Pillory it was a satisfaction to know that mortal spight could not place them lower—pray pardon this it is the 3rd of June[10] I have a letter of yours written on this day—just 2 years ago—a most unkind one—& this is as a punishment—pray do not be angry—think of my situation how extraordinary!—my mother in law actually in the place I held—her ring instead of mine—her letters instead of mine—her heart—but do you believe either she or any others feel for you what I felt—ugly & thin & mad & dispis'd as I am—you never have or will be

[9] Caroline could apparently mimic Byron's voice as well as his penmanship.

[10] 3 June 1814 was Lady Caroline's ninth wedding anniversary.

as lov'd by another—of that I am certain because except your own self no one can love as well & devotedly & entirely as I could—& did—& this you one day will know [. . .]—Farewell Mephistocles[11]—Luke Makey de la Touche Richard the 3 Valmont[12] Machiavelli Napoleon [Prival?] the Wicked Duke of Orleans—for you are a little like them all—& Joseph Lancaster[13] is very ugly—& Kean[14] in Othello—also is ugly—put me in mind of you—When I enter a room I know where you are by a row of beaming eyes all turned askance after you—I literally saw nothing but your ear for a whole hour one night—it is perfectly unlike any ear in Nature—& as Tristram Shandy[15] might say requires a Chapter to itself—I have often been nearer to it than the other night—too near even while I exist to forget moments of perfect happiness—your Wife will be happy—I am certain of it—though others doubt it—because you are a Man any Woman might live with forever & until she tired you—you could not tire her—whatever the crime be of loving that which by our vows we have reverenced I only say this one thing for my vindication & also for that of the hundreds who have & the thousands who will fall by the same "light."

8. Lady Caroline to Lord Byron. [JUNE 1814.]

every feeling in me has been struggling for mastery till I have been mad & now that the little good left me has triumphed I must write—Farewell—not as you say so to your favourites or they to you—not as any Woman ever spoke that Word for they never mean it to be what I will make it—but as nuns & those who die—as Madoc said it to Llewellyn[16]—so will I to you—thanks for your goodness to me which is fixed in my memory & heart never to be forgotten—thanks too for your patience & forgiveness in many trying scenes—& even receive thanks for your cruelty as it has humbled a very proud and vain character whom none but you ever dared contend with before—from a child I have made

[11] That is, Mephistopheles.

[12] Henri de Latouche (1785–1851), guilty of several literary frauds and malicious attacks on his contemporaries. Vicomte de Valmont, heartless hero of Choderlos de Laclos's *Les Liaisons Dangereuses* (1782).

[13] Lancaster is credited with inventing the modern hierarchical school system.

[14] Edmund Kean (1789–1833) Shakespearean actor.

[15] The Life and Opinions of *Tristram* Shandy, by Laurence Sterne (1759-1767).

[16] That is, Robert Southey's *Madoc* (1805), based on the story of 12th century Prince Madoc and Llewellyn the Great of Wales.

everyone bend to me—the least contradiction the least controul made me desperate—a word from those I loved & honoured most was more than I could bear—and I felt so sure of never failing in what was honourable and true that I could not bring myself even to pray to God for his support—could you but guess with such a character as mine so like an untamed Tygress—what I have sufferd within these three years you would perhaps judge me less harshly—if I go into the World or if I stay with my family—& still more if I lie down in Bed that horrid name I merrit pursues me—& I think of what I am but I never yet repented—it is not in my nature—either to feel remorse or shame. You [the word has been written over the word "God"] have judg'd me severely not justly—my principles were most firm till my ill conduct shook them & sooner than feel wrong—I preferred thinking right a mere nominal distinction—in short I lov'd you as no Woman ever could love because I am not like them—but more like a Beast who sees no crime in loving & following its Master—you became such to me—Master of my soul more than of anything else & since I have known you now I believe near 3 years I do not believe that one moment of my time has been engrossed with a single thought but you—

[*12 lines of illegible scribble-out*]

I took my last leave of you when you little thought it & the remembrance of this made me both kind—& cold. But was I cold when first you made me yours—when first you told me in the Carriage to kiss your mouth & I durst not—& after thinking it such a crime it was more than I could prevent from that moment—you drew me to you like a magnet & I could not indeed I could not have kept away—was I cold then—were you so? oh between that first and that last kiss what volumes of contradictory feelings might be placed—all that love & passion can invent from the thoughts of Idolatry down to the cold torpor of indifference and pity on your part & regret & remorse on mine—never while life beats in this heart shall I forget you or that moment when first you said you lov'd me—when my heart did not meet yours but flew before it—and both intended to remain innocent of greater wrong—that time to you is nothing—for it has been repeated more or less by thousands—but for me—never—no never—it remains single & shall ever do so—& while it is so forgive me if my thoughts revert to it at all hours & moments it is set on my heart & soul & brain in character of love & happiness which make me mad to think of—who is like you Byron Where shall I ever hear that voice or see a countenance like that again—don't accuse me of flattery or mean arts. Hope and vanity alone teach there—but what have I to Hope—only this that I may learn to forget you—only this that when you belong to another perhaps to that Mary[17] whom you lov'd in happier days you will not learn to hate me—none have said such severe things of me & to me as you—but none either have ever been as good to me & so kind—to forget you or what I feel for you is not in my nature—but I am disgusted with myself for my ingratitude to a noble generous husband, therefore believe me—I will never more—disgrace either of you—you ought to send back my letters or to burn them for his sake—I think you ought—as to yours, indeed I will give them up & every one of your Gifts—indeed I am serious—for why should I keep them who cannot retain you—& of what pleasure are they to me—when their very sight fills me with such feelings as might break mens tough hearts could they know them—I send you a letter my Mother wrote to me—tother day—I neglect every thing—& when I try & feel happy—either in Company with others or alone—such thoughts come into my soul that I cannot struggle against them. happiness love & guilt must never never exist together—it would scarcely be a crime in me to go & offer myself to some other Man if by doing this I could unchain my soul from you but I cannot bear Men. I feel quite a loathing to them. Sometimes I try if I can talk in that Jargon I us'd to hear but I cannot endure it & the remembrance of what you said puts all they say out—so that men hate me—today at Murrays I heard one read—& it made me sick so did the poem—it is Rogers's. I wish I thought it pretty it affects to [simplicité villagiose?] & the lines about thrushes & love love love—or the manner in which it was read vex'd me—because I wish to admire it—

> [*in Greek*] "Who will play your pipe, o thrice-longed–for one?
> Who will put his mouth to your reeds? Who so bold?
> For even now your lips and your breath breathe."[18]

scuse all my faults in [orthographic characters] & every thing else—am no scholar—have little to commend me—but love you so so well that should not hate me if can 'void it—I go to the 'squerade—shall you—tell your sister to try & not dislike me—I am very unworthy of her I know it & feel it but as I may not love you nor see you—let her not judge me harshly—let her not pass me by as Lady Gertrude Sloane

---

17 Mary Chaworth, object of Lord Byron's youthful affection.

18 Professor Blanche McIntyre of Oxford University tracked down the source of these lines in Greek. They are from Moschus, in his "Lament for Bion," lines 51ff. The fact that the Lament is dedicated to "Bion" may have attracted Lady Caroline, whose own fictional characters often have names that resemble those of familiar figures from her life and experience. I am indebted to Professor McIntyre for this information and the literal rendering of the text.

does—& Lady Ranncliffe—tell her—I feel my faults my crime sooner—but try & make her forgive me—if you can—for I love that Augusta with my heart because she is yours and is dear to you—who ever read as you read—the least sound of your voice makes the heart bleed & men who never feel cry if you read to them—Murray sat and heard you the other night ah why not have put me behind the Curtain then—better listen to that—than see what I witnessed—if I had followed you—you would have made me make the Bed for your new favourites—you are just a Man to exact it & with all my violence you would have made me do it—I have done all but that already—have I not—& really that night I expected the handkerchief would have been thrown every moment—I saw you lift the vail up twice—it was a strange adventure—but you were not kind that night as formerly—you thought of others even while with me—of that I am sure—& the remembrance of that night and your accusation of wildness are disagreeable to me—God Bless my friend—or sooner my hearts enemy—God Bless & preserve thee this night & make even thy dreams blest—

Fed up with his own inability to divest himself completely of his former lover, Byron finally tried to shock her by strongly implying, if not confessing, that he had engaged in homosexual acts and had sex with his half-sister.

9. Lady Caroline to Lord Byron.
[September–October 1814.]

I will go out every where see every thing & try all I can to forget you—to love you now is a double crime—

I do not believe I never will believe you can have had the heart to suffer me to be so treated—what I have gone through—it is neither my wish or intention to repeat—Women who walk in the streets alone in Pagan cloathes must encounter insult & barbarity but from you—henceforward you are safe—the means you took to frighten me from your door are not in vain.[19] I have been very severely ill—however it is over & in future I will go out every where & try & command myself better. You shall be quite freed from me—you are to be married I am told I hear it on all sides & I heard it jestingly as I concluded from you—why should it give me pain if it will give you happiness selfish as I appear to

[19] In other words, stories about his homosexual experiences and of his incestuous love for his half-sister, Augusta Leigh.

you—from my heart I wish you all that those who love you best can wish all that I am sure you will find—the girl you love is beautiful & chaste & has everything likely to make you happy. at least if it is Lady Adeline whom I know but little—who I never more must speak to—for your wife shall never be intended upon by me—I remember too well your bitter words—I am not worthy to appear before her & never shall. Lord Byron while yet I may address you while yet you are free to act for yourself, if you refuse to see me—tell me at least that you had no hand in the cruel treatment I experienced the other night let me not suppose so—for the thought is very bitter—I beg of you to send me back all the letters notes Pictures & drawings you have left of me—it is quite different now. I consider you as belonging to one much better in every respect than I am—but let her not judge me—judge me not either yourself—if ever you have yielded to the violence of feelings you would not controul if ever you should—then remember my suffering & do not dispise me—if in future by word or look or thought I seek you—if even I allow the World to think I still love—then dispise me—but not till then—send back what I ask for & the ring with the dates in particular & the Book I gave you & all the drawings this I do request I have a right to ask or insist but I trust to your honour & good nature that you will not refuse me—the servant who takes this can bring them—do not refuse me—I am not in a state of mind to bear it—cruelty—oh beyond all others—no Man ever yet suffered a Woman to bear so much—pray send back those rings & the drawings and Book all shameful witnesses of my misery & eternal disgrace—farewell for ever oh for ever—I will nor see nor write nor think of you again—but I pray God to bless you & your Wife & to grant you both every possible happiness & delight only this if you have a child—once let me see him only once just to [*illegible*] see him I never can see his father no never more

Fearing Byron's betrothal to someone, Lady Caroline had not yet heard that he planned to marry William Lamb's cousin, Anne Isabella Milbanke.

10. Lady Caroline to John Murray. [Not After September–October 1814.]

Dear Sir—

[. . .] you seemed to regret the wetting I was about to have—I assure you it was remarkably warm and pleasant, besides no drizzly rain that falls on me can wash my misarray as the Lady says to the Friar—I was reflecting all the way home upon a new cause of misery which I have conjured up—I think I shall live to see the day—when some beautiful & innocent Lady Byron shall drive to your door—& I picture to myself the delight with which you will receive her—how every remark of hers will be admired by you & how bright she will appear to you compared to one who is faded & fallen—I really believe that when that day comes, I shall buy a pistol at Mantons[20] & stand before the Giaour & his legal wife & shoot myself, saying as Billy Taylors Mistress[21] did that as I must not live for him I will die—Morrie pour amore est bello morrie![22]—I shall Idolize that Lady Byron but do not you prefer her to me—you will, because the Law will uphold her & there is something so beautiful in virtue & innocence that it sets like a crown of glory round a Woman—& when she has cast it off—she is either contemptable or at best only worthy of pity—if you knew how good I was once how sorry you would be for me now—pray instead of returning my letters burn them—believe me that is the safest & best manner of disposing of them—oh that Lady Byron, how I feel secure that you will prefer her ten hundred times to me—every one will!

Once she knew the name of Byron's bride, Lady Caroline vented to Murray.

11. Lady Caroline to John Murray. 18 November 1814.

Brocket Hall

Dear Murray amidst all the changes & chances of this mortal life let me entreat you not to forget me—pray write me a letter of news & accept the parcel I send in remembrance of one who will never forget the real kindness you have shewn her. thank God my wandering mind is at length found. Thanks to the generosity of a man I hardly dare name—I mean my husband—I am not as wretched as I deserve [. . .] are you acquainted with my Cousin Annabel. She is very learned and very good & the top of her face handsome—certainly handsomer than half of the Biondettas & Black & White Ladies hitherto admired—I wish you to answer this letter forth with & to remember our old contract of the sacredness of our epistles to each other—be doubly careful now as I chuse

[20] John and Joseph Manton were gun craftsmen who excelled at their trade after registering their first patent in 1792.

[21] "Billy Taylor" was a popular street song on the early 1700s. Taylor's wife follows him to sea "dressed up like a man." When he cheats on her, she shoots him to death.

[22] Roughly: "Death for love is a beautiful death."

to have nothing to do or say with "Fulvia"[23] [. . .] I had a letter from him which might have been written by a Lord Chief Justice during the Assizes—I assure you the style froze me—though it was superlatively kind and condescending. How has he disposed of the other unfortunates? I speak of them by dozens, you see. For God's sake do not show this letter do you want a dog a Maid a cook or a Coachman? I can give a character to the first—and the others have been recommended to my protection because they have lost all other.

Caroline pressed Murray for an answer: would he publish her novel, which was set in Ireland during the 1798 rebellion, to be titled "Glenarvon"?

12. Lady Caroline to John Murray. [1814–1815.]

Mr Murray
Albemarle St

Dear Mr Murray—considering the agony which you know must arise from suspense—I am rather vexed at your not writing to me—if it is execrable in your estimation you can say gently that it is not so happy as you expected—I shall not be offended—therefore send me yr criticisms—or at all events call on me soon—I inclose you two Tickets for a Concert to which I cannot go though I promised it as I am obliged to be in the Country—will you take my place—even were you to think the vol. I sent you stupid dull & bad—I do not & therefore shall not be offended the conceit of an Author particularly one new to the name—can stand much humiliation therefore if you would knock me down at once prepare the blow as you would for an ox—all short of that will be taken in too favourable a sense [. . .]

6 Mile Bottom was the home of Byron's half-sister, Augusta Leigh, with whom some believe he had an incestuous affair. Byron stayed there several times in the three months before his marriage to Annabella Milbanke, which took place at Seaham on 2 January 1814. In the following letter, Lady Caroline seems to allude to Byron's staying there, just as she does in another letter in the Murray archive written about this time: "6 Miles Bottom!!! How singular. Where ignorance is bliss—Tis madness to be wise."

---

[23] The nickname Caroline gave Annabella Milbanke. The formidable Fulvia took Marc Antony in 44 BC as her third husband and defended him with military troops and cunning.

13. Lady Caroline to John Murray. [Late 1814.]

6 miles Bottom!!! est possible

Dear Mr Murray I return you many thanks for Parkstrands—which have made me even more melancholy than I was before—no news of my mother for a month—it is the first time that I ever was separated from her. I take it so little well that I am grown weaker faint & unable to write or send—if you have any thing to say to me—write tonight as I am entirely alone & just arrived—yrs. Clytea—& she turned her eyes up to her God as he passed her—& she died—see the Woman who was turned into a sun flower for worshipping the sun

14. Lady Caroline to John Murray. [1814–1815.]

Dear Sir,

[. . .] Mr Murray, my heart is set on the Publication of my novel & the vignettes[24] with it—they are pretty the novel is still very unequal—I am going to recorrect it—answer me fairly as a Man & not in jest—is it your wish to undertake it—Hookham[25] will not do the vignettes as well as I like—he fears the expence & wishes them to be done in an inferior style There are 4 [—] What do you say to it [. . .] tell me now without delay & by the bearer seal your wishes & as such I will follow them—but do not say yes & then give it into other hands—this would be acting like a B[yro]n

Farewell—

Bad company evil communication corrupts good manners [—] a Heathen & Christian proverb

Byron married Annabella Milbanke on 2 January 1815. Caroline sought solace in writing, reading, and sharpening her critique of Byron's personality and works.

15. Lady Caroline to John Murray. [February–March 1815.]

[. . .] my novel is nearly finished—will you read it & honestly return it—it is very incorrect very dull very full of faults but I shall persevere till I finish

---

[24] "Vignettes": decorations Lady Caroline drew for the title pages of the three volumes of *Glenarvon*, which were printed as she wished, though not by Murray, who eventually declined the novel, but by publisher Henry Colburn.

[25] Hookham was a bookseller and printer who also offered message delivery service.

it—& then it may light the next Bon fire any Lady is compelled to kindle if you don't like it and if you do Ile dedicate it to you if you hear any news tonight in mercy send it me—I live on no other Aliment do you wish to oblige an old & clever Lady—if so send me word who wrote the review of the Paradise of Coquettes[26] it is the widow of Sir Wm Jones who wishes to know—Fare well—I cried over Meg Merrilies[27] when she met Brown again—at the little Inn at Cumberland & my tears are not apt to flow—

yours most sincerely
CL

Caroline had tried to resolve her view of Byron: that "he has not a noble heart," though she still loved him: "I have already assured you in Italian Latin & Greek & I now do in plain English that I no longer worship your Idol," she told Murray in a letter of this period.[28] *She regained some of her flippancy, signing her letters with names like "Medora" and "Hermione, Princess of Strasberg." She also continued to press John Murray to publish her novel, which she had been working on now for almost three years. Still totally dependent upon the relatively small allowance she and William received from his father, she also confessed to Lady Melbourne in a letter of this time, that "we are rather ruind about money."*[29]

16. Lady Caroline to John Murray. [After April 1815.]

Write & tell me when I can have the words to the Hebrew Melodies[30] [. . .] My errors have made me inestimable in your eyes but I am not weak and mean and worldly-minded [. . .] I think I know myself well enough to say that I would rather die than deceive her[31] or play the Hypocrite—as

---

[26] Sir Thomas Brown (1778–1820) published *The Paradise of Coquettes: A Poem in Nine Parts* in 1814 (John Murray). The review in question was probably written by Francis Cohen (later known as Francis Palgrave) and it appeared in *The Quarterly Review* 12, 23 (October 1814) published 6 January 1815.

[27] Sir William Jones (1746–1794) was a British Orientalist and jurist. Meg Merrilies was Bertram's gypsy nurse in Walter Scott's *Guy Mannering*.

[28] Lady Caroline to John Murray. [1815.] Murray Archive.

[29] Lady Caroline to Lady Melbourne. [July–October 1815.] British Library Add. MS 45546 ff. 87–88.

[30] The first of a two volume song collection titled *A Selection of Hebrew Melodies, Ancient and Modern* had been published that spring. It was the product of a collaboration between Lord Byron and composer Isaac Nathan. Murray had gotten the lyrics and published them separately. Lady Caroline also had the original publication, for she alludes to specific verses on page 62 of it, in another letter of this period.

[31] Annabella Milbanke, who had married Byron 2 January 1815. Here is the first indication that she felt guilty over her failure to warn Annabella of Byron's transgressions and temper.

she is so closely connected with my family and has such excellent character I shall show her every respect and the same to him but I cannot court her or go to her house or be her friend—this is too German for me & I have peculiar feelings on this head which stand in lieu of principles. Therefore it is from you alone that I wish to receive the slightest favour.

I am very miserable they have just ordered my brave Brother & his Regiment the 12th to Flanders.[32] I did not know it when I began this what a melancholy year this is—

17. Lady Caroline to John Murray. [April] 1815.

I entirely deprecate your opinion concerning Manwaring[33] or sooner the opinion you had borrowed for I am convinced if you had read it through or even half you would have admired it excessively—I judge by myself who never can get over ten pages of any Book[—]yesterday—I finished it—I liked it better than I did Waverly—the story is better told the Hero more interesting the Gypsies delightful the Characters very well drawn indeed—all good in short except the love & the Ladies which are flippant & vulgar as is the Fashion now [. . .] Many a dull thing goes down by a puff—& all in all is fame Witness the Hebrew Melodies[34] which I have though you did not send them me—they are not worthy of him—trust to one who can appreciate his Genius they are very common place lowly performances—il se répête & has long wanted a thorough entire change of ideas[35] [. . .] send me a book or two—& pray destroy my letters—my novel is much prettier than any thing you ever read.

Caroline showed Byron not only that she perceived his vanity, but that she had remade his seal "Crede Biron" ("Believe in Byron") to read "Ne Crede Biron."

18. Lady Caroline to Lord Byron. 4 April 1815.

My Lord

Altho' you have got a lovely new Wife—an Elegant new Carriage—and a Beautiful new Seal with handsome handle of the same mounts in Gold

---

[32] Lt. Colonel Frederick Ponsonby embarked for Ostend as a commander with the 12th Dragoons, known as the Prince of Wales's regiment, after Napoleon escaped from Elba in March 1815.

[33] Walter Scott's *Guy Mannering* had been published February 1815

[34] Murray had published the lyrics of Byron and Nathan's *A Selection of Hebrew Melodies, Ancient and Modern* (1815–1816) separately from the music, over Nathan's objections.

[35] Lady Caroline states an idea common then and now: that at this time Byron was repeating himself.

I add this to let you see tho' others are rich so very fortunate as have a Wife yet there are those who have Seals as well as you—
"Crede Biron"

19. Lady Caroline to John Murray. [After April 1815.]

[. . .] It is a childish pride that our Poets now cherish to note the number of minutes and days in which they write a thing. They hurt themselves by these hasty and ill-digested performances.[36] "She walks in beauty like the night," for example—if Mr. Twiss[37] had written it how we should have laughed! Now we can only weep to see how little just judgement there is on earth, for I make no doubt the name of Byron will give even these lines a grace. I who read his loftier lay with transport will not admire his flaws and nonsense. You will say it is only a song, yet a song should have sense [. . .]

20. Lady Caroline to John Murray. [After April 1815.]

Do you know my heart so well all that you express pass'd—& there it ends—as to the meeting I am pleased with it—as to what follows it is not so wise—he never can be what he appears, he has not in him that which alone could realize so brightly a vision—"he has not a noble heart" therefore I consider all the rest of your letter as nothing because it goes upon a false principle like the House built upon sand the first trial will blow yr praise & the structure down—remember when an enthusiast before—you suddenly awake—there is a black speck in our divinity & like the most venomous of poisons though concealed from the eye it will shew itself at the hour appointed—as to the Lady has character is spotless—her understanding sensible accurate intelligent but when you talk of playfulness—I comprehend not your meaning—if Fulvia[38] Sporteth it must be like the dance of the Elephant that would vainly attempt to rival the Antelope So sportive are all the Hobhouses Hollands Clarks Hertfords & Prince Regents—there is a mournful merriment Jaques[39] says in such frolic as theirs—out d——ned spot—do you remember Mrs Siddons in

---

[36] And yet Lady Caroline tried to pretend she had written *Glenarvon* in a month.

[37] Horace Twiss (1787–1849), contributed laudatory reviews to newspapers, and as ridiculed for his activity. In 1813, he sued John Murray for lack of payment for two unpublished articles intended for Murray's *Quarterly Review*.

[38] That is, Annabella, Lady Byron.

[39] A discontented Lord attending the banished Duke in *As You Like It*.

Lady Macbeth—if all the syrups of the East—and all the waters of the ocean can wash it away—then I again will bow to my "sometime" Idol—& bear the chains whatever of bitter may be mingled with them—in spight of 6 Miles Bottom[40]—but as it is—I wash my hands from ill deeds—[. . .] talking of conceits let me make use of one to illustrate that new married couple—it is like the [root?] of a precious stone placed with a diamond of the first water & price—all that is delicate refined—high in Beauty & polish—as to mind & manner in the latter—the former has it not—trust me there is no stamp of Genius in my Learn'd Cousin[41]—but much good.

In June 1815, Caroline's brother Frederick was severely injured at the Battle of Waterloo and almost died. The bizarre social scene that ensued in Brussels and Paris after the battle is documented here, along with Lady Caroline's flirtations with Michael Bruce and the Duke of Wellington. Bruce had just returned from the Near East, where he had met Byron in 1810 (as the traveling companion of Lady Hester Stanhope), near Athens. Bruce surprised Byron with an impromptu confession of friendship Byron felt he had "done nothing to deserve."[42] *As a fellow Byron-lover, Caroline delighted in Bruce's company, calling him "He of the Desert." Lady Melbourne seems to have competed for Bruce's attentions, much to the disgust of Caro George: "I am doomed to hear her's and [Caroline's] mutual confidences of how the other makes up to him. [Lady Caroline] says the 'truth is he wants me, but I am not to be taken in, so he comforts himself with her.' This family is enough to make one sick."*[43]

21. Lady Caroline to John Murray. [June-July 1815.]

My Dear Sir

I enclose you my drawings & Miss [Thomasina] Webster will send you my Mss—it is in a dreadful state & has only time to correct the 3rd vol which you read all the rest is merely copied from my Brouillon & terrible—I scarce think you can make it out—I am just setting out for Brussels & shall be obliged to you to write to me constantly there as I will to you—I must to the post office

God Bless you & all those who have been so good & kind—I hope my journey may not be in vain—Williams kindness in going with me surpasses every thing I ever heard of—

---

40 As noted, the home of Augusta Leigh, Byron's half-sister.

41 That is, William Lamb's cousin—now Lady Byron.

42 Lord Byron to John Cam Hobhouse, 19 June 1811. *Byron's Letters and Journals*, 2:49.

43 Letter of Mrs. George Lamb, 9 August 1815. Mitchell, *Lord Melbourne: 1779–1848*, 74.

Sketch by Lady Caroline showing French woman in evening gown addressing an English woman who is accompanied by two dogs. By permission of Hertfordshire Archives and Local Studies.

22. Lady Caroline to Lord Duncannon. 7 July 1815.

[. . .] I have just seen Frederic, & thank God he is said to be out of danger. I arrived here half an hour ago. Nothing you ever heard of is like the crowd, but we have procured excellent appartments in this best hotel, not very far from my brother.

How happy I feel at having come. Poor Fred wants the greatest care & attention. He seems very weak, he is laid on his back in Mr. Greathead's house, who has been most good to him. The same surgeon attends him who attends the Prince of Orange.[44] I am to see him tomorrow at 12. I scarce can write, I feel so very nervous but happy. Only his breath seems very affected, but the surgeon says he is doing well. He must not

[44] The Hereditary Prince of Orange (1792–1849), later William II, King of the Netherlands, was wounded at Waterloo.

speak yet. He asked after you all & my mother, & particularly wished me to have brought Augustus.[45] Pray tell him as I have only time to write to you. For the post direct yr. letters to me at 1'Hotel de Flandre, Place Royale, & tell Miss [Thomasina] Webster Lord Uxbridge has lost his leg but is doing well.[46]

23. Lady Caroline to Lady Melbourne. [After 7 July 1815.]

Dearest Lady Melbourne your letter is the only one of any sort we have received & very acceptable it was—I cannot describe to you how totally cut off from news of every sort—it is said that Buonaparte & his Brothers having delivered themselves up to the protection of England are gone there [. . .] The great amusement at Brussels indeed the only one except visiting the sick is to make large parties & go to the field of Battle—& pick up a skull or a grape shot or an old shoe or a letter & bring it home—Wm has been I shall not go—having had an orderly man to explain it sufficiently for me—unless when Fred gets better & goes with me—there is a great affectation here—of making lint & bandages—but where is there not some & at least it is an innocent amusement—it is rather a love making moment the half wounded officers reclining with pretty ladies visiting them is dangerous—I also observe a great coxcombality in the dress of the sick—which prognosticates a speedy recovery—it is rather heart breaking to be here—however—& one goes blubbering about—seeing such fine people without their legs & arms—some in agony—& some getting better—the Prince of Orange enquired much after all his acquaintance he suffers a great deal but bears it well [. . .] Lady F[rances] Webster is too ridiculous—Mr Bradshaw an amiable Dandy close by me says it makes him ill for 2 hours after he has seen her—I conclude you have heard that the D——of Wellington fell desperately in love with her & 2 others, which was the cause of his not being at the Battle in time [—] the D[uche]ss of Richmonds fatal Ball[47] has been much censured there

---

[45] Given Augustus's great disabilities, it seems notable that Frederick Ponsonby missed him.

[46] Lord Uxbridge had just been created Marquess of Anglesey in recognition of his military services.

[47] At the commencement of the Battle of Waterloo, many regimental officers were abruptly called away from parties, including a large ball thrown by the Duchess of Richmond. She was then blamed for having distracted the officers from preparations for the battle that subsequently took so many of their lives.

never was such a Ball—so fine & so sad—all the young Men who appeared there shot dead—a few hours after [. . .]

24. Lady Caroline to Michael Bruce. [September–October 1815.]

Dear Mr. Bruce:

If it is not yet too late to turn & repent write & tell me so—as I having had a small attack of fever could not go & William wishes to join your party—if you have not fill[ed] my place shall I come also fever & all. Suppose you call here & give me the answer—believe me yours sincerely—

Caroline

25. Lady Caroline to Michael Bruce. [October 1815.]

Star of the East I go tomorrow & must entreat you to call on me tonight till one you will find me at Home pray bring the inconstant[48] & any other you may find—how I regret the Bruce on quitting Paris—aye and all else in this delightful capital.

Yours with respect & truth
Caroline

Caroline herself was probably the author of the play manuscripts she sent Lady Byron in hopes Byron himself would read them. The manuscripts have not survived.

26. Lady Caroline to Lady Byron. [Late October 1815.]

My dear Lady Byron—

I was most sorry to be out when you had the kindness to call here—will you accept a Lyoness scarf, it is made of such thin material that I have torn it & nearly spoild it—as they made me wear it on Landing—to prevent the Sharks from [seizing?] it—I am going to Brighton to see my Boy—but I hope to return soon—will you do me the favour of reading the 2 MSS—which I was urg'd to present to one of the managers at Drury Lane—& if they are worth any thing will you show them to your husband—I know

---

48 Benjamin Constant, Madame de Staël's former lover.

nothing of their Author except his having made me this request—George is out of Town—are you offended that I thus venture to torment you—

believe me ever sincerely
& gratefully yours
Caroline Lamb

Melbourne House
Friday—Morning

Will you have the kindness to deliver these MSS to Lady Melbourne when you have looked at them—in case the Man should call whilst I am gone—I conclude they are not likely to answer—but have not read them—only it is kind thus to conclude——Le Secret du Menage at Paris acted by Mad^elle^ Marse is very pretty—I hear Pie Voleuse[49] is better at Drury Lane than the original—would your husband like to have a Book—belonging to Napoleon—with the Eagle on it—

[49] The melodrama *La Pie Voleuse* had played in London in summer 1815 and was enthusiastically received that fall partly because it mirrored the case of Elizabeth Fenning, a servant girl who, on circumstantial evidence, was convicted of poisoning her master's family. Rossini based an opera on the story in May 1817.

CHAPTER SIX

Fare Thee Well

LETTERS, 1816

Although part of her may have wished for it, Lady Caroline was still shocked at the news that Byron had separated from his wife. At first, she was anxious to squash rumors of Byron's homosexual practices—and possibly of his incestuous love affair with Augusta Leigh. She gave him, Murray, and Lady Byron advice by mail, working to get both parties back together.

1. Lady Caroline to John Murray. [MARCH 1816.]

Can you call on me this Evening or tomorrow Morning & do for God sake tell me—have you breathed what I told you to any one, & if not, have you heard the reports—is it really true & do you know why—they say it is certain—every thing is rumoured as cause of it even the worst possible—I have been litterally ill on account of it—pray write.

2. Lady Caroline to Lord Byron. [MARCH 1816.]

Melbourne House

—Thursday—

When so many wiser and better surround you, it is not for me to presume to Hope that any thing I can say will find favour in your sight—but yet I must venture to intrude upon you, even though your displeasure against me be all I gain for so doing—All others may have some object or interest in View I have none but the wish to save you—will you generously consent to what is for the peace of both parties? & will you act in a manner worthy of yourself?—I am sure in the end you will consent—even were every thing now left to your own choice—you never could bring yourself to live with a person who felt desirous of being seperated from you—I know you too well to believe this possible & I am sure that a seperation noble & generously arranged by you will at once silence every report spread against either Party—believe me Lord Byron you will feel happier when you act thus—& all the World will approve your conduct which I know is not a consideration with you—but still should in some measure be thought of—they tell me that you have accused me of having spread injurious reports against you—had you the heart to say this—I do not greatly believe it—but it is affirmed & generally thought that you said so—you have often been unkind to me—but never as unkind as this—those who are dear to you can not feel more anxious for your happiness than I do—they may fear to offend you more than I ever will—but they cannot be more ready to serve you—I wish to God that I could see one so superior in mind & Talents & every grace & power that can fascinate & delight—happier—you might still be so Lord Byron if you would believe that some day you will find love—have you ever thought for one moment seriously do you wish to heap such misery upon yourself that you will no longer be able to endure it—Return to virtue & happiness for God sake whilst it is yet time—oh Lord Byron let one who has loved you with a devotion almost profane—find favour so far as to incline you to hear her—sometimes from the mouth of a sinner advice may be receivd that a proud heart disdains to take from those who are upon an equality with themselves—if this is so—may it now even now have some little weight with you do not drive things to desperate extremes—do not even though you may have the power—use it to ill—God Bless & sooth you—& preserve you—I cannot see all that I once admired & loved so well—ruining himself & others without feeling it deeply—if what I have said is unwise at least believe the motive was a kind one—& would to God it might avail—I cannot believe that you will not act generously in this instance—

Yours unhappily as it has proved for me Caroline

Those of my family who have seen Lady Byron have assured me that whatever her sorrow—she is the last in the world to reproach or speak ill of you—she is most miserable—what regret will yours be ever more if false friends or resentment impel you to act Harshly on this ocasion—whatever my feelings may be towards you or her I have with the most scrupulous care for both yr sakes avoided either calling or sending or interfering—to say that I have spread reports against either is therefore as unjust as it is utterly false—I fear no enquiry.

3. Lady Caroline to J.C. Hobhouse. [MARCH–APRIL 1816.]

Melbourne House

I wish to say one word to you—but if you ever tell—I never can forgive you—you have often been very harsh to me & perhaps I have deserved it—Byron has behaved almost barbarously to me & I can never feel any thing towards him again but resentment—in this quarrel too I differ from you & take her part not his—so do not mistake me. Yet Mr. Hobhouse for old acquaintance sake & a disgust I feel against the violence shewn against yr friend I wish to propose one thing to you—I have enough trinkets & things to raise about 300£ if the Trunks could be redeemed[1] with this I would gladly part with them if not, I shall not interfere [. . .]

4. Lady Caroline to Lord Byron. [MARCH? 1816.]

Lord Byron hear me & for God sake pause before you rashly believe any report others may make—if letter or report or ought else has been malignantly placed in the hands of yr Wife to ruin you I am ready to swear that I did it for the purpose of deceiving her there is nothing however base it may appear that I would not do to save you or yours from this—do not oh do not believe those who would lead you for one moment to think she knows any thing for certain—be firm be guarded—resolve upon seing seeing her—there is nothing—nothing a wife cannot & ought not to forgive—I can never believe that she will betray you—the curse of God will fall on her & her alone if she does—I know not whether it may appear wrong or right to say so—but this I know that if my death could at this moment save you—little prepared as I am I would seek it—& if it is a mere letter—I will swear I wrote it as

[1] Alludes to property seized by Lord Byron's creditors at Piccadilly Terrace on 23 April 1816: the date *The Morning Chronicle* announced his departure. Caroline's offer elicited no response.

a forgery as any thing if it can but prevent her believing any thing against you—all I ask is this be circumspect don't let even your bosom friends know anything—& let it please you to hear that amongst those who have most warmly most zealously supported you against every attack William lamb has been the foremost—oh Byron believe it both himself & me & all our family would gladly bear any calamity any reproach to save or to serve you—Lady Melbourne is unwell & low we have neither of us been out once since this report (not on account of it but because she is ill—) she disbelieves every word against you—& if I tremble more than her—think not at least that I judge you—this alone I ask you—do not rashly credit any lie or invention that old Devil Lady Milbanke may invent—don't even think that Lady Byron may know because she suspects—& if it be a letter deny it at once—there are moments when to deny is a virtue & this is one—be firm & do not let mistaken friends gain your confidence—I scarce know what I say this I know that my Brother Wm told a Man this morning when he spoke unkindly of you—that he thought him both mean & cowardly for doing so—& William Lamb at Brooks[2] said—as far as my denial can have had effect I have said stoutly & without enquiry that all such reports were fake—believe me Lord Byron we all honour you & regard you with attachment & interest that is not to be altered—& though my misconduct & unhappy circumstances have estranged us—you will never find truer or more affectionate relations & friends than in this House—

I must think Lady Byrons conduct blameable & Lady Noels[3] shameful whether it were a mere error or a crime—it is not for the Mother of Anabella to act thus—but dont be severe & whatever happens insist upon seeing her—all the words in the world are not worth one interview—one promise I ask of you—suppose people tell you any thing is know that you think of consequence—swear to me that you will be firm—deny it calmly & to all—do not do not fancy because every appearance is against you that it is known see your Wife—& she cannot have the heart to betray you—if she has she is a Devil—& in mercy be calm—could you know what yr Aunt suffers you would write to her or see her—God bless & preserve you with respect & truth yrs

Caroline

---

[2] Brooks's was a Whig club founded in 1778 by William Brooks with 26 other "macaronis," or dandies whose average age was twenty-five.

[3] Annabella Milbanke's mother.

Reports of Byron's atrocious behavior to his wife in the days before she left him confirmed Caroline's determination to "take her part not his" (see letter 3 above). Byron had been physically and verbally abusive, to the point that Annabella entertained the possibility he might be mad. Byron's poem, "Fare Thee Well" (a bid for sympathy and partly an attack on his wife) was privately printed on 4 April 1816 and then appeared in The Champion *ten days later. Caroline claimed to be appalled, and the tone she takes with Murray does seem sincere, though many biographers have doubted it.*

5. Lady Caroline to John Murray. [April 1816.]

My Dear Sir

it should be a positive proof to you that I no longer am Byron's friend or admirer—what I am now going to say to you—I think it a shame in you to shew these verses[4]—to try & awake feelings for him when his conduct I find has been too mean & too atrocious even for such as I am to tollerate for God sake see me—I think if you have a heart I can make it feel & though to all others I will be silent to you I must I will speak openly—I do entreat you to either appoint some time when you will see me tomorrow or call on me tonight you will find me quite ill—but thank God—it is because I am not yet abandoned & hardened enough to see real virtue & generosity undone and a Villain a Coward & contemptible Villain set up to be admired——you know how I have loved & what I have forgiven—no Woman's feelings no resentment no jealousy occasion my present warmth—

Caroline now approached Lady Byron in sympathy—or with manipulation and revenge in mind, depending upon how one views her inconsistencies. Caroline's faith in Byron had been shaken, and although she still loved him, she claimed to identify with Lady Byron, who might lose custody of her child. Though Annabella mistrusted Caroline, she agreed to talk secretly to her about protecting her child by threatening to disclose Byron's "crimes." Despite having provided Lady Byron with ammunition for her separation negotiations, Caroline still thought Byron would escape without public disclosure.

---

[4] That is, "Fare Thee Well."

6. Lady Caroline to Lady Byron. 4 March 1816.

Lady Byron

It is not for me to write to you or in any way to appear in this most melancholy scene—God protect & preserve you through it—trust in him & in your own good heart & in yr Parents who still remain to watch over and save you—what I could say I will not—my lips are forever seald & all interference on my part either way must be misrepresented—yet I will never be so mean as to deceive you—in the first moment of surprise & regret when I heard with every gross & shameful misrepresentation of yr departure & his dispair—I wrote to him with all the kindness and affection of a friend imploring him to follow you to seek you & to regain you—I even spoke bitterly in my letter of yr Parents who I was informed had forced you to this act—such letter I am miserable at having written if for one moment you or he or any other can think me base enough & false enough to every feeling of humanity & the commonest principle—as to take this part against yours—Lady Byron whatever may be my fate—from this hour nothing on earth shall tempt me in word or thought to have the slightest communication or friendship for one of his character—I have suffered many deserved grief[s] through his Barbarity & my own inexcusable & criminal conduct thank God I have suffered them as in part perhaps they may attone for my weakness & crime but I can assure you that never till this hour did I feel disgust & indifference for him who deserves no other sentiments—so different is the feeling which arises from the blow given to ourselves when we feel that we deserve it from the hand of God—& the unmerited cruelty exercised on one—not only innocent—but by his own account exemplary noble—& all that ought to have been prized & loved—I shall neither call on you nor send to you & you know & must feel my motive & I do most solemnly enjoin you never to any human Being say that I have written to you—your name at this time must not be coupled with mine—you must not even speak of me with the generous kindness you ever have—there may come a time when I shall prove in more than words how I esteem & love & feel for you—but for God sake Hold no sort of communication with me now—only were I to die for it tonight I will not suffer another hour to pass without telling you—that I would stand by you not him were the whole world & every thing in it—in his favour—& if he has the cruelty to tear the child from you I will tell you that which if you merely menace him with the knowledge shall make him tremble—keep every one in the dark as to what you know—they feel secure now but at first he was very much frightened—think of my situation when I saw you an innocent unsuspicious sacrifice to his selfish & cruel vanity—do not fancy that I stood by coldly & calmly to see it—he made every promise of amendment man could make—but still I reproach myself that I did not fly before you & tell you all I knew—all I had sworn never never to reveal—to keep such oath was more scandalous than to have broken it—but I still Loved Byron even then—& had he behaved to you but as he said—I could not have hated & despised him as from my soul I now do & will—Lady Byron though you are spotless & pure & I am all that is fallen & worthless yet hear me—it is on my knees I write to you your friendship your protection can be nothing to me—dont then think I say what I now say for any purpose or to flatter you—but for yr dear childs sake for yr poor Mothers—trust no one—there are serpants round you who can smile on you & bite you to the heart—all will tell you that some have taken yr part but do not believe them—perhaps they have a motive for their behaviour oh beware even of yr own shadow—keep all at a distance—be cold to his friends & relatives—they are more his friends than yours—above all mistrust those who tell you he is ill & unhappy—I will let you know if ever he is really so—I took the allarm upon false reports—but he is only crafty & double mouthed that he may the better deceive you—to Lady Melbourne & HobHouse He holds the proudest language—speaks of you However as you deserve—but asks repeatedly if you were not Happy—lays the charge on yr Parents & false friends—says he knows you love him & shews some letter with tender expressions from Kirby in proof—Mrs Lee[5] too Espouses yr part—it is not natural—how much she takes it—oh mistrust even her—keep all at a distance—say not to one of them what you fear his knowing & above all intimate to him that you have the knowledge & proof of some secret which nothing but dispair shall force you to utter—do not think me cunning & crafty because I thus write to you but you are so innocent so good you can not be aware of these arts—truth & virtue will find its way in Heaven & God will preserve & protect you—but to spare you a scene of horror to spare you the agony of having yr child taken from you & consigned to such hands—I urge you to follow my counsel it is from the heart I write it—& urge it—there is a secret—he dares not face that I would sooner die I think than

[5] Byron's half-sister, Augusta Leigh.

reveal it—but if he thinks that you know it—if he feels he is in yr power he will not dare to push matters to extremity—he will not face a public trial—or if he does—he will yield to all such just demands as you must insist on—

Now Lady Byron I have done for you what I would not for my self or any other—I have placed my life my honour in yr hands—& acted a shabby part by one I thought once I had died merely to please—yet so strong are my feelings for you—so great my indignation—that I will run any risk sooner than not do my utmost to save you—one word more I wish to say to no one living not even to Caro[line St. Jules][6] who loves you as if you were her sister tell that I have written this letter—burn it for God sake—& do not answer it upon any account whatever if questioned by Lady M[elbourne] I wish to be able to say that I have not ever heard from you—Mrs Lamb too even you her own sister could not feel more—& Lady Byron if some indignation springs up in yr mind at finding yr own Aunt less warm in your cause than others—oh remember that he who can make friends & relations think whatever he pleases—has blinded her not now alone but long long before—& it appears to me that kindness & attention may perhaps bring her round from her infatuation—

when guilt remorse & a barbarity little expected from one who had appeard so kind so good to me—drove me to acts of insanity & dispair—Lady Melbourne even at that time espoused Lord Byrons cause & her doing it added to the bitter agony I endured—Farewell my Dearest—& much honoured & loved Cousin—God support & bless you—& pardon me ever yrs Caroline Lamb prego in Dio a lei di Brucciare questa lettera e che niente vi fa scrivere a me[7]—but if you are not offended & feel kindly—when next you see Caroline [St. Jules]—send me a message—such as yr remembrances—but even to her do not say I have written as I wish her to be able to say that she does not know of our having had any communication whatever—Believe me at this moment it is of consequence for were you to adopt my advice & hint at some secret—if it were to be known to come from me—it would seem I had acted the part of a Kings evidence—& God knows what——therefore I stake as it were my life in yr hands———

---

[6] Mrs. George Lamb, the other "Caro"—illegitimate child of Lady Elizabeth Foster, mistress of the Duke of Devonshire.

[7] Roughly: "I pray you for God's sake burn this letter and let nothing make you write to me."

7. Lady Caroline to Lady Byron. 27–28 March 1816.

after the long letter I wrote to you at 3 oclock last night—you will be surprised at my again intruding—but I must say all that is on my mind & that done I shall persevere in my resolution & till the whole of this is settled one way or other—hold no sort of communication with you—but My Dear Lady Byron—I am situated in a manner that seeing all things & knowing much more than any unless yourself—I cannot but be allarmed—in the first place you wish this amicably settled & who would not provided your interest & dignity & child are left you—now in such case do you not perhaps think it were as well to conciliate in some manner yr Aunt—to write her a kind & frank letter—perhaps in some such manner as this—saying My Dear Aunt you will no doubt be surprised & hurt that at a moment of affliction like the present I have not written openly or seen you—but I too have been deeply wounded—& have thought by all I have heard that you have rather taken part against me than with me—there are things which I will never communicate to any—which are wholly my own but in all else I wish to shew you confidence it is not possible for me exactly to say how I wish you to write yr own good feelings may dictate this—but be assured when I tell you that Lady Melbourne is of that warm nature that if she thought you dealt openly with her—she would be touched—& is it a moment for anger—is it indeed worth it—I will not deceive you or say you should trust her—but recollect my Dearest Lady Byron How artful he is & what a manner he has of turning things & pity sooner than hate those whom he deceives—I can assure you too that himself & Mrs Leigh & HobHouse though they all keep repeating—she is faultless oh she is generous good kind noble—say every now & then a word—that makes the more impression from this apparent candour—now God forbid I should Judge anything—I believe Mrs Leigh is your sincere friend but recollect also that she is his sister & that she may feign this warm defence of yr conduct for some purpose—for is it probable else that she should be against him there is a difficult game to play & they are playing it skillfully—I write not in enmity but merely to put you on yr guard—some affectionate letter of yours has already been much misrepresented & made a vast deal of use of against you—some letter of yr maids saying "she threw herself down screaming out oh they have forcd me to this I am lost forever—I am imprisoned—has been stated to many—this is said to have been addrest to Fletcher—Lady Byron you will ruin me forever if you tell one word of this even to yr real friends and what is even more you will do yourself incredible harm—remember the situation in which I stand—were it but thought that I espous'd your cause—would it not hurt it—so she has joined with

Lady C. L against him will be said—the cast off mistress & the Wife make common cause—[. . .] William Lamb desires me to say all that is kind from him—he thinks if you could try & conciliate yr Aunt it were well—but it requires consideration—& be assured that a cold letter or reserv'd manner will only further iritate—she is infatuated about Lord B—she ever has been & she is now more willing to think him Mad at times than wicked—besides which she has an idea that you have a cold character & certainly as the story has been represented to her it is singular [. . .] in your conversation with Lord Holland—appear frank & kind for he has a good heart—but do not trust him as he tells all to Lady H—though he may promise not—do not strive however to hide that you feel deeply—as they have it now all over the Town that you are cold—& do not feel—particularly for yr child—when I say this I speak of the narrow circle I live in—the whole world believe me is disgusted & indignant with him—but have a care for I know him so well that I dread his subtlety—& though both in Heaven—& on earth after a time real virtue shines forth & puts guilt to flight yet he may triumph now by skill & you have suffered sufficiently—already—part with yr maid she is Fletchers Wife! pray remember that!

seem to hint to Lord Holland that you know something very bad—but that dispair alone & the loss of yr child shall tempt you to reveal it say however that if driven to the last extremity if yr generous forbearance is not understood—if yr family instead of supporting you joins with & supports him—if the causes you can & will name are insufficient—oh say that you will come forward yourself & bring such accusations against him that he dares not stand— for God sake speak thus to Lord Holland—you have no conception of the good it will do—you have no thought how much it will tend to facilitate an amicable seperation & believe me Lady Byron were it to come to the worst were I to see your child taken from you I would appear myself against him in Justice & call on the humanity of strangers to prevent so wicked so barbarous an act—

Farewell—burn this for God sake

Scarcely had the flap over "Fare Thee Well" subsided when Murray showed Caroline a poem of Byron's seemingly addressed to his half-sister. She couldn't believe he intended to publish it, and wrote to him.

8. Lady Caroline to Lord Byron. [April 1816.]

At a moment of such deep agony & I may add shame—when utterly disgraced judge Byron what my feelings must be at Murrays shewing me some beautiful verses of yours[8]—I do implore you for God sake not to publish these could I have seen you one moment I would explain why—I have only time to add that however those who surround you may make you disbelieve it you will draw ruin on your own head and hers if at this moment you shew these—I know not from what quarter the report originates—you accused me & falsely—but if you could know all that is said at this moment you would believe one—who though your enemy though forever allienated from you though resolvd never more while she lives to see or speak to or forgive you yet would perhaps die to save you—

Byron hear me & my own misery—I have scarce once thought of what is the loss of one like me to the World—but when I see such as you are ruind forever & utterly [insensible?] of it I must grieve—of course I cannot say to Murray what I think of those verses—but to you to you alone I will say I think they will prove your ruin—

John Murray had finally declined to publish Lady Caroline's novel, so she reached an agreement with Henry Colburn, a successful publisher who had printed works by many women. She had formed a fast friendship with Isaac Nathan, and wanted music printed to go with some of her songs. Colburn received a barrage of correspondence from his new author: "I am quite vex'd at seeing the songs without [Nathan's] music," she told him. He fixed the problem when Glenarvon *was finally published on 9 May 1816.[9] Although Colburn probably knew that the fall–out would be severe, Lady Caroline seems to have been unprepared for the beating she was about to take, and that she would narrowly avoid the strait–jacket and incarceration.*

9. Lady Caroline to Henry Colburn. [APRIL? 1816.]

[. . .] I prefer abiding by my own errors whatever they are than any other persons. I shall be seriously angry if any alteration is made whatever either in punctuation or orthography & and I entreat you to send me the proof sheets. Remember and send the remainder of the 1st vol.—for I have been obliged to alter it all back again—pray be cautious in future [. . .]

---

8 Refers to the impending publication of the lines "Stanzas to Augusta" in April 1816, exposing Byron to danger for his apparently too intimate relationship with his half–sister. Byron subsequently warned Murray *again* not to let Caroline read any advance copy of his work.

9 Lady Caroline Lamb to Henry Colburn. [April?] 1816. Victoria and Albert Museum Forster Collection MSS vol. 28. #48.E.22.

We shall get into a serious scrape if you do not let me have the first two vols. to look over.

The Lambs were serious about controlling Caroline, and it appears her eldest brother and uncle were not averse to the solution of incarceration.

10. Lady Caroline to Lord Melbourne.
April or May 1816.

My Dearest Lord Melbourne I am not ungrateful—& whatever may happen I shall not easily forget Lady Melbourne & your kindness—what would have been my fate had it been otherwise—God forbid I should say any thing harsh of my own relations the only censure I wish to cast upon any one at present is this—let me remain under your protection till William returns [—] I wish to see no one I do not care about going out—but to tell you the plain truth I had much rather be put in prison for any fault I have committed & abide by the law of the Country than trust myself in the power of either Lord or Lady Spencer[10] as to Duncannon[11] he has a very good heart as well as they have a very good sense but he was extremely severe at first & only when he found he could not prevail with Wm to do all he asked he relinquished his point it is no doubt a proper & just punishment that my Pages should be taken away if you & William propose to do it—but nobody else has a right to interfere—& as to any promises I may have been forced to make when a straight waistcoat & a Mad Doctor are held forth to view—they cannot expect I should think them binding [. . .] & really when I read with my own eyes a letter not hinting but absolutely declaring me mad—I may be a little afraid of those who had the inhumanity to write it—it is too sad to hear all this is for my own good—

11. Lady Caroline to Emily Cowper.
[After 9 May 1816.]

since I wrote to you I have seen Lord Melbourne and I know not how to act [—] he is most kind he wishes me to stay here and live quietly and

---

[10] Caroline's aunt and uncle on her mother's side.

[11] As noted, the title of Caroline's eldest brother, as a mark of his expectation of inheriting the Bessborough title.

comfortably George on the other hand openly professes himself to hate me & to wish never to enter into the House if I remain or to let Caro[line St. Jules]—that is a thing I cannot wish he is a favourite [—] I am not [—] settle it therefore as you will amongst you amicably or no—War or peace only do not let masks of kindness be worn while daggers are stuck in the back when least expected—I forgave him much once [—] he might generously forgive me a hasty word—if not—do as you have all long wished drive me from this House and add open Hostility to secret malice—you hurt no one in it but William—and I do not think you care for him—you have exposed my faults to every one spoken of them at all times—have I ever done the same by you? hitherto—you have with considerable art brought things to the present crisis—push them on now a step further and triumph [. . .]

Despite the outrage of family and friends—she was being "cut" and frozen out in public—Caroline was concerned to see her novel do well. "Get rid of the 1st Edition as quick as possible," she wrote Colburn, "that I may correct some very ridiculous mistakes in the second."[12] The first run of 1,500 copies sold out, and Caroline talked to William about the advisability of a new, corrected edition.

12. Lady Caroline to Henry Colburn. [MAY–JUNE 1816.]

I am happy to say that I have obtained leave to publish a second Edition which will be greatly improved without delaying the Printer. I have also written a most beautiful preface—& now wish to have done with the whole thing—it is useless to deny it—everyone knows who wrote the Book—make therefore what use you chuse of it—take the copyright that is if you will give me for it what others have asked me. 500£.

Byron's friend, John Cam Hobhouse, made the mistake of seeming to threaten Caroline with retaliation for what was widely regarded as an attack on Byron.

13. Lady Caroline to J.C. Hobhouse. [MAY–JULY 1816.]

My mother tells me that you had been informed I mentioned your Visit to me & what passed or sooner what you say did not pass between us

[12] Lady Caroline to Henry Colburn. [after 9 May 1816.] Victoria and Albert Museum Forster Collection MSS vol. 28. #48.E.22.

respecting my novel [. . .] I am not malevolent in this instance [—] I may have ruined myself but no other person alive & had I chosen to be ill natured God knows without deviating from truth—had I even spoken of all others with half the sincerity I have of Calantha[13]—I had plenty of means—no mercy is ever shewn me—I am abused misrepresented villified & then it is expected I can bear all things in silence—all that I thought might harm the character of any living being I pulled out of this Book—of all people upon earth Lord Byron is the last to accuse me—how he has treated me were I to tell it might indeed harm him but he is so far from wishing it he knows I never have and never shall betray him he has tried me something harder than many would bear, & I have not yet—this novel may be stupid may be unseemly for me to write may be any thing you please but is assuredly any thing but malevolent—were it known that at the time I published it people wrote to my husband to implore him to part with me & telling him every thing most cruel of me—were it known that an attempt was made to prove me mad, that had not Wm finally resisted I had now been far from here disgraced for ever—under the care of those brutes who never more would have allowed me freedom to claim even assistance—were it further known that they got about Lord Melbourne & made him order me instantly out of the House many would sooner pity me than judge me with the severity they have for all this was before I sent my Book out—you say in your letter to Lady M something as if I were Lady Byrons advocate & confidante I believe you will find yourself utterly mistaken I do not fancy she would even extend her compassion to a reprobate like me—& though from my soul I pity her as I know that which ought to have made me fly to her—prevent her marriage yet some day you will find out that Lord Byrons own impudence alone betrayed to her a thousand circumstances which to this hour I believe Lady Noel & Mrs Claremont[14] have not the remotest idea of—when you suspect me! ask yourself if there are no others who had more interest in this disunion—& whatever my faults do not judge of a heart that hitherto Has disdained every mean revenge & never will adopt that [course?] but in one case when by him that made me I will disclose all even upon oath & die the next moment—I have been insulted & sacrificed long & often enough to prove me at least to Lord Byron something more noble than himself—it is not for Lady Byron that I shall come forth—for why should I do for her what I

---

[13] Calantha is the protagonist of Lady Caroline's novel, *Glenarvon*.

[14] Mrs. Claremont: a friend of the Noels (Milbankes), not related to Byron's lover, Claire Clairmont.

would not do for myself—but there may come a time when the world shall judge between us—ruind & fallen as I may be—& trust me in such contest Lord Byron will shrink before one he dares not even look at face to face so basely so malignantly so barbarously has he behaved—but I have never never yet betrayed him because such is a Womans nature they cannot readily injure even their most bitter enemy—[. . .] I was informed a week ago that you said I should hear something more of this novel than I expected & that Lord Byron might retort—let him—tell him to publish all my letters let him use all his perfidies all his misrepresentations to my ruin [—] it is what I wish[,] what I ask—one single word—one single line is sufficient it frees me at once from every restraint & I then will appear[15]—& if I fall he at least shall fall with me & some others who now trample on me with malicious delight secure in the midst of their cowardice by my disgrace—let those who take from me without mercy my reputation my heart my feelings who spit at spurn & deride me—remember that a lion may be devourd by vermin because sick & feeble & chased—but that it is not want of power if I forbear—yourself Mr Hobhouse came here and laughd & Mr Webster heard you & talked of the P[rince]ss of Madagascar[16] with pleasure & then went to fawn at Holland House which your friend often has attacked as much & with as much Justice perhaps—I am defenseless now—therefore do your worst all of you—I care not—but expect it—Farewell— yours sincerely though you are but an unkind friend to me

Caroline Lamb

14. Lady Caroline to Lady Byron. 8 SEPTEMBER 1816.

My Dear Lady Byron

I acquiesce in your wishes because I respect you enough to believe that you will never turn harshly from me though you may & must condemn me—I have suffered very much since I saw you & now I trust in God

---

15 In another letter to Hobhouse of this period, Lady Caroline made her threat more specific: "let him but publish the tenth part of a single line in any letter I ever wrote him—let him but write verses or books against me—or any of you—or Lady Holland—& if I die for it I vow to God I will on the instant publish not only all his—but the whole exact journal which I have kept of my acquaintance with him" (10 July 1816. Murray Archive).

16 The Princess of Madagascar is a character in *Glenarvon* based upon Lady Holland, and such an effective caricature that for years her friends called her this—usually behind her back.

that I am going to make a vigorous effort to act rightly till I die—William will call on you & I will not—but let me hope that at some future period you will of yourself see me—I shall never speak or allude to any subject that is past & indeed I think you may have confidence in me in this respect—Yet to you before whom I opened my whole heart so entirely & for whom I broke so solemn an engagement I must yet relieve myself from one painful doubt—they say you live almost wholly with Mrs Leigh it astonished me & William—yet promise me—that even if your better judgment—kindness—or any further investigation have altered your opinion of her entirely—promise me to open my eyes also—to say to me "You were deceived—he deceived you—& I know it[″]—for that secret rests on my heart & makes me miserable & I would give any thing never never to have heard or thought it—

one thing more—M[rs] Leighs manner to me is that of hatred—I never for one instant suffered myself to believe you had betrayed me—but I am sure if she did not think I had spoken she durst not & would not thus look on me no not if I were black with every sin—for how should she judge me—this my Dear Lady Byron was on my mind [. . .]

Troubles over Byron's separation and her deteriorating relations with almost everyone except William faded into the background whenever Caroline contemplated Augustus and his seizures.

15. Lady Caroline to Lady Melbourne.
28 September 1816.

You will not wonder Dearest Lady Melbourne that I should feel almost heart broken about Augustus I really am so dispirited I scarce know what to do he has had 4 attacks today 2 very very severe ones—& it is only the 4th day—he is to take one of Evans powders tonight as Mr Lucas says he should at all events give him a cleaning dose—& the moment the 3 are taken he goes to Brighton & if Wm can spare me I shall go too—

I have been very ill—myself but I believe it is greatly encreased by anxiety about my Boy—God Bless you—tell George that Wm & I think Timon [of Athens] just suited to [Edmund] Kean it is almost my favourite play I think the 1st 3 acts require scarce any alterations God Bless you I have not heart to write more

16. Lady Caroline to Lady Melbourne.
[SEPTEMBER–OCTOBER 1816.]

Dearest Lady Melbourne it gives me some little hope that Augustus may be the better for these blisters as he has not had the least return—Mr Lucas seems very uneasy about my heart—it has not ceas'd fluttering since the morning you were here it is a sort of convulsion & he put me on a huge blister yesterday which gave me great pain bigger than this paper over the whole side & today he thinks of bleeding me—I am so sure lowering will encrease it that I have beggd to postpone bleeding a day or two & indeed <u>must</u> from circumstance but it makes me very faint & sick—[. . .] Augustus has a breaking out quite in the middle of his head at the back—my breathing is so much affected by the heart fluttering & beating so that I litterally feel like a person with the Ast[h]ma & I do not find Laudanum or Ether or Valerian of the least use—whilst the blister was drawing I did not feel I did not feel it & last night it was easier—I kept the blister on 24 hours it innundated me—but it is all the worse now Lucas says I am so low that he does not like to bleed me but the pulse stops so—& the heart beats so that he should like to take blood from the left arm what do you advise [. . .]

As usual, Caroline turned for solace to those like John Murray, with whom she had shared the experience of Byron.

17. Lady Caroline to John Murray.
13 OR 15 OCTOBER 1816.

[D]o you remember some time ago when you were Justly indignant with Lrd B & said he was "done for" that I said by no means & also the Machiavelian advice I then gave you—now as it has proved so good in point of Worldly Policy will you allow me to offer you a little more with another view—be not dazzled by his success—be not thrown into wild delight because his genius has shone forth—misfortune & rage have occasioned this & whenever he may speak <u>himself</u> Lord Byron will succeed—self is the sole inspirer of his genius he cannot like Homer Dante Virgil Milton Dryden Spencer Gray—<u>Goldsmith</u> Tasso write on other subjects well[—]but what he feels he can describe extravagantly well—& therefore I never did doubt that he would one day or other write again as at first—but for God sake do not let this circumstance make you forget what a Rogue he is [. . .] the sun may shine upon a bit of broken Glass till it appears like a Diamond but if you take it up you will only cut your fingers—& though the World even were again to be taken in by Lord Byron neither you nor I can be—do not forget the wrongs of such as are opprest—remember that Mother & that child[17] [. . .] I speak of her wrong not mine—I was so wrong myself that I never dared resent what I knew however was not the conduct of a man who had one honest feeling in him—but though the belief of his being at length detected might soften me—by him who created me I swear that if he ever rises more though I may die or ruin myself in the attempt, I will prove no contemptible enemy [. . .]

Michael Bruce, who had been imprisoned in France, threatened with execution, had reappeared in London.

18. Lady Caroline to Michael Bruce.
[After September 1816.]

[. . .] do you know that I am miserable—indeed it is not that I am ungrateful either to God or to William but my hearts in torture & my whole soul the same—it is as if there was a sword run through me—or a fire burning in my brain—no ship that ever was tost on a strange sea without daring to anchor any where or in immediate fear of being lost—ever yet was so distressed as I am—I know not how to live & I dare not die—there is but one thing could sooth and calm me & that were Religion—but I know neither how to believe or how to doubt—my heart inclines me to kneel down & pray—& my pride also rejects it—you said you could calm me & advise me—but you have only made me much worse—There are such thoughts in me at times that if they continue I must go mad human weakness cannot bear up against it and in the night 'tis dreadful—if this is what is called remorse how can people say there is no Hell [. . .] & the people who have seen me so gay & apparently so hardened because pride & spirit kept me up in their presence need not fear—could they see me when alone they would not say the moral to Calantha was bad—its such that I cannot struggle with it long—though it is but a mite or a moth that is burned—yet it suffers agony even should you place it among roses & flowers

---

[17] That is, Lady Byron and her daughter, Augusta Ada.

19. Lady Caroline to John Murray. 12 December 1816.

It is strange but my visit to your House today has made me miserable—after all what a life mine has been & how irregular our acquaintance—you must show me the seal when it is done & the sketch of it before—I believe none will be found better to take the likeness from than Westalls print[18]—The Journal[19] you mentioned—were you serious if indeed you will permit me to look at it I will call on you & read it—I had a thousand things to say to you but they were all forgotten the moment they said you were at home—is not life strange whatever he is however I have abused him—If I believed him at any hour unhappy would I not go through the fire to serve him—that child of his—will it be like him—but what is all this to me—your room speaks of him in every part of it—& I never see you without pain—yet is it not strange it seems to me most unpleasant if I pass any length of time without seeing you & what I can safely say I add—that I think you have been a sincere upright & manly friend to both him & me—through many very trying scenes—if ever you are grieved send for me—for I am yours in my heart & soul—& perhaps I reproach myself for the violence with which I have presumd to judge & condemn another—of all people on earth I am the last to do it—who ever knew so little as myself how to command my own actions yet be assured whatever my faults I feel yr kindness with the utmost gratitude & never never shall forget to name you among my real friends—if you should either in the Morning or Evening have a few moments to spare perhaps you will come here & when you do like to shew me the Journal—remember that you confer on me the greatest favour you can—yrs CL

[18] Richard Westall (1765–1836) had painted Byron in 1813 when Byron was twenty-five.

[19] Caroline refers to Byron's memoirs, which she read before they were destroyed.

CHAPTER SEVEN

Disgrace

LETTERS, 1817–1819

Only after the departure of Lord Byron and the debacle of Glenarvon *did Lady Caroline Lamb feel the full weight of her transgressions. She acknowledged to herself what she repeated obsessively to others: William had saved her. What she never quite revealed was the toll it took on their relationship. Though William had shown he would never give her up—to be declared mad and locked away—he had also realized her permanent disability as a spouse and companion, for she could not be faithful or discreet. At times, he acknowledged his sister Emily was correct—that he ought to let Caroline go. But he still refused a formal separation. Counting on his love and support, which he still gave, Caroline tried to repair what was left of her social life and hang on to her writing career.*

1. Lady Caroline to Lord Granville Leveson Gower. [1817.]

My Dear Lord Granville—

Thank you for your kindness; but had you not come up, it had indeed been cruel. Do forgive me; I cannot bear that Harriet and yourself should be so unrelenting to one who loves you as I do, and who am so near to her in blood and affection. You do not know the circumstances—you cannot. Is it to be supposed that after ten years' marriage and such ill conduct on my part William would thus support me at the risk of all he most prizes for himself, if the case were [as] it is represented? Indeed, indeed, I was desperate and most afflicted when I took this last step, and I am convinced that had you seen me before, you would have felt for me. At all events, before you judge me you should see and question the Boy to whom I was said to be so barbarous, and whom no offers no entreaties, can prevail on to leave me. You should also see my husband, who knows every thing, and is not blinded by my acts or even by love, and who says that he could not in honour give me up. Recollect that at the time I gave this book into the hands of Colburn, whom Mr. Constant had sent to me about his own book, I was so miserable that the man himself spoke with me as he would to a person dying, and took orders what to do as if in that case. I was ordered out of the House in no gentle language: my Mother was spoke to with the most barbarous roughness in my presence. My husband received letters telling him he would be the public ridicule and jest if he supported me—I was proved mad. Mr. Moor assured me I was so, and entreated me to persuade my husband of it. I appealed to a few, but my letters were not even answered. I went to Roehampton; Lady Jersey, to the extreme annoyance of my Father, quite turned her back on me and refused to speak to me. I came back to Town and met Lord Holland, who coldly passed me by. Indeed, indeed, Lord Granville, I could not stand it; these people, too, had all taken Lord Byron's part, had all stood by him, though cruelty and falsehood were heaped upon him. Wm returned, a dreadful scene passed between me and Lord M. and Mama. That night I sent the novel. It was then much more violent—Calantha was not made to die, but it was brought home to real life. Wm Lamb heard of the novel the day it came out. I solemnly assure you upon my honour this passed between us. He came in and said: "Caroline, I have stood your friend till now—I even think you ill used; but if it is true this Novel is published—and, as they say, against us all—I will never see you more." The Books were that Evening on the table—you know the rest; but you do not know how William behaved. They wrote, happily for me, with such malignant violence that they over did it. He read what was termed a libel. He saw and feels, deeply feels, the unpleasant situation it is for turn, but he loves me enough to stand firm as a rock, and to despise such as came forward to ruin one who had never hurt them. Recollect that when we fight for life and liberty we are not cold and prudent. For four years Lady Cowper and Lady Melbourne have supported Lord Byron, to the annoyance of William, recollect that Lady Holland behaved to William, as he thought contemptibly; and also observe that wrongs, crimes, follies, even the last, were raked up even from the days of infancy and brought forth to view without mercy. To write this novel was then my sole comfort, but before I published it I thought myself ruined past recall, and even then I took out all the passages I thought might reflect upon Lady Melbourne and many others. This is not said by way of excuse for what I have done, but merely explanation. Do not judge me with severity, for you cannot know half what I have suffered. And now, Lord Granville, with respect to going out: hear me, and ask yourself if I am to blame. William having once decidedly said: "I will stand by you or fall with you," it was my duty, however painful, to maintain my situation. You cannot but know the shabbiness of many: had I not appeared this year, I was lost. Some, very friendly, advised me to come out—amongst these Lady Salisbury, who has even been most good natured to me. I did not wish to appear to brave others, but merely to maintain myself. All have received me with only too much good nature. It is now, therefore, now that no interested motive, no mean dirty view of getting in or out of society, actuates me—that I thus write to you to ask, to sue even if necessary for pardon, for support, from you and from Harriet;[1] and be assured that if I did not see how anxious William is about it, for myself I should not care if I retired for ever. Besides, you know I am not worldly enough to take measures for what can be purchased at any time by a few balls and dinners. It is not therefore from interest I demand this, but for affection's sake, and because I cannot bear not to see Harriet and Georgiana as formerly. Be not over angry at my writing this, and believe me, Dear Lord Granville, whatever you are to me, ever, with respect and affection,—

Yrs. sincerely,
Caroline Lamb.

In 1817, Madame de Staël died, and, having lost one literary hero, Caroline found another in Italian writer Ugo Foscolo, whose Le ultime lettere di Jacopo Ortis *(1798) is sometimes considered the first modern Italian novel. Like Caroline, Foscolo was small and animated, with a hot temper.*[2] *Caroline invited him to dine and sent him letters containing her drawings and admiration*

2. Lady Caroline to Ugo Foscolo. [1817.]

Few things have pained me so much as your coldness of last night. Chance placed me near you, I found a seat and was rejoicing at the thought that you could spare a moment for a chat—nothing of the

[1] Harrio, Caroline's cousin, now Lord Granville's wife.

[2] So Samuel Carter Hall describes Foscolo in *Retrospect of a Long Life: From 1815 to 1883* 2 vols. (London: Bentley & Son, 1883), 1:99–100.

sort—you left me abruptly and hurt me very much [. . .] one could not exchange two words with you without gaining a great deal. Unfortunately whilst I was profiting, you were wasting your time. Therefore I have not badgered you to visit me, knowing that you would find better elsewhere. [. . .] Adieu, whenever it pleases you, come and see me at Brocket Hall. If you have a moment to spare, let it be offered to me to compensate for last night. William admires you and if I am worth nothing, he is worth a great deal

Caroline Lamb

Melbourne House.
Excuse my orthography.

Caroline must have understood why William felt depressed by his circumstances, still powerless to progress politically and unable to socialize freely unless he left Caroline at home.

3. Lady Caroline to Lady Melbourne.
[After 2 April 1817.]

Viscountess Melbourne

My Dear Lady Melbourne I have not been out since I saw you for I have thought William not very well & so extremely low that unless there is some cause for it which I am not aware of—I must attribute it to health as it is only the 3rd day that I have observed it [—] he says he wishes he was dead & the like [—] I think it would do him good to go in the Country but he seems not to like it [—] that [horror?] comes on at night & he is restless but no fever [. . .] I think he has a fancy that he shall die soon of an illness like Fox [—] I attribute all this to worry of mind & vexation—it was on this account I urg'd you to delay talking of change for unless Lord Melbourne wishes us to take a House now—there can be it seems to me no use to enter upon the subject just at present—but as I well know he ever imputes the basest motive to me & never since I was in this House believd that I did one thing from kindness or right feeling tell him that he need be under no sort of allarm he has the power to turn us out tomorrow if he chuses and as George Emily the Prince Lord Egremont[3] & all his friends advise it I hope he will be happier when he

[3] Lord Egremont was widely acknowledged to be William Lamb's father.

has given William he greatest pain he can inflict [. . .] I will never do any thing more that can harm William but when you turn us out of doors which Lord Melbourne has pledged himself to do [,] I find[,] to many—I owe it to all to publish as far as I can without involving those I love a full explanation of my conduct a full refutation of the calumnies that have been spread against me & my infamous book—and an exact account of Lord Byrons conduct for the last four years—[. . .] I do not like underhand measures—& I have written openly—trust me however I neither seek to deter you from your purpose nor to allarm you—I merely state a fact—as you all do—& God so deal with you all as you have dealt with me—I wish no worse—can I? tell Wm I want to see him particularly can he come?

She attempted to approach Lady Byron, offering advice—to no avail.

4. Lady Caroline to Lady Byron. [5 May 1817.]

My dear Lady Byron—

May I ask you how you are & may I also know whether you would permit me to see you a few moments—I wish very particularly to speak to you—you ought not I think ought not to refuse me—if you knew how sincere an admirer & friend I had been of yours you would not whatever my faults—entirely turn from me—perhaps you may one day know me well enough to think I deserve some little kindness from you—you have given me pain—I have thought you unkind—but I know you enough not to judge you by appearances—you may think the line of conduct you persue towards me deserv'd & yet be assured you are wrong—for on Earth I do believe—I am one of those most sincere towards you—& you may perhaps some day believe this though now you do not—I could I think be of use to you at this instant—I wish to be so—I only wish one moment to see you no selfish motive makes me ask it—if then it is not painful to you—either call on Lady Melbourne—afterwards see me or send for me to call one moment on you—believe me ever with respect & most true affection yrs Caroline Lamb

What I have to suggest indeed indeed may be of use—

Melbourne House Monday Evening—

Lady Me[lbourne]—asked me to go & see you but I never will till you send for me—or call for be assured it is not pour me [*illegible*] that I now ask for one moments interview—I never wish it known—if you mind it.

To Murray she described one of her humiliations.

5. Lady Caroline to John Murray. MAY 1817.

[. . .] I must tell you of my adventures tonight—I set out stark Mad in white satin as Tilburnia to go to see Don Juan seized by the statue & scarce was my dear fatal name pronounced Lady Caroline Lamb when some Jocose footman said ["]sooner Lady Caroline Wolf["] at this too just witticism several warm defenders sallied forth amongst the same precious herd, whilst they were all fighting I was very near kidnapped by 2 Hack chair men who insisted on carrying me each into his respective chair—I being all the time vainly desirous of getting in & not out of the opera House—it so chanced that I was very fine having dined out in diamonds & feathers—when I therefore got safe up with a crowd of civil plumed attendants my unfortunate dog that long car'd for dog covered with mud like Lord Somethings rat—appeared entering the vestibule—at this sight soldiers & servants shouted forth—["]a fox[!"] and began hissing it down [—] Judge of my situation I was either obliged to give up this dear shabby cur who had followed my carriage & me—or own a friend in such disguise that few had dared do so—the butler was however my choice being much too frightened & late after all these adventures I turned back to find my carriage about carried away by a crowd of [link?] boys & drunken chair men one of whom to the indignation of the rest constantly vociferating this is my Lady—yr Lady d– –n you—yes my Lady.—& sure enough he like the dog proved a mendicant pensioner when a blaze of light showed him to me like the ghost—now fare thee well excuse all this nonsense—& come & see me

yrs the
Apostate [. . .]

To Michael Bruce she once again appealed for comfort.

6. Lady Caroline to Michael Bruce. 3 JUNE 1817.

Mr. Michael Bruce, Esq.

If I could believe what you say respecting Lord Byron it would indeed make me miserable as it is I cried for an hour upon reading your letter—but I believe it was chiefly because my mind & body are both weakened—I have so often & so long been the dupe of what I call the meanest of all Arts—that of attempting to create a strong interest by

Sketch by Lady Caroline in her Commonplace book showing a child caressing a dog. By kind permission of the John Murray Archive.

affecting to be on the point of going away from your Country or in an allarming state of Health—that I unwillingly allow myself to feel again for him—& it is at all events of very little importance to him whether I do or no but amidst all the better feelings that continuously recur to my mind—I wish contempt for his conduct were not so strong [—] human weakness cannot endure the thought that we have sacrificed every thing here & possibly hereafter—for one we despise—I should be the last in the World to use such an expression towards any one—& assuredly towards a person who has such high talents but I do not think him the person he appears to others & instead of conceiving him to be the prey of a fine daring spirit—or even strong passion I believe him to be capable of acting all that interests & and to be mean—& groveling where it is for his own advantage [. . .] I believe our hearts & minds make our Health & diseases—no wonder then Ld Byron is in such an allarming state—but it is not so—he will live to make more people miserable—to wring other hearts & to prove that the brightest & most beautiful Talents added to every charm of person & mind & every art of seduction to give them force—are but so many curses & causes of degradation if misapplied—I am unhappy—write to me—Bruce of the desert

7. Lady Caroline to Michael Bruce. [1817.]

[. . .] We have an old Woman here on our grounds who is eighty [—] I asked her the other day what part of her life was the happiest & she made me this very singular but good answer—the last 30 years—for before that I either vex'd myself about what I had—or what I had not—I also cared much about children—who are now dead, or friends who did not care as much for me—but now nothing vexes me—for I value nothing. I am concerned about nothing for I possess nothing I have my health—& believe in the mercy of God—I have never been very wicked—but for what I did that was wrong—I have long since repented & amended—I wish to live for I am truly happy—& when I die—I have no doubt I shall be more so—

The name of this Woman is Dame Nash. She is very clever & lovely & says her adventures might make a Book about as big I make no doubt as that one of which my son Benjamin was delivered after so long & painful a labour[4]—pray write to me some time & believe me ever yours with all that is right for a very good Woman to feel—& not one thought more—who writes every thing you hear of Lord Byron [—] God grant him His blessing and forgiveness—I cannot mine no not even in Death

He has the curses of hearts that are broken of souls that are torn from within & pain on him by night & day he is wicked cruel—mean—coldly cruel—& most Barbarous I do not think I can ever say to myself that I forgive him—as a good Christian would he has behaved so very brutally to those in his power he has no honour—no faith in any transaction—do tell me why you say he is ill—after all I trust in God he is not ill—

She tried to draw comfort from the mercurial Foscolo.

---

[4] Henri Benjamin Constant de Rebecque (1767–1830), Madame de Staël's former lover and author of the introspective and semiautobiographical novel, *Adolphe* (1816).

8. Lady Caroline to Ugo Foscolo. November—December 1817.

Melbourne House. Tuesday.

Mon tres cher Foscolo, I beg you not to give way to hypochondria, I was in that condition for nine months. I was as in a trance at that time and I have never been able to wake up since. These will hardly appear to be the words of a comforter but you have enough spirit to rouse yourself, and you will do so sooner than you think. Do try the regime that really gave me new life—horse exercise. There is nothing to compare with riding, dancing, or some other exercise. Do take care of yourself and let me know your news from time to time. If when you go to Brighton you feel better, come here afterwards. The weather is fine and Mr. Lamb, Doctor Lee,[5] and I will look after you. I only write these few words without expecting a reply and only to say God bless you before your journey

Caroline Lamb

When Byron's Beppo *was published anonymously, she immediately identified the author and wrote Hobhouse about having had a literally visceral response to the poem.*

9. Lady Caroline to J.C. Hobhouse. [March? 1818.]

and so you have never heard of Beppo—I think you said so at Devonshire House supper. Now Heaven fail in granting me pardon for all my offenses if it is not by himself, & in his very best wit as good as any thing Swift ever wrote a flatterer would say better. I read it having taken an Emetic for that head ache which troubled me so much the night I sat beside you & I must own it did delight me so that the Emetic faild in affecting me—now though this is not a pretty illustration of what should be felt in reading Poetry—believe me it is emphatic & expresses much more than fairer words—after all it would be kind in you to tell me if it is his and how he is and whether he is ever again coming to England & when I shall see that

[5] Doctor Robert Lee had joined the household 5 November 1817. As Hilary Dickinson has said, Lee was "a man of high principles but little warmth and sympathy." Augustus was "singularly unfortunate in the personality of the man who was selected to be his tutor" (Dickinson, "Augustus Lamb (1807–1836) and His Tutor, Robert Lee," 52).

new child[6]—I who so rapturously so absurdly & yet so sincerely adored the first for though I hope I hate that man whose genius lifts him up to Heaven but whose unkindness to some who were [*illegible*] to him makes him I think every thing that is cruel and bad—yet as I am sure he has done so little to entitle him to happiness hereafter, I do from my heart like to hear he is well & enjoying himself here—you who have humanity in you may let me know something of him and be assured I shall not on that account consider myself as in the least forgiven or liked by you—besides I have done with every thing of the sort now am grown sickly old judicious & look but very little out of the direct road that leads to the grave. Every one around me seems hastening there & people look sad enough to make even a gay heart melancholy—at Almacks[7] the old were grown grey the middle aged ugly & there was not a youthful or happy look even on one young face—no wonder you preferred staying away—I know you live in other society I know also the state of your feelings for me—perfect cold indifference were it not for a spice of dislike peppered over with a little rankling and yet contemptuous displeasure—now remember life is short—forgive—for there is not on earth one would go further or do more to serve you & him than I would & pray observe that I have been hardly used myself, not to speak of being left cut mocked at teazed—I was nearly sent to a Mad House—at the very time I saw you before that Book[8] which did me no greater disservice to my mind than hurting me in your opinion I think Lord Byron has behaved rather generously to one—he had the power to retaliate in a manner that I could never have shewn my face again—I was in his power entirely—I have done every thing at every time to offend him most. I have besides which is worse teazed him it is rather Manly rather noble—something a little like what I believed him once—not lifting up his sword to crush a fly, for in my mind in Talent in power I am but as such to him—though God knows I think in attachment in generosity I am as far above him if you think it not beneath you to forgive a Woman who asks you to do so & almost confesses herself in the wrong—do so at once—I should die happier & perhaps live to prove to you that I am neither presumptuous nor ungrateful.

yrs most sincerely
CL

---

6 Allegra Clairmont (1817–1822), Byron's illegitimate daughter by Claire Clairmont.

7 The club controlled by Lady Holland and other members of the "gynocracy."

8 That is, *Glenarvon*.

How very very clever I think Beppo—I am quite sure it is his—& still more that Mr. Frere never could have written any thing like it

Lady Melbourne died on 6 April 1818, and Caroline lost both an antagonist and a protector, for her mother-in-law had on many occasions tried to foster Caroline's career simply for William's sake.

10. Lady Caroline to J.C. Hobhouse. [April 1818.]

My dear Mr. HobHouse

I know that you will feel that loss, we have felt so severely—and I think it will please you to know that in almost the last conversation I had with her she spoke kindly of you—you had seen her lately enough to prepare you for this event—but it is her loss & not the suddenness of it that all who knew her must regret for I think a kinder heart & a fairer mind were never to be found any where than there—God bless you—if ever you like to come to this mournfull House remember that whilst William and I are in it you will be welcome.

Yours,
Caroline Lamb

That fall, Caroline heard the news that barrister and legal reformer Sir Samuel Romilly, depressed over the death of his wife, had killed himself.

11. Lady Caroline to Ugo Foscolo. 30 October 1818.

I am grieved at leaving town without seeing you—did you receive my drawing? I waited for you all Tuesday, why have you not been to see me?

Oh, Foscolo, here was I writing to you like this and here is the news of Sir Samuel Romilly's death—I cannot write another word. How heart-rending! Oh God what a world we live in! So happy one day and then so sad! Please come to see me at Brocket, I will try to make you so happy, I will do everything for you, and you will be so welcome.

Do come
Toujours avec sincerite et attachement
Votre Agneau[9]

---

[9] Literally: "Your Lamb."

Romilly's suicide prompted Caroline to write once more Byron. She had apparently forgotten that Romilly was despised by Byron for having advised Lady Byron while under obligation as a barrister to Byron himself. There is no record of a response from Byron.

12. Lady Caroline to Lord Byron.
[OCTOBER–NOVEMBER 1818.]

permit me to write you a few words—you will see by the papers and by letters from England that Sir Samuel Romilly is dead—it was in a moment of phrenzy brought on by grief that he did this—his children they say feel it dreadfully—it is a cruel thing to do—but he had lost his mind I am sure at the time—never do you do this Lord Byron never whatever may happen it is a cruel thing remember it—if even a dog is left on earth who loves you—but I did not write to you to say this—I wrote because his death brought you to my mind—as every thing does—& I remember you at the time when Percival was shot & how much you felt it, your coming here—your seeing William affected—your being deeply so yourself all are present to me as if it were but yesterday, and though every thing is changed since—yet events like these make time between pass & restore former sentiments—

it is but a few months ago we saw Romilly surrounded by friends—happy without being over elated, but much moved when he passed Brookes & then I thought of you—& thought had you been there none would have rejoiced more—& now it appears to me that you more than any here except it be William Lamb can feel for him—yet he is much censured—at the time of the death of Perceval[10] when I had the misfortune to consider you as the dearest friend I possessed on earth when I had willingly died to serve you and felt for you what I truly believe no one ever before did or will—you promised me—do you remember you promised that whatever might happen, whatever my conduct might be you would never cease to be my friend—if this ever occurs to your mind if one remembrance of the past ever comes back to plead for me—forgive me before I die. I have sinned against every one on earth and against you—but from my soul I suffer for all I have done and accuse no one but myself for all I have and shall suffer—may God protect & restore

[10] Lady Caroline harks back to the assassination of Prime Minister Spencer Perceval by John Bellingham in the House of Commons, when Byron had stayed up all night to watch the hanging at dawn. See chapter 4, letter 22.

you—may I live to see you one day return & become all you may be—& whether you believe it or not—In absence in enmity I am & ever have been your sincere and [interested?] friend—

I saw Scrope Davies the other day and Lady F. Webster—they came here in the Evening. HobHouse is at Brighton—your child I am told is clever and beautiful—Lady Byron ill and sorrowful. Lady Noel [Byron's mother-in-law] who came to Brocket to see me about three weeks back seemed proud of that child—and yet said it was very like its father—& seemed not sorry as she said it—she mentioned that the way its head was put upon its neck was like you—God bless you my Lord—the post is going I am grieved for the past—Heaven preserve you—William Lamb though it be strange likes you and almost cries when he reads any thing you have written. Many like you here—and you are dear to your country tho' it, perhaps, is not dear to you—poor Romilly it breaks my heart to think what he has suffered forgive my writing this we are all ill and may soon be dead, and why should enmity be the only thing to live and thrive.

Caroline's arch enemy, Lady Cowper now softened her tone toward her sister-in-law in order to alleviate the social ostracism of William.

13. Lady Caroline to Lady Emily Cowper. [1819.]

I do not know that I much deserve your kind letter my Dearest Emily I do not either know that I have an excuse to offer for any thing I have said or done now or formerly—I am imperious I am I own irritated and irritable but be assured I am in fact more affectionate and more really sensible of my faults than you can well believe I thought George all along had said things on purpose to mortify me [—] I was irritated with him at Brocket I thought him luke warm about William & that he spoke of him saying the whigs did not support him & much else above all too I was vexd at some expressions Caro had made use of to William about my Mother whose invariable generous kind conduct to the D[uche]ss[11] deserved some gratitude I thought but indeed Emily I am of too violent a temper—all is my fault it is none of yours & wherever I am I must make others unhappy which makes me so ten times more—will you believe it your merely writing kindly has quite renderd me

[11] That is, the former Lady Elizabeth Foster, who had been the mistress of the fifth Duke of Devonshire, then married him after her great friend, the Duchess of Devonshire, Georgiana, had died in 1806.

weak & foolish [—] I would do anything you wished and if indeed you will feel some little affection for me some compassion I should say for that my temper is so unfortunately violent I will be as gentle as forbearing as anxious to please you all as possible in future—thank you for this explanation thank you for your extreme kindness and forbearance—thank God every day that you have so sweet so delightful a character you know not the misery of the contrary—one thing further make my peace with George I ever felt for him more than for any other connected with him and have the sincerest attachment & respect for him—I feel I have been deeply to blame many many things surrounded & irritated me—I had friends I would have died for you were one of my earliest you know not how very much I loved you once—it is this it is feeling too keenly it is suspecting evil perhaps never intended that makes me so harsh so violent so odious forgive me Dearest Emily in your hands I put myself this once plead with me for George bring him to dine here tomorrow & by Heavens I will cut my throat before I will suffer my tongue to say one ill word again provoke me as you please [. . .] ever my Dearest Emily your most grateful and most attached friend

Caroline Lamb

As part of her campaign to be reinstated in her family and social circle, Lady Caroline canvassed for George Lamb in a parliamentary election against John Cam Hobhouse in February 1819. George enjoyed a satisfying, if short-lived, victory in part because of the help from his despised sister-in-law.

14. Lady Caroline to Lord Byron.
[February–March 1819.]

Do you remember when Jeannie Deans went to London for her sister the gentle Gertie Robertson[12] gave her a [*illegible*] among the Robbers. Now you should send me one as in my Brisk movements I meet with insults from yr friends of the lower sort which I am sure their master would never sanction—as I must say to you that since I have known you I have ever found you to see all that is honourable kind gentlemanlike

[12] Jeanie Deans, the main character in Sir Walter Scott's *The Heart of Midlothian* (1818), refuses to give false testimony that would have saved her sister, Effie, who has been wrongly charged with child-murder. Jeanie travels to London and obtains a pardon for her sister, who then marries Geordie (not Gertie) Robertson, whose real name is George Staunton, an aristocrat.

and as I think I owe you nothing but good will do feel assured & with this letter do testify that if I exert my humble mite against you it is but for my Relations & Party[13] and not in malice God knows—for whoever may win or lose I shall never feel towards my son—otherwise than I can have done a sinner an affectionate—let me add a grateful friend.

I think it unfair their not letting George speak & all the people say they are kind to stop him from it but I do not believe this.[14] I really believe you wish everything done in a handsome & gentlemanlike way—you have yr India I hear they are eager for you—forgive your Mother if circumstances makes her the other way—I hope you are I am early & active—more so I think than any one but yr self & Sir Francis [Burdett] who speaks heavens like an Angel enough to seduce even me from my allegiance—once more I beg for a pass—& that kindness you shewed when last we met which whatever be the event I shall ever feel for you—

15. Lady Caroline to J.C. Hobhouse.
[February–March 1819.]

I know that during Elections songs & squibs are fair on each side & much bad wit & many severe things must be said—but I am sure that neither you nor Sir Frances Burdett can see without disgust what is now handed about and sent here & every where and must be sanctioned by some of the people in your Committee. What should you think if any of our people were to Vilify yr Mother yr sisters Lady Burdett Lady Hanah or any of the friends interested for you—every one has some vulnerable point no human being in person and Character is wholly free from either ridicule or imputation raillery may be permitted even Caricatures & jests—but do you think to us who have so lately lost a kind & dear friend like Lady Melbourne[15] a person you will know who stood by Byron

[13] In other words, helping both her brother-in-law, George Lamb, and the Whig party by campaigning against Hobhouse in the House of Commons elections of February and March, 1819. The seat in Westminster had been vacated by Romilly's death, and Caroline threw herself into the election, hoping to gain favor with the Lambs and attract Byron's attention by defeating his friend.

[14] George Lamb's eventual success in campaigning for the seat left vacant by Sir Samuel Romilly's suicide in October 1818 was hard-won, with literal mud-slinging. One of Caroline's pages was cut by a stone flung at her carriage in St. James's Street (Palmerston, *Letters of Lady Palmerston*, 19).

[15] Lady Melbourne had died 6 April 1818.

through all his errors & sorrows do you think we can see her name used in a coarse & vulgar & disagreeable manner without feeling most deeply hurt—I know you are too clever & far too much of a Gentleman to have any thing to do with the common placards sent about in the way this is—but as I read part of it in the Statesman I think you could at all events stop its being inserted and ask yourself what your feelings would be if you found the grossest insults & imputations sanctioned by any of our Party against yr Birth or yr relations perhaps you care the less as you may be exempt from every imputation—I assure you no personal fear of what you may say of me actuates this—I am I know in yr power in this respect—but for that very reason I feel perfectly secure against me you never will permit attacks of this sort—then why against one far better & Dearer & who has ever been to you & to him a kind and most firm friend—and is now no more be assured I think it will be unlike all I believe of you if you do not find means to stop it and do not tell me you cannot—because I am sure you can & will

yrs ever sincerely,
Caroline Lamb

CHAPTER EIGHT

Novel Endeavors

Letters, 1820–1823

With Lady Cowper's help, Caroline sought to rehabilitate her social life. Emily got her sister-in-law back onto the list for Almack's balls, mostly in sympathy for William, of course. Shortly thereafter, in early 1820, Lady Caroline arrived at a masquerade dressed as Don Juan and accompanied by several pages dressed as devils. She had recruited extra pages from her contacts at Drury Lane: "I must have a Devil—could you come with me as such. I want a very dear Devil not in bad taste."[1] *Byron later heard about it and wrote Murray from Ravenna: "I only wonder that she went so far as 'the Theatre' for 'the Devils' having them so much more natural at home—or if they were busy—she might have borrowed the bitch her Mother's—Lady Bessborough to wit——The hack whore of the last half century."*[2]

She continued to hope that Augustus might gain enough intellectual and social control to take his place as heir to William's estate. She was also anxious to help George Lamb once again in a parliamentary campaign. John Murray was consulted about this and everything else. "I am thinking of nothing but elections," she wrote him in February 1820—and then in the same week: "I inclose you the case of my dear Boys illness and wish you to ask Doctor Blake what he thinks could be done."[3]

---

[1] This note is attached to a letter in French from Lady Caroline to Ugo Foscolo, and it is endorsed by Francis Cohen, scholar and translator, as "given to me by Ugo Foscolo, 24th Dec[ember] 1819." The Carl H. Pforzheimer Collection of Shelley and His Circle, the New York Public Library, Astor, Lenox and Tilden Foundations.

[2] *Byron's Letters and Journals*, 7:169.

[3] Lady Caroline Lamb to John Murray. February 1820. Murray Archive.

A report circulated in the London newspapers in late August that Byron had returned to England incognito. Lady Caroline pumped Murray for news, but Byron was not in England.[4]

1. Lady Caroline to John Murray. AUGUST 1820.

Brockett Hall

My Dear Sir

you have never written to tell me about him now did you know the pain & agony this has given me you had not been so remiss [. . .] [tell] me how he looks what he says, if he be grown fat if he is no uglier than he used to be if he is good-humoured or cross-grained putting his brows down—if his hair curls or is straight as somebody said if he has seen Hobhouse[5] if he is going to stay long, if you went to Dover as you intended and a great deal more which if you had the smallest tact or aught else you would have written long ago for as to me I shall certainly not see him neither do I care he should know that I ever asked after him only—it is from mere curiosity I should like to hear all you can tell me about him—pray come here immediately.

yrs
CL

Caroline initiated a literary correspondence with Amelia Opie (1769–1853), the prolific novelist satirized by Thomas Love Peacock as "Miss *Poppyseed*" *in* Headlong Hall *(1816), and publisher and philosopher William Godwin.*

2. Lady Caroline to Mrs. Amelia Opie. 1820.[6]

My Dear Mrs. Opie, May I Hope you will do me the favour of coming to me on Tuesday Litterally to no Party—a very small society—all

---

[4] Byron heard the rumors and mentions them to Countess Guiccioli in a letter of 9 September 1820 (*Byron's Letters and Journals*, 7:173).

[5] Hobhouse had stood for his principles against government repression by admitting authorship of a reformist pamphlet so that the printer would not go to prison. He was jailed in Newgate at the time Caroline wrote this letter.

[6] Mrs. Opie wrote on this letter: "1st letter I ever received from Lady C Lamb 1820." Later, she told Caroline how much she admired the tune and lyrics of "Waters of Elle," a song from *Glenarvon*: "I often sing it to my lute harp, & with encreased pleasure because my recollection of you is rendered more vivid by it & as I sing your words I *think of you*" (Bessborough Papers, C1 D4, folder 201).

yr friends,—& if you like to bring a gentle man such are the rules you have a right—provided he is not a dandy—

I have been reading for the first time 2 of yr Tales & am delighted with them. They not only amuse & interest & affect extremely but they amend—and it must be a delightful reflection for a Person who has written for others to feel that they have done good instead of harm. You must tell me when I see you whether you will refuse to give me some of your unpublished poetry. I will not allow you to answer this in a letter—refusals are more easy upon paper than in person. Let me Hope you will come on Tuesday—

Believe me

yrs with respect & truth,
CL

3. Lady Caroline to William Godwin. 15 May 1821.

Brockett near Welwyn

I cannot express to you how pleased I was to see yr note and how much I regret not being able to meet you upon the day you name as I intend staying at Brockett Hall until June to enjoy this most beautiful season of the year. I wish I could induce you to come here instead if that is possible I will send my carriage to Barnet to fetch you any day but just at present—when we shall be with people—write and tell me all you would have said or half—[. . .] yours is a beautiful style—I believe the saying so to you is the repeating what has been said by every one for years—forgive it—I am too calm and stupid & comfortable to think of any thing new or witty believe me However with much interest & respect yrs

CL

To the consternation of her family, Caroline focused upon writing more novels. In addition to Godwin, Opie, and Foscolo, Caroline contacted other well-known writers about her aspirations, including Thomas Malthus (1766–1834), famous for his Essay on the Principle of Population *(1793).*

4. Lady Caroline to Thomas Malthus. [1821–1822?]

Brocket Hall

Dear Mr Malthus—I have been months thinking in what manner I could ask a favour of you but I never yet found courage—it is not that you look as if you would be unforgiving but I feel I have no claim on the good nature I am sure you possess—now I will not waste your time by a longer preface but you must promise two things—one that you will refuse me at once if you do not like to do what I ask and at all events that you will keep my secret—every one longs to see themselves in black & white & even the lowest of us are ambitious of this honour though they generally repent it—I have set my heart on it but could only aspire to write a novel & considering the very bad ones daily appear it did not seem presumptuous to make the attempt—but having tried I find that it is far from as easy as I expected & my vanity makes me a little anxious to have some one who has talents & good nature sufficient to point out many faults & set me at least in the way of Succeeding—not that I mean ever to acknowledge it & particularly I wish no one of my friends or family to hear of it before they read it that I may hear what is said—now therefore tell me—have you a little moment of your precious time to waste & if so may a mere Butterfly lay claim to some portion of it—& if this is granted will you read with an eye to what others would think & not to what you might from your nature like to say to a "Woman"—as I found a novel difficult I have tried two—and since the Fashion is to call every thing in the manner of Pride & prejudice, sense & sensibility, I have named mine Principle & passion—but I have made it two stories—principle or the Brothers is full of events rather terrific & in Monk Lewis's[7] style—all the people whether the Daemons or the angels male or female act from determination—passion or the Impulse of the moment which I request you to take charge of is quite without events or story & therefore requires the greater care in point of language & manner—I should like it above all to be free from common place ideas—& vulgarities & mock wit—now you will think me very vain & very presumptuous in addressing myself to you—it would be like a person asking Buonaparte to dress a doll—or paint a skreen [. . .] I feel quite a dread now I have written this—all I ask is that you will burn it & forget the request if it is improper & any how do not name it to another—believe me

Very sincerely yrs
Caroline Lamb

Malthus, whom Caroline had met at a ball in 1810, apparently replied that he was unfit for the job of advising her on her novel and directed her to another reader ("Lord John"). Caroline replied that she would "follow advice," though she was

[7] M.G. Lewis (1775–1818), author of the gothic novel, *The Monk* (1796).

"very disappointed." Instead of Lord John, however, she once again consulted Ugo Foscolo.

5. Lady Caroline to Ugo Foscolo. [1821.]

Thank you for yr beautiful kind letter. May I ask a favour? I have written a tale, not a novel, it is full of mistakes, and I feel that perhaps it is no good, but in any case Murray has been so kind as to print it for you to read. Do me this favour, let your Maid-of-all work read it to you and tell me frankly "I like or do not like this or that." Only you and Mr. Lamb have the sound judgement and admirable simplicity to tell the truth. Without any flattery you will be doing me a real favour by reading this little work for me—but don't speak of it, not a word! I hope you will not refuse me, believe me always my Dear Foscolo

Yr Friend
Caroline Lamb

In fall 1821, Lady Bessborough traveled in Italy with her youngest son, Willy, and his wife Barbara and little boy. Caroline received the ominous news from her mother that little Henry Ponsonby was seriously ill.

6. Lady Caroline to Lady Bessborough. [September–October 1821.]

Dearest of own hearts blood thank you for your letter [. . .] I hope little Henry is better—yr account of him makes me very anxious [. . .] Dearest, I would you were in England. There is a strange wild story called Ada Reis, written, they say, by an American,[8] and if I can get Murray to let me send you a rough printed proof of it, I will, as it will amuse you but I understand that he minds particularly its being seen or getting about, so if it goes to you do take care [. . .] The Duchess is expected here soon & Caro [George] immediately—I hope We shall all meet this year at Paris—

ever yours
Caroline Lamb

Tuesday, but too late for the post.

---

[8] *Ada Reis* was Lady Caroline's own work, her third and last novel, which would be published by John Murray in 1823.

Murray had printed special advance copies of the manuscript of Ada Reis but he hesitated to bring it out, much to Caroline's frustration.

7. Lady Caroline to John Murray. 26 November. 1821.

Private I implore—!

My dear sir answer this question fairly have you regrets at having undertaken Ada Reis—I have reread it and altered some things I wish it to be printed immediately—and you might let it steal out quietly—pray show it no one—and if you really upon your heart dislike doing it as I know you are not over fond of a row & although I think it will fall like a lump of lead into a lake—yet as there is no knowing only say let me off & make some argument with whoever I choose to name by which the immense expense I have put you to may be remunerated & let it come out else where—I own that I should have felt flattered at having it with your name—but if you really think it might be unpleasant just say so—now I beg you not to be offended at what I say and above all not to show my letter to any on Earth—there is one other thing I have to tell you as Graham Hamilton[9] will soon be out I much wished this to be at the same time—but I leave all to you—only answer as frankly as I write and say yes or no [. . .] I have also written a short account some years ago of some of the people I saw & liked most[10]—This also I will send you but may I depend [. . .] upon no living person ever hearing one word of it [—] recollect how sacred a thing letters are & what scandal it would give were I known to have done any such thing—but as I wish what I have written one day published to whom could I safely entrust it but to you—when therefore you have perfect leisure read it—you will perhaps be surprised and pleased to find not one word of scandal or satire in it as to the letters there are some from Ld B[yron] some from William[,] my Mother[,] Sydney Smith[,] Lady Holland the Duke of Dev[onshire]—and they will do no dishonour to the writers—this letter I consider as of confidence & written in confidence. Do me the favour therefore to send it me back as I did Cain & will the memoirs[11] & pray remember if Moore

---

[9] Henry Colburn would publish Lady Caroline's second novel, *Graham Hamilton*, in 1822.

[10] The fate of this manuscript, if Lady Caroline ever sent it, is not known.

[11] Murray had given the manuscript or printer's proof of *Cain*, Byron's verse-drama, to Lady Caroline to read. More importantly, he had let her read Byron's infamous memoirs, and this letter shows she had them in her possession in fall 1821. Murray, Hobhouse, and Moore burned the memoirs after Byron's death in 1824.

Hobhouse or any one else see it it will be serious to me I ask you to be cautious in the same of all you hold dear on earth and pray answer me immediately about Ada Reis—I am resolved about its coming out [. . .]

Henry Ponsonby had died, and news had come that Lady Bessborough was extremely unwell. Caroline had a premonition of what was about to happen—indeed, her mother had already died when she wrote this letter.

8. Lady Caroline to John Murray. 27 November 1821.

Sir, Is it not strange when I wrote my letter to you in the night and found it was upon black paper I felt alarmed—today is come news of grief to me—my Dearest Mother & Brother & Lady Barbara have suffered much in their way to Florence from the sickness and lastly the death of lady Barbara's son a beautiful Boy of 2 years—I know you will feel for them—God grant my Mother Health and on her life mine hangs[12] therefore my arranging my papers thus for you may be an omen that you will sooner than you think for receive them in my narrative there is a letter of yours and a few words about you—let these pass they redound to yr. credit and as every thing in after years is brushed up I should like it to be known that in no one instance you flattered or encouraged vice—yr letter is really beautiful [. . .]

9. Lady Caroline to John Murray. 28 November 1821.

My Dear Sir—for Heavens sake do enquire at Ld Bathursts and Mr Arbuthnotts if there are any accounts from Italy. I think there are letters for me sometimes they remain in the offices—you cannot conceive since I wrote to you & this enclosed how dreadfully anxious I have been my dearest Mother is very ill—[. . .] I must just tell you an act of kindness of William Lamb—he has been looking over and correcting Ada Reis for me—he is most kind & believe me I feel it my dear sir if in truth I have yr answer and you receive my trunk & letters & papers sealed. May I rely on yr solemn promise that whilst I live without leave no eye but yours shall look at them

yours most truly
CL

---

[12] Lady Bessborough had already died on 11 November 1821, but Lady Caroline did not yet know.

There is a Mr Smith in Ld Bathurst office who often hears from Dr. Walker—Perhaps he has now do I entreat you ask

News of Lady Bessborough's death finally arrived on 28 November 1821.

10. Lady Caroline to Lady Emily Cowper. [AFTER 28 NOVEMBER 1821.]

Dearest Emily

I am quite calm but I can't see to write much—Dr. Lee has copied my dear Brother Wms letter to me[13] [—] send this copy from me to Georgiana Morpeth when you have read it & tell her to send it to the Duke from me—pray do this—& do not any of you come a day sooner on my account calm and quiet is all for me now yr dear Brothers kindness is very great—I only heard all this last night.

11. Lady Caroline to the Sixth Duke of Devonshire. 25 DECEMBER 1821.

Christmas day—

all left this House at 8 this morning—my poor Brothers were deeply affected—I do not know whether I am or not—I feel a calm I never yet felt [. . .] you yourself will attend my Dear Mama—it has pleas'd me more than is reasonable—Harriet came here yesterday but was so much agitated—I did not like to see her—I was ill only once & that was yesterday & kind Miss [Selina] Trimmer who came only for an instant says she will leave me no more till all is done that must be—her staying thus when most inconvenient to herself & her coming with me & her being so pleas'd to see you makes me hope you will not mind this addition to our mournful family I am ever yours my own & I may say from my heart Dearest dearest Cousin—
yrs
Caroline Lamb

[13] William Ponsonby wrote Lady Caroline on 12 November 1821, right after Lady Bessborough died: "I dread, my dearest sister, the effect which the sad intelligence you will have heard before you receive this, may have upon you . . ." A copy of this letter in an unknown hand is held in the Devonshire MSS. Chatsworth [UK], sixth Duke's Group f. 599.

12. Lady Caroline to the Sixth Duke of Devonshire.
28 December 1821.

I trust I shall be able to do all I ought but human nature is weak[—]I am so & suppose I feel that I cannot do what Miss Trimmer has been suggesting is right—suppose I really cannot will you promise to forgive me if after all I fail—& do not go[—]it makes a great difference to me—this public meeting of the Funeral & sitting by it at the same time I will tomorrow tell you how I feel only leave it open for me not if I find I can not—I should like also to know exactly what will take place—pray tell me all—

ever yrs
Car Lamb

Caroline was, as she had warned her family, unable to attend her mother's funeral.

13. Lady Caroline to Frederick or William Ponsonby.
[December 1821.]

Dearest Brother

I depend upon you that I shall once more see those dear remains of our own kindest Mother before they are removed—Tupper assures me I am only very nervous & his draughts are to make me quite well—so that I shall wait till you fetch me down—

14. Lady Caroline to Mrs. Amelia Opie.
1 January 1822.

Brocket Hall

You will be surprised and vexd when I tell you that after arriving at Derby I was not well and did not go[14]—I remained in Bed [—] a kind friend read the service to me [&] I heard the Bell and even the organ [. . .] I have lost such a friend—next to William I loved her better than anything in life—but if it please God to spare him & I can grow good

[14] As noted, Caroline failed to attend her mother's funeral.

enough to dare die—I shall not consider myself as unhappy besides which I have passed such a very happy life & enjoyed so many blessings & so much kindness that it is wrong to repine [. . .] I wrote two stories lately—it was my wish you should have seen them—I think your judgment so good that if you were to [say] burn them they will do mischief or alter such passages I would do it—but I know it is a great torment looking over others writings & and the writers vanity is often mortified if truth be spoken yet I believe I should not in this respect. With respect and truth,

Lady Caroline Lamb,

The story of my stories is this—I was ad[jured?] as I will write to write a simple proper story within certain bounds & rules [. . .] Genius is not necessarily the companion of the disorderly & odd—& I fear my wild story is not in good taste.

15. Lady Caroline to William Godwin. 3–5 March 1822.

Sir,

May I after a long silence ask after your Health. Mine is neither well nor ill but the loss I have experienced is irreparable[15]—never was anyone kinder. However it is so & there an end—What I wish to ask you is simply this will you look me out a few of your elementary Books for Augustus who owing to his illness has not until now begun Latin or Greek. [. . .] Mr. Lamb has been all kindness to me & it is for me he goes now & then in this way to Brockett when the H[ouse] of Commons lets out its House. I remain ever with respect & truth

Sincerely yours
Caroline Lamb

In 1822, Lady Caroline published Graham Hamilton, *her second novel with Henry Colburn. She had two copies especially bound for herself and her husband, but told Colburn that "publishing has more pain with it than pleasure—suppose it be reckoned stupid—bad—How can I bear it?" She continued frustrated that her books were published anonymously. "It was my wish to put my name," she reminded Colburn, "I had rather stand by what I write however bad, but as I*

[15] That is, her mother's death.

must consider others [. . .]" She had several pieces of fiction under way, including a story to be titled "Rose & Mary." "In case I die," she told her publisher, "I wish to tell you what I want to be done with the 100£ for Rose & Mary. I want you to have it secured with what interest it can for an orphan child I have adopted and called Ellinor Mowbray—it is none of my own I swear but of a friends." Colburn obliged Caroline by printing a few copies of a small book that collected all the song lyrics in Glenarvon.[16]

16. Lady Caroline to William Godwin. 18 April 1822.

Brocket Hall

Thank you for being pleased with your visit and not displeased with Graham [Hamilton]. The circumstances of my writing it—and the Tale I wish you to see, were these. Ugo Foscolo said try if you like to write—to take one simple plot describe one character as I have done in my Jacobo Ortis [—] do not seek events—if you find them in yr way take them—I said I would try but the feeling was like writing a letter upon ruled paper and to ease myself I wrote Ada Reis during this time which pleased me better but which I fear is nonsense—after all I had better read than write and what were better than all, I read in a chinese book today—converse with clever people when I say a chinese Book I mean a book with 2 chinese stories in it the one is very curious & amusing about Too and Twan—it is called the "Shadows in the Water" two people kept separate fall in love thus by seeing each others shadows—William is certainly not a person who lets himself out kindly he is really shy—very very shy an odd thing for a man who has liv'd as he has much in the World but not having been abroad & having liv'd with a set of people he knows intimately I think he very seldom speaks much with those he seldom sees he was however very much pleasd with you & yr stories were not I assure you lost upon him—perhaps when the fine weather & flowers come back you will pay us another little visit—pray do & at all events thank you for yr good nature upon this occasion—I hope to hear from you soon you interested me very much about Coleridge—I wish I had ever known him—his translation of Wallenstein[17] is in my opinion perfectly beautiful [. . .]

---

[16] Lady Caroline to Henry Colburn. [1822.] Victoria and Albert Museum Forster Collection MSS vol. 28. #48.E.22.

[17] Coleridge had translated Friedrich Schiller's *Wallenstein* from the German as *The Piccolomini* and *Death of Wallenstein* in 1800.

In 1822, Caroline exchanged a number of letters with her cousin G about medicines and the psychology of good health.

17. Lady Caroline to Georgiana, Lady Morpeth, Future Sixth Countess of Carlisle. [1822.]

Dearest G—as I cannot call on you and talk medically today I do entreat you to send me word by Mrs. Lamb[18] how you are pray do not write & if you still feel any thing on your brain ask [Dr.] Warren if it were not good to tonsure you & apply a blister or leeches there[19]—I am all for relief on the spot though I know the old saws of blood circulation every where & lessening the quantity being sufficient yet my belief is that local bleeding and blistering according to the old idea in the time of Hypocrates is every thing—pray read little or none—but ask Ld M[orpeth] to read you the lost Peri[20] & see of the lines about the boy kneeling & the man of crime are not passing beautiful read it too with your heart and not with rules of criticism—I think many parts of Lalla Rookh perfectly beautiful & the idea and often the poetry but he has heaped such a mass of affection about it & affects such discord to make his harmony more sudden & conspicuous that it requires much good humour to admire[—]pray Dearest G do as the women who want pretty children do—think of every thing cheering—& if that terror on your nerves recurs remember one thing that the most healthy are as likely to die in a moment as the most apparently sick & weak—also—think how good you have been—above all how kind—& imagine if it pleases you that you are going to die and settle every thing that most agitates your mind & pray to God and then remember that all of us stand in the same state as you—that you are no nearer to the hour appointed to die because you have been ill than if you had not been so—that many left numbed cold in agony are now walking about

---

18 A servant.

19 Caroline recommends the tonsure (cutting Georgiana's hair in the clerical style of shaving the top of the skull only) to enable the blister and leeches. In another letter of this period, Caroline says that "cupping upon the temples" and the drawing of "not more than a thimble full of blood" through the application of six leeches helped her headache and rapid heartbeat, but when all else fails, take "Ginger tea hot and five drops of laudanum in a spirit of Castor" (Castle Howard MSS J18/35/98).

20 The third part of Thomas Moore's oriental poem *Lalla Rookh* (1817), is titled "Paradise and the Peri."

well witness Lord Carlisle[21] whom I saw yesterday and that if the time has come the strongest in an hour must fall—say to yourself for example that a Woman crossing the square with her children the other day was killed by a gig[22] going on her when she had not a fear of it & that one million of people at death's door the Duke & Duchess of Newcastle[23] and others are quite well—Montagu[24] never left his room without considering himself as sure to die—Mozart the same—Rousseau very much so[—]the two latter made themselves miserable in this reflection—the former satisfied last night the palpitation in my heart was so violent that I could scarce endure it I felt I must die—I reasoned in vain but when I thought so—had I the consolation you have—could I look back to a life of goodness purity and mildness could I say to myself those around me have been made happy—I have fulfilled every duty to the best of my power & if I have erred I have prayed for pardon to God No Dearest Gall I can ever say is that which the publican said and that I do say God be merciful even unto me a sinner—this being the case think yourself happy contemplate the death you fear & remember that twenty thousand fits cannot produce it—nor any doctor on earth retard it—at least fear death when it is at hand to strike and though those terrors which we indulge are more the effect of shattered nerves and sordid stomach than any thing else—calm yourself then Dearest G—& when that is done so far exert yourself as to drive out—take with you some draught to take if you faint—and remember that in a carriage or on a couch—in bed or out—God the same sees us protects us & resolves on what is to be—I have written all this because I know the horrors of your sufferings—for five years I almost bent under them & often often I have thrown myself into every hurry and folly only to forget the apprehensions which these strange & horrid nerves give—pray do not read this all at once or let it be about—seek to interest yourself a little in something & when you feel allarmed particularly at night remember what I have suggested & you will find yourself composed

Yours
Caroline Lamb

---

21 Lady Morpeth's father-in-law, Frederick Howard, fifth Earl of Carlisle (1748–1825).

22 Two-wheeled horse drawn cart.

23 The fourth Duchess of Newcastle died in 1822.

24 Perhaps John Montagu, fourth Earl of Sandwich (1718–1792)?

18. Lady Caroline. Michael Bruce. [1822.]

My dear Mr. Bruce

I have to thank you for your real kindness as it enabled me to see my Brother alone a few moments which he much wished [. . .] would to God I had been an Adam Blair & not a Mrs Campbell[25] [—] after all at the close of life there is nothing like a good Conscience—I would give Heaven be Witness what I would & to tell at this moment that I had not neglected every duty wasted Happiness and time and above all rewarded such a Man by ingratitude & unkindness violence & much more—as you are toreceive my dying behest I treat you with this Rhapsody which I pray you excuse[26]—I am only miserable—because I dare not die—and like Adam Blair cannot say my prayers [—] do you know that wicked as it may be I should not so much mind errors of the wandering heart if I had been gentle and made William happy. But as it is I am miserable—and when I die he will not even be able to love my remembrances—all this I say only to you—do not repeat it & pray burn my letter & do take pains to get these two after you have read them delivered to their respective owners—I am most truly yrs

Caroline Lamb

Isaac Nathan had become another of Lady Caroline's true friends—the sort of male admirer she seemed unable to do without. Caroline and William were godparents to one of Nathan's daughters, whom he had named Caroline.

19. Lady Caroline to Isaac Nathan. [1822–1823?]

Nathan,

I am, and have been very ill; it would perhaps cure me if you could come and sing to me, "Oh Mariamne"—now will you? I entreat you,

---

[25] Adam Blair, in *Some Passages in the Life of Mr. Adam Blair*, by J.G. Lockhart (1822), is a callow minister whose wife, Isobel, dies of grief after the deaths of three of their four children. Charlotte Campbell, an attractive woman who once hoped to marry him, turns up, and Blair travels to the estate of her husband, from whom she is alienated but not divorced. Blair has sex with Charlotte, then runs off in self-revulsion and becomes ill. Charlotte nurses him, catches the illness herself, and dies. After years of penance, Blair returns to his church a real minister.

[26] Lady Caroline included a watercolor and ink drawing of one cherub holding another who has been shot in the heart with an arrow, and on the back wrote a poem that ends: "One kiss—one last fond kiss he cried, / She gave him what he wished—and died."

the moment you have this letter, come and see me, and I promise you that if I get well I will come to your Theatre—but I use no bribe, I merely ask—come and soothe one who ought to be happy, but is not. I enclose this to Miss Richardson.[27]

Yours with much truth,
Caroline Lamb

20. Lady Caroline to Isaac Nathan. [1823].

From the Conservatory at Brockett Hall,
In the beautiful Month of May.

My Dear Sir,

I think your book delightful, and am much flattered by your sending it to me. I have not yet sent it to Lady John, as I wished to write with it. I shall send to purchase a copy immediately, and shall take every opportunity of recommending it. I think I must ask you to come here one day next week, when every thing is in bloom: thank you for my song.[28] I gave one copy to Lady Cork, who is here, and she has nieces who play and sing very well. This weather is delightful. Believe me, when I tell you, if I can serve you at any time, or in any way, I shall be most happy. I mean to send Mrs. Nathan Ada Reis, in return for remembering me. Tell my God-daughter to love me.

And believe me,
Yours, with truth,
Caroline Lamb

In the fall of 1822, Caroline conceived of a new publishing project—a lady's "pocket-diary" to be titled "Penruddock,"[29] and sold before New Year's. John Murray, already burdened with Ada Reis, *was conscripted belatedly to publish it. Pocket diaries were purchased by the mistresses of households as a resource and a record of important engagements, recipes, and expenses. Along with a ring of*

---

[27] An acquaintance of the Lambs who is alluded to by Caroline in her correspondence as early as 1821 and as late as 1826.

[28] Possibly "Weep for what thou hast lost, love," which Nathan had set to music for printing in *Ada Reis* (1823). Other possibilities include "Sir Henry De Vaux," a lyric also from *Ada Reis*, or "Sing Not For others, but for me."

[29] The title comes from Richard Cumberland's sentimental drama, *The Wheel of Fortune* (1795). As a boy, Byron had played the main character of Roderick Penruddock, whose enemies come within his power when he receives a windfall inheritance from a successful gambler.

keys, they symbolized women's domestic dominance. If successful, they were updated and republished annually. Unfortunately, this effort languished, and the New Year had long passed before it was in press. "Will you at all events have Penruddock advertised to quiet me[?]" Caroline wrote to Murray of her "new account Book," saying impatiently, "I hope Parker will let me have the proofs soon."[30] Penruddock *was one of numerous projects she hoped Lady Morgan might help her publish.*

21. Lady Caroline to Lady Morgan. [SPRING 1823.]

My Dear Lady Morgan would I had a good pen but as I have not one I write from my bed with a bad one—to thank you for yr kind reception of Adamo el Reis—you must tell Lady or Mrs Fletcher that Condulmar not Ada is Ld Byron that is if there be a Byron in the Tale and as to the Radicals in Hell they must be some where you know & where the Deuce in these Aristocratic days can they be—I entreat you write a fair critique for me of Ada Reis, it is the only thing I ever wrote which no one has (I mean of my family) abused [—] my Dearest Angel Mother lovd it [—] that is the idea [—] & as to yr saying it is a youthful thought I wonder at [you?] it appears to me a melancholy truism—the dregs of a vitiated imagination and disappointed heart—William Lamb rather admires it—Lady Dacre Miss Porter and yourself have written to me to praise it—and I myself rather admire it just as old men Love a little child & its fancies—I pray you therefore say all you can for it [—] my next is the Witch of Edmonton[31] I have written 3 between—
Sir Eustace de Grey, wild & uncorrected—
Rose & Mary common place & dull—
Charles & Julia imitative of Adam Blair[32] but a failure &
Arthur Pennruddock a work upon domestic oeconomy which nobody dares publish as it is against the present system of Great Houses & servants—

I should much like you to read & revise this last—if approvd of have it printed abroad or in Ireland—as here it cannot come out—I think you

[30] Lady Caroline Lamb to John Murray, January 1823. Murray Archive.

[31] She had asked her cousin Hart if she could dedicate the novel *The Witch of Edmonton* to him (letter to the sixth Duke of Devonshire. 12 July 1823. Devonshire MSS. Chatsworth [UK], sixth Duke's Group, f. 817A).

[32] Lockhart's *Some Passages in the Life of Mr. Adam Blair* (1822). See letter 18 above.

might put in many things I shall be proud whatever happens if my name to it—

after this the juvenile ardour is gone for ever
my gay unthinking days are gone
And I am now a weary Crone
sitting beside my fire sighing
Living but with—The dread of Dying—
My Early friends or dead or changed—
My Health not good my mind deranged
nothing to stir—imagination
nothing to cause me great vexation
you shall not—answered by—I will
a little ill—a little pill
[. . .]

22. Lady Caroline to Lady Morgan [1823.]

My dearest lady,

As being a lady whom my adored mother loved, your kindness about Ada Reis I feel the more, as everybody wishes to, run down and suppress the vital spark of genius I have, and, in truth, it is but small (about what one sees a maid gets by excessive beating on a tinder-box). I am not vain, believe me, nor selfish, nor in love with my authorship; but I am independent, as far as a mite and bit of dust can be. I thank God, being born with all the great names of England around me; I value them alone for what they dare do, and have done, and I fear nobody except the devil, who certainly has all along been very particular in his attentions to me, and has sent. me as many baits as he did Job. I, however, am, happily for myself, in as ill a state of health as he was, so I trust in God I shall ever more resist temptation. My history, if you ever care and like to read it, is this—My mother, having boys, wished ardently for a girl; and I, who evidently ought to have been a soldier, was found a naughty girl— forward, talking like Richard the Third [. . .]
I had three children; two died; my only child is afflicted; it is the will of God [. . .]

Lady Caroline had made a concerted effort to comfort John Murray in August 1821, when his wife suffered illness: "I entreat you do not give way to despondency and as I have often sought you when I have felt ill & miserable do come & see me or allow me to see you." Now she pressured him to publish Penruddock, *even though the New Year's buying season was well over.*

23. Lady Caroline to John Murray. [EARLY 1823.]

My Dear Sir you can do me a very great favour—Frederic Ponsonby / My Brother / now banishd to Corps and soon going to India that is in a year or two is most anxious to see any Book really good & will take care of it & bring it back he has a most careful servant who has livd with him ten years & who is bound to us to do this—I have just bought & by favour of Mr Wilmot sent him the War by Southey—I wish you could add to this the New Canto![33] of Don Juan and Moor[e]s poem[34] if you have one—& if not a quarterly review——& if Mr Parker could give it him a <u>Pennruddock</u>[35] as it would I think amuse him [. . .] I am in great anxiety about yr not writing me what Gifford says[36] I think it is a civil way of giving me my Death Warrant—if Penruddock does not

24. Lady Caroline to Lady Morgan. [APRIL–MAY 1823.]

All I have asked of Murray is a dull sale or a still birth. This may seem strange, and I assure you it is contrary to my own feelings of ambition; but what can I do? I am ordered peremptorily by my own family not to write. All you say is true, and so true, that I ask you if one descended in a right line from Spenser, not to speak of the Duke of Marlborough, with all the Cavendish and Ponsonby blood to boot, which you know were always rebellious, should feel a little strongly upon any occasion, and burst forth, and yet be told to hold one's tongue and not write, what is to happen? You cannot do me a greater favour than to recommend <u>Ada Reis</u>. I will send you three copies, and with them the letters I have received from Gifford, Lady Dacre,[37] and several others whom you know. [. . .]

---

[33] This may refer to a work satirizing Lord Byron's *Don Juan* that has been attributed to Lady Caroline, but which some doubt is really hers: *A New Canto* (London: William Wright, 1819).

[34] Most likely Thomas Moore's *Lalla Rookh* (1817) or *The Fudge Family in Paris* (1818).

[35] *Penruddock*, as noted, was a woman's pocket-diary. Murray was the publisher of the *Quarterly Review.*

[36] William Gifford, editor of the Tory *Quarterly Review*, had been asked to look at the manuscript of *Ada Reis* in late 1822.

[37] Lady Barbarina Dacre (1768–1854), a verse playwright and translator.

25. Lady Caroline to William Godwin. [April–May 1823.]

Brockett Hall

You would not say if you were here now that nature had not done her best for us [—] every thing is looking beautiful every thing is in bloom— it is impossible for me to come just yet to London but I will if I live in June yet do not fancy that I am here in such Health walking about & being sociable & bountiful—I am like the wreck of a little boat for I never come up to the sublime & beautiful—merely a little gay merry boat which perhaps stranded itself at Vauxhall or London bridge or wounded itself without killing itself as a brother Johnny does in a Tallow Candle [. . .]
God Preserve You

yrs
CL

I am dying to know what you think of Ada Reis & dread hearing for fear you should not approve

Caroline felt confirmed in her career as a writer. In September 1823, she wrote Henry Colburn that if he republished Glenarvon *or* Graham Hamilton, *"you have my order to put my name to them as I never again mean to publish anything without."*[38] *She received some fan mail, including a letter from Edward Bulwer, then about twenty years old, who thought* Glenarvon *a wonderful book.*

26. Lady Caroline to Edward Bulwer. 22 May 1823.

[. . .] It is quite beautiful and I feel very much flattered by your letter. I should have written to you before this but I have been very unwell and am come here to get better. This beautiful weather must I think cure any one and yet I feel as if nothing would for long do me good. I wish I did not dread to die. When I wrote the book you like[39] my career was over. I was miserable and in a state however in which I might have dared to die. I have lived since and to little purpose. Mine has been an absurd, unprofitable and erring life. However it is no use to obtrude all this on you—you are like Zevahir in Ada Reis.[40]

---

[38] Lady Caroline Lamb to Henry Colburn, 4 September 1823 from Brocket. Victoria and Albert Museum Forster Collection MSS vol. 28. #48.E.22.

[39] Almost certainly *Glenarvon*, which impressed Bulwer immensely.

[40] Zevahir (also known as Phaos and Zamohr) is the spirit of goodness in *Ada Reis*, who appears less and less frequently to the heroine, Fiormonda, as she loses emotional control.

In general, Caroline was generous in trying to assist others. She had set up a "circular letter" to raise funds for William Godwin, and at this time was trying to help a Miss Bryan gain a position as a governess for Lady Cloncurry's children, using Lady Morgan as an intermediary.

27. Lady Caroline to Lady Morgan. OCTOBER 1823.

My dear Lady Morgan,

Thank you and thank Sir Charles[41] for all his kindness about my fairy tale, Ada Reis, although I think he uses a rod even whilst he is merciful. I must now tell you about Miss Bryan. She has caught cold, and been very, very ill. I would not, for the world, have Lady Cloncurry wait for her; but if she chances to be without a proper person when well, Miss Bryan would assuredly go. However, it is no loss to the girl, as I feel sure she wishes to die or to marry Wronsky, and therefore do nothing further about her. She is sensible, handsome, young, good, unsophisticated, independent, true, ladylike, above any deceit or meanness, romantic, very punctual about money, but she has a cold and cough, and is in love. I cannot help it; can you? [. . .]

Well aware that she seemed fundamentally unable to alter herself or her behavior, she imagined herself reborn after falling from a horse—only to fall back into her old ways within a few days.

28. Lady Caroline to an Unknown Correspondent. 18 DECEMBER 1823.

Brocket

[After a fall from a horse]

For one week I never swallowed anything. The moment of danger is now passed, and I believe, in truth, I died; for assuredly a new Lady Caroline has arisen from this death. I seem to have buried my sins, griefs, melancholy, and to have come out like a new-born babe unable to walk, think, speak; but perfectly happy. So, finding myself—after I had wished for death and died—alive again, I made them carry me out into the air in a blanket, and then, to the astonishment of every one, ordered my horse

---

[41] Lady Morgan's husband.

next day, and sat upon it and would ride, and now am well, only weak. I have positively refused to take any draughts, pills, laudanum, wine, brandy, or other stimulants. I live upon meal-porridge, soda water, milk, arrowroot, and all the farinaceous grains; My mind is calm—I am pleased to be alive—grateful for the kindness shown me; and never mean to answer any questions further back than the 15th of this month, that being the day of this new Lady Caroline's birth: and I hate the old one. She had her good qualities, but she had grown into a sort of female Timon—not of Athens—bitter, and always going over old, past scenes. She also imagined that people hated her. Now the present Lady Caroline is as gay as a lark, sees all as it should be, not perhaps as it is; and having received your very clever letter, full of good sense, means to profit by it; but at present, like her predecessor, and like one of your country-men, is going about wanting work. I have nothing necessarily to do. I know I might, and ought to do a great many things, but then I am not compelled to do them. As to writing, assuredly, enough has been written, besides it is different writing when one's thoughts flow out before one's pen, and writing with one's pen waiting for thoughts.

William Godwin's role as mentor, tutor, and parent, seemed to sustain her when William Lamb had let his own lapse. What must Godwin have thought and felt upon receiving the following letter, however?

29. Lady Caroline to William Godwin. [1823–1824.]

My Dear Sir,

[. . .] Mr. Bulwer Lytton a very young man & an enthusiast wishes to be introduced to you he is taking his degree at Cambridge on his return pray let me if I live make him acquainted with you I shall claim yr promise of coming to Brockett would yr daughter and son accompany you—Hobhouse came to me last night how strange it is I love Ld Byron so much now in my old age in despight of all he is said—to have said—that I also love Hobhouse because he so warmly takes his part—pray write to me—for you see yr advice has had some effect—I have been studying yr little books with an ardour & a pleasure would surprise you there is a brevity which suits my want of attention & a depth of thought which catches at once & does not puzzle my understanding—a simplicity & kindness—which captivates & arouses every good feeling & a clearness which assist those who are deficient as I am in memory & attention—I am delighted

so are my brothers—the few men who are about me are all eager to get yr books but what has vexd me is that the 2 children & 4 young Women to whom I endeavoured to read them did not chuse to attend—How I like the beautiful little preface to the History of Rome—oh that I were 12 quite good & quite well to be yr pupil—
I'de "drudge like Selden[42] days & nights
And in the Endless labour die"

after all what is the use of any thing here below but to be enlightened & to try & make others happy—from this day I will endeavour to conquer all my violence all my fear—but you are destined to be my Master—the only thing that still checks my ardour is this— for what purpose &
for whom should I endeavour to grow wise—
what is the use of anything—what is the end of life & when we die what difference is there here between a Black beetle & me
oh that I might with the feelings I yet possess—without one vain one ambitious motive at least
feel that I was in the way of truth & that I was of use to others—the only thoughts that ever can
make me lose my senses are these—
a want of knowledge as to what is really true
a certainty that I am useless
a fear that I am worthless
a belief that all is Vanity & vexation of spirit & that there is nothing new under the sun—
The only prayer I ever say beside the sinner & the only life I shall ever leave written by myself of myself is that I have done those things which I ought not to have done & have left undone those that I ought to have done—fare well—

[42] The lines are by Richard Bentley (1708–1782), a classicist who had attacked Pope's translation of Homer. John Selden (1584–1654) was an English Historian and Antiquary.

CHAPTER NINE

Remember Me

LETTERS, 1824–1825

Isaac Nathan's wife, Rosetta, died in childbirth on 19 January 1824, and he wrote down his feelings in Hebrew and sent Caroline a rough translation, asking her to put them into verse.

1. Lady Caroline to Isaac Nathan.
[AFTER 19 JANUARY 1824.]

My dear Sir,

I only received your note yesterday evening, and until you tell me in what metre I cannot do what you desire; I was however so struck with the simplicity and melancholy of what you sent me, that I just wrote these very imperfect lines. Will you write and explain to me how you wish them done, and I will make another attempt.

Yours with much truth,
Caroline Lamb

[she enclosed her poem beginning, "As the flower early gathered . . ."]

On 19 April 1824 Lord Byron died. News reached England by 14 May, and Caroline knew not long after. With her health failing, Caroline was profoundly shocked by the tidings from Greece of Byron's unexpected demise. He had been working on behalf of the Greek resistance movement.

2. Lady Caroline to J.C. Hobhouse. [MAY 1824.]

My Dear Mr HobHouse it is strange that 13 years cannot make a silly person wise—however all is over now—romantic & enthusiastic & revengeful feelings all past and gone & if I were but well I would either write or speak like a rational being—I wish you to tell me what you think Ld Byron would prefer—the desires of the dead should be sacred if you wish his letters to be burned as I am in a bad state of Health they shall be all burnt before you & myself & my Brother William—I however should like to keep one or two they are merely letters expressions of affection you may see them & some verses to myself—as to my letters I trust all to yr generosity—you have provd yourself a most kind friend to Ld Byron & to me I am sorry to find myself so very much overpowered at an event which after 10 years of indifference or perhaps enmity on his part ought to have excited no feeling in me but a similar one—however there is no accounting for our nature [—] I loved him dearly—I do so still—I told Murray to tell you that I read his journal[1] with sorrow & perhaps anger but upon my honour & soul I took no copy of any part of it—others have I have not I swear—nor any one connected with me [. . .] really my Dear Mr Hobhouse when I think of how imprudently both Ld Byron & myself wrote all I ask you for his sake is—get every thing in yr own hands & burn whatever you think proper in some of my correspondence with him if you read it you will find me saying—d——HobHouse & such expressions but then it was because he said you wanted to part us—pray excuse my faults they are God knows Heavy enough upon my mind—I shall not live long to you I leave even the Rose-Carnation he first gave me at my Mothers God Bless you & I pray you burn this letter or you shall if you wish have my Journals at yr house—do either come & see me here for a day—or write to me—& pray write & tell me when Fletcher comes—

get all my things out of Lady Byrons & Mrs Lees & Fletchers hands—have them yourself you have my authority for it & I seriously wish it—although I must tell you that Lord Byron said Mrs Lee & Lady Byron had read all my letters verses——

ever yrs with gratitude
& respect
Caroline Lamb

Brockett Hall
Sunday

---

[1] That is, Byron's memoirs, which Hobhouse, Moore and Murray burned on 17 May 1824.

3. Lady Caroline to Lydia White.[2] [May 1824.]

My Dear Miss White I do not like at such a moment to intrude upon any one immediately connected with Ld Byron—I am out of Town to all intents and purposes I am shocked beyond idea—

although no one will perhaps believe it—I have lost the kindest friend & the bitterest enemy any one ever had all enmity however had ceased even before this most afflicting event. I do not like to trouble you, yet as you are always kind to me—know Moore, Hob House, and Mr. Murray—be so good as to say that I wish for Lady Melbourne's letters for William seald & they shall be burnt if they like in their presence—my own letters & two pictures of me & my drawings I particularly request I may receive myself—pray do not trouble yourself too much about this but if you see either Mr Murray or Mr HobHouse—I am sure it will be done yrs affectionately, Caroline Lamb

In July, Caroline encountered Byron's funeral procession—she claimed it was by accident, though a stop of the hearse had been scheduled in Welwyn for the night of the 12th.

4. Lady Caroline to John Murray. 13 July 1824.

Brocket Hall

My Dear Sir

I have been more ill than I can express or I should have written to you—I wish I could see you—It is surprising to me that I have not heard from Hobhouse—Will you write & tell me every Particular of what has pass'd since I saw you. Lord Byron's Hearse came by our gates Yesterday—You may judge what I felt—Pray write to me

Ever your sincere friend
Caroline Lamb

Caroline's subsequent letters to Godwin are painful. Similarly, her letters to Lady Morgan, while full of plans and hopes for further writing, turn often to death, loss, and despair.

---

[2] Lydia White, a bluestocking hostess who overcame illness to maintain her social and literary relations through salon-gatherings, to whom Lady Caroline dedicated *Ada Reis*.

5. Lady Caroline to William Godwin. 24–25 October 1824.

My Dear Sir—

from the moment when I saw you last under such excessive agitation until the present moment I have been as you said I might be if I would—calm & perfectly well—& tollerably happy—is it not strange then that I can suffer my mind to be so overpower'd & mostly about trifles—can you think of me with anything but contempt—tell me would you dislike paying me a little visit? I will not allure you by descriptions of a Country life if you come I imagine it is to pay me a friendly visit & if you do not I shall feel secure you have good reasons for not coming—the whole of what passed which set me so beside myself I forget & forgive—for my own faults are so great that I can see & remember nothing beside—yet I am tormented with such a superabundance of activity & have so little to do—that I want you to tell me how to go on—it is all very well if one died at the end of a Tragic scene after playing a desperate part—but if one lives & instead of growing wiser—one remains the same victim of every folly and passion—without the excuse of youth & inexperience—what then? pray say a few wise words to me—there is no one more deeply sensible than myself of kindness from persons of high intellect—& at this point of my life I need it—I have nothing to do—I mean necessarily there is no particular reason why I should exist—it conduces to no ones happiness & on the contrary I stand in the way of many—besides I seem to have lived 500 years & feel I am neither wiser better nor worse—than when I began—my experience gives me no satisfaction—all my opinions & beliefs & feelings are shaken as if suffering from frequent little shocks of earthquakes—I am like a boat in a calm in an unknown to me unsought for sea without compass guide or even a knowledge whither I am destined—now this is probably the case of millions but that does not mend the matter & whilst a fly exists it seeks to save itself after destroying itself—therefore excuse me if I do the same—pray write to me—and tell me also what you have done about my journal—thank you for the frame—will you pay for it & send it me in any account we have at your House—I am very anxious about my Dear boy—I must speak to you of him—every one as usual is kind to me—I want for nothing this Earth can offer—but self controul—forgive my writing so much about myself & believe me most

sincerely yrs
Caroline Lamb [. . .]

Sketch by Lady Caroline showing a monstrous wraith with a torch stabbing to death a figure supine on a rock in the ocean, and with the caption "Le desespoir met fin a ses jours." By permission of Hertfordshire Archives and Local Studies.

In fall 1824, Thomas Medwin published a book of "Conversations" with Byron, and he included a vitriolic poem Caroline had never seen before, written in response to one of her forays into Byron's apartments after their affair had supposedly ended. She had scribbled in his copy of Vathek *the phrase "Remember me!" What she could not know is that there had been an earlier version of this poem—that he had changed his first response from anger—even hate—over shared guilt to complete condemnation of her. The original poem read thus:*

"Remember thee," nay—doubt it not—
Thy Husband too may "think" on thee!
By neither canst thou be forgot,
Thou false to him—thou fiend to me!
"Remember thee"? Yes—yes—till Fate
In Lethe quench the guilty dream.

Yet then—e'en then—Remorse and Hate
Shall vainly quaff the vanquished stream.[3]

The revised poem is a curse:

Remember thee, remember thee!
Till Lethe quench life's burning stream,
Remorse and shame shall cling to thee,
And haunt thee like a feverish dream!
Remember thee! Ay doubt it not.
Thy husband too shall think of thee!
By neither shalt though be forgot,
Thou false to him, thou fiend to me![4]

She thought that she had heard everything that might be said against her by anyone, including Byron, and now this. She wrote at length to defend herself to Medwin, whom she treats respectfully, though she had told Hobhouse that it would have been better to publish Byron's journal rather than burn it, for Medwin's book was "full of vulgarity & errors—even as to dates."[5]

6. Lady Caroline to Thomas Medwin. November 1824.

Sir

I hope you will excuse my intruding upon your time. With the most intense interest I have just finished your Book which does you credit as to the manner in which it is executed, and after the momentary pain in part which it excites in many a bosom, will live in despight of censure and be gratefully accepted by the Public as long as Lord Byron's name is remembered—yet as you have left to one who adored him a little legacy and as I feel secure the lines "remember thee—thou false to him then friend time"—were his—and as I have been very ill I am not likely to trouble any one much longer—you will I am sure grant me one favour—let me to you at least confide the truth of the past—you owe it to me—you will not I know refuse me.

---

[3] *The Works of Lord Byron: A New, Revised, and Enlarged Edition* (1898–1905), 3:60. No original exists. The text we have from E. H. Coleridge is dated 22 February 1813. For a thorough explanation of the case (saving only the identification of "Bd." as "Biondetta"), see Andrew Stauffer, "Byron, Medwin, and the False Fiend," 265–76.

[4] Byron, *Complete Poetical Works*, 3:84.

[5] Lady Caroline to John Cam Hobhouse. [October-November 1824.] Murray Archive.

It was when the first Child Harold came out upon Lord Byron's return from Greece that I first had the misfortune to be acquainted with him. at that time I was the happiest and gayest of human beings I do believe without exception— I had married for love —and love the most romantic and ardent—my husband & I were so fond of each other that false as I too soon proved he never would part with me—Devonshire House at that time was closed from my uncles death for one year—at Melbourne House where I lived the Waltzes and Quadrilles were being daily practised—Lady Jersey, Lady Cowper, the Duke of Devonshire, Miss Milbank, and a number of foreigners coming there to learn. You may imagine what forty or fifty people dancing from 12 in the morning until near dinner time all young gay & noisy were. in the evenings we either had opposition suppers or went out to Balls and routs—Such was the life I then led when Moore and Rogers[6] introduced Lord Byron to me. What you say of his falling up Stairs and Miss Milbank[e][7] is all true—Lord Byron 3 days after this brought me a Rose and Carnation and the very words I mentioned in Glenarvon—with a sort of half sarcastic smile saying—Your Ladyship I am told likes all that is new and rare for a moment—I have them still, and the Woman who through many a trial has kept these relics with the romance of former ages—deserves not that you should speak of her as you do—Byron never could say I had no heart—He never could say, either , that I had not loved my husband—In his letters to me—he is perpetually telling me I love him the best of the two, and my only charm, believe me, in his eyes was that I was innocent, affectionate and enthusiastic—Recall these words, and let me not go down with your book as heartless—Tell the truth: it is bad enough but not what is worse. It makes me so nervous to write that I must stop—will it tire you too much if I continue? I was not a woman of the world. Had I been one of that sort, why would he have devoted nine entire months almost entirely to my society—have written perhaps ten times in a day: and lastly have pressed me to leave all and go with him—and this at the very moment when he was made an Idol of—and when, as he and you justly observe, I had few personal attractions. Indeed indeed I tell the truth, Byron did not affect but he loved me as woman never was loved. I have had one of his letters copied in the Stone press[8] for you: one just before we parted. See if it looks like a mere

---

[6] Thomas Moore and Samuel Rogers.

[7] That is, Lady Byron, the former Annabella Milbanke.

[8] That is, she had the letter lithographed.

lesson—Besides, he was then very good, to what he grew afterwards; & his health being delicate, he liked to read with me and stay with me out of the crowd. Not but what we went about every where together, we were at last invited always as if we had been married—It was a strange scene—but it was not vanity misled me—I grew to love him better than Virtue, Religion, all prospects here.—He broke my heart. Still I love him—witness the agony I experienced at his death & the tears your book has cost me. Yet, Sir, allow me to say, although you have unintentionally given me pain I had rather have experienced it than not have read your book. Parts of it are beautiful, and I can vouch for the truth of much as I read his own memoirs before Murray burnt them. Keep Lord Byron's letter to me (I have the original) Some day add a word or two to your work from his own words, not to let every one think I am heartless. The cause of my leaving Lord Byron was this: my dearest mother now dead, grew so terrified about us, that upon hearing a false report that we were gone off together she was taken dangerously ill & broke a blood vessel. Byron would not believe it, but it was true. When he was convinced we parted I went to Ireland & remained there 3 months. He wrote every day, long kind entertaining letters, it is there he asked Murray to look at, and extract from, when he published the journal; but I would not part with them—I have them now—and they would only burn them, & nothing of his should be burnt. At Dublin, God knows why, he wrote me the cruel letter part of which he acknowledges in Glenarvon (the 9th November 1821.) He knew it would destroy my mind, and all else, it did so—Lady Oxford was no doubt the instigator. What will not a Woman do to get rid of a rival? She knew that he still loved me—I need not tire you with every particular. I was brought to England a mere wreck, & in due time Lady Melbourne & my mother being seriously alarmed for me, brought me to town, & allowed me to see Lord Byron. Our meeting was not what he insinuates—he asked me to forgive him: he looked sorry for me. he cried. I adored him still, but I felt as passionless as the dead may feel—Would I had died there! I should have died pitied & still loved by him, & with the sympathy of all I even should have pardoned myself, so deeply had I suffered. But, unhappily, we continued occasionally to meet. Lord Byron liked others, I only him. The scene at Lady Heathcotes is nearly true—he had made me swear I was never to Waltz—Lady Heathcote said, ["]come Lady Caroline you must begin, & I bitterly answered—Oh yes! I am in a merry humour.["] I did so. but whispered to Lord Byron, "I conclude I may Waltz <u>now</u>" and he answered sarcastically, "with every body in turn, you always did it better than any one. I shall have a pleasure in seeing you." I did so, with what feelings you may judge. After this, feeling ill, I went into a small inner room where supper was prepared: Lord Byron & Lady Rancliffe entered after! Seeing me, he said, "I have been admiring your dexterity" I clasped a knife, not intending anything, "So my dear" he said "yet if you mean to act a Roman part, mind which way you strike with our knife. be it your own heart not mine—you have struck there already," "Byron," I said, and ran away with the knife. I never stabbed myself. It is false. Lady Rancliffe & Tankerville screamed and said I would; people pulled to get it from me; I was terrified my hand got cut & the blood came over my gown. I know not what happened after—but this is the very truth—After this, long after, Ld Byron, abused by every one, made the theme of every one's horror, yet pitied me enough to come & see me, and still, in spite of every one, William Lamb had the generosity to retain me—I never held my head up after—never could. It was in all the papers, & put not truly. It is true I burnt Lord Byron in Effigy, & his book, ring, & chain. It is true I went to see him as a Carman, after all that! But it is also true, that, the last time we parted for ever, as he press'd his lips on mine (it was in the Albany) he said, "poor Caro, if every one hates me, you, I see, will never change, no, not with ill usage!" I said, "yes I am changed, & shall come near you no more" For then he showed me letters, & told me things I cannot repeat, & all my attachment went. This was my last parting scene, and well I remember it. It had an effect upon me not to be conceived.—3 years I had worshipped him—Shortly after he married, once, Lady Melbourne took me to see his wife in Piccadilly. It was a cruel request, but Lord Byron himself made it. It is to this wedding visit he alludes. Mrs Leigh, myself, Lady Melbourne, Lady Noel & Lady Byron were in the room. I never looked up. Annabella was very cold to me—Lord Byron came in & seemed agitated—his hand was cold, but he seemed kind—this was the last time upon this earth I ever met him.

Soon after, the Battle of Waterloo took place. My brother was wounded, & I went to Brussels. I had one letter while at Paris from Lord Byron, a jesting one: hoping I was as happy with the regiment as he was with his "Wife Bell." When I returned, the parting between them occurred—& my page affair.[9] & Glenarvon—I wrote it in a month

---

[9] Refers to an incident in which Lady Caroline lost her temper with one of her pages who loved tossing squibs (tiny firecrackers) into the fire. When he did it once too often, she threw a cricket ball which hit him on the head, drawing blood. According to her own account, she panicked, running out into the street screaming, "Oh God, I have murdered the page!"(Morgan, *Lady Morgan's Memoirs*, 2:201–2). This event became symbolic of Caroline's madness.

under circumstances would surprise every body; but which I am not at liberty to mention. Besides, it has nothing to do with your book and would only tire you. Previous to this, I once met & once only, Lady Byron. It was just after the separation occurred. She was so altered I could scarcely know her. She appeared heart broken—What she then said to me I may not repeat. She was however sent away. She did not go willingly—She accused me of knowing every thing, & reproached me for not having stopped the marriage. How Could I! She had been shewn my letters, and every one else—It is utterly false that she ever opened the desk—the Nurse had nothing to do with the separation—From that hour Lady Byron and I met no more, & it was after this, that, indignant, miserable, I wrote Glenarvon. Lady Byron was more angry at it than he was. From that time, I put the whole as much as I could from my mind. Ld Byron never once wrote to me—and always spoke of me with contempt. I was taken ill in March this year—Mrs Russell Hunter and a nurse sat up with me. In the middle of the night I fancied I saw Ld Byron. I screamed jumped out of bed and desired them to save me from him. He looked horrible and ground his teeth at me; he did not speak. His hair was straight; he was fatter than when I knew him, & not so handsome. I felt convinced I was to die. This dream took possession of my mind. I had not dreamed of him since we had parted. It was, besides, like no other dream except one of my mother that I ever had. I am glad to think it occurred before his death as I never did & hope I never shall see a ghost. I have even avoided enquiring about the exact day for fear I should believe it—it made enough impression as it was. I told William, and my brother, & Murray at the time. Judge what my horror was, as well as my grief, when long after the news came of his death, it was conveyed to me in two or 3 words. "Caroline, behave properly, I know it will shock you. Ld Byron is dead." This letter I received when laughing at Brockett Hall. Its effect or some other cause produced a fever from which I never yet have recovered. It was also singular that the first day I could go out in an open carriage, as I was slowly driving up the hill here, Ld Byron's hearse was at that moment passing under these very walls, & rested at Welwyn. William Lamb, who was riding before me, met the procession at the Turnpike, & asked whose funeral it was. He was very much affected and shocked. I of course was not told; but, as I continually asked where & when he was to be buried, & had read in the papers it was to be at Westminster Abbey. I heard it too soon, & it made me very ill again.

7. Lady Caroline to William Godwin. [December 1824.]

Thanks for your letter—come here if possible and bring the Journal[10] one moment—yr books too—let me have them—I will try & bind my weakened wavering understanding to something worth—but where is the object—pray have you read Medwin's Book—the part respecting me gives me much pain—this is strange—why need I care—I do however [. . .] I feel flattered by yr letter—a little flattery is now perhaps of use—for I have been deservedly—no doubt—deeply & painfully humiliated

William finally resolved to obtain a legal separation from his wife. The acrimonious negotiations dragged on through the spring and into the summer. Caroline lashed out at those she believed were seeking to banish or marginalize her.

8. Lady Caroline to an Anonymous Correspondent. [April–June 1825.]

Dear [blacked out]

I have sent your kind invitation to Mr Lamb who is in town—as to myself I am very ill and very miserable on my death bed I believe at Brockett Hall—could I have attended your Party you know not with how much pleasure I should have done so—particularly if I were to see a few kind friends there—and as I feel no doubt you will have many—I assure you had I been well enough I should have tried to steal away one or two for myself. Believe me with sincere interest and

regard yours,
Caroline Lamb née Ponsonby

Brockett Hall—do me a favour—ask of those you think great schollars the meaning of the word amicable separation after 20 years of mutual attachment resentment and much forebearance eagerness to part and making it up again—but no I will explain it. It is to Idolize to flatter to be entirely governed by a Woman who every day errs and is never restrained nor reproved whilst she is young in Health & accounted clever—it is to retain her by protestation of kindness and love when others wished to take her away—it is to laugh at her termigant humours independent ideas proud spirit—& encourage her in these and when perhaps by her own

[10] Presumably Lady Caroline's journal or diary, supposed to be several volumes, now lost.

fault she becomes miserable—ill & lonely—to find out all her errors blaze them to the world & have straight waistcoats. Physicians with all the Aristocracy of the country to say she had better go—go where?

will you find that out & do not as John Bull Frederic Lamb Lady Cowper & others would say answer to the D——l let them go there if they like—I will not if I can help it—excuse me for troubling you—& pray mark that in this truly amicable arrangement I am accused alone of being passionate (—when ill used)—did they never find that out before!

"I however still love the hand upraised to shed my blood."[11]

9. Lady Caroline to Lord Cowper. [April–June] 1825.

My Dear Ld Cowper thank you—I am too ill to write tell Emily to tell William if he will only see me one instant I shall do whatever he pleases—tell him if he pleases he may bring [*illegible*] a straight waistcoat [. . .] I am on my bed perhaps my bed of death.—I will not accept half this money now—but I will not be unkindly used. tell William and Emily to come & see me. I can hardly speak or write—I never will press William for money now—Haggard[12] has my keys my journal I have got back. I entreat you to let Emily & William come and see me—I am more ill than I can express. thank you & the Duke for your kindness—but I can agree to nothing untill I see William—

Caroline

The Duke [*illegible*] arrived last night—
I am too unhappy—

10. Lady Caroline to the Sixth Duke of Devonshire. [1825.]

If you have not otherwise disposed of yr boxes at the play it were kind to let me go there tonight—or when you can—I believe I stay here till Saturday—remember me remember me[13] those bitter lines are a legacy which grieves me allow me therefore to send you the copy of the last

---

[11] A slightly misquoted line from Pope's *Essay on Man* (Epistle 1, sec. 3) that Caroline had entered into her Commonplace Book in 1812, saying Byron had often repeated it to her: It alludes to a puerile "lamb" that "licks the hand just raised to shed his blood."

[12] A long-time groundskeeper at Brocket Hall.

[13] See commentary preceding letter 6, in this chapter.

letter written to me by Lord Byron "when we two parted in silence & tears["][14]—it was written the very week after we supped at Devonshire House & my Mother was ill—Dearest Duke—do sometime or another see me & hear me—I am very much mistaken if you will have other opportunities for I feel too much to live long—& although I have sinned—yet as I belong in a manner to you—you need not fear conversing with me I have some few things to say to you—& when I was really ill at Brocket & you had your Hay fever I sent for you—no wonder some folks then thought me mad—& adopted measures which might have made me so—however all that is past & forgotten or sooner forgiven—I now ask you to see me whilst I am myself & in Town & the best way if it pleases you is to come alone with me to the play—because then if I bore you the play will amuse you——& by the by I scarcely ever passed so pleasant an Evening as when Emily took me to The Maid of Milan Clari[15]—is it not too beautiful—if you can tame me to see it again only name the night & I will attend you, but I wish to see you—to you—to you only I will give up my journals Ld Byron's letters verses every thing to burn—you must make HobHouse give up mine—you are like a King in the family[16] & I want the whole thing to be done really—it is unfair but he will not give up my letters unless I give up Ld Byron's—now as my guilt is remembered & published—is it not upon my part folly to agree to this demand—yet if you will condescend to consider my case & you advise it—I will do whatever you think best I inclose Ld Byron's letter to me—I have had ten copies made of it since Medwin's book came out—it is fit after this & a thousand before like it that he should speak of me as he does—Dearest Cousin forgive me—I feel violently is that madness? I have cried—but not been deceived—I

[14] This poem was first published in 1815 as sheet music by composer Isaac Nathan, who was Lady Caroline's friend and Byron's collaborator on *A Selection of Hebrew Melodies, Ancient and Modern* (1815–1816). Caroline claims it was written to her in 1812, not in 1815, as Jerome McGann says in his edition of Byron's *Complete Poetical Works,* 7 vols. (Oxford: Clarendon Press, 1980–1993), 3:475–76.

[15] *Clari, The Maid of Milan*, by John Howard Payne (1791–1852), prolific American actor and playwright, born in New York City, who wrote more than 50 plays. *Clari* was first performed at Covent Garden 8 May 1823, and it contains his most famous song, "Home Sweet Home."

[16] Lady Caroline wanted to avoid legal separation from William at all costs. She begged and cajoled her cousin Hart (now sixth Duke of Devonshire), to avert or at least "retard" the process, and satirized herself as "no more mad than a March Hare only now & then rumbustial when misunderstood," adding the commands, "be kind" and "pity me." (Lady Caroline to the sixth Duke of Devonshire. April 1825. Devonshire MSS. Chatsworth [UK], sixth Duke's Group, ff. 1128 and 1129.)

love you from my heart of hearts. I thank you for yr kindness & from my soul I forgive all such as have been otherwise—knowing how much I have tried all yr patiences out, it has pleased God to restore me my Health & spirit—let me know yr wishes & make good use of it—do not tell any one what I say to you but see me—& believe me ever yours with the truest affection—Caroline Lamb

The anniversary of her marriage on 3 June, which she "celebrated" alone at Brocket with a number of local tenants, was the nadir.

11. Lady Caroline to Lady Morgan. 2 June 1825.

Melbourne House

My Dear Lady Morgan,

[. . .] Oh, God, it is a punishment severe enough; I never can recover it; it is fair by William Lamb to mention, that since I saw you he has written a kinder letter; but if I am sent to live by myself, let them dread the violence of my despair—better far go away. Every tree, every flower, will awaken bitter reflection. Pity me, for I am too unhappy; I cannot bear it. I would give all I possessed on earth to be again what I once was, and I would now be obedient and gentle; but I shall die of grief [. . .] hearing this is a sad ending to a too frivolous and far too happy a life. Farewell; if you receive the portrait, return it, and send the letter; it is his parting one when I went to Ireland with mamma (I mean Lord Byron's). She was near dying because she thought I was going to leave her. William, at that time, loved me so much that he forgave me all, and only implored me to remain. My life has not been the best possible. The slave of impulse, I have rushed forward to my own destruction [. . .]

At the time of her anniversary, she permitted a young poet named Wilmington Fleming to visit, and he come "prowling about and writing verses to me of the most flattering kind," as she later said.[17] *Fleming had written begging letters to her, unable to believe that she really had little to give. She allowed him to read her journals, and somehow he got mixed up in her confused plans to publish them.*

---

[17] Lady Caroline to Colburn [before March 20, 1826.] Victoria and Albert Museum, Forster Collection MSS vol. 28. #48.E.22.

12. Lady Caroline to Wilmington Fleming. [March–April 1825.]

I assure you you wrong me I saw Mr. Murray and will try to serve you in every way I can—I received no money but just what the servants wanted for their food—I have been much too ill to write or see you—call tomorrow bring me the journals I gave you—I hope to think of something for your advantage write & tell me frankly your History and what [*illegible*] you d[esire?] yrs.[18]

CL

Fleming's begging letters turned to blackmail the next year, but after John Cam Hobhouse became involved, he disappeared. In the mean time, Caroline came to her own and Isaac Nathan's defense when one of her songs was misattributed to the actress Mrs. Jordan.

13. Lady Caroline to Isaac Nathan. 11 June 1824.

Melbourne House

My Dear Sir,

excuse my writing to you in great haste but I was surprised that the song I gave you even before Mr. Colburn published Graham Hamilton—beginning "if thou could'st know what 'tis to weep["] a song my Dearest Mother loved—and which you remember I composed when ill should now be published in London & I apprehend in France as being made by Mrs. Jordan on her death bed—pray say to them who have done this all you know about the matter & remember I gave you alone my leave to put any songs I wrote in the only 3 novels I ever published—to music—

believe me yrs with
respect & truth
Caroline Lamb

Caroline encouraged Augustus to study the Bible so he could be confirmed as a "Religious and a good Boy," and she pressed William to hire a Mr. William

[18] In March 1825 Fleming sent Lady Caroline a poem on Byron's death titled "The Poet's Grave." Fleming inscribed the poem to her, the wealthy and talented patroness of the arts, and begged for money. She sent him a few pounds, she later said, then imprudently let him take her journals to read.

Trimmer as Augustus's tutor to teach him what we today would call "life skills."[19]

14. Lady Caroline to Augustus Lamb. 26 June or July [1825.]

My dearest boy, I thank you much for your letter and am glad to hear you are well and have given up the snuff which in such quantities as you take it must injure your Health—I Hope you will abstain from taking that vast Tower of Bread with that immense sea of Tea as I am convinced the mammoth and the Ostrich alone could digest anything like the quantity—will you also be pleased to tell your kind friends with whom you now are that whilst at Brockett Miss Wheeler took every care of you [. . .] I do sincerely Hope that you will not be ungrateful enough to lay your bad Tricks & attacks & bad words to our door, as I think I may with truth say that you were reminded in rather severe terms once or twice by me that such pinching people & dogs and such other Idle habits were neither agreeable to us at Brockett nor to your Father nor to Mr Stuart. Do try and seriously break yourself off from doing these things they can give you no pleasure and they give all living things upon whom you inflict them real pain—I shall send you some balls which will save many heads & windows. Your Father kindly sent me some—Miss Wheeler actually spit blood & is not yet well from the blow she received in her chest from your cricket ball—all your books are locked up and safe—your Father I Hope will not go just yet not till it is cooler I am going to London for a few days & shall probably pay you a visit very early some morning or very late some Evening—I mean about 7. I Hope you do not go out in this hot weather until late and that you keep your Hair short & omit your neckcloth—pray ask Mr [Barham?] now and then to write & tell me how you are—your Uncle William Ponsonby has gained his Election with great applause—Fanny Ponsonby has the Hooping Cough but is doing well God bless you Dearest boy remember me to Mr & Mrs Stuart & believe me your own affectionate Mother Caroline Lamb

19 Lady Caroline to her son Augustus. [June-July 1825] Hertfordshire Archives. D/ELb F76/10.

Caroline finally departed Brocket on 12 August. The final agreement was that she should be paid £2,500 per annum during William's lifetime and £3,000 thereafter. She embarked on a steam boat for Calais.

15. Lady Caroline to William Lamb.
8 September [1825.]

Calais

May I request you to attend to my wishes respecting my Mare the young Horse & Tom Croft—my Health depends upon riding & the expense of keeping these Horses is less than the money I am obliged to pay for hiring even a gig [. . .] Thank you for keeping the boy so much with you. I always told you it would be better for him than sending him to stupid places where he remains with women & children[,] learns nothing and grows silly—my conduct spirit & pride shall prove to you that I deserved more mercy at yr hands than you have shewn—yr cruelty will one day recur to your mind—& may my curse bitter and entire fall upon the rest, as for you I never will curse you but if it be permitted to me to return I will come and look at you even as Ld Byron did at me—the more I think of the mean barbarous manner in which I have been sacrificed the less I can understand how you could bring yourself to sanction it—I still maintain that the proceedings have been as illegal as they were cruel, that taking advantage of my long & severe illness with the assistance of the basest and most Hypocritical of men—by intimidation and every sort of unkindness I was forced from your fathers House—Lady Cowper upon her bed of death and Frederick Lamb and that abhorred scoundrel Jack Milbanke shall remember me—[. . .] Farewell you may trample upon me as much as you please I would not be you for all yr present momentary Happiness—cruelty, even in this world is ever punished—and you are cruel—cowardly—& selfish—the abhorred deed is here I have not looked at it—no message came with it—The Devil take the deed that took my Willy from me—I have a pretty little picture of you from Harding [*illegible*] whilst doing it—remember me to my own sweet kind boy, no one wrote to me on his birthday—have you had much sport do you still keep an account of the birds you kill—write to me pray do—

In October, Caroline returned for the signing of the papers, which permitted her to reside in London. William's sister Emily hated this prospect and prompted

Caroline's Doctor, Mr. Goddard, to diagnose her as officially "insane."[20] *Caroline feared rightly that "Goddard is out looking for some place in the Country to put me away in."*[21] *Despite Lady Cowper's efforts to place Caroline and Augustus with caretakers outside London, on 17 November 1825 William leased 39 Conduit Street for one year at the exorbitant tariff of £546. Caroline now lived near the lending library and offices of Henry Colburn. She was also not far from John Murray's publishing house at 50 Albemarle Street. Clearly in decline, she continued thinking about "Lord Byron, that dear, that angel, that mis-guided and mis-guiding Byron, whom I adore, although he left that dreadful legacy on me—my memory."*[22]

---

[20] Dr. Goddard to William Lamb. 19 October 1825. Hertfordshire Archives D/ELb F33/1.

[21] Lady Caroline to the sixth Duke of Devonshire. 26 October 1825. Devonshire MSS. Chatsworth [UK], sixth Duke's Group, f. 1217.

[22] *Lady Morgan's Memoirs*, 2:206–8.

CHAPTER TEN

Last Words

Letters, 1826–1828

By early 1826, Lady Caroline's entanglement with Wilmington Fleming prompted her to write a letter to a Mrs. Blaquiere of Great Marlborough Street, who was somehow involved in the negotiations with Henry Colburn to get back the remnants of Lady Caroline's journals.[1] *She also wrote to Edward Bulwer, who continued to be fond of her despite the heavy disappointment she had inflicted upon him earlier by treating his love cavalierly and refusing to sleep with him.*

1. Lady Caroline to Edward Bulwer. 2 August 1826.

I should have answered your letter long ago had I even one innate Idea—but I am convinced there is no such thing—how then can I write even imagination must have some materials upon which to work I have none the passions might produce sentiments of some sort but mine are all calm'd or extinct—memory—a waste with nothing in it worth recording—happy Healthy quiet contented I get up at 1/2 past 4 ride about with Haggard[2] & see Harvest men at work in this pretty confined green Country—read a few old Books, see no one hear from no one and occasionally play at Chess with Dr Goddard or listen to the faint

[1] Lady Caroline to Mrs. Blaquiere[before 20 March 1826]. Victoria and Albert Museum, Forster Collection MSS vol. #48.E.22. Mrs Blaquiere's husband Edward represented the London Greek Committee seeking to help the Greeks in their war for independence. Blaquiere towed Byron's casket to *Florida* on 24 May 1824.

[2] The groundskeeper at Brocket.

High warblings of Miss Richardson—This contrast to my sometime hurried life delights me besides I am well and that is a real blessing to oneself & companions—when you saw me and were so kind to me—how ill how miserable I was if there be a place of punishment hereafter assuredly the lost souls must feel as I did then—

Pray write to me as you then did even although your opinion of me and affection boyish affection be utterly destroyed—your letters were beautiful and soothing—I detest wit and humour and satire I fear you are given to all this and have lost the freshness of youthful feelings the noble sentiments and the warm vivid hopes and aspirings of an uncorrupted and unworldly heart. I drew my good spirit in Ada Reis from you as I imagined you pray do not turn into a bad one—what are you writing now? May I be allowed to know—Fare well give my adoration to the Dear sea—whose every change I worship and whose blue waves I long to dip in—provided two old women take me out again safely—excuse this stupid letter and write me a long and amiable one—Lady Dacre and Mrs Sullivan came over to see me the day before yesterday—it is the first time since my exile from Home—tomorrow William Lamb says he will come. He has been at Hastings with which he was delighted as far as scenery goes and climate but he found himself there knowing no one and having nothing to do without wife or Parliament or trouble—he ought now to have found true enjoyment he pined for quiet yet if I mistake not he is less happy than when he was plagued by these apendages—if there are two p's in that word imagine one & pray excuse my spelling—yours with sincere interest and disinterested attachment—

Lady Caroline's health continued to fail throughout 1826 and into the spring of 1827, when William Lamb was posted by Prime Minister Canning as Chief Secretary to Ireland. She dreaded the separation: "Being unhappy today," confessed to Dr. Goddard, "I have drunk a whole bottle of wine which I bought for myself all at once [. . .] I did it upon hearing Mr Lamb wished to speak to me. I was still able to do every thing he wished."[3] *Caroline got her courage up and prevailed upon William to take Augustus with him, though she knew it might mean she would never see her son again. She wrote on 29 August 1827 to commiserate with Augustus after he took a fall, and told him that the Brocket staff were preparing to serve mutton, beef, and beer to 125 people.*[4] *In September 1827, she received a visit from the Duke of Wellington and set up a chess game*

---

[3] Lady Caroline to Dr. Goddard [spring 1827.] Hertfordshire Archives D/ELb F62.

[4] Lady Caroline to her son Augustus. From Brocket, 29 August 1827. Hertfordshire Archives. D/ELb F76/16.

between Augustus and Dr. Goddard to be carried on by correspondence.[5] *That fall she became too ill to write much in her own hand, but not so downhearted that she could not amuse herself in reporting that she had named one of her dogs "Byron," and that it had "devoured a bird whole entire feathers and all."*[6]

Now needing full-time medical care, Caroline underwent a procedure called "tapping," in which needles were inserted to reduce water accumulation in the tissues due to "dropsy"—progressive organ failure causing retention of water.

2. Lady Caroline to William Lamb. [Fall 1827.]

Dearest William:

This is the first time I can write. I have suffered much, and I hope patiently, since I wrote last. Tapping is by no means an agreeable sensation. It does not give pain like a tooth drawn, but it turns you deadly cold and sick. The operation was more troublesome than usual; this is the first day I feel easy. All the county have been to see me. My dear brother has read to me and soothed me, and is coming back. I never met with such affection and kindness as from all persons of both our families, and dear Emily and Caroline; but what pleased me most was your dear letter saying you loved and forgave me. God bless you, dearest. My love to Augustus. All here doing well.

Ever yours,
Caroline

3. Lady Caroline to William Lamb. 3 November 1827.

Augustus has not been well [—] perhaps he leads too regular a life and does not take enough exercise and too much tea & bread & butter—Everybody I have seen makes great enquiry after you and after him—I am quite surprized to hear you have game from Brocket, pray if you can get a pair easily send me some grouse [. . .] My brother Wm is not well at Harrogate. I take my simple medicines and as Dr Goddard is writing for me he will probably tell you what they are (Blue Pill & squills and sweet sp of nitre with an infusion of cascarella bark)[7] God bless you my

---

[5] Lady Caroline to Augustus Lamb. 20 September 1827. Hertfordshire Archives. D/ELb F76/9.

[6] Lady Caroline to Augustus Lamb. [fall 1827.] Hertfordshire Archives. D/ELb F76/12.

[7] "Blue pill" was cyanide or perhaps mercury, given most often for syphilis, but also as a general prophylactic for the severely ill. Cascarella (or cascara) bark, a licorice-flavored root that acted as a laxative, was given to her in a glass of sherry.

Dearest William—I will write to you myself very soon do not forget to write a line often to me—everything at Brocket is going quite well. Yours most affectionately and gratefully, Caroline Lamb

William was kept informed by Dr. Goddard and by Lady Morgan, who happened to be in Ireland that fall. He knew that Caroline had become unnaturally calm.

4. Lady Caroline to Lady Duncannon. 5–6 December 1827.

Dearest Maria as I cannot sit up I am obliged to use a pencil—I never hear Duncannon's name without crying my own dear dear brother—but I owe it to myself to say that except Wm. Lamb Lady Cowper, my kind brother William—all the under people & Dr. Roe told me he was the person spoke most severely against me and wanted me locked up in a Mad House, so that I fear his very name—I consider my painful illness as a great Blessing—I feel return'd to my God & my duty & my Dearest husband, & my heart which was so proud & insensible is quite overcome with the great kindness I receive—I brought myself to be quite another person & broke that horrid spell which prevented my saying my prayers. So that if I were better, I would go with you & your Dear children to church. I say all this Dearest Maria, lest you should think I flew to Religion because I was in danger—it is no such thing my heart is softened I see how good & kind others are & I am quite resigned to die—I do not myself think there is a chance for me

Finally, Caroline's doctor warned William that little time remained for Caroline.

5. Dr. Goddard to William Lamb. 13 December 1827.

My Dear Sir,

I regret very much that I have but a melancholy account to give you today of Lady Caroline's health. Saturday she seemed in good spirits; but on that night she began to complain of pain in her side, accompanied with cough and shortness of breath. These symptoms are, I think, partly accidental, and may not continue; but should they, they will certainly give us great cause of alarm. There is another change, also; she is inattentive to what is going on. She speaks with difficulty, and seems unwilling to see many people. You may gather too plainly from all these symptoms the unwelcome news that her ladyship is getting worse; her sufferings she still bears with fortitude, and complains but little.

I remain, dear Sir,

Your obedient and humble Servant,
G. Goddard.

William could not come immediately, however. He wrote to Caroline from Dublin after Christmas, then made plans to travel as soon as possible. She received visits from Lady Cowper, her brother Willy, Caro George, and Edward Bulwer, who found her "dreadfully altered."[8]

6. William Lamb to Lady Caroline. 6 January 1828.

Phoenix Park, Dublin

I received your little line yesterday, & I have also received with great pleasure Dr. Goddard's account that you were better. My heart is almost broken, that I cannot come over directly, but your brother, to whom I have written, will explain to you the difficult situation in which I am placed. How unfortunate & melancholy that you should be so ill now & that it should be at a time when I, who have had so many years of idleness, am so fixed & chained down by circumstances. Augustus is very well. I gave him today Dr. Goddard's letter, with which he was much pleased [. . .]

William and Augustus arrived in time to see Caroline rally briefly and talk with them. She survived a few days longer, dictating letters to friends.

7. Lady Caroline to Lady Holland. [January 1828.]

I can only write one line to thank you for your generous conduct—will you accept from my heart my deep regret for the past—it makes me most unhappy now—I trust I may see you if not believe me with every affectionate and grateful feeling

Yours
Caroline Lamb

[8] Edward Bulwer to his wife Rosina. 10 January 1828. Knebworth Archive, Letters of Edward Bulwer, Box 71. I am grateful to Cindy Lawford for supplying this information.

"To write," Lady Caroline had told Lady Morgan, "was once my resource and pleasure."[9] *But now pen and pencil were laid aside for good. On 25 January 1828 Caroline died. William had stepped out for a moment, and she passed quietly away.*

Caroline's body was interred in the crypt beneath the lectern at St. Ethelreda's church in Hatfield. In her will, she bequeathed to her friend and fellow writer, Lady Morgan, the picture of Byron by George Sanders which she had so much desired. Five months after Lady Caroline died, Lord Melbourne passed away at age eighty three. William finally assumed the family title and his place in the House of Lords.

William later wrote that he felt, "in a manner which I have often heard others describe, but in which I have never felt before myself, and did not think I could feel, a sort of impossibility of believing that I shall never see her countenance or hear her voice again, and a sort of sense of desolation, solitude and carelessness about everything, when I forced myself to remember that she was really gone."[10]

---

[9] *Lady Morgan's Memoirs*, 2:211.

[10] Ziegler, *Melbourne: A Biography*, 105.

Who's Who

Bessborough, Lady (Countess). Henrietta Frances Spencer Ponsonby. Mother of Lady Caroline and her three brothers, John, Frederick, and William. With her lover, Granville Leveson Gower, she also had two other children.

Bessborough, Lord (third Earl). Frederick Ponsonby. Father of Lady Caroline Lamb. Held title of Lord Duncannon until his father, the second Earl, died in 1793.

Bruce, Michael. Acquaintance of Byron's who had an affair with Lady Caroline after meeting her in Paris in 1815.

Bulwer-Lytton, Edward. Novelist and poet, he developed a youthful crush on Lady Caroline and almost became her lover late in her life.

Byron, Lady. Anne Isabella ("Annabella") Milbanke. Wife of Lord Byron and cousin of Lady Caroline's husband, William Lamb.

Byron, Lord (sixth Baron). George Gordon. Poet and political activist, he had many love affairs, including one with Lady Caroline Lamb in 1812, and died helping the Greek revolutionary movement.

Cavendish, Georgiana (Little G, or G). Lady Caroline Lamb's cousin, the elder daughter of Georgiana, Duchess of Devonshire. Later Lady Morpeth. Later the sixth Countess of Carlisle.

Cavendish, Harriet Elizabeth (Harryo or Harrio). Lady Caroline Lamb's cousin, the younger daughter of Georgiana, Duchess of Devonshire. Later Lady Granville.

Churchill, Susan Spencer. Illegitimate daughter of Harriet Caroline Spencer, a relative of Lady Caroline's, who became the ward of William and Lady Caroline Lamb.

Cooper, Lady Barbara Ashley. Married Willy Ponsonby, Lady Caroline's favorite brother.

Cowper, Lady. née Emily Lamb. Later, Lady Palmerston. Sister of William Lamb. Upon Cowper's death, she married a future prime minister of England, Lord Palmerston.

Devonshire, Duchess of. Georgiana Spencer Cavendish. Aunt of Lady Caroline.

Devonshire, Duchess of (*see Lady Elizabeth Foster*).

Devonshire, fifth Duke of. William Cavendish (nicknamed "Canis"). Uncle of Lady Caroline.

Devonshire, sixth Duke of (Hart). William Spencer George Cavendish. Cousin of Lady Caroline. Nicknamed "Hart," because he held the honorific title of "The Marquis of Hartington" until the fifth Duke died in 1811.

Duncannon, Lady Maria (John's Wife, formerly Maria Fane).

Duncannon, Lord John Ponsonby. Lady Caroline's eldest brother.

Fane, Maria (*see Lady Duncannon*).

Fleming, J. Wilmington. Obscure poet to whom Lady Caroline gave her journals to read and who later tried to use them for blackmail.

Foscolo, Ugo. Italian novelist. He advised Lady Caroline on her writing.

Foster, Lady Elizabeth. Lived with the fifth Duke and Georgiana, the Duchess, bearing the Duke two children, then married the fifth Duke after Georgiana's death.

Goddard, Dr. B. Lady Caroline's personal physician through the last years of her life.

Godwin, William. Author, publisher, and social philosopher, husband of Mary Wollstonecraft and father to their daughter, Mary Shelley (author of *Frankenstein*). He became Lady Caroline's close friend and mentor after they began corresponding in 1819.

Grammont, Corisande de (*see Lady Ossulston*).

Granville, Viscount. Granville Leveson Gower. Lover of Caroline's mother, with whom he had two children before he married Caroline's cousin, Harrio.

Grey, Lord Charles. Famous tea maker and lover of Georgiana, Duchess of Devonshire, who bore him a child, almost ruining herself when her husband discovered she was pregnant. Formerly Lord Howick.

Harrio or Harryo (*see Harriet Cavendish*).

Hobhouse, John Cam. Political liberal and close friend of Byron as well as longtime acquaintance and correspondent of Lady Caroline Lamb, witnessing many scenes during and after Caroline's affair with Byron in 1812.

Holland, Lady. One of Lady Caroline's closest bluestocking (or liberal-feminist) friends. Caroline had an affair with her son, Godfrey, and later satirized Lady Holland as "The Princess Madagascar" in her novel *Glenarvon*.

Howick, Lord (*see Lord Charles Grey*).

Lamb, Augustus. Only child of William and Lady Caroline Lamb, born epileptic and retarded.

Lamb, Caroline Adelaide St. Jules. Exact contemporary of Lady Caroline Lamb and illegitimate child of Lady Elizabeth Foster and the fifth Duke of Devonshire, she married William Lamb's brother, George and was nicknamed "Caro George" to distinguish her from Lady Caroline Lamb.

Lamb, Lady Caroline. Born Caroline Ponsonby. Attained the title of "Lady" when her father became third Earl Bessborough. Also called "Caro William" to distinguish her from George Lamb's wife, the former Caroline St. Jules.

Lamb, Emily (*see Lady Cowper*).

Lamb, George. William's younger brother and a hack journalist and amateur playwright.

Lamb, William. Lady Caroline's husband. Later Lord Melbourne, prime minister of England under Queen Victoria.

Lee, Dr. Robert. Augustus Lamb's personal physician and tutor from 1817 to 1822.

Leigh, Augusta. Lord Byron's half-sister, with whom he was accused of having an incestuous affair that resulted in the birth of an illegitimate daughter.

Leveson Gower, Granville (*see Lord Granville*).

Little G (*see Georgiana Cavendish*).

Malthus, Thomas Robert (1766–1834). Author of *An Essay on the Principle of Population* (1798), to whom Lady Caroline appealed for help with her fiction-writing.

Melbourne, Viscount. Peniston Lamb. William Lamb's father, who lived until after Caroline died, so that she never became "Lady Melbourne" and so that during her lifetime William never achieved financial independence.

Milbanke, Anne Isabella (*see Lady Byron*).

Morgan, Lady. Formerly Sydney Owenson. Novelist, feminist, and friend of Lady Caroline.

Morpeth, Lady (*see Georgiana Cavendish*).

Morpeth, Lord. Married Caroline's cousin, Georgiana Cavendish.

Nathan, Isaac. Jewish tenor, composer, and publisher who collaborated with Lord Byron on *A Selection of Hebrew Melodies* (1815–1816) and with Lady Caroline Lamb on almost a dozen songs, including music printed in two of her novels. Lady Caroline became godmother to his daughter.

Ossulston, Lady. Corisande de Grammont, a French émigré who grew up in the Devonshire household with Lady Caroline.

Oxford, Lady. Jane Elizabeth Harley. Lady Caroline's friend and tutor, who betrayed her trust by having an affair with Byron after he had dropped Caroline.

Palmerston, Lady Emily (*see Lady Cowper*).

Ponsonby, Caroline (*see Lady Caroline Lamb*).

Ponsonby, Frederick Cavendish. Lady Caroline's older brother, a war hero at the battles of Talavera and Waterloo.

Ponsonby, John William. Lady Caroline's eldest brother, became Lord Duncannon and married Lady Maria Fane.

Ponsonby, William ("Willy") Francis Spencer. Lady Caroline's younger, favorite brother, who married Lady Barbara Ashley Cooper.

Preedy, Rev. James. Performed the marriages of William to Lady Caroline and (after being tricked into believing her was only repeating the ceremony) of Lady Elizabeth Foster to the fifth Duke.

St. Jules, Caroline (*see Caroline St. Jules Lamb*).

Sheridan, Esther Jane Ogle. Nicknamed "Hecca," Richard Brinsley Sheridan's second wife, who participated in a bizarre scene on the night Lady Caroline gave birth to her son Augustus.

Sheridan, Richard Brinsley. Playwright, politician, and lover of Caroline's mother, Lady Bessborough.

Spencer, George John, second Earl Spencer. Lady Caroline's Uncle.

Spencer, Lady Georgiana. Lady Caroline's grandmother.

Staël, Madame de. Novelist and essayist, a major influence in French and European literature who interacted with both Byron and Lady Caroline.

Trimmer, Selina. Governess for the Devonshire and Bessborough households.

Webster, Sir Godfrey Vassal. Son of Lady Holland by her first marriage and lover of Lady Caroline in the two years before she met Byron.

Webster, Thomasina. Augustus Lamb's beloved nurse and governess.

Wellington, Arthur Wellesley, first Duke. Hero of Waterloo (1815), who had a liaison with Lady Caroline in Paris after his great victory.

White, Lydia. Bluestocking hostess to whom Lady Caroline later dedicated her third and last novel, *Ada Reis* (1823).

Chronology

1779	March 15	William Lamb born.
1781		Caroline's brother John William Ponsonby (later Lord Duncannon) born.
1783	July 6	Caroline's brother Frederick Cavendish Ponsonby born.
1785	August 16	Caroline Rosalie St. Jules (later "Caro George") born.
	August 29	Harriet Elizabeth Cavendish ("Harryo" or "Harrio") born.
	November 13	Caroline Ponsonby (later Lady Caroline Lamb) born.
1787		Caroline's brother William ("Willy") Francis Spencer Ponsonby born.
1788	January 22	George Gordon, sixth Lord Byron, born.
1790		William Spencer Cavendish, Marquis of Hartington ("Hart," later the sixth Duke of Devonshire) born.
1791	November	Caroline leaves for Europe with her mother and Aunt Georgiana, the Duchess of Devonshire, who has been banished by the Duke ("Canis") for becoming pregnant by her lover, Earl Grey.
1793	January	Louis XVI of France guillotined.
	March 11	Lord Bessborough dies, making Caroline's father the third Earl Bessborough and her officially "Lady Caroline."
	May	Caroline's Aunt Georgiana and Lady Elizabeth Foster are permitted by the Duke of Devonshire to return to England, but her mother, Harriet, is too ill to travel.
	October	Marie Antoinette guillotined.
1793–1794		Caroline suffers a life-threatening illness in Italy, and her mother, Harriet, falls in love with Granville Leveson Gower.
1794	August	Caroline's mother is well enough to travel home to England.
1799		William Lamb takes his degree at Cambridge and goes to Glasgow to study.
1802	August	Caroline and William Lamb meet and are infatuated.
1803	May 18	Britain declares war on France.
1805	June 3	Caroline and William Lamb are married.
1806	February 1	Caroline delivers a girl, who dies shortly after. William elected Member of Parliament for Leominster.
	March 30	Caroline's Aunt Georgiana, Duchess of Devonshire, dies.
	November	William opens Parliament and Caroline sneaks in dressed as a man to watch proudly.
1807	August 29	Caroline's son Augustus born.

1809	May 17	George Lamb marries Caroline Rosalie Adelaide St. Jules.
	October 19	Lady Elizabeth Foster marries fifth Duke of Devonshire (Canis).
	December 24	Granville marries "Harrio" (Lady Harriet Elizabeth Cavendish).
1810	March/April	Caroline begins an affair with Sir Godfrey Vassal Webster that becomes known to her mother and mother-in-law. She tries to break it off, but it continues into the next year.
1811	February 5	Regency bill becomes law, and the Prince of Wales assumes the royal duties because George II is incapacitated by porphyria.
	July 29	Fifth Duke of Devonshire, dies, making "Hart" the Sixth Duke.
1812	March 10	*Childe Harold's Pilgrimage* officially published.
	March 25	Byron attends a waltzing party at Lady Caroline Lamb's. Their affair begins.
	August 12	Caroline runs away and Byron manages to bring her home.
	September	Caroline is taken to Ireland by her family.
	November	Byron delivers the blow: Caroline is no longer his lover.
1813	January	Caroline forges Byron's handwriting to obtain a painting from John Murray.
	July 5	Caroline cuts herself in a chaotic scene at Lady Heathcote's ball.
	August 10	Austria declares war on France.
1814		Caroline's brother Willy marries Lady Barbara Ashley Cooper.
	March 18	Caroline's grandmother Lady Spencer dies.
	Spring	Caroline meets Isaac Nathan, who arranges music in honor of her brother Willy's engagement.
	May 4	Napoleon exiled; arrives on Elba.
	July 1	Caroline attends a masked ball at Burlington House held by Watier's Club to honor the Duke of Wellington's victory over Napoleon.
1815	January 2	Byron is married at Seaham to Anne Isabella ("Annabella") Milbanke
	March 20	Napoleon returns to power in France.
	March 28	The Byrons settle at 13 Piccadilly Terrace (house of the Duchess of Devonshire).
	April	Nathan and Byron's *Hebrew Melodies* volume 1 published.
	June 18	Napoleon defeated at Waterloo.
	August 11	Viscount Melbourne created Lord Melbourne.
	August 12	Granville Leveson Gower created Viscount Granville. William and Caroline visit Brussels and Paris.
	October 16	Napoleon exiled to Saint Helena.
1816	March	Lady Caroline visits and advises Lady Byron on her separation while also trying to get Byron to reconcile with his wife.
	April 18	Nathan and Byron's *Hebrew Melodies* volume 2 published.
	April 21	Byron signs deed of separation from his wife.
	April 24	Byron leaves London for the Continent.
	May 9	Lady Caroline's first novel, *Glenarvon*, published by Henry Colburn.
	July 7	William elected Member of Parliament for Northampton.
	November 18	Canto 3 of Byron's *Childe Harold* published in London.
1817	July 14	Madame de Staël dies.
1818	March	Susan Spencer Churchill born to Harriet Caroline Spencer; the illegitimate child becomes Lady Bessborough's ward.
	April 6	Lady Melbourne dies.

	Spring	Emily Cowper (William's sister) fights to get Lady Caroline admitted to Almack's Club.
1819	February/March	Lady Caroline canvasses for William's brother, George, in a parliamentary election, which he wins against John Cam Hobhouse.
	July 15	Byron's *Don Juan* Cantos 1 and 2 published.
	October	Lady Caroline's *A New Canto* (satire of *Don Juan*) published.
1820	January 29	George III dies.
	February 16	George III buried.
	April 27	George IV opens Parliament.
	Summer	Lady Caroline appears at Almack's dressed as Don Juan with attendant devils (pages in devil costumes).
	August	Queen Caroline's trial for adultery with her courier, Bartolommeo Bergami, begins and will last through November. She is barely acquitted.
1821	July 19	George IV's coronation at Westminster Abbey, to which Queen Caroline fails to gain entry.
	August 7	Queen Caroline dies estranged from the King.
	August 8	Byron's *Don Juan* Cantos 3–5 published.
	Fall	Caroline's *Gordon: A Tale* (another satire of *Don Juan*) published.
	November 5	The infant son of Lady Caroline's brother William and Lady Barbara dies in Parma, Italy.
	November 11	Lady Bessborough dies in Florence, Italy.
1822	January 28	Annabella's mother (Lady Noel) dies and Lord and Lady Byron assume the additional name of Noel.
	April 19	Byron's illegitimate daughter by Claire Claremont, Allegra, dies.
	Fall	Caroline's *Graham Hamilton* published by Henry Colburn.
1823	March	Caroline's *Ada Reis* published by John Murray.
	April	Caroline's pocket-diary, *Penruddock*, published by John Murray.
1824	March 30	Lady Elizabeth Foster, Duchess of Devonshire, dies.
	April 19	Lord Byron dies in Greece.
	May 17	Byron's memoirs burned at John Murray's offices in Albemarle Street, and it is disclosed that Murray let Caroline read them.
	June 29	The *Florida* arrives in England with Byron's remains.
	July 12	Byron's funeral cortege leaves London and passes through Welwyn, Hertfordshire, where Caroline encounters it.
	July 16	Byron's funeral.
	October 23	Medwin's *Conversations of Lord Byron* published and Caroline reads his vitriolic "Remember Thee" for the first time.
1825	Summer	William finally yields to family pressure to separate from Caroline, who signs separation agreement, meets obscure poet Wilmington Fleming, and departs for Calais.
	October	Lady Caroline back in London; Doctor Goddard makes diagnosis of insanity.
1826	January	Lady Caroline returns to Brocket Hall, Welwyn.
1827	April	William appointed Chief Secretary to the Lord Lieutenant for Ireland, takes Augustus with him.
	September	Caroline severely ill.

1828	January 15	William notified Caroline likely to die.
	January 25	Lady Caroline dies, William and Augustus having arrived in time to speak with her.
	July 22	William's father dies at age 83 and William becomes Lord Melbourne.
1836		Caroline and William's son, Augustus, dies.
1848		William Lamb dies.

List of Letters with Sources

Chapter One Letters, 1797–1804

1. Lady Caroline Ponsonby to Lady Georgiana Cavendish. 7 January 1797. Castle Howard Archives J18/35/100.
2. Lady Caroline Ponsonby to Lady Georgiana Cavendish. 21 January 1797. Castle Howard Archives J18/35/91.
3. Lady Caroline Ponsonby to Lady Georgiana Cavendish. 25 September 1797. Castle Howard Archives J18/35/98.
4. Lady Caroline Ponsonby to Lady Georgiana Cavendish. [November– December 1797.] Castle Howard Archives J18/35/89. Archival docket says 1797. Christmas Eve was on a Sunday in that year, and the Bessboroughs were indeed back at Roehampton in fall 1797.
5. Lady Caroline Ponsonby to Lady Georgiana Cavendish. [1797–1798.] Castle Howard Archives J18/35/99. Juvenile handwriting dates it to same period as other letters of 1797–1798.
6. Lady Caroline Ponsonby to Lady Georgiana Cavendish. [1797–1798.] Castle Howard Archives J18/35/90A. Juvenile handwriting dates it to same period as other letters of 1797–1798.
7. Lady Caroline Ponsonby to Lady Georgiana Cavendish. [1797–1798.] Castle Howard Archives J18/35/94. Juvenile handwriting dates it to same period as other letters of 1797–1798.
8. Lady Caroline Ponsonby to Georgiana, Lady Morpeth, future sixth Countess of Carlisle. [1802.] Castle Howard Archives J18/35/32 D[evonshire] House. The year is 1802 because *Edinburgh Review* was founded in that year. There were invasion scares of 1801, and in 1802 the Treaty of Amiens was signed on March 25.

Chapter Two Letters, 1805–1809

1. Lady Caroline Lamb to Georgiana, Lady Morpeth, future sixth Countess of Carlisle. [18–20 June 1805.] Castle Howard Archives J18/35/9. Caroline states almost three weeks after her marriage.
2. Lady Caroline Lamb to the Marquis of Hartington. 23 June 1805. Devonshire Archives. Chatsworth [UK], fifth Duke's Group, f. 1814.1.
3. Lady Caroline Lamb to Georgiana, Lady Morpeth, future sixth Countess of Carlisle. [August–November 1805.] Castle Howard Archives J18/35/1. Caroline was pregnant, but not at Priory yet.

4. Lady Caroline Lamb to Georgiana, Lady Morpeth, future sixth Countess of Carlisle. [October–November 1805.] Castle Howard Archives J18/35/29. Plays in which William Lamb performed at the Abercorns in the Priory, Stanmore, shortly after Lady Caroline Lamb's marriage to him.
5. Lady Caroline Lamb to Georgiana, Lady Morpeth, future sixth Countess of Carlisle. [October–November 1805.] Castle Howard Archives J18/35/30 Visiting Abercorns and brother's imminent wedding in November.
6. Lady Caroline Lamb to Georgiana, Lady Spencer. 9 December 1805. Printed in Bessborough and Aspinall, *Lady Bessborough and Her Family Circle*, 140–42.
7. Lady Caroline Lamb to Georgiana, Lady Morpeth, future sixth Countess of Carlisle. [April 1806.] Castle Howard Archives J18/35/88.
8. Lady Caroline Lamb to Georgiana, Lady Morpeth, future sixth Countess of Carlisle. [September 1806.] Castle Howard Archives J18/35/71. Other dated letters in this sequence have content clues.
9. Lady Caroline Lamb to Georgiana, Lady Morpeth, future sixth Countess of Carlisle. [14 September 1806.] Castle Howard Archives J18/35/[77]. Other dated letters in this sequence have content clues.
10. Lady Caroline Lamb to Georgiana, Lady Morpeth, future sixth Countess of Carlisle. 14 November 1806. Castle Howard Archives J18/35/78.
11. Lady Caroline Lamb to Georgiana, Lady Morpeth, future sixth Countess of Carlisle. 26 November 1806. Castle Howard Archives J18/35/39.
12. Lady Caroline Lamb to Georgiana, Lady Morpeth, future sixth Countess of Carlisle. [26–27 November 1806.] Castle Howard Archives J18/35/69. Dates to previous letter.
13. Lady Caroline Lamb to Lady Bessborough. 14–15 January 1807. Bessborough Papers, Chichester. Printed in Bessborough and Aspinall, *Lady Bessborough and Her Family Circle*, 156–57.
14. Lady Caroline Lamb to Georgiana, Lady Morpeth, future sixth Countess of Carlisle. [January–March 1807.] Castle Howard Archives J18/35/76. Caroline was married, pregnant, and making a book for G.
15. Lady Caroline Lamb to Georgiana, Lady Morpeth. 16 March 1807. Castle Howard Archives J18/71/1.
16. Lady Caroline Lamb to Georgiana, Lady Morpeth, future sixth Countess of Carlisle. [Spring 1807.] Castle Howard Archives J18/35/31. Caroline was pregnant, and her sister-in-law, Maria, Lady Duncannon, had married in November 1806.
17. Lady Caroline Lamb to Georgiana, Lady Morpeth, future sixth Countess of Carlisle. 3 August 1807. Castle Howard Archives J18/35/43.
18. Lady Caroline Lamb to Georgiana, Lady Morpeth, future sixth Countess of Carlisle. 13 October 1807. Castle Howard Archives J18/35/44.
19. Lady Caroline Lamb to Lady Bessborough. 30 October 1807. Bessborough Papers, C1 D4, folder 161.
20. Lady Caroline Lamb to Lady Bessborough. 24 April 1808. Printed in Bessborough and Aspinall, *Lady Bessborough and Her Family Circle*, 168–69.
21. Lady Caroline Lamb to Lady Bessborough. 21 August 1808. Printed in Bessborough and Aspinall, *Lady Bessborough and Her Family Circle*, 170–71.
22. Lady Caroline Lamb to Mr. Baker, her tailor. 25–26 October 1808. British Library Add. MS 38855 f. 225.
23. Lady Caroline Lamb to Georgiana, Lady Morpeth, future sixth Countess of Carlisle. 30 September 1808. Castle Howard Archives J18/35/49.
24. Lady Caroline Lamb to William Lamb. 27 May 1809. Hertfordshire Archives D/ELbF32/3.

25. Lady Caroline Lamb to Lady Bessborough. 28 July 1809. Printed in Bessborough and Aspinall, *Lady Bessborough and Her Family Circle*, 185–86.
26. Lady Caroline Lamb to Lady Bessborough. August 1809. Printed in Bessborough and Aspinall, *Lady Bessborough and Her Family Circle*, 186–87.
27. Lady Caroline Lamb to Lady Holland. [fall 1806 or later.] British Library Add. MS 51560 f. 124. Probably later, though archivist docket says "before 30 Jan. 1806." Tone more consistent with her later freaks of behavior at parties.
28. Lady Caroline Lamb to Lady Bessborough. 14 August 1809. Printed in Bessborough and Aspinall, *Lady Bessborough and Her Family Circle*, 187–88.
29. Lady Caroline Lamb to William Lamb. 4 September [1809] from Ryde. Hertfordshire Archives D/ELb F32/4.30.
30. Lady Caroline Lamb to the Marquis of Hartington. 29 September 1809. Devonshire Archives. Chatsworth [UK], fifth Duke's Group, f. 1954.
31. Lady Caroline Lamb to the Marquis of Hartington. 11 October 1809. Devonshire Archives. Chatsworth [UK], fifth Duke's Group, f. 1957.
32. Lady Caroline Lamb to the Marquis of Hartington. 9 November 1809. Devonshire Archives. Chatsworth [UK], fifth Duke's Group, f. 1962.
33. Lady Caroline Lamb to Georgiana, Lady Morpeth, future sixth Countess of Carlisle. 17 November 1809. Castle Howard Archives J18/35/51.
34. Lady Caroline Lamb to the Marquis of Hartington. 27 December 1809. Devonshire MSS. Chatsworth [UK], fifth Duke's Group, f. 1965.

Chapter Three Letters, 1810–1811

1. Lady Caroline Lamb to the Marquis of Hartington. 21 January 1810. Devonshire MSS. Chatsworth [UK], fifth Duke's Group, f. 1966.
2. Lady Caroline Lamb to Lady Melbourne. April 1810. British Library Add. MS 45546 ff.13–15.
3. Lady Caroline Lamb to Lady Melbourne. [April–June] 1810. British Library Add. MS 45546 ff. 21–22. Handwriting and tone, content similar to other letters of April–June in this sequence in the British Library.
4. Lady Caroline Lamb to Lady Holland. After 11 July 1810. British Library Add. MS 51560 f. 135.
5. Lady Caroline Lamb to Lady Holland. After 14 July 1810, British Library Add. MS 51560 f. 137.
6. Lady Caroline Lamb to the Marquis of Hartington. 21 July 1810. Devonshire MSS. Chatsworth [UK], fifth Duke's Group, f. 1983.
7. Lady Caroline Lamb to the Marquis of Hartington. 31 July 1810. Devonshire MSS. Chatsworth [UK], fifth Duke's Group, f. 1983.
8. Lady Caroline Lamb to Georgiana, Lady Morpeth, future sixth Countess of Carlisle. 10 August 1810. Castle Howard Archives J18/35/52.
9. Lady Caroline Lamb [Brocket Hall] to the Marquis of Hartington. 2 October 1810. Devonshire MSS. Chatsworth [UK], fifth Duke's Group, f. 1990.
10. Lady Caroline Lamb to Lady Holland. 18 October 1810. British Library Add. MS 51560 f. 147.
11. Lady Caroline Lamb to the Marquis of Hartington. 10 November 1810. Devonshire MSS. Chatsworth [UK], fifth Duke's Group, f. 1993.
12. Lady Caroline Lamb to Lady Holland. before 16 [or 11?] April 1811. British Library Add. MS 51560 f. 159.
13. Lady Caroline Lamb to Lady Holland. May 1811. British Library Add. MS 51560 f. 164.
14. Lady Caroline Lamb to Lady Holland. 29 May 1811. British Library Add. MS 51560 f. 177.

15. Lady Caroline Lamb to Lady Holland. 4 June 1811. British Library Add. MS 51560 ff. 184–186.
16. Lady Caroline Lamb to Lord Holland 27 June 1811. British Library Add. MS 51558 f. 7.
17. Lady Caroline Lamb to Lady Holland. [July 1811.] British Library Add. MS 51560 f. 187.
18. Lady Caroline Lamb to Lady Holland. [July 1811.] British Library Add. MS 51560 f. 190.
19. Lady Caroline Lamb to Lady Holland. 6 August 1811. British Library Add. MS 51560 f. 194.
20. Lady Caroline Lamb to Georgiana, Lady Morpeth, future sixth Countess of Carlisle. 25 October 1811. Castle Howard Archives J18/35/53.
21. Lady Caroline Lamb to the sixth Duke of Devonshire. 14 November 1811. Devonshire MSS. Chatsworth [UK], sixth Duke's Group, f. 36.
22. Lady Caroline Lamb to Miss Owenson [Lady Morgan]. 1811. Printed in *Lady Morgan's Memoirs*, 1:442–43.

Chapter Four Letters, 1812–1813

1. Lady Caroline to Lord Byron. 9 March 1812. Bodleian, Dep. Lovelace Byron 155, f. 73.
2. Lady Caroline Lamb to Lord Byron. [11 March?] 1812. Bodleian, Dep. Lovelace Byron 155, f. 74. Duncan Wu reported that he was unable to locate the manuscript of this poem among the Byron-Lovelace papers in the Bodleian Library. While I never saw the original, the archive responded to my query of October 2002 that the original is on deposit.
3. Lady Caroline Lamb to Lord Byron. 27 March 1812. Murray Archive. This letter was written on fancy stationery with a blue edge, embossed at the corners with shells and around the edges with scrolls. 27 March was a Friday.
4. Lady Caroline Lamb to Lord Byron. [March–June 1812.] Murray Archive.
5. Lady Caroline Lamb to Lord Byron. [May 1812.] Bodleian, Dep. Lovelace Byron 155, f. 76.
6. Lady Caroline Lamb to Lord Byron. [April–June 1812.] Murray Archive.
7. Lady Caroline Lamb to Lord Byron. [April–June 1812.] Murray Archive.
8. Lady Caroline Lamb to Fletcher, Byron's valet. [April–June 1812.] Murray Archive.
9. Lady Caroline Lamb to Lord Byron. 9 August 1812. Bodleian, Dep. Lovelace Byron 155, ff. 79–81.
10. Lady Caroline Lamb to Lady Melbourne. [12 August 1812.] British Library Add. MS 45546 f. 53. This note was almost certainly written and sent back to Melbourne House after Lady Caroline ran away on 12 August 1812, before Byron himself returned her to her family.
11. Lady Caroline Lamb to Lady Melbourne. [13 August 1812.] British Library Add. MS 45546 f. 29 ff. 31–32.
12. Lady Caroline Lamb to Lord Byron at the Albany. [15–23 August 1812.] Murray Archive.
13. Lady Caroline Lamb to Lady Melbourne. [Almost certainly August 1812.]
14. Lady Caroline Lamb to Lady Melbourne. 28–29 September 1812. British Library Add. MS 45546 ff. 34–35.
15. Lady Caroline Lamb to Lady Melbourne. 15 October 1812. British Library Add. MS 45546 ff. 38–39. Lamb Papers.
16. Lady Caroline Lamb to Lady Melbourne. 14 October 1812. British Library Add. MS 45546 f. 37.
17. Lady Caroline Lamb to Lady Melbourne. 13–17 October 1812. British Library Add. MS 45548 f. 56. The letter bears a 20 Oct. 1812 Postmark, but is dated from Kilkenny, where the Bessboroughs stayed from 13–17 October. This letter is scrawled and smeared as if she had wept over it.

18. Lady Caroline Lamb to Lady Melbourne. [October 1812.] British Library Add. MS 45546 f. 41.
19. Lady Caroline Lamb to Lady Melbourne. 4 November 1812 British Library Add. MS 45546 ff. 46–48.
20. Lady Caroline Lamb to Lady Melbourne. [fall 1812?] British Library Add. MS 45546 ff. 70–71.
21. Lady Caroline Lamb to Lady Holland. [February 1813.] British Library Add. MS 51560 f. 199. Archivist docket seems correct.
22. Lady Caroline Lamb to Lady Melbourne. [Before 24 March 1813.] British Library Add. MS 45546 ff. 56–60. Dated from next letter.
23. Lady Caroline Lamb to Lady Melbourne. Bath. 24 March 1813. British Library Add. MS 45546 ff. 65–67.
24. Lady Caroline Lamb to Lord Byron, draft of a letter in her blue Commonplace Book. [May 1813?] Murray Archive. The book was begun in 1812, seemingly before she departed for Ireland. This letter probably dates to May 1813, when Caroline knew Byron was planning to leave in June to follow Lady Oxford to the continent.
25. Lady Caroline Lamb to Lord Byron. [before 5 July 1813] British Library Add. MS 45548 ff. 132–35.
26. Lady Caroline Lamb to John Murray. [May–July 1813.] Murray Archive.
27. Lady Caroline Lamb to John Murray. 7 October 1813. Murray Archive.
28. Lady Caroline Lamb to John Murray. 9 November 1813. Murray Archive.
29. Lady Caroline Lamb to John Murray. [fall 1813.] Murray Archive.
30. Lady Caroline to John Murray. [28 December 1813]. Murray Archive.
31. Lady Caroline Lamb to Lord Byron. [1813.] Murray Archive.
32. Lady Caroline Lamb to Lord Byron. [1813–1814?] Caroline alludes to "the Picture" she wanted in 1813 and to sketches of Madame de Staël, whom she did not meet until 1813.
33. Lady Caroline Lamb to Lord Byron. [1812–1814?]. Murray Archive.

Chapter Five Letters, 1814–1815

1. Lady Caroline Lamb to John Murray. [1813–1814.] Murray Archive. Date is tentative.
2. Lady Caroline Lamb to John Murray. 25 January 1814. Murray Archive.
3. Lady Caroline Lamb to John Murray. [February 1814.] Murray Archive. *The Corsair* was published 1 February 1814.
4. Lady Caroline Lamb to John Murray. [February 1814.] Murray Archive. *The Corsair* was published 1 February 1814.
5. Lady Caroline Lamb. Letter to her uncle Lord Spencer, 13 May 1814. British Library Althorp Papers 76113, unfoliated.
6. Lady Caroline Lamb to Lord Byron. [1814.] Murray Archive. Empress Josephine died in 1814.
7. Lady Caroline Lamb to Lord Byron. 3 June [1814.] Murray Archive. Caroline mentions a letter written to her two years before to the day, which was the approximate time she passed Annabella's poems to Byron for his reaction.
8. Lady Caroline Lamb to Lord Byron. [June 1814.] Murray Archive. Archivist docket: late 1814 or early 1815—she has known him "near 3 years"—but that is probably summer 1814, if she exaggerates slightly, and she speaks of the 'squerade, which could be Watier's Club Ball at Burlington House, 1 July 1814.
9. Lady Caroline Lamb to Lord Byron. [September–October 1814.] Murray Archive. Caroline has heard Byron is engaged but does not know to whom.

10. Lady Caroline Lamb to John Murray. [not after September–October 1814.] Paper watermarked "1814." Caroline has heard Byron is engaged but still does not know to whom.
11. Lady Caroline Lamb to John Murray. 18 November 1814 Murray Archive.
12. Lady Caroline Lamb to John Murray. [1814–1815.] Murray Archive. Regards manuscript of *Glenarvon*.
13. Lady Caroline Lamb to John Murray. [late 1814.] Murray Archive. From October 1814 to May 1815 Lord and Lady Bessborough traveled to the south of France to winter there for Lady Bessborough's health.
14. Lady Caroline Lamb to John Murray. [1814–1815?] Murray Archive. *Lara* (with Samuel Rogers's *Jacqueline*) was published by Murray in 1814, and went through a number of editions; Murray published the fifth edition in 1815. If LCL saw a copy just after its publication, the date of this letter would be 1814 rather than 1815.
15. Lady Caroline Lamb to John Murray. [February–March 1815.] Murray Archive. Walter Scott's *Guy Mannering* appeared in February 1815.
16. Lady Caroline Lamb John Murray. [after April 1815.] Murray Archive.
17. Lady Caroline Lamb to John Murray. [April] 1815 Murray Archive. After Nathan's *Hebrew Melodies*.
18. Lady Caroline Lamb to Lord Byron. 4 April 1815. Bodleian, Dep. Lovelace Byron 155, f. 82.
19. Lady Caroline Lamb to John Murray. [after April 1815.] Murray Archive. After Nathan's *Hebrew Melodies*.
20. Lady Caroline Lamb to John Murray. [after April 1815.] Murray Archive. After Nathan's *Hebrew Melodies*.
21. Lady Caroline Lamb to John Murray. [June–July 1815.] Murray Archive. Watermark 1811, but Frederick Ponsonby was wounded at Waterloo on 18 June 1815—also concerns *Glenarvon*.
22. Lady Caroline Lamb to Lord Duncannon. 7 July 1815. Printed in Bessborough and Aspinall, *Lady Bessborough and Her Family Circle*, 244.
23. Lady Caroline Lamb to Lady Melbourne. [after 7 July 1815.] British Library Add. MS 45546 ff. 85–86. Caroline stayed the balance of the month of July after her brother Frederick was wounded at Waterloo.
24. Lady Caroline Lamb to Michael Bruce. [September–October 1815.] Papers of the Bruce Family. Bodleian Library, University of Oxford. MS Eng. c. 5753, f.119.
25. Lady Caroline Lamb to Michael Bruce. [October 1815.] Papers of the Bruce Family. Bodleian Library, University of Oxford. MS Eng. c. 5753, f.121. Caroline is "quitting Paris."
26. Lady Caroline Lamb to Lady Byron. [late October 1815.] Bodleian Dep. Lovelace Byron 78, f. 147. Immediately after Caroline's return from Paris.

Chapter Six Letters, 1816

1. Lady Caroline Lamb to John Murray. [March 1816.] Murray Archive.
2. Lady Caroline Lamb to Lord Byron. [March] 1816. Murray Archive.
3. Lady Caroline Lamb to J.C. Hobhouse. [March–April 1816.] Murray Archive.
4. Lady Caroline Lamb to Lord Byron. [March? 1816.] Murray Archive.
5. Lady Caroline Lamb to John Murray. [April 1816.] Murray Archive.
6. Lady Caroline Lamb to Lady Byron. 4 March 1816. Bodleian Dep. Lovelace Byron 78, ff.157–61.
7. Lady Caroline Lamb to Lady Byron. 27–28 March 1816. Bodleian Dep. Lovelace Byron 78, ff.162–67.
8. Lady Caroline Lamb to Lord Byron. [April 1816.] Murray Archive.

9. Lady Caroline Lamb to Henry Colburn. [April?] 1816. Victoria and Albert Museum Forster Collection MSS vol. 28. #48.E.22.
10. Lady Caroline Lamb to Lord Melbourne. April or May 1816. British Library Add. MS 45546 ff. 89–90.
11. Lady Caroline Lamb to Emily Cowper. [After 9 May 1816.] British Library Add. MS 45548 ff.157–58.
12. Lady Caroline Lamb to Henry Colburn. [May–June 1816.] Victoria and Albert Museum Forster Collection MSS vol. 28. #48.E.22.
13. Lady Caroline Lamb to J.C. Hobhouse. [May–July 1816.] Murray Archive.
14. Lady Caroline Lamb to Lady Byron. Sunday 8 September 1816. Bodleian, Dep. Lovelace Byron 78, ff. 175–180.
15. Lady Caroline Lamb to Lady Melbourne. 28 September 1816. British Library Add. MS 45546 f. 93.
16. Lady Caroline Lamb to Lady Melbourne [September–October 1816.] British Library Add. MS 45546 ff. 114–16.
17. Lady Caroline Lamb to John Murray, 13 or 15 October 1816. Murray Archive. 18 November was official publication of *Childe Harold III*, for which Murray paid £2,000, but Caroline saw proofs or an advance copy.
18. Lady Caroline Lamb to Michael Bruce. [After September 1816.] Papers of the Bruce Family. Bodleian Library, University of Oxford. MS Eng. c. 5753, ff. 133–34.
19. Lady Caroline Lamb to John Murray. 12 December 1816. Murray Archive.

Chapter Seven Letters, 1817–1819

1. Lady Caroline Lamb to Lord Granville Leveson Gower. [1817.] Printed in Granville, Granville Leveson Gower, First Earl. *Private Correspondence of Earl Granville: 1781–1821.* 2 vols. Ed. Castalia, Countess Granville. London: John Murray, 1917. 2:541–43. Caroline says she has been married ten years, and 1816 would be her eleventh anniversary, but that is a generic statement ("a decade")—and she says she hopes to reemerge in society, so 1817.
2. Lady Caroline Lamb to Ugo Foscolo [1817.] Printed in Vincent, *Ugo Foscolo: An Italian in Regency England*, 72.
3. Lady Caroline Lamb to Lady Melbourne. [after 2 April 1817.] British Library Add. MS 45546 ff. 119–22.
4. Lady Caroline Lamb to Lady Byron. [5 May 1817.] Bodleian Dep. Lovelace Byron 78, f. 153.There is a typed transcription of this letter in Dep. Lovelace Byron 359.
5. Lady Caroline Lamb to John Murray. May 1817. Murray Archive.
6. Lady Caroline Lamb to Michael Bruce. 3 June 1817. Papers of the Bruce Family. Bodleian Library, University of Oxford. MS Eng. . 5753, ff. 135–37.
7. Lady Caroline Lamb to Michael Bruce. [1817.] Papers of the Bruce Family. Bodleian Library, University of Oxford. MS Eng. c. 5753, f. 138. A probable continuation of the previous letter.
8. Lady Caroline Lamb to Ugo Foscolo. November–December 1817. Printed in Vincent, *Ugo Foscolo: An Italian in Regency England*, 74. Dr. Lee (mentioned in the letter) joined the Lamb household 5 November 1817.
9. Lady Caroline Lamb to J.C. Hobhouse. [March? 1818.] Murray Archive. *Beppo* had been published anonymously 28 February 1818.
10. Lady Caroline Lamb to J.C. Hobhouse. [April 1818.] Murray Archive. Lady Melbourne had died on the 6 April 1818.

11. Lady Caroline Lamb to Ugo Foscolo. 30 October 1818. Printed in E.R. Vincent, *Ugo Foscolo: An Italian in Regency England*, 73.
12. Lady Caroline Lamb to Lord Byron. [October–November 1818.] Murray Archive.
13. Lady Caroline Lamb to Lady Emily Cowper. [1819.] British Library. Lamb Papers, Add. MS 45548 ff. 153–55.
14. Lady Caroline Lamb to Lord Byron. [February–March 1819.] Murray Archive.
15. Lady Caroline Lamb to J.C. Hobhouse. [February–March 1819] Murray Archive.

Chapter Eight Letters, 1820–1823

1. Lady Caroline Lamb to John Murray. August 1820. Murray Archive.
2. Lady Caroline Lamb to Mrs. Amelia Opie. 1820. British Library Add. MS 50142 f. 4.
3. Lady Caroline Lamb to William Godwin. 15 May 1821. Oxford, Bodleian Library [Abinger] Dep. C. 529.
4. Lady Caroline Lamb to Thomas Malthus. [After 1819 and most likely in the 1821–1822 period in which she was writing both *Graham Hamilton* and *Ada Reis*.] British Library Add. MS R.P. 4687 (ii) Box 108. Photocopy. Original in the Carl H. Pforzheimer Collection of Shelley and His Circle, The New York Public Library, Astor, Lenox and Tilden Foundations.
5. Lady Caroline Lamb to Ugo Foscolo. [1821.] Printed in Vincent, *Ugo Foscolo: An Italian in Regency England*, 75.
6. Lady Caroline Lamb to Lady Bessborough. [September–October 1821.] Printed in Bessborough and Aspinall, *Lady Bessborough and Her Family Circle*, 263–64.
7. Lady Caroline Lamb to John Murray. 26 November 1821. Murray Archive.
8. Lady Caroline Lamb to John Murray. 27 November 1821. Murray Archive.
9. Lady Caroline Lamb to John Murray. 28 November 1821. Murray Archive.
10. Lady Caroline Lamb to the Lady Emily Cowper. [After 28 November 1821.] Devonshire MSS. Chatsworth [UK], sixth Duke's Group, f. 559.
11. Lady Caroline Lamb to the sixth Duke of Devonshire. 25 December 1821. Devonshire MSS. Chatsworth [UK], sixth Duke's Group, f. 581.
12. Lady Caroline Lamb to the sixth Duke of Devonshire. 28 December 1821. Devonshire MSS. Chatsworth [UK], sixth Duke's Group, f. 583.
13. Lady Caroline Lamb to Frederick or William Ponsonby. [December 1821.] Bessborough Papers, C1 D4, folder 161.
14. Lady Caroline Lamb to Mrs. Amelia Opie (1803–1873). 1 January 1822. British Library Add. MS 50142.
15. Lady Caroline Lamb to William Godwin. 3–5 March 1822. Oxford, Bodleian Library [Abinger] Dep. c. 507.
16. Lady Caroline Lamb to William Godwin. 18 April 1822. Oxford, Bodleian Library [Abinger] Dep. c. 507.
17. Lady Caroline to Georgiana, Lady Morpeth, future sixth Countess of Carlisle.[1822.] Castle Howard Archives J18/35/100 [1822 because of *Lalla Rookh* (1817) and the death of the fourth Duchess of Newcastle (1822).]
18. Lady Caroline Lamb to Michael Bruce. [1822, not 1815–1817 as archivist docket says.] Papers of the Bruce Family. Bodleian Library, University of Oxford. MS Eng. c. 5753, ff. 144–45. *Adam Blair* was published in 1822.
19. Lady Caroline to Isaac Nathan. [1822–1823?] Printed in Nathan, *Fugitive Pieces and Reminiscences of Lord Byron . . . also some Original Poetry, Letters, and Recollections of Lady Caroline Lamb*, 150. Original in the Australian National Library, Sydney.

20. Lady Caroline to Isaac Nathan. [1823.] Printed in Nathan, *Fugitive Pieces and Reminiscences of Lord Byron . . . also some Original Poetry, Letters, and Recollections of Lady Caroline Lamb*, 153.
21. Lady Caroline Lamb to Lady Morgan. [spring 1823.] Houghton Library *43M-93. By permission of the Houghton Library, Harvard University. Docket says 1827, but the allusion to Penruddock places it in 1823, after *Ada Reis* was published by John Murray.
22. Lady Caroline Lamb to Lady Morgan. [1823—Ada Reis.] Printed in *Lady Morgan's Memoirs*, 2: 210–13.
23. Lady Caroline Lamb to John Murray. [Early 1823.] Murray Archive. *Ada Reis* was being reviewed by Gifford, *Penruddock* not yet published.
24. Lady Caroline Lamb to Lady Morgan. [April–May 1823.] Printed in Torrens, *Memoirs of the Right Honourable William, 2nd Viscount Melbourne*, 1:130.
25. Lady Caroline Lamb to William Godwin. [April–May 1823.] Oxford, Bodleian Library [Abinger] Dep. C. 529. *Ada Reis* mentioned as just published.
26. Lady Caroline Lamb to Edward Bulwer (1803–1873). 22 May 1823. Hertfordshire Archives D/EK C24/21/1.
27. Lady Caroline Lamb to Lady Morgan. October 1823. Printed in *Lady Morgan's Memoirs*, 2:178–79.
28. Lady Caroline Lamb to an Unknown Correspondent. 18 December 1823. Printed in Torrens, *Memoirs of the Right Honourable William, 2nd Viscount Melbourne*, 1:132.
29. Lady Caroline Lamb to William Godwin. [1823–1824.] Oxford, Bodleian Library [Abinger] Dep. C. 529. Watermarked 1822, but before Byron's death was known to Caroline in May 1824.

Chapter Nine Letters, 1824–1825

1. Lady Caroline Lamb to Isaac Nathan. [After 19 January 1824.] Printed in Nathan, *Fugitive Pieces and Reminiscences of Lord Byron . . . also some Original Poetry, Letters, and Recollections of Lady Caroline Lamb*, 155–56.
2. Lady Caroline Lamb to J.C. Hobhouse. [May 1824.] Murray Archive.
3. Lady Caroline Lamb to Lydia White. [May 1824.] Murray Archive. Byron's death on 19 April was known by Hobhouse 13 May 1824.
4. Lady Caroline Lamb to John Murray. 13 July 1824. Murray Archive. Apparently dictated.
5. Lady Caroline Lamb to William Godwin. 24–25 October 1824. Oxford, Bodleian Library [Abinger] Dep. C. 529. Marked by Godwin as "Rec'd Oct. 25, 1824."
6. Lady Caroline Lamb to Thomas Medwin. November 1824. Murray Archive this is an enclosure in a letter to Henry Colburn, requesting that Colburn publish it and send it on to Medwin. Copies exist in the Bodleian Library and the Victoria and Albert Museum, as well as this hand transcription in the John Murray Archive. A transcription is also printed in *The Works of Lord Byron: A New, Revised, and Enlarged Edition, With Illustrations* (1898–1905), 2:451–54.
7. Lady Caroline Lamb to William Godwin. [December 1824.] Oxford, Bodleian Library [Abinger] Dep. c. 529.
8. Lady Caroline Lamb to an Anonymous Correspondent. [April–June 1825.] British Library Add. MS 38855 ff. 233–34.
9. Lady Caroline Lamb to Lord Cowper. [April–June] 1825. Hertfordshire Archives D/EP F427/15.
10. Lady Caroline to the sixth Duke of Devonshire. [1825.] Devonshire MSS. Chatsworth [UK], sixth Duke's Group, f. 1130.

11. Lady Caroline Lamb to Lady Morgan. 2 June 1825. Printed in Lady Morgan's Memoirs, 2:203–4.
12. Lady Caroline Lamb to Wilmington Fleming. [March–April 1825.] British Library Add. MS 50142.
13. Lady Caroline Lamb to Isaac Nathan. 11 June 1824. Lithographic facsimile of this printed in Nathan, *Fugitive Pieces and Reminiscences of Lord Byron . . . also some Original Poetry, Letters, and Recollections of Lady Caroline Lamb*, 161–64.
14. Lady Caroline Lamb to Augustus Lamb. 26 June or July [1825.] Hertfordshire Archives. D/ELb F76/11. Though there is some doubt, this is probably an 1825 letter.
15. Lady Caroline Lamb to William Lamb. 8 September [1825.] Hertfordshire Archives D/ELb F 2/5. Lady Caroline had left 12 August 1825 and writes from Calais.

Chapter Ten Letters, 1826–1828

1. Lady Caroline Lamb to Edward Bulwer. 2 August 1826. Hertfordshire Archives D/EK C1/5.
2. Lady Caroline Lamb to William Lamb. [Fall 1827.] Printed in Torrens, *Memoirs of the Right Honourable William, 2nd Viscount Melbourne*, 1:297.
3. Lady Caroline Lamb to William Lamb. 3 November 1827. Hertfordshire Archives D/ELb F33/7. Dictated to Dr. Goddard.
4. Lady Caroline Lamb to Lady Duncannon. 5–6 December 1827. Bessborough Papers, C1 D4, folder 161. Docketed: "Received Dec. 7th, 1827."
5. Dr. Goddard to William Lamb. 13 December 1827. Printed in *Lady Morgan's Memoirs*, 2: 249.
6. William Lamb to Lady Caroline Lamb. 6 January 1828. Printed in Bessborough and Aspinall *Lady Bessborough and Her Family Circle*, 290.
7. Lady Caroline Lamb to Lady Holland. [January 1828.] British Library Add. MS 51560 f. 213.

Manuscript Sources

Bessborough Papers	Papers of the Bessborough Family. Private Archive.
British Library	The Althorp, Lamb, and Melbourne Papers of the British Library, in Additional Manuscripts (Add. MS).
Castle Howard	Papers of Lady Georgiana, sixth Countess of Carlisle in the Castle Howard Archives.
Devonshire Manuscripts	Letters and other papers of the fifth and sixth Dukes of Devonshire held in the archive at Chatsworth, Derbyshire.
Harvard University	Houghton Library, Harvard University.
Hertfordshire Archives	Papers of the Lamb [Melbourne] family held in the Hertfordshire Archives and Local Studies Office, County Hall, Hertfordshire.
John Murray Archive	Letters and other papers of Lady Caroline Lamb, Lord and Lady Byron, and John Murray, London.
New York Public Library	The Carl H. Pforzheimer Collection of Shelley and His Circle, the New York Public Library, Astor, Lenox and Tilden Foundations.
Oxford University	Abinger Collection and Papers of the Lovelace/Byron family on deposit with the Bodleian Library of Oxford University.
Victoria and Albert Museum	Letters of Lady Caroline Lamb in the Victoria and Albert Museum Forster Collection MSS vol. 28 (Pressmark 48.E.22).

Printed Sources

Airlie, Mabell, Countess of. *In Whig Society: 1775–1818*. London: Hodder and Stoughton, 1921.

———. *Lady Palmerston and Her Times*. 2 vols. London: Hodder and Stoughton, 1922.

Askwith, Betty. *Piety and Wit: A Biography of Harriet, Countess Granville, 1785–1862*. London: Collins, 1982.

Bakewell, Michael, and Melissa Bakewell. *Augusta Leigh: Byron's Half-Sister*. London: Chatto & Windus, 2000.

Bessborough, Earl. *Georgiana, Duchess of Devonshire*. London: John Murray, 1955.

Bessborough, Earl, and Arthur Aspinall. *Lady Bessborough and Her Family Circle*. London: J. Murray, 1940.

Blessington, Marguerite, Countess of. *Conversations of Lord Byron*. (1834). Ed. Ernest J. Lovell, Jr. Princeton: Princeton University Press, 1969.

Blyth, Henry. *Caro: The Fatal Passion: The Life of Lady Caroline Lamb*. London: Rupert Hart-Davis, 1972.

Byron, George Gordon, Lord. *Byron's Letters and Journals*. Ed. Leslie Marchand. 1 vol. Cambridge: Belknap Press of Harvard University Press, 1973–1995.

———. *His Very Self and Voice: Collected Conversations of Lord Byron*. Ed. Ernest J. Lovell, Jr. New York: Macmillan, 1954.

———. *Lord Byron's Correspondence: Chiefly with Lady Melbourne, Mr. Hobhouse, the Hon. Douglas Kinnaird, and P. B. Shelley*. Ed. John Murray. 2 vols. London: John Murray, 1922.

———. *The Works of Lord Byron: A New, Revised, and Enlarged Edition, With Illustrations*. Ed. Rowland E. Prothero and Ernest Hartley Coleridge. 13 vols. London: John Murray; New York: C. Scribner's Sons, 1898–1905.

Calder-Marshall, Arthur. *The Two Duchesses*. London: Hutchinson, 1978.

Campbell, Mary. *Lady Morgan: The Life and Times of Sydney Owenson*. London: Pandora, 1988.

Cecil, David. *Melbourne*. New York: Bobbs-Merrill, 1954.

Chapman, Caroline, and Jane Dormer. *Elizabeth and Georgiana: The Duke of Devonshire and His Two Duchesses*. London: John Murray, 2002.

Clubbe, John. "*Glenarvon* Revised—and Revisited." *Wordsworth Circle* 10 (1979): 205–17.

Dallas, Robert C. *Recollections of the Life of Lord Byron, From the Year 1808 to the End of 1814*. London: Charles Knight, 1824.

Dickinson, Hilary. "Augustus Lamb (1807–1836) and His Tutor, Robert Lee: Theoretical and Methodological Issues in Historical Sociology." *Occasional Papers in Education and Interdisciplinary Studies: University of Southampton* 1 (1992): 43–53.

Dunckley, Henry. *Lord Melbourne*. 2nd ed. From the series Prime Ministers of Queen Victoria. London: Sampson Low, Marston, Searle & Rivington, 1890.

Eisler, Benita. *Byron: Child of Passion, Fool of Fame*. New York: Knopf, 1999.

Elwin, Malcolm. *Lord Byron's Family: Annabella, Ada, and Augusta 1816–1824*. Ed. Peter Thomson. London: John Murray, 1975.

———. *Lord Byron's Wife*. London: Macdonald, 1962.

Fleming, Wilmington. *The Destroying Angel, A Fragment; The Captive's Boy and Other Poems*. London, 1825.

Foreman, Amanda. *Georgiana: Duchess of Devonshire*. New York: Random House, 1998.

Foster, Vere. *The Two Duchesses*. London: Blackie, 1898.

Gower, Henrietta Elizabeth Leveson. *Hary-O: The Letters of Lady Harriet Cavendish, 1796–1809*. Ed. Sir George Leveson Gower and Iris Palmer. London: John Murray, 1940.

———. *Letters of Harriet, Countess Granville, 1810–1845*. 2nd ed. Ed. Hon. F. Leveson Gower. 2 vols. London: Longmans, Green, and Company, 1894.

———. *A Second Self: The Letters of Harriet Granville 1810–1845*. Ed. Virginia Surtees. Wiltshire: Michael Russell, 1990.

Gower, Iris Leveson. *The Face Without a Frown: Georgiana, Duchess of Devonshire*. London: Frederick Muller, 1944.

Graham, Peter. *Don Juan and Regency England*. Charlottesville: University Press of Virginia, 1990.

Granville, Leveson Gower, First Earl. *Private Correspondence of Earl Granville: 1781–1821*. Ed. Castalia, Countess Granville. 2 vols. London: John Murray, 1916.

Grebanier, Bernard. *The Uninhibited Byron: An Account of his Sexual Confusion*. New York: Crown, 1970.

Grosskurth, Phyllis. *Byron: The Flawed Angel*. New York: Houghton Mifflin, 1997.

Hobhouse, John Cam (Lord Broughton). *Byron's Bulldog: The Letters of John Cam Hobhouse to Lord Byron*. Ed. Peter W. Graham. Columbus: Ohio State University Press, 1984.

———. *Recollections of a Long Life: With Additional Extracts from his Private Diaries*. Ed. by (his daughter) Lady Dorchester. 4 vols. London: John Murray, 1910; New York: AMS Press, 1968.

Hofkosh, Sonia. "The Writer's Ravishment: Women and the Romantic Author—The Example of Byron." *Romanticism and Feminism*. Ed. Anne K. Mellor. Bloomington: Indiana University Press, 1988. 93–114.

Howell-Thomas, Dorothy. *Lord Melbourne's Susan*. Old Woking: Gresham Books, 1978.

Jenkins, Elizabeth. *Lady Caroline Lamb*. London: Victor Gollancz, 1932.

Joyce, Michael. *My Friend H: John Cam Hobhouse, Baron Broughton of Broughton de Gyfford*. London: John Murray, 1948.

Kelsall, Malcolm. "The Byronic Hero and Revolution in Ireland: The Politics of *Glenarvon*." *The Byron Journal* 9 (1981): 4–19.

Lamb, Lady Caroline. *Ada Reis*. 3 vols. London: John Murray, 1823; Paris: Galignani, 1824.

———. *Glenarvon*. 3 vols. London: Henry Colburn, 1816. Facs. 1st ed. Jonathan Wordsworth. Oxford and New York: Woodstock Books, 1993. Facs. 3rd ed. New York: AMS Press, 1975.

———. *Gordon: A Tale; A Poetical Review of Don Juan*. London: T. and J. Allman, 1821.

———. *Graham Hamilton*. 2 vols. London: Henry Colburn, 1822.

———. *A New Canto*. London: William Wright, 1819.

———. *Verses from Glenarvon, to Which is Prefixed the Original Introduction Not Published With the Early Editions of that Work*. London: Henry Colburn, 1819.

Lovell, Ernest J., Jr. *Captain Medwin: Friend of Byron*. Austin: University of Texas Press, 1962.

MacCarthy, Fiona. *Byron: Life and Legend*. London: John Murray, 2002.

Marchand, Leslie. *Byron: A Biography*. New York: Knopf, 1957.

Marshall, Dorothy. *Lord Melbourne.* London: Weidenfeld and Nicolson, 1975.

Masters, Brian. *Georgiana, Duchess of Devonshire.* London: Hamish Hamilton, 1981.

Mayne, Ethel Colburn. *The Life and Letters of Anne Isabella, Lady Noel Byron.* New York: C. Scribner's Sons, 1929.

Medwin, Thomas. *Conversations of Lord Byron. Revised with a New Preface by the Author for a New Edition, and annotated by Lady Byron . . . and others who Knew the Poet Personally.* Ed. Ernest J. Lovell, Jr. Princeton: Princeton University Press, 1966.

Melbourne, Elizabeth Milbanke Lamb, Viscountess. *Byron's "Corbeau Blanc": The Life and Letters of Lady Melbourne.* Ed. Jonathan David Gross. Houston: Rice University Press, 1997.

Mitchell, Leslie G. *Lord Melbourne: 1779–1848.* Oxford: Oxford University Press, 1997.

Moore, Doris Langley. *The Late Lord Byron: Posthumous Dramas.* Philadelphia and New York: J. B. Lippincott, 1961.

Moore, Thomas. *Letters and Journals of Lord Byron: With Notices of His Life.* 2 vols. New York: J. J. Harper, 1830.

Morgan, Sydney Owenson, Lady. *Lady Morgan's Memoirs: Autobiography, Diaries, and Correspondence.* 2nd ed. 2 vols. London: William H. Allen & Co., 1863.

Nathan, Isaac. *Fugitive Pieces and Reminiscences of Lord Byron: Containing and Entire New Edition of the Hebrew Melodies, With the Addition of Several Never Before Published; the Whole Illustrated with Critical, Historical, Theatrical, Political, and Theological Remarks, Notes, Anecdotes, Interesting Conversations and Observations, Made by that Illustrious Poet: Together with His Lordship's Autograph; also Some Original Poetry, Letters and Recollections of Lady Caroline Lamb.* London: Whittaker, Treacher and Co., 1829.

Nathan, Isaac, and Lord Byron. *A Selection of Hebrew Melodies, Ancient and Modern.* (1815–1816.) Ed. Frederick Burwick and Paul Douglass. Tuscaloosa and London: University of Alabama Press, 1988.

Olney, Clark. "*Glenarvon* Revisited." *University of Kansas City Review* 22 (1955): 271–76.

Palmerston, Emily, Viscountess [formerly Emily Cowper and Emily Lamb]. *The Letters of Lady Palmerston: Selected and Edited from the Originals at Broadlands and Elsewhere.* Ed. Tresham Lever. London: John Murray, 1957.

Paston, George [E. M. Symonds], and Peter Quennell. "*To Lord Byron*": *Feminine Profiles Based Upon Unpublished Letters 1807–1824.* London: John Murray, 1939.

Paul, C. Kegan. *William Godwin: His Friends and Contemporaries.* 2 vols. Boston: Roberts Bros., 1876.

Pierson, Joan. *The Real Lady Byron.* London: Robert Hale, 1992.

Ponsonby, Sir John. *The Ponsonby Family.* London: The Medici Society, 1929.

Rogers, Samuel. *Recollections of the Table-Talk of Samuel Rogers.* Ed. Morchard Bishop. Lawrence: University of Kansas Press, 1953.

Sadleir, Michael. *Bulwer: A Panorama—Edward and Rosina, 1803–1836.* London: Constable, 1931.

Smiles, Samuel. *A Publisher and His Friends: Memoir and Correspondence of the Late John Murray.* 2 vols. London: John Murray, 1891.

Soderholm, James. *Fantasy, Forgery, and the Byron Legend.* Lexington: University Press of Kentucky, 1996.

Stauffer, Andrew. "Byron, Medwin, and the False Fiend: Remembering 'Remember Thee.' " *Studies in Bibliography* 53 (2000): 265–76.

Strickland, Margot. *The Byron Women.* London: P. Owen, 1974.

———. "An Early Pioneer." *Parents Voice* (1985): 22–23.

Stuart, Dorothy Margaret. *Dearest Bess: The Life and Times of Lady Elizabeth Foster, Afterwards Duchess of Devonshire, from her Unpublished Journals and Correspondence.* London: Methuen, 1955.

Torrens, W. M. *Memoirs of the Right Honourable William, 2nd Viscount Melbourne*. 2 vols. London: Macmillan and Company, 1878.

Vincent, E. R. *Ugo Foscolo: An Italian in Regency England*. Cambridge: Cambridge University Press, 1953.

Wilson, Frances, ed. *Byromania: Portraits of the Artist in Nineteenth- and Twentieth-Century Culture*. London and New York: Macmillan Press and St. Martin's Press, 1999.

Wu, Duncan. "Appropriating Byron: Lady Caroline Lamb's *A New Canto*." *Wordsworth Circle* 26.3 (1995): 140–46.

Ziegler, Phillip. *Melbourne: A Biography of William Lamb, 2nd Viscount Melbourne*. New York: Knopf, 1976.

INDEX

["LCL" refers to Lady Caroline Lamb]